SUCCUBUS

Written by Brandon Blake Varnell
Edited by Linda Branam
Illustrated by Lawrence Mann

Dedication

There are so many people who've helped me during the process of writing this book. My parents, my beta readers, my amazing editor, my super awesome illustrator, and, of course, all of the people who've been reading my books. I never would have been able to get this far without any of you.

Chapter 1

Christian peered through a large gap in the metal roof, the edges of which were frayed and torn, as if God's hand had reached out from heaven and ripped it asunder. The interior, a warehouse, appeared to be spacious but almost empty. *Almost.* Although the large room was devoid of boxes, crates, and other equipment, there was something down below that he could easily make out. Something that didn't belong in a warehouse.

His target: *a vampire.* To most people, the creature below would have been considered beautiful. Its form carried an elegance that few could match, and its eyes glowed with an otherworldly iridescence. Silvery-blond hair sat almost gently upon its head and pale, nearly translucent skin shone with a brilliant luster in the light of the full moon.

Christian saw no beauty in it. How could something that drank human blood ever be beautiful?

His target wasn't alone. Arrayed in a semicircle stood half a dozen vampires. Their pale, nearly translucence skin shone in the darkness, and their eyes glowed with an otherworldly iridescence: some blue, some black, some red.

One of the vampires spoke. "Greetings, brother." Its voice was rough and coarse, as if it hadn't had anything to drink in days.

Maybe it's fasting. Christian almost snorted at the thought.

"'Tis a grand night, brother," his target replied.

"Were you spotted?"

"No."

"Good. How has thy search gone? Hast thou discovered another delightful treat for us?"

Christian moved silently to better position himself for what was to come. The creatures hadn't noticed him yet—not that he had expected them to. Few abominations ever looked up. He'd slain dozens of foes this way; the ease with which he had taken their lives had been almost laughable.

"I have indeed; a lovely girl who works the closing shift at a small thrift store. She has no family, no friends, and she longs to feel the affection of another. Easy prey. She'll not be missed."

As he mentally prepared himself for his coming task, Christian listened to the almost stereotypical vampire conversation. He really didn't know what it was with this species, but almost all of them spoke like they lived in the sixteenth century. Couldn't their manner of speech be a little more up to date? Even bishops and priests had stopped speaking like bad actors in some Shakespearean play decades ago. The least these vampires could do was give the same courtesy.

I think Tristin is beginning to rub off on me.

"Good, good. What time doth this woman leave work?"

"Eleven in the evening."

"Excellent. Now then, tomorrow we shall—"

Christian had heard enough. After a mental countdown and a quick prayer, he allowed himself to free-fall head first through the hole.

As he dropped, he twisted his body until his feet pointed toward the ground. At the same time, he reached behind him for the two objects on his back: Twin swords, each with a diamond-shaped pommel and a cross-guard shaped like a crucifix with a single ruby in the center. Steel hissed as he pulled his weapons from their sheaths.

He hit the ground with a harsh thud, bone-jarring and forceful enough to make him gasp. He shunted the pain aside and bent his knees to absorb most of the impact, while the rest was absorbed when he pushed himself into a forward roll. He felt his shoulders jolt as he rolled along the ground. Then he leapt to his feet, right in front of his first kill: The vampire that he'd been following.

He had just enough time to see the startled look in his target's eyes before he brought his twin weapons to bear. A flash of light reflected off the surface of his blades as he swung them forward, too quick for human eyes to follow. They traveled in a blurred line, tracing an almost gentle arc horizontally through the air, the movements spellbinding in their grace.

Then he moved past the vampire, his feet sliding along the floor, kicking up dust as he twisted around to face the rest of his opposition. Blood dripped from the two blades in his hands. They were straight blades, double-edged. The surfaces not covered in thick, dark-red liquid reflected the moonlight spilling in through the hole overhead.

One second passed. Then two. Time seemed to stand still before, with surprising slowness, the vampire's head slid off its shoulders and fell to the ground. As the head rolled toward the other vampires, the rest of the body fell as well, first to its knees, then toppling the rest of the way with two dull thuds.

Christian felt a moment of regret at having killed, but he shoved his emotions into the deepest recesses of his soul.

This is for the good of mankind.

There was a long moment of silence. The other vampires stared at him in shock, eyes wide and mouths gaping to reveal sharp fangs.

With a flick of his wrists, Christian forced the blood staining his blades to fly off and splatter against the ground. One of the vampires—the leader, Christian guessed—noticed the crucifix cross-guard.

"Shit! It's an Executioner!"

That seemed to be the cue for the others, jolting them out of their trance-like states. They bared their fangs and unleashed sibilant hisses like a nest of angry vipers.

"Kill him!"

Christian remained where he was as four of the five remaining vampires surrounded him. He stood there, his swords held loosely at his sides, his defense intentionally full of gaps. Even an amateur could see the various weaknesses in his stance to exploit. He observed his enemies with keen eyes, taking in their positions, their stances, the expressions on their faces. Some distance away stood the fifth vampire, arms crossed, watching him.

Coward.

A slight shift in movement was the only signal Christian received before they attacked. All four charged forward, converging on him, attempting to box him in. Their bloodlust rolled over him in waves.

Less than a second later, three of the four reached him. They attacked. Perhaps they believed that simultaneous attacks from all directions would leave him unable to fight back.

He didn't know. He didn't care. Because it didn't matter. None of the attacks hit. Christian reacted long before the vampires reached him, long before they attacked, almost as if he had predicted their movements.

Christian tilted his head back, avoiding a swipe to his face by a pair of long claw-like nails. He removed the offending limb with a swing of his sword, severing the hand at the wrist.

The vampire screamed as blood poured from the stump. Christian then disemboweled the creature, swinging the sword in his left hand into its stomach, tearing through skin and muscle with ease.

As Christian's sword finished slicing through the now dead vampire's torso, he moved to the left. Sensing movement, he bent at the waist, avoiding a foot that shot out in a reverse heel-kick that would have shattered his spine had he not leaned back. As he avoided the attempted kick, one of the vampires moved past his previous position in an obviously failed attempt to tackle him.

That particular vampire ended up losing its head when Christian came back up and swung the sword in his right hand. Dark-crimson blood spurted from the severed neck as the head soared through the air, disappearing into the darkness of the warehouse. The aberration's body continued running for several feet before it seemed to realize it no longer had a head and subsequently tumbled to the ground. It rolled along the dirty floor, bouncing several times, and then came to a stop.

Air currents flowed at his back. Christian turned. Sparks flew when he thrust out his sword, not blocking the claws that nearly gouged out his face, but redirecting them. Then he thrust out the sword in his right hand, stabbing the vampire through the chest. As the monster released a death gurgle, he kicked it off his sword. The vampire fell onto its back and remained still.

The fourth vampire to have charged in had held back. Maybe it had expected the other three to fail. It could have also been confident that its friends would be up to the task of slaying him, or perhaps it just wanted to wait for an opening. Its footsteps echoed from behind Christian.

Christian danced to the right. He lashed out with the sword in his left hand, severing the vampire's right arm at the elbow. While his enemy screamed in anguish, he swung the blade in his left hand across the vampire's throat, leaving a deep, gaping wound.

The abomination's eyes widened. Its only remaining hand and the stump that *used to have a hand* moved to its throat. It gurgled and coughed, choking as carnelian liquid gushed from the open wound like a faucet, pouring down its neck and collarbone, staining its shirt. It stared at him with wide, shocked eyes. And then it fell backward, striking the hard ground with a thud, which rang out several decibels louder than it should have. The body twitched once, twice, and then became still.

Just one more and this will end.

"What are you fools doing?! Kill him! Kill him!!"

Christian's eyes darted to his left. There was another vampire, one that must have been standing guard outside. It came in fast, so fast that Christian's eyes were incapable of keeping track of the supernatural creature while it moved.

That was okay. He didn't rely on his eyes to fight. They were useless against opponents whose speed surpassed anything a human could match.

A noise alerted him to movement on his right. Footsteps. The leader still stood several feet away. Was there another guard?

Ducking low, Christian avoided a claw swipe from the vampire coming in from his blind spot. The creature's thrust flew over his head, its movement so swift it created a powerful gust of wind, causing his hood to soared off his head.

Christian rolled backward while still crouched low, ignoring the pain that flared up in his spine. He avoided the other vampire, which tried to smash his head in with a heel-drop. Instead, all his enemy hit was the ground, which cracked and dented from the power of its strike.

Kipping up to his feet and moving to the right, Christian avoided a thrust that would have impaled him through his left eye and then retaliated, swinging the blade in his right hand. The vampire tried to dodge, but Christian had foreseen this possibility and adjusted his sword's movement accordingly. He impaled his victim through the chest, the tip of his blade emerging from the vampire's back.

The vampire looked down at the wound in shock, as if unable to believe its own demise. It shuddered once, and then it died.

With movements that were just as quick as his piercing thrust, Christian yanked the blade from the dead vampire, allowing the creature's corpse to fall to the floor.

"Damn you!" The voice came from behind him.

Tilting his head, Christian avoided a thrust claw that tried to impale him through the back of his skull. He reversed his grip on the blade in his left hand and thrust it behind him. A croaked gurgle echoed behind him. He yanked the blade out of soft, pliant flesh, spun around, and then swung the sword in his right hand, severing the creature's head. It flew off as Christian sidestepped the now headless body and let it crumple to the ground.

Just one more. Where was the leader?

The sound of running feet caught his attention. Christian snapped his head toward the exit, where he could see the last vampire attempting to flee.

Not on my watch.

With a single fluid motion, Christian sheathed his blades and moved his hands into the cloak concealing his frame. He reached for the two objects holstered to his thighs, his fingers closing around grooved handles with a trigger. Pulling them out revealed a pair of handguns—one black and the other silver.

He pointed them both at the fleeing vampire and pulled the triggers. The sound of gunfire filled the air. A dozen bullets were unleashed in half as many seconds, a hailstorm of gunfire. The tiny projectiles, nothing more than streaks of incandescent blue light, crossed the killing field in less than a hundredth of a second.

The vampire didn't stand a chance. The bullets tore through its body with ease. The force with which they were delivered made the creature stumble forward and fall to the ground, the bullets embedding themselves deep within its body.

Then they ignited. Like flares going off in the night, the bullets inside the vampire exploded with the power of a dozen miniature suns. Its mouth opened in a silent scream. It flopped along the ground like a fish, sucking in oxygen. Its body quaked and spasmed as flesh, muscle, bone, and even blood dissolved faster than the time it took to blink. A few seconds after being shot, the vampire was gone—not even ashes remained.

Christian stood amid the bodies of those he had slain. He took a deep breath, held it for one second, then two. Slowly, he released it, and all the tension that he'd built up during the intense fight disappeared.

The battle was over.

Mission accomplished.

Holstering his guns, Christian looked around at the blood on the floor, at the corpses, and for a moment, he felt nothing but pity. These creatures were once human. Humans who, through incredible misfortune, had encountered a vampire that turned them, gave them their lust for blood.

It was sad to think about, and sadder still that he'd been forced to kill them. All Christian could do for them now was pray. He knelt down on the floor, hands clasped, and prayed for God to forgive him for the lives he'd just taken, for it was not their fault they had ended up like this.

His praying done, Christian stood up and pulled a thin phone with a touch screen from the back pocket of his pants. Opening the main menu, he selected one of the only two applications that he used it for: Calling.

Pressing the phone to his ear, Christian waited for someone to answer. He didn't have to wait long, thankfully.

"Hello," a male voice answered. "Welcome to the Catholic Church Hotline, where we take care of all your godly needs. My name is Tristin, and I'll be your priest for this evening. If you have any sins that you would like to confess, then please—"

"Cut that out, Tristin. You know it's me."

"Oh, Christian." Tristin feigned surprise. "It's so nice to hear from you. It's been so long since our last clandestine phone call, and you hung up before I could ask if—"

"Look," Christian said patiently, or as patiently as he could when dealing with Tristin. "I'm just calling in to let headquarters know that my mission is complete. The vampire coven infecting the abandoned sector of Los Angeles at Colyton has been eradicated."

A low whistle sounded from the other end. "An entire vampire coven, huh? That's impressive. I thought you only had one target."

"I did, but it turned out the target was part of a coven. I felt it would be prudent to dispose of them all before they became aware that someone was onto them or they decided to move."

"Going above and beyond the call of duty, as always," Tristin joked. "How many were there this time?"

"…… There were only eight in this coven."

"Only eight, he says. You do realize that when we take out covens, even small ones, we usually need at least three or four other Executioners to do it, don't you?"

Christian detected a hint of sarcasm in the other man's voice. He ignored it. "I fail to see your point."

"I guess I don't have one," Tristin replied in a cheery voice, and Christian twitched. "I'm just saying that it's impressive. That style of yours sure is scary—crazy, insane, and suicidal beyond belief—but also scary. Anyway, I've just sent word to the Cleaners. They're on their way right now to dispose of the evidence, so you should head on back to HQ. You know that Samantha is going to want her report."

"Understood."

"So, about that thing I was talking about the other day. Would you care to—"

Christian hung up before he could hear the rest of Tristin's words.

Taking one last look at the bodies, he left the warehouse. No one would discover the evidence of his fight. The Cleaners were most efficient when it came to disposing of corpses, and they always arrived on the scene quickly. He guessed they would show up in maybe five minutes, seven at the most.

Morning was coming. The sun peeked through the city, a towering jungle of glass and steel, its many skyscrapers standing tall like giant monoliths. Sunlight outlined the structures in a reddish-orange glow. In a few short hours, morning would truly be upon them.

Christian boarded a bus at the nearest stop, leaving behind an abandoned warehouse and over half a dozen corpses.

Chapter 2

The jarring of the bus woke Christian from his slumber.

Blinking several times, he groggily focused on his surroundings. He was sitting in the back of the bus, a habit that he had picked up during his third mission, in which he had been almost killed by a vampire who'd sneaked onto a bus with him. From his position, he could see several people of different ethnic and cultural groups. America had always been considered a melting pot, where many different nationalities and religious groups converged. He wondered what these people would think if they knew that America, and the world at large, had more than just different types of humans living among them.

God only knows what kind of chaos that would unleash. Best not to think about it.

Christian looked out the window at the world passing by. He noticed that the bus was on Center and Temple Street. This was where he got off.

After yanking on a small cord dangling over his head, Christian stood up as the bus rolled to a stop. He carefully shifted his sheaths to make sure they were at least partially concealed by his cloak—he got enough looks for just the cloak—and exited the bus.

The sights and scents of the city pervaded his senses as he ambled down the street. Crowds of people shared the sidewalk with him—the woman gripping her child's hand as she tried to keep him from running off, the old man who walked with a stooped back and used a cane, the mass of blue-collar workers getting on and off buses and walking out of subway stations. The congestion of the walkways was second only to the bumper-to-bumper traffic on the roads.

The city was far too busy for his tastes. The people of Los Angeles had no concept of relaxation, and the city reflected the state of its people.

By the Almighty, I wish this place at least had a nice park where I could sit down and read one of my light novels.

He arrived at the main headquarters of the Executioners' California Division. The building, like most buildings belonging to the Catholic Church, was reminiscent of a cathedral. It towered over him, nothing like the skyscrapers surrounding it, but imposing in its own way. Large white bricks gleamed in the sun as if freshly painted, and the many Corinthian columns lining the entrance shone with a brilliant luster. A stained glass window above the entrance depicted the birth of Jesus Christ.

No one would deny that it was a beautiful building, but Christian had always thought it a little too obvious a place for the headquarters to be located.

Entering the building through a single door located in a small alley on the left brought Christian into a modern waiting room. Several chairs lined the outermost wall near the entrance. The white floor tiles sparkled under the overhead lights, and multiple paintings hung from the walls.

In the back of the room equidistant from the north and south walls, a young woman sat behind a desk.

Her long brown hair lay smoothly against her head, and matching brown eyes hid behind a pair of rimless glasses. Her gray business suit flattered her figure, allowing her to look professional while maintaining a womanly appearance. While her outfit lent her a sense of professionalism found in most middle-aged men and women, she was actually two years younger than him.

She looks more like a businesswoman than a member of the Church.

Christian walked up to the desk. The woman hadn't noticed him yet, busy as she was typing on a computer. He waited for several seconds, but when it became clear that she wasn't even paying attention, he coughed into his hand.

"Claire."

The woman looked up from her work. Her eyes widened in surprise, then gave a delighted smile when she realized who was standing before her.

"Christian, you're back. Tristin was just telling everyone about how you completed another mission. Congratulations."

I will not kill my comrade. I will not kill my comrade. I will not kill my comrade.

"Thanks. I guess." Christian returned the smile with an uncertain one of his own. He liked Claire, really, but the way her eyes sparkled when she spoke with him made him uncomfortable.

"You do very good work. I heard from Tristin that you took out an entire coven this time. I'm sure God is pleased with the work you do as well."

I'm going to kill him.

"Thank you," Christian said, withholding a grimace. "May I go on in now? Or is Samantha busy?"

"Go ahead." Claire gestured toward the hallway on her left. "She's expecting you."

"Thanks again."

As Christian moved toward the hallway, Claire called after him. "You'll have to tell me about your latest mission when you finish talking to Samantha. I would love to hear about it."

Christian didn't answer her. Not only did he feel uncomfortable when people tried talking to him about his job, but it was against protocol to reveal anything related to his missions with someone who did not hold a certain rank in the Catholic Church's hierarchy. Claire was just an aide. Her job was to act as a secretary, help answer inquiries, and keep the day-to-day operations running smoothly—not to know the details of his missions.

Besides, she shouldn't know the gory details. *The least I can do is spare her from those horrors.*

He walked down the long hallway, his booted feet clicking against the black marble tiles. The hallway wasn't very high, reaching just a few feet above his head.

He passed several doors before stopping at the end of the hall in front of a double door. The dark wood stood in stark contrast to the golden plaque in the center and the white walls of the hallway surrounding it. Embedded into the plaque was a single name, written in elegant cursive: *Samantha D'Arc.*

Christian knocked on the door.

"Come in," a female voice called from the other side.

Opening the door and walking in, Christian took a moment to gather his wits by studying the room's interior.

The white walls were practically bare of ornamentation: only a sword blessed by the pope himself, an antiquated-looking gun, a medal shaped like a crucifix, and a single photograph of the pope. There were no chairs or couches, just a couple of filing cabinets stacked against the wall, and a desk located in the very back.

The desk was the most ornate item in the room. It was large, crafted in the shape of a crescent, and made from finely grained rosewood. Several golden motifs of a crucifix, the symbol of the Catholic Church's Executioners, lined the bottom edges and legs.

Sitting behind the desk was a young woman. Dark, straight, almost raven-black hair flowed down her head, nearly reaching her waist, and long bangs covered her left eye. The single piercing blue eye that remained visible flickered back and forth, reading a report on her desk. Her thin lips were set in a small frown of concentration.

She wore the robes designating her as a commander of the Executioners, though the outfit looked more like a military uniform than a robe. Its crisp, dark-blue pants and long-sleeved shirt were fastened together with straps instead of buttons. The difference between this outfit and standard military garb—aside from the straps—lay only in the dark-blue cape that fell to her ankles.

Christian walked farther into the room, his footsteps undoubtedly alerting the woman to his presence.

"I'll be with you in just a moment," she said, not looking up from what she was reading.

He stopped a few feet from the desk and stood with his feet spaced shoulder-width apart, his hands clasped behind his back. Christian knew her routine by now. Whenever Samantha became like this, it was impossible to get her attention short of making the roof collapse on her.

"My apologies for making you wait," Samantha said as she finished going through another few sheets of paperwork.

"No apologies necessary. I understand that you're busy."

Samantha's head snapped up at the sound of his voice.

"Oh… Christian." She sounded surprised. "I'm sorry. If I had known it was you, I would have stopped working. You should have said something."

"I didn't want to interrupt."

Samantha smiled. "That's just like you. Always putting others ahead of yourself."

Christian shifted uncomfortably. Samantha must have noticed because she straightened a moment later, and her face smoothed into the impassive and collected gaze of a leader.

"I'll receive your report now."

"Right."

Christian took a second to collect himself and then gave her a report of his encounter with the vampire coven. Samantha listened, nodding at some places and frowning at others. When he finished, she leaned back and sighed.

"An entire coven," she muttered, looking tired. "I can't believe an entire coven was hiding out in Los Angeles, and we never realized it until now."

"The Intelligence Division definitely dropped the ball on this one."

Samantha shook her head. "The Intelligence Division wasn't at fault. We've received reports that several covens have been migrating to the western United States for some reason. I didn't believe any of them would have the gall to move so close to an Executioners regional office, but it seems I was mistaken."

"They probably didn't know. It's not like we have a sign pointing at us or anything."

"Maybe, but it should be common knowledge among the supernatural population that all major cities in the US have a regional office. Even if we don't advertise ourselves, it should be more than obvious by this point. No, I believe this is something else. It's almost like something has them spooked."

"Spooked?"

"It's nothing. Why don't you head to the barracks and take this time to relax? I'm sure I'll have more work for you soon."

"Ma'am!"

"And please don't call me ma'am. I'm only a few years older than you are. We were even trained to be Executioners at the same time."

"My apologies, ma—Samantha."

"Better. Now, go rest up."

"Yes, ma'am."

"Christian…"

"… Sorry."

***

Several hours later, Christian sat in his room writing up his report. Despite having given one orally to Samantha, he still needed to file his report with the Intelligence Division. They would create the copies. One would be sent back to Samantha, and another would be filed for future reference.

It was nearing noon. His report was almost done; there were just a few more details to work out, a bit more information to give. After that, he could get some rest. He might not have been injured during his mission, but fighting vampires always tired him, especially because he refused to use performance-enhancing drugs like most of the other Executioners.

His cloak hung on the coat hanger located in the corner of his room near the door. He now wore only a black sleeveless shirt and black pants. His boots and gloves had also been taken off, leaving him barefoot and his hands uncovered. While it was a simple pleasure, he reveled in the sensation of his extremities being unconfined by clothing.

Samantha would probably say I was being uncouth. The thought made him chuckle.

As he wrote up his report, recalling the battle so he could give more details, he thought back to how he'd first become an Executioner. After his home had been lost to him when he was six, he'd been taken in by the Catholic Church. On his tenth birthday, they began training him in the art of combat.

Orphans who grew up in one of the Church's orphanages ended up working for the Church in some way—usually. A few went on to become clergymen and priests. Some worked as secretaries and aides. Others rose to prominence and became bishops.

Christian had gone on to become an Executioner. The normal citizens, those who attended sermons to worship God, knew nothing about this secret sect of the Church. It was for their own protection.

Executioners were given the task of eliminating abominations from the world. They killed the unholy creatures that had no qualms about snuffing out human lives: vampires, werewolves, demons, trolls, goblins, chupacabra, mermaids, sirens, succubi, and so on. For the sake of humanity, Executioners stained their hands in blood. To protect the innocent, they committed one of the sins that the Ten Commandments forbade: Thou shalt not kill.

Even though he disliked killing, Christian took his job as an Executioner very seriously. He never wanted to see someone else suffer because some aberration decided to slaughter innocent people for their own sick amusement.

His pen moved with fluid grace as he put the finishing touches on his report. After reading it over and making sure it contained all the pertinent information, he set the sheet back on the desk.

A loud yawn escaped him and, after stretching his arms above his head to try to work out the stiffness in his muscles, he looked at the clock. It was an hour past noon.

He stood and moved away from his desk, stumbling toward the bed. His bedroom, much like Samantha's office, was rather Spartan, possessing little in the way of furniture or decorations. The Catholic Church did not believe in having more possessions than was strictly necessary. Humility was a virtue to be upheld. The newer members, those who had only became Executioners recently, didn't care about those virtues, but he did.

The only object in his room that could be considered in excess was the sleek, advanced-looking tablet sitting on his desk. It was his only personal possession, aside from his weapons and clothes.

As he crossed the room, Christian divested himself of his clothes and left them on the floor where he dropped them. He reached his bed and quickly crawled underneath the covers. He fell asleep, and in his sleep, Christian dreamed of fire and smoke, of lives lost and lives taken. His dreams always were the stuff of nightmares.

Chapter 3

Fire was everywhere. It consumed everything. No matter where I looked, all I could see was the bright red flames that engulfed my home. All around me there roared a blazing inferno that caused my skin to blister and my body to burn.

It was not just my house that was on fire. Everything else was on fire, too. The entire town I lived in was burning. The once humble dwellings of my neighbors were caught in a blaze. The house belonging to the funny old man who always told jokes had collapsed on itself. Walls reduced to rubble. Roofs crumbling as flames crackled and popped.

I could hear screams in the distance. Cries for help. Cries of despair. I wanted to scream, too, but couldn't.

Smoke filled the sky, as well as my lungs. It clung to my skin and clothes. It clogged my throat. I couldn't breathe, I could scarcely think, as I stumbled through the acrid blackness.

"Mom! Dad!"

I called out to my parents in desperation, or I tried to. The smoke made it difficult. Several times, I found myself choking as I attempted to shout.

"Mom! Dad!"

Smoke or not, call I did. Over and over again.

"Mom! Dad!"

I called because I couldn't believe they were not here with me. I had to believe they were around here, somewhere, someway, somehow. They couldn't have vanished. They had to be here.

"Mom! Dad!"

They had to be!

"MOM! DAD!"

But there was no one. No one but myself and the infernal flames and the cries of the damned. My parents were gone.

Tears gathered in my eyes. Yet even those were consumed by the heat of the flames, the liquid evaporating almost as soon as it was produced.

Where were my parents? What had happened to them? Why was I alone?

***

Knock! Knock! Knock!

"Wakey-wakey, rise and bakey!"

Christian's sleep was rudely interrupted by childish words produced by an annoyingly familiar male voice. Opening his eyes, he looked around, groaned, and then rolled over onto his side and tried to go back to sleep. Maybe if he ignored the voice, his tormenter would leave him alone.

"Come on now, sleepyhead! Get that butt out of bed!"

The knocking persisted, as did the voice. Worse still, the owner of said voice had started rhyming. That the man banging on his door had now resorted to terrible rhyming only served to give Christian a headache. There was no way he couldn't *not* answer the door, not unless he was willing to deal with the mother of all migraines.

"Christian! Christian! Come on, Christian!"

With an exasperated groan, Christian stumbled out of bed and made his way to the door.

He flung the door open with startling violence and cast a withering glare at the man who dared to interrupt his sleep.

"What?!"

"You're always so cheerful when you first wake up," Tristin, the person on the other side of the door, said with his ever-present grin. Wavy blond hair hovered over light blues eyes, and framed a handsome face. Pretty boy. That's what this guy was, one of those Prince Charming types, the ones that made women flock to them just by standing around. And Tristin never failed to bask in their attention.

Though just how all those women dealt with his personality was beyond Christian.

Tristin chuckled in response to the scowl Christian sent him.

"Nice to see you acting so lively today. You may want to put some clothes on, though, as I doubt others will appreciate your state of undress as much as I do."

It took Christian a moment to process those words into something that he could understand. After several seconds of silently staring at the other man like he had two heads and a pair of bat wings coming out of his back, he looked down at himself, and squawked when he realized something that his sleep-deprived mind had not comprehended yet.

He was still in his boxers.

"Hold on a second." An embarrassed flush crossed his cheeks as he slammed the door in Tristin's face. He made his way across the room, grabbed his pants, and shoved himself into them before once more opening the door.

Christian cast another tired glare at the young man who'd come knocking. Now that he was a little more awake, he noted that Tristin wore his full uniform as a member of the Intelligence Division. The dark long-sleeved turtleneck shirt complimented Tristin's sun-kissed skin. It was a dark charcoal color, the same color as the man's pants. A small shoulder cape covered his left shoulder to the bicep. Strapped to his right thigh was a small 9mm pistol, standard issue.

"What do you want, Tristin?" Christian asked, his voice snappish. He was not in the mood to deal with this man. "It's too early in the morning to deal with your antics."

"For starters, it's not morning; it's two o'clock in the afternoon."

"Whatever," Christian grumbled. He rubbed a hand over his face and through his hair. "My question hasn't changed. What do you want? I swear, if you're just here to annoy me—"

"As much as I enjoy bantering with you, I'm actually here because Samantha asked me to come get you."

Christian was nonplussed.

"What? Samantha?" He frowned at Tristin, his eyes squinting. By the Almighty, he was tired. "Why would she tell you to get me? Why didn't she just page me or something?"

"Two reasons." Tristin held up an index finger. "One: I just so happened to be delivering a report when she decided she needed to speak with you. Two: you weren't answering your phone."

"Oh." Christian paused He wondered if his cheeks were as red as they felt.

"Yeah, I figured you would be exhausted after hunting down those vamps and were probably still asleep." Tristin shook his head in slight disbelief. "I still can't get over how many you killed this time. Nine. That must be a new record."

Christian sighed. He wasn't up to listening to Tristin put his accomplishments on a pedestal. While the man didn't seem to have a case of hero worship, he'd never been good at dealing with praise. The fact that it was now coming from Tristin, the most annoying person in existence, just made that praise worse.

Time to change the subject.

"You said Samantha wanted to see me?"

"Yep," Tristin said, popping the *p* at the end. "She said that she wanted to see you as soon as possible." He paused, and then took a quick whiff of the air around him. His nose wrinkled. "You'll probably want to take a shower first though; you reek."

Christian was embarrassed, but he didn't let Tristin on to that fact.

"Yeah, well, that's what happens when you're so tired that you collapse after fighting over half a dozen vampires."

"Indeed," Tristin nodded sagely. "By the way, and this is just a suggestion, you should also—"

Christian didn't hear the rest of Tristin's words.

Because he'd just slammed the door in the other man's face.

***

For the second time in twenty-four hours, Christian stood before his commanding officer. This wasn't as unusual an occurrence for him as it was for others. He was often called in to meet with Samantha, though he had never been called twice within a six-hour period. That was odd. He didn't say anything, however, assuming correctly that she would inform him of the reason that he had been called so soon after completing his last mission.

"I have another mission for you," Samantha said after taking a moment to look at him with a touch of concern. She probably noticed the bags under his eyes. They were not prominent, but they were certainly dark enough to be noticeable. "I know that you just got back from a mission, and

I'm sorry for having to dump this on you so soon, but we don't have anyone else to turn to. You were specifically requested for this mission."

"It's fine, I don't mind working a little more than usual. I know how important our work is." Christian suppressed a frown. Maybe it was just him, but his superior appeared to be uneasy. She spoke with an odd inflection in her voice that he had never heard before.

It's probably just my imagination.

Samantha gave him a strained smile before quickly schooling her features, masking her emotions. Opening a drawer on the left side of her desk, she reached in and pulled out a single item: a photograph, judging by its shape, size, and composition.

"Your mission is to kill this target." She slid the photograph across the desk to him.

Christian picked it up and studied the photo, wondering who he'd have to kill this time.

A prominent frown soon appeared.

The picture was of a girl, an incredibly stunning girl with brilliant blue eyes, fair skin, and a smile to die for. Long blond hair cascaded past her shoulders in gentle waves, framing a face that combined incredible innocence and extraordinary sensuality. *Beautiful* did not begin to aptly describe her.

He looked up from the photo, gazing into Samantha's eyes, frowning.

"This is not a vampire." It wasn't a question.

"No, she is not," Samantha said slowly. "She is a succubus."

"Ah." Christian nodded. "That explains why she doesn't have any vampiric traits." It also explained why her beauty appeared so human. "She's a—wait." He paused. "What?"

Samantha sighed. "She's a succubus."

"A succubus?" Christian stared. Samantha gave him a nod. "A succubus?" he repeated, as if he'd hear something different by asking a second time.

"Yes, Christian." Samantha sounded just as off-kilter as he felt. "Your next target is a succubus."

"You do realize that succubi are outside my jurisdiction? They're outside the jurisdiction of all men." Succubi posed an inherent danger to males; that's why female Executioners were chosen to hunt them. They hunted mermaids and sirens as well.

"I am well aware that men are normally not allowed to hunt succubi," Samantha told him. "However, there have been slight… problems that make sending females to dispose of this one troublesome."

This time Christian was sure he had not imagined it. His superior definitely felt uneasy. Did something about this mission bother her? Or was she simply uncomfortable sending a man to do a woman's job? Few were the times that he wished to be capable of hearing the thoughts of others. This was one of those times.

"What kind of problems?"

"The deadly kind."

Christian looked down at the photo again. The girl in the picture didn't seem deadly or dangerous, but he knew better than to judge a light novel by its cover.

He looked back up at Samantha.

Seeing that she had his attention, his superior continued. "So far we have dispatched two female Executioners. Our first was Jeanne Oria, a newer recruit. Our reports indicated that the target was an easy mark and would be a good first kill for one of our more inexperienced members to gain some much needed experience."

"I'm guessing Jeanne never returned," Christian deduced, looking back at the picture in a new light. All Executioners, even newer recruits, were extensively trained in their chosen field before being allowed on missions. If the girl in the picture had managed to kill an Executioner, then she must be a dangerous individual indeed.

And yet, he felt there was something off about Samantha's words. They rang true, yet he knew that she was not telling him something.

"You're correct." Placing her elbows on the desk, Samantha laced her fingers together and rested her chin on her hands. "About a week after Jeanne made contact with the target, she disappeared. We never saw or heard from her again. At about the same time, our target disappeared as well."

Christian listened to Samantha closely, absorbing all the knowledge he could. You never knew what sort of seemingly useless bits of information would come in handy.

"About a week after that we found the target again. She had not moved far, just a few miles from her hometown on Rhode Island. We don't know if she had been trying to shake us off her trail, or if she just didn't care whether we found her. But we weren't going to look a gift horse in the mouth. Because our raw recruit died, this time, we decided to send in a more experienced member—Sara Exalise."

Christian raised an eyebrow. "The famed 'Huntress,' if I'm not mistaken."

Sara was well known among their ranks as someone who never let a mark escape, and she always killed her targets in the most brutal manner possible. Her hatred of abominations was as famous as the bow she wielded. She was not one of the XIII like himself, but she was powerful enough to have earned a nickname.

"Considering what happened to Jeanne, we didn't want to take any chances."

Christian nodded. He could see why they would send someone like Sara. While he had never met the woman personally, it was often said that her talent at using a bow was on par with his ability to dual wield guns and swords. There had actually been rumors that the higher-ups were thinking of changing the XIII to the XIV by adding her as a member.

And yet...

"I take it there were some problems?"

"That would be putting it mildly." Samantha's sigh spoke of exhaustion. "Only two days after Sara left for her mission, she disappeared. A month later, she was found out at sea by a passing patrol boat, her neck torn open and her chest covered in lacerations from what we assume were a set of claws."

"I see," Christian murmured, glancing at the picture once again. The girl looked so innocent and pure. It was hard to imagine that she was a monster that sucked the sexual essence out of men, or that she was capable of killing two Executioners.

Which was probably how she had killed them in the first place. They likely underestimated her because she looked so innocent.

"It sounds like there is more to this case than meets the eye."

Samantha nodded. "That is what we believe as well. When we realized how dangerous the situation was, we decided to send someone else to do the job—Anthony Trekovski."

"Isn't his section in charge of eliminating incubi?" asked Christian. Incubi were the male version of succubi. Just like a succubus sucked out the sexual essence of men, incubi did the same thing, but to women instead.

"He is. We felt that having someone who had experience with similar creatures would at least be better able to defend themselves against a succubus's sexual aura." Samantha breathed a deep sigh. Her shoulders sagged almost imperceptibly. "Exactly one week after we sent him, Anthony vanished along with the target, who's reappeared on the opposite side of the United States just two months ago."

"And so you've decided to send me?" Christian raised an eyebrow. "Someone who has no experience with killing succubi *or* incubi."

The jurisdiction of the Executioner section that he belonged to exterminated vampires, werewolves, and demons, and while those types of monsters were the most dangerous physically, they were not mentally dangerous like some of the others—certain demons that manipulated the mind aside. The powers of the creatures that Christian hunted lay solely in their ability to greatly increase the strength, speed, and the durability of their bodies. Or, in the case of certain demons, wield supernatural powers that caused wide-scale devastation.

"HQ is beginning to get desperate," Samantha told him, a solemn note in her voice. "With one of our best dead and another missing, we're being forced to turn to someone who we feel can get the job done. You have never failed in a mission before, and you are now the most powerful Warrior of your generation. You're also incredibly stubborn, which should help counteract the succubus's *Aura of Allure*. Honestly, right now, you are the only person we can turn to."

There was still something that Samantha wasn't telling him. She knew something that he didn't, and it was obviously something that she couldn't tell him, because if she could, she already would have. Whatever it was, it obviously made her uneasy.

"And what would happen should I die?"

Samantha sucked in a breath. "Should you die, then we will be forced to label her as an SS-class threat and order all of our forces to stay away. It wouldn't be the first time that we've been forced to admit defeat."

Such a thing had happened on occasion. Christian knew this. A number of vampires and werewolves had been given the SS-class threat, the Executioners proclaiming them too powerful to slay, and there were even more demons that no one human could ever hope to kill. These creatures often lived for well over a thousand years, gaining unimaginable power as a result. Fortunately, the monsters that gained that kind of strength tended to be reclusive, disdaining human contact.

Christian closed his eyes, contemplating everything he had been told thus far.

"I'm not going to force you to accept this assignment." He opened his eyes to find Samantha studying him, her concern more than evident. If he didn't know better, he would have said that she was pleading with him *not* to take the mission. "If you don't want to, just say the word, and I'll let the higher-ups know. They might raise a fuss, but they won't be able to do much else. The Bishopric knows they cannot afford to lose you. If—"

"I'll do it," Christian said. Normally, he would never dare to interrupt his superior, but he felt that the current situation warranted it. Samantha was questioning his ability to complete a mission. If there was one thing that he took seriously, it was his job, his duty. He was a slayer of monsters. He protected the innocent from the horrors that hid among them. That was his mandate.

"Christian?"

"I'll do it," he repeated. I'll find this succubus and ensure that she can never harm another human again." His eyes hardened and his fists clenched. "I'll exterminate her."

"Christian…"

"Don't try to make me change my mind on this. I have the power to make a difference, so I should put it to good use."

Samantha's stare suddenly went flat. "You picked that up from one of those weird books of yours, didn't you?"

Christian turned his head, evading Samantha's blank stare. "…Maybe."

After another moment, Samantha sighed. "I see there's no stopping you. You've always done what you felt was right regardless of the consequences to yourself."

"The job of an Executioner is to protect humanity from the creatures that would inflict great harm upon them," Christian said. "I won't let myself shy away from danger when my contribution could help further our cause. For the good of the human race, I will do God's will and protect those who cannot protect themselves."

"Very well." Samantha straightened in her chair and looked at him with all the authority of her station. "Christian, in three days' time, you are to head for Seal Beach in Orange County, where the Intelligence Division has reported the target is currently located. I would suggest heading to the Science Division before that, and getting yourself equipped as well. Your regular weapons won't be as effective on this mission; they're too obvious."

"I understand."

"Here." Samantha handed him a folder. "This contains all the information we've uncovered about your target: names, associates, where she goes to school and what she is studying; everything that we were able to find is in here. It's not as much as we normally have, but it should help."

Christian took the folder and tucked it under his right arm. He would look at it later tonight. Crossing his left arm over his chest and placing his hand on his heart, he bowed to his superior.

"I will do as you suggest."

"Very well. You are dismissed."

The expression on Samantha's face was indecipherable as she looked at him. Conflicting emotions swirled in her eyes. Christian couldn't tell what the woman was thinking, but part of him realized that it was probably for the best that he remain ignorant.

Turning on his heel, Christian made for the door.

"Christian?"

He paused, his hand resting lightly on the handle, and looked back at Samantha. Her lips twitched for a moment, and he could tell that she was fighting the compulsion to worry them between her teeth. It was a nervous habit that she'd picked up from when she was younger.

"May God bless you on your journey."

A moment passed. Then two. Christian gave her a nod.

Then he left, closing the door behind him. The last thing he saw was his superior's discontented expression.

Chapter 4

The Executioners was a vast organization. It had been founded by Pope Sixtus IV in the 1400s after the Church had discovered that Dracula, or Vlad the Impaler, was a vampire.

While it was not the oldest of the Catholic Church's religious sects, nor one of the largest, it was the best funded and most widely dispersed. Their organization spanned the entire globe, with many agents working undercover, doing God's will for the good of humanity.

The organization was divided into several divisions, apart from the Executioners themselves: The Science Division, the Intelligence Division, the Administrative Division, the Medical Division, and the Security Division. Then there were the Executioners themselves. The Cleaners also didn't belong to any division, but that was simply the nature of their job.

Within the Executioners, members were divided by a caste system: Assassins, Warriors, and the Casteless.

Christian was a Warrior. Martial combat was the lifeblood of his caste. No mission for him or his fellow Warriors ended in anything but violence.

Assassins were responsible for killing aberrations that did not rely on power and strength to kill, but cunning and guile. Succubi, incubi, mermaids, and sirens, among others, were the Assassins' prey. This particular group had more women than men, since most of the creatures they killed were well known for their talent at seducing men to their deaths. Only incubi, the male version of a succubus, required a male assassin to dispose of.

Lastly were the Casteless, those who had yet to prove themselves in combat. They were generally newer recruits who had seen little to no action. Members of the Casteless typically killed small-time monsters: undines, griffins, and pixies were among the few weak monster types that Casteless members were sent against. All members of the other two groups had been Casteless until they had proven their worth through accomplishing numerous missions.

There was a stark difference between Assassins and Warriors. Warriors were combat specialists, trained extensively in the use of various weaponry and hand-to-hand combat. Assassins were taught how to get close to a target, befriending their prey and then killing their target once they had dropped their guard. They were also specialists of long-range combat, and many members were experts at using sniper rifles. It was said that a member of the Assassins could kill someone before their target even realized they were in danger.

Christian was not an Assassin. He had no talent at getting close to his targets and killing them when they least expected it, never mind befriending them. He also didn't know the first thing about killing from long distances. Mid-range with his guns, yes, but he couldn't shoot those any farther than about five hundred meters.

That's why the first thing he did after leaving Samantha was head over to the Science Division. They were the ones in charge of producing all of the weapons and equipment that the Executioners used to complete their missions. He hoped they would have something that he could use that wouldn't require extensive training.

***

A dinging sound alerted him to the elevator reaching its destination. The door before him slid open, and he exited.

The hallway before him looked much different from the one Samantha's office was located in; sturdier, and much more plain. The walls, floor, and ceiling were made of thick concrete, all painted a drab gray. There were no decorations in this hall.

Christian's feet thudded dully on the hard floor as he walked. He ignored the few people in lab coats that passed him by, as well as the strange looks they gave him. He hadn't been here since he'd received his four specialized weapons from Samantha herself. The first time he had ever come to the Science Division was also his last time.

That was six years ago. He had been fourteen at the time.

At the end of the hall, he came to a stop in front of a large set of steel double doors. They were twice his height, and nearly three times as wide as they were tall. There was a complex locking mechanism on the doors that consisted of circular protrusions. Several steel bars ran horizontally and diagonally across the door's frame.

Standing in front of a pair of handprint scanners on either side of the door were two guards. They wore uniforms like those one might expect to see in the military or the police. Unlike most of the Executioners, who had a tendency to personalize their wardrobe, members of the various divisions wore normal uniforms. Members of the Security Division, like these two, had clothing that consisted of plain, dark-blue military fatigues and a long-sleeved button-up shirt of the same color. Strapped across their backs were advanced-looking automatic rifles.

"Identification?" one of them asked.

"Christian, identification number 0666906."

"Hold on for a moment." The one who had asked the question typed Christian's identification number into a small touchscreen tablet. After a few seconds, the tablet beeped. "Confirmed. You're allowed to enter."

The two turned around and placed their hands on the scanners. After several seconds, there was a loud beep, followed by a clicking noise and some hissing as the hydraulics on the door kicked in. The four circular protrusions began to rotate. As they moved, the steel bars covering the door retracted into the walls, ceiling, and floor. Slowly, ponderously, the double doors broke apart.

"I don't think I need to tell you this, but I would advise caution when you're in there," the guard on the left warned him.

"I'll take that under advisement," Christian said dryly. The Science Division was well known for creating incredibly dangerous items that were as harmful to the people using them as to those they were meant to be used against. There were actually more deaths in the Science Division than among the Warriors, Assassins, and Casteless combined.

As Christian crossed the threshold, the hallway opened into a monstrously sized room. The ceiling stood high above his head, covered in massive steel girders and a network of pipes. He didn't know the exact measurements of the room itself, but it easily spanned the length and width of at least three football fields.

All around the room were dozens of people in lab coats. They appeared to be working on various technological advancements. Some held small, innocuous-looking devices; a cell phone, a ring, a necklace with a cross on it. None of the items looked particularly dangerous—until they detonated with enough concussive force to knock down everyone around them. Sometimes they exploded while still in the hands of the one developing them.

In other cases, he saw people testing a variety of firearms, including one woman who looked as if she was wielding a wrist-attached flamethrower. At least he thought it was a wrist-attached flamethrower. He couldn't tell because the woman was running around, her body lit up like an out-of-control bonfire.

The loud *vrooming* of cars alerted Christian to the racetrack some several dozen meters away, where cars used for specific missions were tested. All the various types of vehicles they built had a number of armaments on them, including but not limited to machine guns, grenade launchers, jet propulsion systems, and rims that shot needles... needles that exploded on contact.

Just a few feet from him, one particular individual suddenly exploded in a spray of violence and gore that splattered against the floor. The man had been handling some kind of capsule, though just what it did was something that Christian couldn't fathom, other than it being lethal.

Christian didn't know how the people in this room could just continue about their business, as if nothing was wrong, when one of their number suddenly exploded in a display of blood and brain matter. A part of him was positive that he didn't want to know, either.

"Ah, you must be Christian."

Turning to the voice that called his name, Christian came face to face with a young man who couldn't be much older than he was. Greasy blond hair reminded Caspian of Kirito, a character in a light novel that he'd read a few years back, whose hair was similar to that of a bird's nest. Inquisitive gray eyes stared at him from behind a pair of rectangular spectacles. Like every other member of the Science Division, he wore a lab coat.

"I've been expecting you. Samantha called ahead and let me know that you would be coming. My name is Sebastian Michaelis. It's a pleasure," the young man said, pushing his glasses up his nose with his index and middle finger.

"Pleased to make your acquaintance." Christian nodded a greeting. He didn't offer his hand to Sebastian, which appeared fine with Sebastian. A second later, Sebastian spun on his heel and beckoned Christian to follow him.

"I have been authorized to give you a weapon that I feel will be useful to you on your next mission."

"So you know what my mission is?" Christian asked as they passed a scientist who appeared to be injecting himself with some kind of liquid. The man's arm bulged beneath his lab coat seconds before the veins in his arm exploded violently, sending a shower of crimson blood splashing across the floor. Christian grimaced as the scientist began wailing. Sebastian just ignored it.

"Yes, yes, you're being asked to kill a succubus." Sebastian's grin told Christian how amused this knowledge made him. "Difficult business that, especially for a man. You do know about their *Aura of Allure*, don't you?"

"Of course." Even if his job wasn't the extermination of succubi, he had still learned about them. "The *Aura of Allure* is a trait that all succubi possess. Based on reports from experiments done by your division, succubi cannot turn it on or off, nor do they have any control over it. It's a passive ability that attracts men by increasing the amount of pheromones in the air and is always active. No male has been able to resist, though we know through your division's reports that the *Aura of Allure* doesn't work on other supernatural creatures."

"You are indeed correct." Sebastian nodded. "It's good to see someone who has done their homework. Another thing to note is that the *Aura of Allure* cannot be blocked or defended against, not by a man, at least. That's why women are sent to kill succubi."

"You don't have to tell me twice," Christian muttered to himself. "I still don't know why I'm being sent on this mission, in spite of the obvious danger posed."

"I'm sure Samantha has her reasons."

Christian wasn't so sure that Samantha had any part in this mission, but he chose not to voice the thought. Some might consider such thoughts treasonous.

He followed Sebastian as the young scientist wove through a throng of experiments, all of which seemed to involve the use of enhancement drugs. Christian did his best to ignore the scientists he passed. Some of them looked like they were about to start rampaging across the room and kill everyone there, which was probably why they were tied to chairs with thick chains that not even an Ancestor could break.

That was one of the many inherent risks when using enhancement drugs; they often left those who used them feeling inexplicable amounts of rage and bloodlust.

"Anyway, it's because of the succubus's Aura that I need a weapon that can take my target out at range," Christian determined. "I haven't studied a succubus's *Aura of Allure* in depth, but I know there is a limit to how far it can extend."

"It depends on the succubus in question," Sebastian told him. "Most succubi have a range of two dozen meters or so, but some can have a range as far as several kilometers, and a few only have a range of one or two meters."

They exited the Research and Development lab and entered another hallway. It was much smaller than the hall Christian had entered through, and it was made of white tiles instead of cement. The walls on either side of him were lined with long, tinted windows that he could not see through. This, he knew, was where the weapons that passed inspection and were ready for use were stored.

"Come along." Sebastian walked briskly down the hallway. Christian followed. They arrived at one of the many doors, which slid open as they reached it.

The room they entered was sterile. The walls, floor, and ceiling were all white. So was the table in the center of the room, and the large rectangular cabinets off to the side. The only color in the entire room, aside from them, were the many blinking lights located on the cabinets. It reminded Christian of a laboratory instead of storage space, or maybe even a morgue, morbid as the thought was.

"I have one weapon in particular that I think will be most useful to you for your next assignment." Sebastian walked over to a cabinet and pressed his thumb against one of the blinking lights. He held it for two seconds. A beep sounded, followed by a hiss and several loud clicks. Grabbing onto the handle, the weapons developer pulled the cabinet open.

Reaching in, he pulled out a large gun, long and sleek, painted jet black.

The first thing that Christian noticed about the weapon was the scope on top. It didn't look at all like a regular scope; it was square for one thing, and the lens looked more like a camera than an actual scope. The gun was also a bolt-action, meaning it could only fire a single shot, but it was lighter and more easily maintained than a semi-automatic. Unlike most guns, the barrel on this one was long, easily around twenty-four-inches, and possessed a heavier cross section, as well as external longitudinal fluting and a threaded muzzle. The stock at the end of the gun had been raised slightly to accommodate the high position of the scope.

Christian recognized the weapon, even if he had never used one. "That's a sniper rifle."

Sebastian adjusted his glasses once more. Christian didn't know why, but he had this sudden urge to hit the young scientist. There was just something about that action that really bothered him.

"This is not just any sniper rifle. It's based on the AS50. Of course, we have made several improvements and modifications to it. Its design is sleeker, it's easier to carry, and you can take it apart in order to hide it inside a moderately sized suitcase."

The young developer's glasses gleamed almost ominously as he looked at the weapon.

"On top of that, this rifle is made of the same alloy used to create those guns and swords that you use. Because of its composition, it is not only far lighter than most weapons, but also cannot be detected by metal detectors."

"So it's made out of Orichalcum," Christian hummed.

"Indeed it is."

Orichalcum was a rare, valuable substance that could not be produced naturally. The Church had stumbled upon how to make it sometime in the sixteenth century, after arresting an alchemist named Robert Boyle, who had been attempting to create a Philosopher's Stone by sacrificing several hundred humans. The method for creating Orichalcum had apparently been found in one of the many books written by Robert Boyle during his quest for immortality.

Christian was surprised they had built a weapon out of Orichalcum that wasn't for a member of the XIII. He knew all of the other XIII members. Thus, he knew that none of them used sniper rifles in their missions.

Had this weapon been built for Sara Exalise before she was killed? Didn't she use a bow and arrows?

"I've never used a sniper rifle before," Christian said cautiously. The only guns he'd ever used were handguns.

"Not to worry." Sebastian pointed at the large scope attached to the rifle. "This is the networked tracking scope. It has a tracking system known as the XactSystem. The scope contains a heads-up display that shows a variety of factors, such as wind speed and direction, target distance, gravity, the rotational velocity of the earth, and more. It also calculates when to fire for the most accurate shot." He sent Christian a sly glance. "Even a complete novice like yourself can become as good a shot as most professional snipers when using this system."

Christian grunted at the minor jab to his admittedly nonexistent sniper skills. It wasn't his fault he'd never so much as touched a sniper rifle. He was a Warrior, not an Assassin; he'd never had any need to learn how to use a weapon like this.

"This weapon doesn't seem all that dangerous compared to some of the other stuff I saw in the development lab," he commented.

"Ah, well, that's because I haven't gotten to the good part yet." Sebastien gave a mad-scientist sort of smile. "This weapon doesn't just act as a sniper rifle, but a plastic explosive as well. If you ever need to leave somewhere in a hurry, and can't take this with you, just press this red button by the ammo cartridge, and it will set a prime charge to explode the next time someone comes within one meter of it."

Silence.

"It also has a blast radius of five square meters."

More silence.

"Has anyone ever told you that you and everyone else in the Science Division are certifiably insane?" Christian asked.

"Many times." Sebastian's glasses glinted in the light as he pushed them up his nose.

Chapter 5

The simulation chamber located within the Executioners headquarters was unique. It used advanced holographic simulations to recreate the many scenarios their members might find themselves in when out in the field. Created and developed by a member of the Science Division several years before, it was the most advanced training ground in the world. There were only six others like it, each located in one of the main headquarters of the Executioners. Two were in America, while the others were in Africa, Italy, Russia, and Japan.

Christian had been using the simulation chamber for the past two days.

It had taken the form of a city. Imposing skyscrapers that reached for the heavens were all that could be seen for miles. Down below was a maze of streets filled with cars and pedestrians in equal measure.

He was lying on his stomach, on one of the many skyscrapers located within this holographic city. His sniper rifle sat in front of him on a tripod, and he was looking down its scope.

"'Even a novice like yourself can use it,' he said," Christian grumbled as he continued adjusting his aim. "'Nothing to worry about,' he said. 'It's easy,' he said." The information on the HUD changed again, forcing him to adjust his aim… again. "This is the last time I listen to that crazy scientist."

Contrary to what Sebastian had said, the XactSystem scope was *not* easy to use, nor was it user friendly. The heads-up display had so much information that it made Christian's head spin. Not only that, it made him constantly readjust its settings, since the variables changed continuously. No matter how many times he changed the position of his rifle to account for the different many variables that affected whether the bullet would reach its target, it still refused to give him the perfect shot.

He had been coming to this room each day to familiarize himself with his new weapon.

So far, he was not having any luck.

He hadn't hit a single target.

"'It's the most user-friendly program a rifle could have,' he said. 'So easy to use even the most technologically deficient fool could master it with ease,'" Christian continued to grumble as he made minute adjustments to the tilt and direction of his new weapon. His eyes flickered around, glancing at the many different bits and pieces of information that flashed across his HUD. A change in the wind's direction made him maneuver the sniper rifle a little to the right, and then a building appeared in front of him, blocking his shot. Clicking his tongue, he waited for the scope to account for this new variable. It shouldn't take more than a second for it to—

"Hey, Christian!"

"Tch!"

The simulated world disappeared, and Christian found himself lying on the floor of a room that looked like the inside of a cube. Every surface was gray. Several lines of glowing blue ran across the surface, along with a number of small lights that followed the lines. The lines and lights created an intricate pattern of sharp angles that covered the entire room. Christian didn't know how they worked, but he knew that these were the nodes that created the holographic constructs used in training simulations.

He let go of the sniper rifle, leaving it on the ground as he stood up. When he had finally gotten to his feet, he sent an annoyed glare toward the person who had interrupted his training.

"Tristin, what do you want?"

"Oh, man, that's harsh." Tristin, despite his words, did not look the least bit upset. Actually, he wore a large, face-splitting grin. "And here I thought you'd be happy to see me. Especially since I was going to ask if you wanted to join me and my new girlfriend for dinner tonight."

"I'll pass," Christian said dryly.

Tristin simply laughed off Christian's clipped reply. "That's so like you, Christian. Colder than winter in the Arctic. You really should get out more. Being cooped up in this place except when you're not on missions can't be good for you." His eyes lit up a second later. "I know! We should get you a nice girl to settle down with."

"You know as well as I do that members of the Executioners are not allowed to have intimate relationships with others," Christian said. "The only reason Samantha even tolerates your lewd behavior is because you're not an Executioner, and you have no intention of settling down."

"Hm, that is true," Tristin admitted. "But that doesn't mean you can't at least have a little fun. All the other Executioners know how to have a good time. If you want, I could even introduce you to Alexandria. I'm sure you two would get along famously."

"Not happening." Christian gave the other man a flat stare.

Tristin sighed. "Ha, you are being stubborn about this as always. You do know that sex is allowed, right? Ever since we started recruiting people outside of the faith, the laws against sexual relations have been more or less abolished."

"I would never debase myself by having sex with some random woman that I have no intention of marrying. Nor would I debase a woman by sleeping with her without having the intention of marrying her."

"Fine, fine," Tristin waved a hand in the air dismissively. "Suit yourself. Can't say I didn't try."

"Whatever." Christian ran a hand through his hair. "Did you come here for any reason other than to bother me?"

"Oh! Yes, I did, actually." Tristin grinned at him. "You only have a little less than ten hours before you have to leave for your next mission. Now, I know that you're really dedicated to doing the best you can on your missions, which is why you're trying to learn how to use that long, hard, thick gun over there, but you should know that a couple days' worth of training isn't going to teach you how to become an ace sniper."

That much had already become obvious to him. He didn't need Tristin to tell him that.

"So what am I supposed to do, then?"

The grin that split Tristin's face did not bode well for Christian. Not at all.

***

Standing beneath the shower head, his hands pressed against the wall as water coursed down his back and matted his hair to his forehead, Christian tried not to let his exhaustion get to him. The warm spray caused all of the muscles in his back to relax. It did a good job of soothing his aches and pains, but did little to soothe his frayed nerves.

Dealing with Tristin was always a chore. He didn't know why the guy was always bothering him. It was as if the man got off on agitating him. Christian was sure that Tristin knew his antics annoyed him to no end, which just made everything the guy did all the more upsetting.

Closing his eyes, Christian tried to will away his thoughts and focus on getting clean.

A few minutes later, he turned off the water and walked out of the communal showers, a towel wrapped around his waist. He walked over to the sink, his feet pattering against the blue and white tiles.

Pressing his hands against the marble countertop, Christian studied himself in the mirror. Raven-dark hair stuck out at odd angles, as if he had just gotten out of bed. He brushed at the bangs that hid his heterochromatic eyes; one emerald green and the other crimson. A straight nose sat above thin lips and a sharp chin and jaw.

His skin was light, not quite pale, but not tan either. He spent too much time indoors or outside during the night for the sun's rays to affect him. Scattered across his body were several scars, their pale pigmentation barely visible against his skin, only showing when the light hit them at a certain angle.

Those scars were reminders. Lessons that he took to heart. Each one had been earned early in his career, when he was still raw to the rigors of combat. All except one.

Christian traced a finger across one particular scar, the only scar that he had ever received outside of a mission. The scar that he had gained before becoming an Executioner. The last reminder of his past life. Of his unforgivable sin.

With a shake of his head, Christian dispelled those thoughts and moved away from the mirror. Thinking like that was dangerous, and it was not something that he should be doing. It was also unbecoming of an Executioner to lament over the past. It could not be changed. Only the future mattered.

It didn't take long to reach his room. The communal showers located in the Warriors' barracks were just a few minutes' walk from his assigned quarters.

Much like a military, each caste had barracks of their own. They weren't true barracks, because they were located underneath the cathedral that hid their base of operations. And while the Executioners all shared a single floor together, each caste was separated by wings. The Assassins' barracks was in west wing of the second basement, while the Warriors' barracks was in the eastern wing. The casteless, being the largest of their group, had the entire third basement to themselves. Meanwhile, the divisions within the Executioners—Science, Intelligence, and the Cleaners—lived outside of the Executioners headquarters.

Upon reaching the privacy of his room, Christian hung the towels on a rack, and put on a pair of boxer shorts. He climbed into bed and actually remembered to pull up the covers this time. He fell asleep soon after.

And in his sleep he dreamed of fire, of death, of salvation, and of sin.

Chapter 6

Corpses. They littered the street, the bodies of those who had died in the fires that consumed my town, laying strewn about like broken dolls that had been tossed aside and then trampled on by a giant. Mangled, charred corpses that looked like they'd been cooked for far too long in a furnace. Their forms were black and burnt beyond recognition. If it weren't for how they were shaped in the general semblance of a human, I wouldn't have believed that they were once people.

The stench of burning flesh filled my nose as I walked through the streets. I stumbled around more often than not.

My tears had long since dried up. Even if I could cry, the heat from the flames surrounding me would have evaporated them the moment they formed in my eyes.

I could scarcely feel anything anymore. I knew that I should be sad and angry and lost and helpless, but all I could dredge up was this deep-seated sense of emptiness. I felt nothing. I was nothing.

My strength began to wane. My legs gave out. I fell backward, and my head hit the charred pavement with a harsh crack. I didn't feel it, however, *as there was nothing left to feel. No pain. No emotions. Nothing. Just an endless void that had once been my heart.*

I stared up at the sky, what sky I could see, at least. Most of it was blocked by the rising smoke from the fire. My ears picked up the sounds of explosions in the distance, and I thought I heard laughter as well, but couldn't be sure. Everything was beginning to get hazy.

Is this the end?

Was I going to die in this place? Alone and helpless?

I don't want to die…

A flicker of feeling came back. I didn't want to leave this world. What existed after death but nothing? Death was the end, and when you were dead, there was nothing left. That was it. It was over. I didn't want it to be over.

Please… somebody… help me…

I prayed. I had never done it before, but in that moment, I prayed for a miracle.

***

Jerking his head up, Christian looked around, scanning his surroundings, even as he reached for his gun. It was only after fully waking up that he realized where he was and what he was doing.

He was on the train heading for Seal Beach. The jolt that had startled him awake must have been the train passing over a rough spot on the tracks. There was no fire; despair wasn't clinging to him like a bad lover; he was safe.

He relaxed. His hand moved away from his gun—where it would have been, he corrected himself. It wasn't there right now. His guns and swords were locked up in their case, where they would remain except in case of an emergency. This mission wasn't one that he could accomplish while carrying guns around, especially not a pair of customs like his. It wasn't a covert operation in the dead of night, and he didn't want people asking too many questions.

Turning his head to look out of the window, he was greeted by the sight of a city. He wondered which, though. A glance at his watch revealed that thirty minutes had passed since the train began moving. It took forty minutes to reach Seal Beach by train, meaning he was ten minutes from reaching his destination. That meant he must at least be in Anaheim.

Christian turned from the window and took a gander at the compartment that he was sitting in. One of the many benefits of being a member of the XIII was definitely how they had their own private quarters when traveling. The compartment was nice, and the seats comfortable. They were colored a deep red, almost crimson, which complimented the dark wood used for the compartment walls. A light embedded into the curved white ceiling provided him with illumination, the bulb flickering occasionally.

Situated in a small alcove above his head was his weapons case. Christian thought about getting it down and double-checking his equipment, but decided not to. He might have a modicum of privacy in this compartment, but he was still on a train, and there was no telling when someone would come by to check on him.

Instead of looking at the equipment that he'd taken with him for this mission, he reached for the much smaller traveling case located at his feet. Its silver surface gleamed slightly in the sunlight.

With a few deft clicks, he undid the locks and opened the case to reveal his tablet. It was a sleek device, black and glossy, and it was his most treasured possession—his only possession, really.

With an almost reverent air, Christian lifted the tablet from the soft, velvety cushion that it rested on. He set the case back down, and then turned the tablet on. It didn't take long for the screen to load up, and it took even less time to type in his password. After that, it was just a matter of selecting the application that he wanted to use, in this case his KLReader.

As a large scroll of text appeared on the screen, Christian allowed himself a smile. He soon lost himself within the pages. The sound of the train speeding over the tracks accompanied him as he read about a young man who was forced to confront his dark past.

***

Samantha marched through the corridors of the St. Basil Catholic Church with a determined stride. She ignored the people passing by, even when they stopped to greet her. Unlike members of the clergy, especially those not involved in the darker aspects of the Church, she had neither the time nor the patience for inane pleasantries.

It wasn't long before she passed through a single door and arrived in a small office that was much less Spartan than hers. Decorating the walls were expensive-looking paintings, the kind that she expected to see in a museum, not a church. She had no doubt that they were copies, as the originals cost millions, but even copies were expensive, and her nose almost wrinkled at the opulence.

Masking her features so as not to show any of the distaste she felt, Samantha walked up to the desk, where a nondescript man of indeterminate age was seated. His hair was gray, and wrinkles lined his eyes and mouth. A bulbous nose protruded from his face, shadowing his large lips. Tristin had once called them fish lips, she recalled. The term was surprisingly accurate. His outfit consisted of stately white robes with purple trimming; the robes of a Bishop.

"Ah, Samantha," the man greeted her, his voice amiable. Samantha was not fooled by his pleasant demeanor, not for a second. "I hope God has blessed your day so far?"

"That would depend on what you consider blessed, Bishop Vertrou." Samantha spoke in a calm, controlled voice. "I was hoping we could forgo the formalities. I want to know why you gave me orders to send my subordinate on that mission."

"You never were one for pleasantries, were you?" The Bishop's sigh held trace amounts of annoyance. Old men like him loved to banter for reasons that were beyond her. Samantha had no desire to play his games, so she said nothing. She merely waited for him to continue. "You are referring to our choice in sending Christian on that quest to slay the succubus, yes?"

"Of course I am." Samantha tried not to let her emotions slip, but something must have shown on her face, because Vertrou gave her a disapproving look. She quickly mastered herself and schooled her features. "There is a good reason we do not send men on missions to slay succubi."

"I am well aware of that," Vertrou replied dryly.

"Then why did you have me send him?"

"A test."

Samantha almost blinked. "A test? You sent him on a mission so you could test him?"

"Yes."

Samantha stared at the Bishop in shock for but a moment. It only took her a few seconds for her to process his words and come to the correct conclusion. This man wanted Christian dead. It was the only reasonable explanation for sending a man to do a woman's job, though for what reason Bishop Vertrou wanted him dead was beyond her.

Her eyes narrowed and her lips thinned as she fought the urge to scowl. "What exactly are you testing him on? If this is a test of loyalty, then I can assure you that Christian is the most loyal member under my command. Out of all the Executioners in the California Region, he is the only one who truly follows God's teachings."

"That remains to be seen," Bishop Vertrou said. Samantha's mouth opened almost immediately to let loose a snappish reply. She probably would have, too, had the bishop not spoken first. "While I am aware of his loyalty to the Executioners, the Church has grown… concerned that he may stray from the path of God."

"You can't possibly believe that." Samantha didn't bother hiding her scowl this time. "Christian is one of the few Executioners who reads from the Bible daily. He prays religiously, asking God to forgive him for the sins he's committed while on mission, and he is the only person that I know who knows the Bible inside and out. How could you possibly say that he isn't a true follower of the Church?"

"Easily," the Bishop sniffed. "There are things about that man that you do not know. Things that would make you question everything you've ever thought about him."

"What kind of things?"

"I am afraid that I cannot tell you." As Bishop Vertrou smiled at her, Samantha felt an almost overwhelming desire to strangle him. She knew that he was getting some form of twisted amusement out of toying with her like this. "You do not have the clearance necessary to know that information."

"Christian is one of my subordinates," Samantha argued. "As someone under my command, it is my right to know everything that pertains to him."

"*Your right?*" The Bishop raised an eyebrow. "Young lady, I do believe you are gravely mistaken in this matter. While you may be in charge of the Executioners for this Region, do not forget that it is the Bishopric who ultimately makes all the decisions regarding yourself… and those under you. Now, if that is all, I would like you to leave. I am a rather busy man."

Samantha gritted her teeth and made every effort she could not to glare at the man. For a second, just one second, she thought about giving him a piece of her mind. Then common sense kicked in, and she decided not to push her luck.

Doing a quick about-face, she left the room, her dark hair whipping about behind her. She walked back down the hall, through the cathedral, and then out of the building entirely. She did not look back.

As she closed her car door and started the engine, Samantha felt a sense of foreboding. She didn't know what was going on, and she didn't know what kind of information the Church had on her subordinate, but she sincerely hoped that Christian would not be made to suffer for it.

***

After exiting the train station, Christian made his way to the hotel where reservations had been placed for him in advance, courtesy of the Catholic Church. He could have hailed a taxi, or even taken a bus, but it was a nice day out, and he wanted to familiarize himself with the city's layout. It would be important for him to know his way around, just in case things went south while on this mission.

Seal Beach was located in the westernmost corner of Orange County. Like many coastal cities in California, it consisted of various architectural styles. Because it wasn't a large city, containing a population of roughly twenty-thousand people, there were no large skyscrapers or particularly massive buildings. The biggest attractions the city had to offer, aside from its beaches, were the Naval Weapons Station military base and the pier, which was the second longest wooden pier in California.

Christian spent almost two hours wandering the streets, checking his surroundings and enjoying the weather, before finding his way to the hotel. A number of shops he passed looked interesting, and though the city didn't possess a large population, a good many people walked along the sidewalks —tourists, judging by the clothes.

By the time he arrived at his lodgings, the sun was setting. He glanced at the large hotel, which spread out instead of up. It consisted of three stories, topped with a mostly flat roof. The walls, constructed from a combination of brick and concrete, contained a noticeable shift between the two materials, blending them in such a way that it appeared as if they'd decided to change materials halfway through construction, but were too lazy to tear down the original structure. Spires jutted from the building's four cornerstones, giving a grand visage to what would have been an otherwise unremarkable building.

Checking into the hotel was easy. The clerk at the front desk, a young woman with a nice smile, efficiently checked him in. He soon stood inside the room that would be his base of operations for the foreseeable future.

Off-white walls and a ceiling of the same color surrounded him. Light beige carpeting shifted under his feet as he closed the door behind him. A glance to his left revealed a flat-screen television on a wide dresser. Opposite the dresser sat a wide twin bed with red covers and white sheets. A door on his immediate right led to what was most likely a restroom. In front of him, on the opposite side of the room, a window revealed the city's splendor during a sunset.

Not bothering to put his clothes or other items away, Christian unloaded all the equipment he had brought with him. He always liked to check his supplies after arrival to make sure he wasn't missing anything.

He stared at the objects lying on his bed. There were his custom handguns, two beautifully crafted weapons, one of silver and the other darker than the night sky. They were shaped like a pair of Desert Eagles, had a comfortable grip, and were designed for quick draws and firing. Despite their powerful design, they possessed very little recoil, allowing him the ability to fire rounds in rapid succession without his aim going askew.

He had earned these guns and his swords several years ago, after completing the most difficult mission he'd ever been given. The silver one was called Gabriel. The black one was Phanuel.

Sitting beside his custom handguns were his close-range weapons of choice: a pair of customized swords. Unlike most blades these had no classification. They looked like traditional European short swords, with twenty-three-inch-long blades and six-inch handles. The difference lay in the diamond-shaped pommels and crucifix crossguards. The swords' names were Michael and Raphael. Both guns and swords were made out of Orichalcum.

Among the items he had laid out, there was also the sniper rifle. He had no clue what he was going to do with it, as he still could not fire it with any degree of accuracy. There was also a long scope with a tripod that he could use to observe the city from a distance, provided he could find a building high enough to use it.

The only other items on the bed were his holsters, the sheaths for his swords, the case for the sniper rifle, and several cartridges of ammunition. He didn't have any grenades or explosives, though he did have two flashbangs in case he needed to make a quick getaway. He hopefully wouldn't need them to deal with the succubus.

Once all of his weapons were accounted for, Christian stowed them where they would not only be hidden, but easy to access at a moment's notice—under the bed.

While he did this, his thoughts turned to his target, and he reviewed the information he had on her. The succubus's name was Eve Viava. Reports indicated that she had lived with a woman called Valerie Viava in New Shoreham, Rhode Island, until her fifteenth birthday, when her adopted mother was killed. Eve had disappeared, only to reappear several months later in a different town, under a different name.

A month later, the Church confirmed Eve to be a succubus, and Jeanne was sent to kill her. Jeanne disappeared and Sara was sent after Eve before being killed. Trekovski disappeared weeks later and Eve vanished again, not reappearing for nearly three years, having traveled across the United States to Seal Beach under the assumed name of Lilith Vie.

Sighing as he put away the last pieces of the dismantled sniper rifle, Christian stood up and moved to the bed. He then let gravity take him until his back hit the mattress, bouncing several times before settling down.

He wondered about the deaths of Valerie and Sara. Reports indicated that Valerie had been killed after having her throat torn out via a set of claws, and Sara was found floating in the Atlantic Ocean, her throat lacerated by claws as well.

Succubi didn't possess claws, and their physical abilities remained within the boundaries of human limitations, which meant Valerie and Sara had *not* been killed by Lilith, but by someone else, or *something* else.

As he stared at the ceiling, Christian wondered if the strange feeling coiling in his gut was a premonition or just indigestion.

Chapter 7

A new day dawned in Seal Beach. The sun rose over the horizon, casting a multitude of colors across the sky and sea. Blue, red, orange, and varying degrees of purple made both atmosphere and ocean appear to be far more than their molecular composition would suggest.

It was at this time, as the sun began its climb, that Lilith Vie found herself taking a nice, hot shower. A satisfied moan escaped her lips as she stood under the warm spray. There was something innately pleasant about standing under the spray of hot water, allowing the warm droplets to caress her back and run down her body. It was one of her two biggest guilty pleasures.

When she finished, Lilith exited the shower and grabbed a towel off the rack. She wrapped it around her body, grabbed another towel, and used it to dry her hair.

Upon passing the sink, her eyes strayed to the mirror. It was fogged over, but she could still see herself well enough. Blue eyes. Blond hair. A button nose. A generously proportioned body. People often told her that she was the most beautiful girl they had ever met… well, other girls told her that—the few girls that bothered talking to her, at any rate. Lilith had never gotten along with her own gender, for one reason or another. And she didn't even speak to men, for many reasons, but mostly because they always thought with something other than their heads whenever they were in her presence. The last time she had *willingly* spoken with a man had ended with…

Lilith shook her head, dispelling the unwanted memories. She had more important things to do than dwell on something that had happened in her past. As her mother always used to say. *"You can't change the past, but you can live in the present to create a better future."*

With her thoughts set and her decision made, Lilith exited the bathroom and walked into her bedroom. The cream-colored walls were lined with pictures of Lilith and the only friend that she had made since coming to Seal Beach. A window above her desk overlooked a small park, allowing rays of light to illuminate her room.

She walked over to the dresser, putting on her panties and a bra, then moved to the closet, where she pulled out a light blue sundress and grabbed a simple pair of sandals. For a moment, she thought about wearing the long, ugly overcoat that she had bought for the purpose of hiding her body from view. A glance out the window told her this wouldn't be a good idea. It looked like it was going to be a warm day.

Besides, it's early. I doubt there will be that many men out and about at this time.

Once dressed, she stepped into the apartment's living area. Like most two-bedroom, two-bathroom apartments, the living room and kitchen were a single area, rather than two separate rooms. The only way to tell where the living room ended and the kitchen began was where the tiles shifted into carpet.

"Good morning, Lilith." Somebody was already in the room when she entered; it was a woman who looked to be a few years older than her. Maria Longfield, the only person she could call her friend.

The two of them had met only two months before, back when Lilith had first moved in. Maria had already become one of her favorite people—which might have been due to her deplorable lack of friends, but Lilith liked to believe that it was simply because they got along so well.

Maria's long brown hair was tied into a ponytail, and she was wearing her running clothes: black skort and a red sports bra with black straps. On her feet were a pair of expensive-looking running shoes. Lilith knew that her friend had those shoes custom-made for her.

"Morning, Maria." Lilith greeted her friend, with a bright smile. "Going for another run this morning?"

Maria gave her with a quick smile, before looking back down at the Garmin watch on her wrist and pressing one of the buttons on the side.

"That's right, I have to run twenty miles today."

Lilith shook her head in envy and admiration. Maria was one of those hardcore athletic girls. In high school, she had been the star runner of her cross-country team, and upon graduating had been given a full scholarship by the University of California, Irvine. She was in her last year there, a senior majoring in Health and Science, and minoring in Health Informatics.

"I don't know how you do it," Lilith told her honestly.

"Dedication," Maria replied in the "duh" kind of tone that she used when someone said something that she thought was stupid, or at least lacking in common sense. "You could do it, too, if you had the dedication to train with me every day." Her eyes twinkled at Lilith and a mischievous smile quirked her lips. Lilith felt an apprehensive chill run down her spine. "Perhaps you could even start training right now. Why don't you run the first two miles with me?"

Sweat formed on Lilith's brow, both at the mere thought of running two whole miles, and at her friend's invitation. She had no desire to run several miles, or even a single mile, ever. She wasn't the type who enjoyed working up a sweat. If she wanted to get out of this, she would have to think fast.

"Oh, I would love to, really, but, uh, would you look at the time! I really should be going now! Work and all that! Bye!"

Without waiting for a response, Lilith slipped out the door and headed down the stairs. Maria's muted laughter reached her from behind the closed door.

She and her two roommates lived on the second floor of a small apartment complex less than twenty minutes walking distance from the beach. It was a nice place to live. Everything was well maintained: the grass was trimmed, the buildings were clean, and the play area for children looked brand new, despite being nearly ten years old. Lilith really did love it there.

Perhaps what she loved most about this complex was its lack of men. It was an all-female complex owned by a former sex-abuse victim. Discovering an apartment complex that didn't allow men had been difficult, but well worth the effort.

She did wonder why her two roommates lived there. Maria had a boyfriend—or at least she had when Lilith last checked. They might have broken up already, as her friend discarded the men she dated about as often as she changed her running shoes. And Stacy… the less said about that girl's sex life the better.

Checking her watch, Lilith saw that she had half an hour before she needed to be at work. With that in mind, she decided to grab a bite to eat at her favorite local café. In her haste to leave her apartment, she had completely forgotten to eat breakfast.

***

Christian sat bolt upright in bed, his body covered in sweat, his hair matted to his head, and his chest heaving. His mind was haunted by last night's nightmare, the same one that he had been reliving ever since the Catholic Church rescued him from the ashes of his hometown.

Even now, he could feel the blistering heat of the flames as they burnt his body, and the repugnant scent of fumes as smoke filled his lungs. It was something that he had lived with ever since it happened, and it was probably something that he would never be able to get rid of. Such was the price he paid for having committed the sin of living while everyone else had died.

Wiping the accumulated sweat from his forehead, Christian stood up and entered the restroom. As he waited for the water to heat up, he glanced at himself in the mirror, studying his haggard appearance and the bags under his eyes. He looked away with a grimace.

He did not complain about his appearance. Haggard though it was, this, he felt, was part of his punishment. In some ways, Christian thought he was getting off too lightly. So many people had lost their lives because of him, because he hadn't been strong enough. Looking a little sleep deprived was not nearly punishment enough.

His shower took longer than usual. While his mind was alert and his body wasn't aching from the abuse he so often put it through, he didn't have any real desire to leave. His body, it seemed, wished to remain under the steaming water blasting against his back. It soothed him. The water washed away not just the sweat that covered him like a layer of oil, but also swept away the last vestiges of his troubling dream.

However, he knew that at some point, he would need to leave, to return to the cold world outside of this small space. And the sooner he finished taking his shower, the quicker he could begin his mission.

As he scrubbed himself down, a plan formed in his mind. There was a lot that needed to be done. He had to do some more scouting, find out where this succubus lived, and come up with a plan to confront her. That would the hardest part of his job, but it was something that he would save for later.

The first thing he would focus on was getting a feel for the city and studying its layout. He had done a bit of that yesterday, but there was still a lot of ground to cover. Seal Beach might have been small, but it was still a city of 13.4 square miles.

He also needed to know the succubus's routine. He couldn't devise a plan to exterminate her without knowing her daily schedule. That meant knowing where she went, what she did, which routes she took, and what time she took them. Unlike how he dealt with vampires, werewolves and demons, he couldn't just attack this one at night and kill her in battle. He needed to be subtler, more cunning, get in close to kill her quietly when she least expected it.

By the Almighty, he hated assassinations. He didn't have the talent for it. Why couldn't Samantha have just given him another vampire to kill?

Christian dried off quickly. Exiting the restroom and walking over to the dresser, he grabbed his clothing for the day. He pulled on a plain white t-shirt and tossed a checkered gray button-up shirt over it, leaving it unbuttoned for a casual appearance. Then he put on blue jeans and a pair of black sneakers with white stripe. Once dressed, he looked at himself in a mirror that hung from the small closet.

The clothing he wore had been Claire's suggestion. She had somehow discovered that he was going on a mission outside of his normal mission parameters—he smelled Tristin's hand at work—and suggested this outfit.

He had to admit, Claire had good taste in clothes. He should be able to blend in perfectly. He would have to thank her when he returned.

Nodding to himself, he headed out of the hotel.

He didn't bring his weapons. Christian felt naked without them, but he knew that carrying them in town was out of the question. It would be odd enough having two guns strapped to his thighs. He didn't want to even think about the kind of reaction he would get if people saw a pair of swords on his back. Until he decided to make a move on the succubus, the weapons would remain locked inside his room.

That didn't mean he was going completely unarmed. He had a butterfly knife hidden in his left shoe. It wouldn't do much against a werewolf or a vampire, but he felt better having *something* to defend himself with.

He pulled out his tablet as he walked and accessed Google Maps. He located a small café not far from the hotel. It would be a good place to have breakfast before getting the lay of the land.

***

Upon entering The Crema Café, Lilith took a quick glance around. The combination of dark-brown and cream-colored walls created a nice contrast. Gray tiles made the floor seem mundane, were it not for the many tables and booths strewn about the interior, all of which were made of multi-colored glass. Like most bakeries and restaurants, the entrance was composed almost entirely of glass, allowing prospective customers to peer in before deciding to enter.

A large glass display near the register showcased the many different baked goods and desserts sold there. Behind the counter, people walked back and forth, preparing for the day; putting bread rolls and donuts into the ovens, using a large mixer to create batter and frosting, and decorating a variety of cakes.

Because of the early morning, few people were present. Four local residents sipped their coffee while reading the morning newspaper. It looked as if she had beaten the morning rush.

Even better, there were only two men, and they were huddled in a booth near the back. So long as she didn't get near them, they wouldn't try anything—at least, that was her hope.

"Oh, Lilith. I see you've finally decided to come pay us a visit again."

Lilith was shaken from her thoughts upon hearing the familiar voice. With a smile, she turned toward the elderly woman with gray, nearly white hair, and brown eyes. Her features were youthful, though she did have several wrinkles around her eyes, crows' feet, and a few along her mouth. Those few wrinkles came from smiling. They were the wrinkles of a woman who was content with her life. Lilith hoped that she could look like that when she was this woman's age, as it would be proof that her life had turned around for the better.

"Auntie Kay," Lilith greeted. Kay Carmella wasn't really her aunt, but everyone who visited the café called her that. She was also one of the few women who didn't resent Lilith, which made her one of only three adults that Lilith conversed with regularly.

"It's been a while since you last visited." Auntie Kay's congenial smile put Lilith at ease. "At least a week. I was beginning to think you'd never come back, though I wouldn't blame you if you didn't, considering what happened last time."

"I'm really sorry about that." Lilith tried to not let her guilt show. "If I had known that my presence would cause so much trouble, then I—"

Auntie Kay held up a hand. "There is no need to apologize. You couldn't have known what would happen, nor could you have known about my new employee."

"Yes, but—"

"The fault is mine for not telling my employee that he wasn't allowed to go near you. I know how men react around you, and more important, I know how you react around men. Yet I foolishly forgot to inform him to keep away from you. Had I said something before you arrived, that incident might have been avoided."

The incident Auntie Kay referred to had happened the week before. Lilith had come in and ordered her usual fare before sitting down at a table. A young man working there saw who the order was for and, thinking that he could chat her up, decided to bring the food to her.

The disaster that followed was one Lilith wished to forget. She was sure that the young man whose pride, ego, and face that she had bruised, wished he could forget it as well.

Lilith shook her head. She was grateful that Auntie Kay was willing to stick up for her, but it had been her fault, regardless of what the aging woman or anyone else said.

"So, the usual?" asked Auntie Kay.

"Yes, please."

"It'll be up in just a few minutes. Why don't you find a spot to sit down and wait?"

"Thank you."

As Auntie Kay moved behind the counter and disappeared into the back, Lilith walked to a table—one as far from the men as possible. She sat down and crossed her legs. Placing her hands in her lap, she tried to make herself inconspicuous.

Lilith felt a chill wash over her. She could feel the eyes of the two men on her. They didn't approach her, but she knew they were staring.

A small shiver ran down her spine. Despite trying not to let it bother her, discomfort wormed its way into her gut. She shifted in her seat, looking anywhere but at the two men. If there was one thing that she had learned, it was that making eye contact with a male invited trouble. She fortunately didn't have to wait more than a few minutes before Auntie Kay arrived with a to-go bag.

"Here you are, hon," she said, placing the bag on the table. Lilith took in the scent wafting from the bag. As always, the food smelled delicious. It was almost enough to make her forget about the two men staring at her. Almost.

"Thank you," Lilith said. Auntie Kay smiled.

"There is no need for thanks. And you've already done that once today."Blood rushed to Lilith's cheeks.

After paying for her meal, Lilith hurriedly left the store. She wanted to get to work as soon as possible. It was the one place where she would be safe from the opposite sex—in a manner of speaking.

Had she been paying more attention, she probably would have seen—or at least been more aware—of the person rounding the corner ahead of her. Perhaps then, her life would not have taken such a dramatic turn.

***

Seal Beach really was a beautiful place, Christian mused. It was a perfect fusion of modern architecture and quaint shops in a tropical setting. It was also relatively quiet and peaceful; nothing at all like Los Angeles.

At this time of day, LA would have been bustling, with crowds of people walking down the street and cars honking in jam-packed traffic. The repugnant scent of a thousand bodies mixing together would overwhelm his senses, leaving him doing everything humanly possible not to gag.

Such was not the case in Seal Beach. Only a few people walked down the street: a small family getting an early start on the day, a young couple going out for breakfast, and a middle-aged man talking on his cell phone. That was about it. Only a few cars driving down the road. Christian counted no more than twelve.

Yes, this place was truly a bastion of peacefulness and tranquility. If only he could have been stationed here instead of Los Angeles. It was regrettable that this place didn't warrant an Executioners office.

Christian looked down at the map on his tablet. His location was shown as an arrow, his destination as a blue dot. A green line connected the arrow to the dot, showing which streets he should travel. The Crema Café was less than a mile from his location.

According to the reviews that he had read when checking his phone, this was one of the most popular cafés in the vicinity; good food, a peaceful atmosphere, and excellent customer service—just what he was looking for. Maybe he could even read a chapter or two of his light novel when he arrived. That would be nice.

"Ah!"

As he turned a corner, a much smaller body crashed into him. A feminine yelp knocked him from his thoughts, and also knocked him off balance. Being bigger than whoever crashed head-first against his chest, he didn't stumble backward more than a few steps, though he did almost drop his tablet. Only his quick reflexes stopped it from cracking against the pavement.

Shaking his head and internally berating himself for his lack of awareness—a Warrior should always be aware of his surroundings—Christian looked down to see who he had crashed into…

… and froze.

A young woman around his age sat on the ground before him. Blond hair cascaded down her back like an effervescent waterfall, the sunlight reflecting off each strand, granting her an otherworldly, almost heavenly, appearance. Her face, illuminated by the sun, looked like it had been lovingly crafted by angels. A cute button nose sat below azure-blue eyes. Above the gentle rise of her chin were pink Cupid's bow lips, which glistened in the light as if she was wearing shiny lip gloss.

Christian glimpsed beautifully crafted thighs and shapely calves. Her small feet were adorned with sandals that left her cute little toes free to wiggle about. A light blue sundress flattered her figure.

Her beauty was *not* the reason that Christian froze. There was no mistaking this girl. He'd made sure to memorize her picture before coming here. While she was far more beautiful in person, there could be no doubt in his mind about her identity.

Was it fate, or perhaps will of God that he would meet his target so soon after arriving in town? Truly, the Almighty Creator must have been smiling down at him, delivering his target right into his grasp.

Now that he had found her, all he needed to do was get her alone somewhere, someplace where no one else would tread, perhaps an alley, where he could finish her off. A butterfly knife to the heart was not the most efficient way to kill someone, but it would have to do.

"Ouch." The voice sounded like the tinkling of wind chimes. He focused on the girl sprawled on the sidewalk. She was rubbing her apparently sore backside. "What hit me?"

"I'm really sorry about that," Christian said, his tone polite. If he wanted to get her somewhere alone, he needed to play this cool. "Here, let me help you up."

Before he could even offer the girl his hand, she froze.

He wondered if something was wrong. Maybe that fall had injured her more than he had assumed.

Those thoughts were dispelled when the girl looked up at him. Christian was shocked at the terror etched on her face. Her eyes were wide, her pupils were dilated, and her mouth hung open in abject horror. He had seen this look before, on the faces of monsters right before he killed them.

The most telling sign of her fear was not the look on her face, though it certainly completed the image, but the way her body shook, as if the mere sight of him caused her body to lose control of its muscles.

Why does she look so afraid of me? I haven't done anything to warrant such fear yet.

"Miss, are you—"

"Kya!"

Christian's face scrunched up at the odd noise. "Kya?"

He watched, surprised, as the succubus scrambled backward, away from him. She was still on the ground, using her hands and feet to crawl away like some kind of crustacean. Her face remained frozen in terror. What was going on?

"Um… excuse me?"

He took a step forward.

"M-m-m—it-it's a-a MAN!" the girl shouted, and scrambled to her feet.

Christian could do nothing but stare as the blonde beauty bolted, running away from him like Satan was nipping at her heels. She disappeared around the next corner.

After several seconds of staring at the now empty sidewalk, Christian summed up his thoughts in a few short words.

"What in God's name just happened?"

***

Lilith didn't know how far she ran. The only thing that mattered was getting away from that man. All she wanted to do was run so far that there was no chance of him catching up to her, provided he was even aware enough to chase her down. She hoped that she was lucky, and that he was too stunned by her to move.

She eventually stopped between two buildings, her forehead covered in sweat. She quivered in fear and exhaustion as adrenaline left her system, draining her of what little energy she had possessed.

She leaned against the red brick wall of a small convenience store, breathing heavily. Her legs felt weak. They were shaking, and she wondered how long it would be before they gave out on her.

It took her a long while to regain her composure. The task was harder than she remembered it being, but that didn't surprise her in the least. Ever since the incident that had destroyed her life, Lilith had been unable to even look at a man without feeling the stirrings of fear, never mind going near one. She'd had a few close calls since then, and each one left her a shaking wreck. The last time she encountered a man, Maria had been forced to come to her college because she'd locked herself in a science lab, refusing to come out unless Maria was there.

Thankfully, her workplace didn't have any male employees, though a few dads stopped by to pick up their children. She did her best to not be present when they showed up.

Several seconds passed before the shuddering ceased. With one final glance in the direction she had run from, Lilith began walking to work. She needed to get her mind off what had just happened, and the best way to do that was to spend time doing something that required her full, undivided attention.

***

Christian was still reeling from the events that had transpired with his target. He kept trying to wrap his mind around what he had witnessed. Try as he might, he couldn't quite comprehend what that had been about.

That girl, the one that he felt sure was his target, had run away from him with terror in her eyes. He was positive that she didn't know his identity. How could she? But if that was the case, then why did she run away?

With a shake of his head, he entered The Crema Café, his mind pondering the events of a few seconds ago. The café was pleasantly busy. A few people sat around the scattering of tables and booths, chattering away. There was a bit of a line in front of the register, where people were ordering meals. Waiters and waitresses walked to and fro between tables and groups of people, smiling at customers and making idle conversation.

Christian moved to the back of the line. When his turn came, he decided to go with the oatmeal banana buttermilk pancakes and a coffee. The young girl at the register, who couldn't have been older than sixteen, gave him a small holder with a number on it, told him to find a seat, and assured him that his order would be right up.

He decided to sit outside. It was too crowded inside for his taste—he'd had more than enough of crowds from living in Los Angeles—and it was a beautiful day anyway. Enjoying the mild weather and clear blue sky sounded a lot better than being stuck in a small space full of tables and people.

While he waited for his food to arrive, Christian tried to read his light novel. It was beginning to get good. Kazuma, the main character, was just about to have a showdown with his father, who had kicked him out of their family nearly a decade before the start of the story. Christian was anxious to find out what happened next.

Unfortunately, despite how much he normally enjoyed reading light novels, the encounter with the girl that Intelligence claimed was a succubus remained on his mind. In spite of not wanting to think about what happened, he did, and it hampered his ability to focus on anything else, leaving him unable to even enjoy his favorite pastime.

"Here ya go, hon." The voice and a plateful of delicious-looking pancakes being placed in front of him shook Christian from his musings. He looked up to see an elderly woman serving him. She put an empty cup on the table next to the plate, and then looked at him with a kind smile.

"Coffee will be ready in just a minute. Is there anything else that I can get you?"

"No." Christian shook his head, but was suddenly struck by inspiration. He quickly called to the woman just as she was about to leave. "Actually, there is something that I'd like to ask you."

The woman turned around. "Oh? What would you like to ask me?"

"I accidentally bumped into this girl on the way here. She dropped her stuff and forgot to pick it up." He reached down and grabbed the bag full of food that his target had dropped in her haste. He had picked it up and, not knowing what else to do, took it with him. "I wanted to give it back to her, but don't know where I should go to find her."

"Ah, you met Lilith." The woman had an understanding look about her. Christian had the distinct impression that she knew something he didn't.

"Lilith?" He feigned ignorance.

"The girl you ran into; long blond hair, blue eyes, absolutely gorgeous. Makes supermodels cry in envy."

"Yes, that's the one."

"Hon, you'd best just forget about returning that to her. Even if you did manage to find her, she'd just run away again."

"I'm not sure I understand." Christian didn't need to feign confusion this time. "Why would she run away from me?"

"You must be new here or you wouldn't be asking that," the old woman said. "The reason you won't be able to come anywhere near her is because Lilith has androphobia. She's deathly afraid of men."

Oh, well, that made sense. His target was afraid of men. If that was true, then it was only natural that she would run away from… him…

… Wait. What?

Chapter 8

Tristin Baluf was what most people would consider an odd individual—odd being one of the least defamatory terms used to describe him. He followed no religion, had no creed, and yet he still worked for one of the largest religious organizations in the world.

Very little was known about Tristin. Even the Church didn't have the slightest inkling as to where he came from. They knew little about his past, despite doing thorough background checks on everyone working under them, and he would love nothing more than to keep it that way.

Being an orphan, Tristin had been raised at one of the many orphanages belonging to the Church, a small one located several miles outside of Boise, Idaho.

It was there that he met Christian and discovered his fascination with the other boy. Ever since they had first met all those years ago, the two of them had been thick as thieves. Christian would disagree, but Tristin never really listened to what his best friend said, especially when it contradicted his own version of reality. They did just about everything together, to the point where it eventually became expected that where Christian went, Tristin would follow. And when the Church had discovered Christian's natural affinity for combat and decided to take him in for training, it was only natural that Tristin would go with him.

There was a problem that prevented Tristin from joining the Executioners of the Church, however.

He couldn't fight. At all. He had zero talent for any type of combat, be it long range, close range, or anything in between. He couldn't even handle a gun without nearly shooting himself in the foot. Once, he had almost shot his own eye out.

There was only one way that Tristin would have been allowed to become an Executioner, and he didn't have any desire to take enhancement drugs that would increase his battle performance at the cost of turning him into a berserker. He'd seen some of the people who took those drugs, and it wasn't pretty. Besides, he didn't really like fighting anyway.

That had left him in quite the quandary. He wanted to follow Christian into the Executioners, but without the talent for combat that his friend possessed, and with no desire to take performance enhancers, he wouldn't be allowed into that group. That meant he'd had to find some way to circumvent the system.

Fortunately for him, he had another talent, one that was almost as valuable as the ability to fight: the ability to gather intelligence and disseminate information. Despite how he got on a lot of people's nerves, none could deny that he was one of the best at gathering all the necessary data required for an assignment and delivering it in a timely and efficient manner. He might have a little too much fun with the job—annoying people until they snapped always amused him—but that didn't mean he performed at anything other than his best.

Thanks to his talent as an intelligence agent, he had been welcomed into the Intelligence Division of the Catholic Church's Executioners.

It was an admittedly boring job, especially when there was no work to be had, and he was forced to wait until something came up, but Tristin guessed that was the price he paid for staying with his friend.

Tristin glanced down at the communications station in front of him. Like all the technological equipment used by the Executioners, the comm station was one of the most advanced pieces of tech in the world. The large console had been built into the wall. The vast majority of the comm was taken up by a large screen; a touchscreen that he could use to pull up a variety of information from the Church's intelligence network. This allowed him to help Executioners on their missions by providing constant, up-to-date information.

It looked a lot like something from *Star Trek*, what with all of the blinking lights, high-definition screen, and cool-looking knobs and buttons that seemed to serve no purpose other than as decoration. A part of Tristin even wondered if the guy who made it had been some kind of Trekkie.

He could also use it download music and games so he wouldn't be bored, but he had to be careful when doing that. The last time he'd been caught playing his favorite MMO, Knights of the Cross, when on duty, Samantha had really let him have it. Tristin still had the bruises from that encounter.

The rest of the console was taken up by the actual communications array. There were a lot of buttons. It looked almost like a keyboard, except instead of being used to type something on the screen, they were used to send and receive calls from Executioners out in the field.

And one of those buttons was flashing red.

With a grin, Tristin put the headset hanging around his neck back over his ears and pressed the button. Leaning back in his chair, he said, "This is Doctor Tristin F. Baluf speaking to you live from six-six-point-six, the lo-o-o-ove station. If you have any questions you'd like to ask Doctor Baluf, then please be my—"

"Would you cut that out?!" the person on the other end shouted at him. *"And don't use that number as a part of your shenanigans!"*

Tristin chuckled mildly at his friend's anger. It was always so easy to rile Christian up.

"My bad, my bad. It won't happen again."

"Somehow, I don't believe you." Christian's voice was flat. Tristin could almost see the deadpan expression on his friend's face. It was enough to make him smile.

"So what can I do for you, Christian? Don't tell me you've already completed your mission. It's only been a day."

His friend was good, *scary good*, but not that good. And he wasn't dealing with vampires or werewolves this time, but a succubus. While not capable fighters, they had many weapons at their disposal that a member of the male persuasion would be hard-pressed to beat.

"No, I have not completed my mission."

Tristin raised an eyebrow. Christian was calling him without having completed his assignment? That was odd. His friend never called except upon the completion of a mission.

For some reason, Tristin had the strangest feeling that his friend did this so he wouldn't have to speak with him. He shrugged the thought off, however. It was a preposterous notion, after all. Why wouldn't his best friend want to talk to him?

So, if Christian wasn't calling in to tell him about the mission's completion, then that could only mean…

"Has there been a problem with the mission?"

It was almost as preposterous as Christian not calling until his mission was finished because he didn't want to talk to Tristin, but there was a first time for everything, right? Perhaps this was one of those first times.

Oh, I'm going to be Christian's first. How exciting.

"Yes, there is a problem with the mission." Christian sighed over the line. Even without being able to see him, Tristin just knew that the younger male was running a hand through his hair. It was an old habit from when they were children. Whenever Christian was stressed or tense, he would run a hand through his hair. *"I think we've got the wrong target."*

"Excuse me?"

"You heard me. I think we've got the wrong target."

Tristin sat up a little straighter. He remained silent for a moment, pondering his friend's words before actually speaking. Christian wouldn't say something like this unless he was one-hundred percent sure in his beliefs. If he said that they had the wrong target, then he likely had a really good reason for thinking that way.

"What makes you say that?"

"… She's afraid of men."

Silence followed. Tristin would have stared incredulously at Christian had they been speaking face to face. As things stood, he settled for gawking at the console.

"I'm sorry, what? Could you repeat that, please? I could have sworn you just said that your target is afraid of men."

"That's exactly what I said."

"Your target, a succubus, is afraid of men?"

"Yes."

"A *succubus* is afraid of men?"

"That's what I said." He could almost see Christian rolling his eyes. He could certainly hear the annoyance in his voice, but he'd learned to ignore his friend's tone whenever the young Warrior was exasperated by something—particularly when that something was him.

For once in his life, Tristin found himself at a loss for words. The idea that a succubus, a creature that fed off the sexual energies of men, was afraid of men was unfathomable. It was almost as incomprehensible as his friend calling only when absolutely necessary because Christian didn't want to talk to him.

"I'm not sure I understand. How could this be possible?"

"I don't know," Christian voiced helplessly. *"All I know is that she's deathly afraid of men. I accidentally bumped into her on the way to breakfast, and the moment she got a good look at me, she screamed and ran away."*

"She screamed and ran away?"

"Yes."

"Pfft! He-he-he... ha-ha-ha-ha-ha! Oh, God! This is just too funny! Christian, slayer of vampires, werewolves, and demons! A man so powerful and feared that even succubi quake in their boots at the mere sight of him!"

"This isn't a laughing matter!"

"Yes it—he-he-he—yes it is!"

"Stop laughing!"

"S-sorry—hehehehe-he—ha... ha..." Tristin took a deep breath, trying to stifle his laughter. He already received plenty of strange looks from the other people working in the Intelligence Division. Best not give them something else that they could use to question his sanity with. "Whoo... okay, I think I'm good now."

"Really?" Christian's voice was the definition of skeptical. Tristin could almost imagine the dry look on his friend's face.

"Yes, really... at least I think so."

"Whatever." Christian sighed before getting back to business. *"Listen, I need you to double-check our information and make sure I've actually got the right target."*

"I could do that, but are you sure it's necessary?" asked Tristin. "Couldn't this girl just be faking it? You know, acting like she's afraid of men so that you wouldn't suspect her of being a succubus?"

"I don't see why she would. It's not like she knows who I am, and according to what I've learned from asking around, she's been like this ever since she started living in Seal Beach. I highly doubt she would spend all that time pretending to be afraid of men on the off chance that she ended up meeting a male member of the Executioners."

"True enough, I suppose."

"Besides, you can't fake terror like that," Christian added.

"Well, I guess you would know," Tristin admitted. "All right, I'll gather up all the information we have on this and verify its accuracy. It might take a while, so just sit tight while I look into things on my end."

"Thank you."

"Oh, wow." Tristin grinned into the headset. "Did you just thank me?"

A second later, a loud beeping was heard as Christian hung up on him. Tristin chuckled. Some of his co-workers wondered why he was so dead set on getting on his friend's nerves—and even more thought he was crazy for doing so. None of them realized just how much fun it was.

It was like poking a sleeping lion with a stick. In most cases, the lion would simply swat the stick away. However, annoy it too much, and it was more than likely to tear off the hand holding the stick—along with the arm it was attached to. It was fun in a potentially lethal kind of way.

Leaning back in his seat, Tristin basked in the afterglow of successfully irritating his friend. He would look up that information that Christian wanted later. When he felt like it.

For now, *Knights of the Cross* was calling to him.

***

Christian ended the call and scowled. That conversation could have gone a lot better.

Then again, what else should I have expected?

Resisting the urge to crush the cell phone in his grip, he slipped the device back into his pocket and began stomping down the sidewalk.

Dealing with Tristin was always a chore, one that he felt he would be better off without.

The people walking down his side of the street were quick to move out of his path as he stomped toward his destination, wherever that was. It was only after several minutes of angrily stomping across the city that he decided to calm down by heading to the nearest park to relax. According to the map he'd downloaded earlier, it wasn't that far.

He could have gone back to his hotel room, but after dealing with Tristin, he didn't think sitting alone in his room would do his mood any good. Finding a nice quiet place amid nature would be infinitely more beneficial for his poor disposition.

He soon entered the park, his shoes lightly treading well-maintained and perfectly green grass. Several trees sparsely populated the area, and a wide variety of flowers added an array of colors that Christian found soothing. Several children played on a swing set, and a few toddlers were having a grand time in a sandbox. Standing a few feet away, watching the children and conversing among themselves, a group of adults stood; parents, he concluded. Christian felt a pang of envy for those kids, but he pushed it down.

Finding a nice spot underneath a tree, Christian sat down, setting the bag in his left hand next to him and putting the case containing his tablet on his lap. He took the tablet out and turned it on.

Christian tried to enjoy the story, but in spite of the tranquil setting, he found himself unable to do so. His eyes scanned the lines of text, but he didn't see the words.

And so Christian sat there, not paying attention to the world around him, his mind focused on something that only he could see.

I can already tell. Today is going to be a really long day.

***

"A is for apple. B is for bear. C is for circus, and D is for dare."

Sitting in a chair, Lilith smiled at the small group of children sitting in a circle around her on a light blue rug. All the children were very young, no older than five. She was singing the "Alphabet Song," and all of them eagerly followed along with her.

Each of them sang loudly and off-key, but she didn't care. It was the effort they put into it that made their singing beautiful, not whether they could sing on-key or not.

"E is for elephant. F is for fickle. G is for great, and H is for hello."

After regaining her composure from her close encounter of the male kind, Lilith had made her way to Little Seal's Preschool, where she worked part-time as a teacher. It was a small preschool, consisting fifty or so children varying in age from two to five. Because she only worked Mondays, Tuesdays, and Wednesdays, she didn't make a lot, but it was enough to get by.

She was considered an assistant teacher because of her part-time employment. But after the other teachers saw how good she was with children, they gave her a class of her own, though they still considered her an assistant.

Because she didn't have to work with any men on this job, she didn't make a fuss over how little she got paid. Plus, she liked working with children. She seemed to have a knack for it.

"I is for inside. J is for jump. K is for kindness, and L is for love."

The song continued, going from M (Mom) all the way to Z (zebra). When the song ended and everyone finished singing (they all sang at different times and tempos, so it took a while for all of them to finish), Lilith stood up and clapped her hands.

"All right, everyone! Class is over now. Time to pack up your school bags." Smiling when she received a number of "aww's" from the children, Lilith said, "There's no need to be sad. Tomorrow we're going to be counting numbers and learning about addition, and I've got a new song for you that I know you'll all love."

It wasn't long before the kids were all packed up and ready to go. They were ushered outside to the playground by one of the other teachers; an older woman with her hair done up in a frizzy bun, wearing a long gray skirt. As the children filed out of the room, one little child broke ranks and ran back toward her.

"Kevin." Lilith smiled down at the boy. While she was afraid of men, she didn't hold any fear or dislike of little boys. They were too young to be affected by whatever ailed the adult and teenage population—hormones, she assumed. "Is there something you need?"

"Dis is fa you." Kevin held up a pink paper heart. On it were the names Kevin and Lilith. Both were spelled wrong, with Kevin being spelled "Kefin" and Lilith missing an "i" and the "h" at the end. The heart had been one of the assignments that she'd had them do today for arts and crafts.

Lilith knelt down and took the paper heart from Kevin's hand. She then graced the boy with her wondrous smile.

"Thank you. I'll be sure to keep it somewhere I can see it every day."

"You're welcome. I'm gonna marry you one day!"

Okay, so maybe even little boys were still somewhat affected by her. At least she didn't have to worry about them trying anything… untoward with her.

"You'll have to wait until you're much older to marry me," Lilith said, amusement lacing her voice. "And by the time you're old enough to marry, I'll be an old maid."

"Nuh-uh!" The little boy shook his head in adamant denial. "Ms. Lilith will always be young and beautiful!"

"Well, thank you." Lilith's smile was the very definition of amusement. "Now, you'd best be off. I'm sure your mom will be coming to pick you up soon."

"M'kay! Bye, Ms. Lilith!"

The boy ran out the door, which the older teacher had kept open while Kevin was declaring his intentions of marriage toward Lilith. Sighing, she sat back down in her chair, and glanced around the room.

It wasn't large, maybe about the size of her living area. She gazed at the colorful and vibrant posters covering the cream-colored walls. Some she had bought to use as visual aids, but others had been created by her class. A number of round tables were scattered around the room, tiny chairs sitting along their circumference. Several feet away from the tables was a desk, which she sometimes sat behind when not helping the kids learn.

After several minutes of just sitting there, silently contemplating anything and everything, Lilith stood and made her way out of the room. The older woman was waiting for her.

Janice Altier wasn't someone who Lilith would call old. At thirty-one years of age, Janice's frizzy brown hair didn't have any gray in it, and her face still maintained a youthful appearance. Her face was the kind that could easily get lost in the crowd, but was by no means ugly. Plain. That was probably the best word to describe her.

"Kevin's given you another declaration of his love, I see," she said as Lilith closed the door behind her, the smile she wore one of mirth. "This is his seventh time, if I'm not mistaken."

When Lilith first started working at the preschool, Janice had not liked her. She'd been critical of everything Lilith did, berated her over even the smallest mistakes, and insulted her every chance she got. Having already experienced the hatred that her gender showed toward her, Lilith had done her best to ignore the older woman and focus on helping the children.

Janice's dislike for her hadn't changed until about three weeks ago. An older gentleman had shown up to pick up his son. Lilith had been unfortunate enough to be stationed at the front desk at the time. The older man had started hitting on her, gotten angry when she tried to run away, and then tried to molest her. Lilith had kneed him in the balls and escaped. Janice had found her several hours later, huddled under a desk in an unused classroom, shaking and crying.

Janice had stopped being discourteous after that, and they began getting along decently enough, although Lilith wouldn't call them friends, but they weren't enemies either.

"He still hasn't beaten Russel yet." Lilith didn't know whether to be feel amused or resigned about the situation. Maybe a little bit of both. "He's given me ten."

"And Mike has given you twenty-three." When Lilith just sighed again, the other woman responded with a smile. "All the children are quite taken with you. It almost makes me wonder what they'll do when you graduate college and get a real job."

Lilith withheld a grimace at the thought of graduating college. She wanted to graduate; she didn't enjoy college because of the large number of hormonal men attending, but she didn't know what she would do after graduating. How could she find a job when most, if not all of them, required her to work with the opposite sex?

"We'll just have to see, I guess," Lilith said.

After saying goodbye to Janice and several of the other teachers—most of whom ignored her, she noticed—Lilith began the journey back to her apartment. It was a twenty-minute walk from Little Seal's Preschool.

The afternoon sun blazed overhead, turning the air warm and humid. A breeze blew through the streets and between the buildings, creating a pleasant contrast against her skin.

As she walked, she recalled the events of this morning, how she had run away from that man in fright. A part of her felt a tad foolish. Even if the person she had bumped into had ill intentions toward her, it was rather shameful on her part to just run off screaming like that—not to mention embarrassing. And it had been in public, too. How many people had seen her reaction and were now gossiping about that strange girl who ran away from a man, screaming like a banshee?

Lilith dispelled such thoughts and focused on her surroundings. She was walking by a park, one of many that dotted the city. She could see children running to and fro, having an all-around good time. A group of parents conversed some distance away, watching the children, and a young man was sitting underneath a tree with a tablet in his hands.

Just then, the young man looked up and their eyes locked. Lilith froze. It was him! The man she had run into this morning!

His eyes flickering in recognition, the male partly responsible for the incident this morning stood up, and began walking toward her. This was not good! This was so not good! Had he followed her all the way here? What should she do? Should she run away again? Wouldn't he just catch her if she did? And how did he even know that she would pass by this playground?

As he closed the distance, Lilith dithered in indecision. With her mind paralyzed in fear, she could do little but stand frozen in place, a statue of ice amid a sea of viridian grass. The young man seemed to recognize the signs, for he stopped just short of two meters from her.

"Hello," he said, his voice coming out in smooth overtones that would have probably been soothing had she not been so frightened.

Despite her growing distress, Lilith still heard his words and respond in kind. It was an action done more out of reflex than anything else.

"Ah, um, h-hello," Lilith stuttered. She tried taking several deep breaths, but they came in quick pants. She was getting close to hyperventilating. Why couldn't this man just leave her alone?

"I wanted to apologize for bumping into you this morning," he continued.

"O-oh?"

"I'm really sorry about what happened. It was never my intention to frighten you."

Lilith's fear stilled and made way for another emotion: surprise. This was new. No one had ever apologized before, and he wasn't attempting to get close to her either. Most men would have already tried groping her by now, but this man just stood there, calm, composed, completely unaffected by her presence.

What's going on?

"That's... it's okay," she managed to speak again, surprising herself. Shouldn't she be running away by now? "I'm, uh, sorry for screaming at you."

"Oh, no, don't worry about that." He waved off her apology with a smile. "I understand that men make you uncomfortable. Kay told me," he added upon seeing her expression. "And it was my fault for bumping into you. I'm new here, and I wasn't paying attention to where I was going."

"Ah," Lilith gasped and, for reasons that were beyond her, she tried reassuring the man. "No, no, I was in a rush to get to work, so really, it's my fault for not being more careful about where I was going."

The man ran a hand through his messy locks of hair, the slight twitching of his lips the only sign that he was amused.

"I guess we're both sorry, then."

"Yes." Lilith smiled uncertainly. "I guess so."

What was going on? Why was this man still talking to her? Why was she still talking to him? She didn't understand. This should have been the part where he tried molesting her, and she ran away in fear, shouldn't it? That's what always happened to her when she was around men.

"Anyway, I don't want to make you any more uncomfortable than you probably already are," he continued. "I just wanted to give this back to you."

"Is that...?" Lilith trailed off as he held up a familiar to-go bag, light brown and quite large, with THE CREMA CAFÉ stamped on it.

"Yeah, you dropped it when you..." he trailed off, his face scrunching up, as if he was searching for the right words to describe how she had fled from him in terror. "Well, after we bumped into each other."

Lilith stared at the bag in shock. This entire situation was getting more unusual by the second. She didn't know what to think anymore.

"I have some doubts about whether or not it's any good now." His expression became a bit sheepish, and maybe even a tad self-deprecating. "But I thought I should return it to you all the same."

Lilith stared at the bag for a long moment. She said nothing, nor did she make any move to grab it. He seemed to realize why she was so hesitant, because he set the bag on the ground a moment later, and took several steps back.

"I'll just leave it here, then. You can take it, or not. I just thought it would be polite to return it to you."

Slowly, Lilith walked up to the bag. She knelt down and picked it up, her eyes never straying from the young man's heterochromatic gaze. He didn't move from where he stood, allowing her to pick it up and scuttle back.

"Thank you," she said, her voice as soft and gentle as the breeze blowing through the park. The young man gave her a small half-smile. Lilith wondered why her heart skipped a beat.

"You're welcome."

Silence descended upon them. Awkward. Tense. Stifling. Neither seemed to know what to say or do, and it caused the atmosphere to grow thick.

"Well…" The young man broke the tension, coughing into his hand, a light flush of pink staining his cheeks. "I really just came to give that to you, so I'll be going now."

Lilith didn't know whether to feel relieved or disappointed.

"Okay. Goodbye."

"Goodbye, and God bless you."

"God?" Lilith's face scrunched up in confusion as she watched the young man walk away. He hadn't struck her as the religious type, but then, what did she know about religion? She hadn't believed in God since the day she lost her mother.

A little while later, after the man had left, Lilith continued walking home. For some reason, she kept the bag containing the breakfast that she never ate, even though the food had definitely spoiled by now.

After she returned home, Lilith would look inside the bag and discover that, instead of food, there was money inside—enough to cover the meal that she had lost after bumping into that enigmatic young man.

Interlude 1

Darkness blanketed the sky. The stars did not shine, and the moon was but a pale imitation of what it would be in places that were less developed. The heavens were blocked by the smog that humanity had covered the atmosphere with. God would not reach these people.

A figure stood on a tall building, its long robe was darker than the night sky, wreathing his body like black flames caught in a breeze. The robe was large enough to hide whether the figure was male or female. The face was covered by a hood, masking all but its eyes.

Its eyes. From within the hood their eyes glowered at the world below them. Two crimson orbs like bloody pools stared at the city below in disgust.

Long ago, his kind had inspired great fear. Humans fled before them in terror, mere prey for them to feast on. That time had long since passed and he, like many others, had been forced to hide in the shadows. No longer were they the once great and proud race of centuries past. They had been reduced to bottom feeders, picking off the scraps that humans left behind.

The decadent filth that was humanity had long since overpopulated this world. And not just humans. Oh, no. There were many others who populated this world, mucking it up with their grime. Once he gained enough power, all those lesser species would perish.

He would keep the humans, however, for they had their uses. He would breed them like cattle and suck them dry. They would sustain him, increasing his power, and he would let them live. He was, after all, a merciful lord.

Ah, but there was one among this group of pestilence that he would save, one that he would acquire for himself. He would find her, and he would break her, and then she would stand by his side. She would be his Queen.

"My dear Eve, no matter how far you run, I will always find you."

Chapter 9

"Three numbers are such that the second is six less than twice the first, and the third is five more than the sum of the first two numbers. The sum of the numbers is two-hundred and thirty-four. Find the numbers."

Lilith worried her lower lip as she stared at the computer in front of her. The text on the monitor seemed to mock her for her inability to answer the algebra problem that it presented. Despite having been staring at the problem for the past fifteen minutes, as well as reading it out loud several times, she was no closer to discovering the answer than she had been when she first started.

The index finger of her left hand tapped a staccato rhythm on the table, a habit that she had picked up for moments like this, while she held a strand of hair between the fingers of her right hand and twirled it around. Her left leg jiggled up and down, so quickly that it sounded like the beating of a hummingbird's wings. Frustration had set in a long time ago.

Pointless. This was all pointless. No matter how long she stared at the screen, Lilith found herself no closer to solving this equation. And it was the first problem of her math homework! If she couldn't even solve the first problem, then how was she going to solve the others?

Math had never been her strongest subject. It would not be inaccurate to say that she royally sucked at math. In fact, she didn't just suck at math; she was so splendidly horrible that mathematicians everywhere cringed whenever she attempted to solve a mathematical equation. Lilith was more of the artistic type. Drawing and illustrations were her specialty, not math and science. Why was she even required to take math courses when they weren't needed for her degree?

It had only been two months since Lilith began attending classes at California State University. She wanted to say that she enjoyed going to college, but the truth was that she couldn't stand it. The classes were nice, but wholly unenjoyable because of the obvious reason of there being one male too many. All of the boys in her classes spent more time stripping her with their eyes than paying attention to the instructors. It was so bad that she not only sat in the back of the classroom, but she'd begun wearing the most unflattering clothes she could find so people wouldn't notice her.

It's too bad that hadn't worked out like she'd been hoping it would. Even when disguised in clothes that hid her entire body from view, people still stared at her.

The beginning of the year had been especially bad. The first time that she had gone to the campus, she had become the object of unwanted attention.

Every male in the vicinity had ogled her like a piece of meat. The women had glared at her, as if she was to blame for their boyfriends' wandering eyes, which Lilith didn't understand. It wasn't like she enjoyed the attention. She hated it. If she knew how to make them stop, she would have gladly done so a long time ago.

If that had been the worst thing that had happened, she might have been able to grin and bear it. Unfortunately, not only had she been the center of attention, but several guys who'd apparently been stronger willed than most had assaulted her.

Lilith still shuddered when she remembered that incident. Even now she could feel the way they had grabbed her, could remember the terror she felt as they forced her against the wall. She remembered how the boys had surrounded her, keeping her caged between them, unable to move, unable to run. To this day her mind still reeled in horror as she recalled how she had tried to scream, only for them to clamp her mouth shut and keep her arms pinned above her head, leaving her helpless to their machinations.

If it hadn't been for a teacher passing by—a female, thank God—Lilith was positive that they would have tried something right there in the hallway. She had been lucky to walk away with only bruised wrists and an even healthier fear of men.

After she talked with the school director, they had worked out a solution that at least partially satisfied her. Lilith's instructors would email all the lesson plans and homework that didn't require her attendance, and she would complete her assignments at home. She would then email the homework back, get graded for it, and have the next assignment sent to her. So long as she kept a three-point-five GPA and turned all of her assignments in on time, they would let her continue doing the majority of college work from home. The only time that she would have to attend was during tests.

This arrangement had worked out pretty well so far. There were a few bumps in the road—she couldn't ask her teachers for in-person help on her schoolwork, and e-mail didn't work as the instructors didn't always respond to her in a timely manner.

That issue was mostly rectified thanks to Maria, who was ridiculously intelligent on top of being an amazing athlete. She helped Lilith with her math and science homework, which was where she struggled the most.

Unfortunately, Maria wasn't there right now. She was out on another run, and Lilith had no clue when she would be back.

"Would you stop that? It's annoying."

Another problem, and part of the reason for her agitation, was her second roommate: Stacy Moon. She and the other girl had never gotten along. They didn't argue much, but Lilith was sure that the only reason Stacy didn't make a bigger fuss about her presence was because Maria made the rules—mainly because she paid most of the bills and actually liked Lilith.

Stacy was a seventeen-year-old girl who had run away from home. Lilith didn't know much about her past other than that. Truth be told, she didn't really want to know. The girl was unpleasant to her at the best of times and downright insulting at the worst of them.

Her dark hair was styled in a short pixie cut, several streaks of pink running through it. She was decked out in gothic clothes: black pants, a black lace bodice, black armbands, and black boots with about a dozen straps that gave her several extra inches in height. A black choker clung to her neck, completing the ensemble, and the dark clothes created a stark contrast to her pale, nearly ghost-white skin.

She and Stacy tried avoiding each other whenever possible. They just didn't mesh. The other girl was the type who enjoyed staying up well into the night partying, while Lilith was an early bird. Just about the only thing that she knew about her estranged roommate was that Stacy worked at a nightclub called Up Lounge in Anaheim.

Lilith had no clue how the young girl had gotten a job there, though she knew the goth-clad female used a fake ID to sneak into clubs. She never really bothered asking. Even if she disapproved of someone so young getting a job at a dance club that served alcohol, it really wasn't any of her business.

"Stop what?" Lilith asked absently, eyes narrowed at the monitor, as if glaring at the equation would make it solve itself.

"Don't 'stop what' me! Stop making so much noise! It's distracting, and I'm trying to watch TV."

Lilith looked up from her work, and turned her head to see the girl sitting on the couch. Her propped legs and slouched posture annoyed Lilith. Everything from the way she sat to the way her clothes were rumpled, and even the slack expression on her face screamed lazy. On the other side of the room, the television played some kind of reality TV show.

"It's not something I can help." Lilith looked back down at the homework mocking her from the monitor screen. "Besides, I'm at least doing something productive. All you're doing is lazing about."

"I don't see what that has to do with anything." Even though Lilith was no longer looking at the other girl, she could practically feel the scowl being directed her way. "So you're doing something productive. Big deal. I pay more of the bills than you do."

"That doesn't mean much. Maria pays more than both of us. Plus, I go to college and you don't. What's more, I was here first. If you think I'm annoying, then you could always just go outside. A day in the sun might do you some good."

It also might give her the worst sunburn known to mankind, but Lilith honestly didn't care. Out of all the girls that she knew, Stacy was the one that she liked the least. Not only had the girl dropped out of high school after running away, but she lived a

wild lifestyle. Why the cops hadn't arrested her yet was a mystery.

How Maria had put up with her for so long was an even bigger mystery.

"Are you trying to start something?!"

Lilith sighed in barely contained annoyance. "No. In case you haven't noticed; I'm *trying* to do my homework. I don't have time to start something, nor would I want to. I was simply pointing out that you don't have to remain here if you don't like listening to me."

"I'm not going outside."

"Then don't complain."

"Tch!"

Before the situation could deteriorate further, the door to the apartment opened, and a sweaty but satisfied Maria walked in. For her run that day, she had chosen to wear black running shorts and a pink shirt that showed off her midriff. Lilith was not bisexual, but even she had to admit that her friend looked gorgeous in her running clothes. Maybe that's why Maria never felt jealous around her.

"Don't tell me you two are fighting again." Maria sounded exasperated. Despite having gone on a twenty-two mile run, she didn't seem the least bit winded. Her breathing was even and slow. The only sign that she'd done anything physical was the way her skin glistened in the light.

"Not at all," Lilith lied. "We're just having a difference of opinion."

"What she said," Stacy opined from her place on the couch.

Maria just sighed. "What am I going to do with you two?"

Lilith didn't have an answer to that, so she didn't say anything. And it was clear to both of them that Stacy had no intention of answering her, either.

When neither of them gave her a reply, Maria headed toward the shower. She returned nearly ten minutes later dressed in pink booty shorts, sandals, and a sleeveless shirt with a Captain America shield emblazoned on the front.

Her friend wasn't a hardcore Marvel fan—at least she didn't think so, but she knew that Maria thought the guy who played Captain America in the movies was hot. It was the only reason they had gone out to see the movie when it first came out in theaters.

Footsteps came from behind Lilith as she was still trying to solve the first question to her homework.

"Having some trouble?" Maria's asked, causing Lilith to sigh.

"Aren't I always?" The reply wasn't necessarily scathing, but it did have a touch of sarcasm to it. Maria didn't let it bother her.

"I can give you a hand if you want."

"Yes, please!"

"All right, but first, I think you should take a break." Lilith looked up from her homework to stare at Maria's grinning face. "You haven't had lunch yet, have you?"

As if in answer to her question, Lilith's stomach growled, sounding more like the roar of vicious predator than a stomach. When Lilith's cheeks became suffused with red, Maria nodded, her grinning face one of triumph.

"Thought so. Let's go grab some lunch. I'll help you when we get back."

"Yeah, okay." Lilith stood up, and, after shutting off her computer, she turned away from the offending object. She really could use a break. Not only was she sick of staring at math problems, but her eyes were burning. "Where are we going?"

"The Crema Café, of course," Maria said in that "duh" voice of hers. "That's one of the only places we *can* go."

Lilith's shoulders drooped a bit. "I'm sorry. I know the only reason we're not going somewhere else is because of me."

Although The Crema Café wasn't exclusive to women, it was the only place where she felt safe. This was largely because of Auntie Kay, who was very accommodating, and did her best to make sure that none of the male workers or patrons bothered her.

"Hey, hey, it's all right." Maria wrapped an arm around Lilith's shoulder and smiled. "I don't mind, and I'm really just in the mood for a frappuccino. You know that I can never stomach real food after a run."

"I guess." Lilith still felt a bit guilty, but she gave her friend a smile nonetheless. "Thank you."

"He-he, you're welcome."

***

Because they had arrived in the middle of the day, most of the community was at work. That meant there were only a few patrons at The Crema Café when Lilith and Maria entered. The two of them were still the center of attention from the moment they walked in, maybe even before that.

It was a common occurrence whenever they went out, whether alone or together. Both were considered incredibly beautiful. Maria had that athletic build that men loved; a flat stomach, toned legs and arms, and a face that was to die for. Her breasts were a little small because of how fit she was, but that didn't detract from her looks in the slightest. Lilith wouldn't say it out loud, but if she were a man or into girls, she wouldn't mind being intimate with her friend in the slightest.

And then there was Lilith. Maria called her The Bombshell, insisting that she was flawless in every way, from her perfectly proportioned body to the stunning features of her otherworldly face. Lilith didn't know how much of that was true, though she did know that men found her attractive—it was hard not to with how they acted around her. Still, being called a "Bombshell," even the person calling her that was female, was embarrassing.

As they walked into the store, Lilith moved closer to her friend's side, and grabbed Maria's arm in a vice grip. Her friend allowed this—just another reason that Lilith liked Maria so much.

"You know, I sometimes feel like you're just using me as a shield," Maria joked.

Lilith flinched. "I'm sorry."

"Hey now." Maria patted Lilith's right hand. "You know I don't mind. I was just kidding."

Lilith gave her a weak smile. "Right."

The men in the cafe hadn't stopped staring since they'd entered. Only Maria's *take one step closer and I'll punch your face in* glare kept them in place. Lilith tried her best to ignore them as she and her friend walked up to the register. Fortunately—and also unfortunately—the person manning the register that day was a girl.

"I'll have a strawberry banana smoothie with protein powder," Maria said. Lilith looked at her oddly.

"I thought you wanted a frappuccino?"

"I've changed my mind."

"One strawberry banana smoothie with protein powder, got it," the young pig-tailed girl behind the register said. She then directed her gaze to Lilith, the smile on her face becoming strained. "And what about you?"

"Um." Lilith tried to concentrate on the menu, but it was hard. She wasn't feeling very comfortable, maybe because the patrons were now behind them. She could feel more stares being directed at her backside. "I would like your... Pesto Chicken Panini."

"All right, one Pesto Chicken Panini. Are you two ordering together or separate?"

"Together," Maria said before Lilith could say "separate." She sent her friend a look, but Maria just grinned at her.

"Okay, here's your number. Just find a seat and we'll bring your order up once it's ready."

"Come on." Maria turned around, the holder with their number in hand, and began walking away from the cash register. "Do you want to sit inside or outside?"

Lilith followed her friend while turning the question over in her head. As she was trying to determine what she wanted, her eyes strayed across the room, seeking an answer from her surroundings. Halfway through her inspection, she froze. There, seated at one of the tables, a small steaming cup and a pot of coffee sitting before him, was the raven-haired man that she had run into yesterday.

He didn't look at her, even though his chair was facing her. He didn't even seem to have noticed her yet, which was odd. No male had ever been able to ignore when she walked into a room, even if they were facing away from her, like all men had some kind of sixth sense that let them know she was near. The tablet that she had seen him with the other day sat on his lap, and his irises skimmed across the screen. What was he reading? she wondered.

"Hey, Lilith. Have you thought of where you want to sit yet? Lilith?"

When Maria noticed that she had stopped moving, she turned back around. Lilith stood frozen like a block of ice. With a concerned look, her friend followed Lilith's gaze and immediately zeroed in on the young man.

A sly smile crossed her lips. "Oh, my. Oh, my, oh, my. I hadn't realized that you've finally become interested in the opposite sex."

"What?"

Lilith's attention snapped away from the man and to her friend. She stared at Maria with an expression of uncertainty, her mind replaying Maria's words in her mind. When she finally finished analyzing what her friend had said, her eyes widened, while at the same time her cheeks gained a healthy dose of color.

"I-it isn't like that." She was careful to keep her voice down so no one would hear her. Too many people were already watching them. No need to add more fuel to the fire. Plus, she didn't want *him* to also notice her presence.

"It's not?" Maria's eyes were alight with mirth. Her brown orbs twinkled merrily and with more than a bit of mischief. She had the look of someone who'd just been told Christmas had come early.

Lilith didn't like that look. Not one bit. "No, it's not."

"Then what is it like?"

"Ah… well, I just sort of… ran into him… the other day, I mean…" Lilith answered lamely.

The look on Maria's face demanded a lengthier explanation. "You ran into him?"

"We kind of… crashed into each other… literally, I mean. And I may have… sort of… kinda… overreacted a bit. Just a little."

"I see, I see."

Lilith felt an inexplicable urge to hide at the sight of Maria's widening grin. There was something frightening about that look.

"So basically, you reacted like you do every time a man gets too close, and ran away screaming like a banshee who discovered crack."

If there hadn't already been heat surging to her cheeks, there most certainly was now. Her face felt hot enough to cook a panini on it. Did her friend really have to bring that up?

"I don't do that every time I run into a man." Lilith tried to defend herself. When Maria gave her a steady stare, her defenses crumbled. Her shoulders slumped, and she gave her friend a pathetic look. "Okay, so maybe I do act like that. I can't help it, though. You know how men frighten me."

"Trust me, I am well aware of that," Maria said dryly. She then glanced sideways at the young man across the room. "That still doesn't explain why you reacted so strongly when you saw him."

Lilith glanced at the man as well. Now that she wasn't quite freaking out, she could see his features more clearly. He was definitely what most girls would describe as handsome. He had slightly pale skin, strong features, and looked like he kept himself in good shape, if the definition in his arms and the way his shirt strained against his pectorals and broad shoulders were any indication. His midnight-black hair was wild and untamed in a devil-may-care sort of way. Lilith imagined many girls would enjoy running their hands through that hair.

Perhaps his most arresting feature were his eyes, which stood out prominently, even from a distance. They practically glowed, outshining even the lights overhead. The left eye reminded her of an emerald, bright and vibrant. Meanwhile, the right eye was a deep scarlet, reminiscent of a ruby. Rather than detract from his looks, the starkly contrasting colors enhanced them. Even Lilith had to admit that his eyes were gorgeous.

Ridding herself of all these strange thoughts, she redirected her attention to Maria, who also eyed the young man with an appreciative gaze.

"I met him twice." Maria blinked, and then turned her head and looked back at Lilith. "Once when I was leaving this place, and again when I was on my way home." Her gaze flickered to the young man, who still hadn't looked up. "He… he apologized for bumping into me when I was on my way home from work, and then he gave me the bag of crepes I had dropped earlier that morning."

"He gave you the food you had dropped?" Maria raised an eyebrow. "That seems like an odd thing to do. Wouldn't it have spoiled by then?"

"There was money in the bag," Lilith informed her. "Enough to cover the cost of the food."

"Oh, my." Maria was smiling again. "It seems he is quite the chivalrous young man."

Chivalry was considered a dead concept in this day and age. From what Lilith understood, most women considered a man who acted chivalrous to be chauvinistic. Having been on the receiving end of every man's unwanted advances for the past several years of her life, Lilith didn't even know what that concept meant anymore.

"He didn't try to assault me."

Maria paused. She knew what Lilith meant. For whatever reason, Lilith had a strange effect on men. Either they became drooling idiots or attempted to sexually assault her. Neither of them understood why.

"Really?"

"Yes."

"Well," Maria started slowly. "It had to happen eventually, right? I mean, there has to be at least one man in this entire planet that doesn't turn into a drooling mass of flesh or a salacious beast when they're in your presence." Slowly, ever so slowly, the smile returned in full bloom. "Perhaps he's the one you're destined to be with."

"D-don't joke like that," Lilith stuttered, her face aflame. "There's no such thing as fate or love at first sight or anything like that. That's just a bunch of fairy tales made up by Disney to entertain little girls who dream of being swept of their feet and—are you even listening to me?"

No, Maria wasn't listening. Clasping her hands together and bringing them up to her chin almost as if she were about to pray, Maria did an approximation of a swoon. "I can just picture it now: two lost souls who never thought they could fall in love with a member of the opposite sex meet, and find comfort in each other's arms. It sounds so romantic!"

"R-romantic?!" Embarrassed did not begin to describe how mortified Lilith felt. In that moment, all she wanted to do was crawl into a hole and die. "I don't… it's not… I mean I couldn't…"

Maria whirled on her, the grin still present. "Regardless of what you could or couldn't do, you should at least thank him for reimbursing you for the money you lost."

"Eh?" Lilith blinked at Maria's sudden change in topic. Slowly, a frown appeared as she contemplated her friend's words. "That… that does seem to be the right thing to do, doesn't it?" She worried her lower lip with her teeth. "But…"

"But nothing! Go over there and thank him!"

Maria must have grown tired of her indecision. The next thing Lilian knew, her friend had pushed her toward the table where the young man sat.

Lilith stumbled toward the table where the young man sat. She just barely kept from losing her balance and falling onto the floor in front of the table. Not that this made her feel any better. Why did her friend have to be so pushy sometimes?

Smoothing out the nonexistent wrinkles in her knee-length skirt, Lilith opened her mouth… and promptly froze. It wasn't fear that kept her from speaking—at least not completely. Her silence was caused by something entirely new.

She had no idea what to say. This would be the first time that she had ever willingly spoken to a man in years, outside of e-mail (some of her teachers were men). What could she say to him? *Thank you for giving me enough money to cover the cost of the food you made me drop?* Somehow, that didn't sound appropriate, or polite. It actually sounded kind of rude.

While she was busy thinking about what she should say, the young man in question finally noticed her. He looked up from his KLReader to stare at Lilith. For several long seconds, he said nothing, merely looked at her as if not quite sure what to make of her presence.

After a moment of him staring at her and her staring at nothing, he asked, "Can I help you?"

"Kya!" Startled, Lilith let out a short scream.

The action in the room ground to a halt. Everyone who had not already been staring at her stopped what they were doing and gawked. The men began to drool, the women to glare. Lilith hardly noticed this time. Her wide eyes were fixed upon the person before her.

"Sorry," he apologized, looking abashed. "I didn't mean to startle you."

"Oh! Um, no, no!" Lilith squeaked. She shook her head, trying not to give in to the increasing desire she felt to turn around and flee the café. "It's okay. I was… was… um… thinking?" Lilith had no clue if she was asking a question or making a statement. She didn't know much of anything at the moment. Her brain was on the fritz.

The young man raised a single dark eyebrow. "Thinking?"

"Y-yes. Thinking."

"… Okay." He seemed content accept what she said, or at least not concern himself enough to question her further. Lilith didn't know how to feel about that.

As his eyes focused on her, Lilith wondered why she was even doing this. She shouldn't be talking to him. He was a man. She didn't like men. They were perverted, had no sense of shame, and drooled over her like she was a pinup model who didn't possess any feelings of her own. They lied and had no qualms about hurting her if it meant getting what they wanted. She couldn't trust them.

And yet…

"Is there something I can do for you, Ms…"

Lilith stiffened. "No!" she squeaked pitifully.

The young man stared at her some more. "Then why are you here?"

When Lilith flinched, he shook his head and tried again. "I'm sorry, that was extremely rude of me, and I didn't mean it like that. I meant, why are you here talking to me? I thought you hated men."

"I did—I mean I do!"

"If you hate men, then why are you…"

"Because I…" Lilith stalled. Her face heated up like a furnace. God, this was so embarrassing! "I wanted to… to… to…"

"Yes?"

"Iwantedtothankyou!"

A blink. For several seconds that was the only answer she received that let her know that he heard her. His face scrunched up for a moment, like he was trying really hard to figure out what she had just said. Not that she blamed him. The speed with which she had spoken caused her words to jumble together like a cat getting tangled in a ball of yarn. His face cleared a few seconds later.

"You're welcome," he said simply. "Though I don't know what you're thanking me for."

"For the money you left me." Lilith spoke more slowly this time. Her voice had also grown

soft, barely more than a whisper. Only the silence blanketing the room allowed him to hear what she said. "It was very kind of you to pay for the meal that I dropped when we ran into each other."

"Oh, that." He shook his head. "You don't have to thank me for that. I was the one who bumped into you, so it's only right that I make it up to you."

"But, if I hadn't been in such a hurry, we wouldn't have ended up crashing into each other," Lilith insisted.

"And if I had been paying a little more attention to where I was going, you wouldn't have bumped into me."

"You still didn't have to pay for my food," she pressed, not at all sure why she was making such a big deal out of this, or why she was even still talking to him.

"Maybe not," he agreed. "But I would have felt bad if I didn't do anything."

"I see." Lilith looked down at her sandal-clad feet. Her toes wiggled absently as she thought about his words. Seconds later, she was looking at him again. "Even if you say that, I want to thank you anyway. It was a very nice gesture."

His smile came naturally—this time Lilith was sure of it. Her heart had definitely skipped a beat.

"You're very welcome."

Another silence filled the air. Lilith stood there in indecision. Should she continue talking to him? He didn't seem like a bad person, and he wasn't acting like an idiot. It could be a trick… but no, she knew what men who were affected by her looked like. This man didn't look like he was losing his mind to depravity and lust. If anything, he looked like he just wanted to continue reading whatever was on his tablet, which he glanced at every so often.

Lilith swallowed heavily as he stared at her. Her heart pounded against her chest, a war drum threatening to break free. She was afraid, but at the same time, she wasn't. This fear felt different from her normal "*Oh, my god it's a man*" fear. She didn't understand. Why? Why didn't she want to run away?

"So… um… what are… what are you reading?" she asked hesitantly.

"It's called *Kaze no Stigma*," he told her. "You probably haven't heard of—"

"You're reading *Stigma of the Wind*?" Lilith asked in shock.

He looked at her in mild surprise. "You've heard of it?"

"I have all twelve volumes under my bed," she said in excitement, right before realizing that she had just admitted to owning several volumes of a Japanese light novel—which only nerds and geeks read. And admitted it loud enough for several dozen people, including her friend Maria, to hear. "I mean… I thought they looked interesting, so…"

"I love reading Japanese light novels."

Lilith blinked. "R-really?"

"Yes." He smiled. "I've always loved reading. It's been a hobby of mine since I was little. I've read so much that there are very few original stories that I haven't read. I had been looking for something new to read when I stumbled upon my first light novel in the manga section of a bookstore. I've been hooked ever since. Light novels are very different from American novels and novellas."

Lilith felt a smile creeping onto her face. "That's what got me into them, too. Plus, most American novels are either those gloomy dystopian series or vampire and werewolf stories."

"Ugh, don't remind me." The young man looked positively ill. "How anyone could possibly enjoy those vampire books are beyond me. Whoever heard of a vampire that sparkles in the sunlight? It's completely inaccurate. Vampires burst into dust when the sun hits them. They don't sparkle like a pretty boy who's been shot in the face with a glitter cannon."

"I know!" Lilith readily agreed, her head bobbing up and down for emphasis. "And then there are the werewolves whose sole reason for existing in a story seems to be losing their clothes after they transform. It's like they were made simply to give teenage girls something to drool over."

"I know!" The young man repeated Lilith's earlier words, looking positively ecstatic to see someone who agreed with him. "The dystopian stories are okay," he added after a moment's pause. "Though I'll admit, there are far too many of them. Stories like that are only good after the first couple of series. Once you've read a couple dozen, you find that they're all more or less the same story, and the only real difference is the characters involved, and they tend to be carbon copies of other stories' characters anyway."

"I couldn't agree more," Lilith said. She looked at the tablet in his hands, and curiosity overtook her. "So, what volume are you on?"

"I just finished volume one."

"Oh, that means you just finished reading about Kazuma's and Ayano's battle with the Fūga clan."

"Yes."

"What other light novels have you read?" asked Lilith, sitting down across from him.

The young man looked thoughtful. "Let's see, I've read *Spice and Wolf, Accel World, Another, Ballad of a Shinigami,* and…"

As the conversation continued, Lilith completely forgot that she was talking to a man. She'd finally found someone who shared her passion, and she would be damned if she let this opportunity slip by!

***

Nathan Storm was a delinquent. He acted like one, dressed like one, and spoke like one. Everyone who lived on this side of Seal Beach knew better than to cross him. As the leader of one of the only gangs in town—a small biker gang that mostly stuck to petty vandalism and thefts—the people in the area were suitably wary of coming near him.

He also enjoyed fighting. To him, there was nothing better than the thrill that came from his fist meeting another person's face. The satisfying crunch as someone's nose broke against his punch. Nathan's love for combat was so great that he had even been kicked out of his dojo for instigating unnecessary violence and needless brutality.

There was only one thing that Nathan loved more than violence and combat: Lilith Vie. Ever since she had come into this town he'd been captivated by her. Just the thought of those big blue eyes, soft lips, wide hips, slim waist and voluptuous breasts made him want to howl. She was everything that he wanted in a woman.

He even had plans to make her *his* woman. It had taken a while for him to figure out a way to accomplish this, but after weeks of careful thought and planning, Nathan believed that he had come up with a suitable method to claim her.

Of course, all that planning was now ruined because of the sight before him. He stood on the sidewalk, his eyes glaring through the windows of The Crema Café, and watched as some nobody talked to *his* woman. Even worse, Lilith was talking back! She was actually speaking to a man!

Nathan was well aware of Lilith's fear of men. That's the whole reason he hadn't approached her yet. If he did, she would run, and he wanted her to become his willingly.

It didn't look like that was possible anymore, though. Someone had beaten him to the punch. How and when this happened he didn't know, but he wasn't going to stand for it.

As he glared at the light-skinned young man with glowing red and green eyes, another plan formed in his mind. It would put him several weeks back on his original plan to make Lilith his woman, but that's how life worked sometimes. He couldn't do anything about Lilith until he dealt with this new annoyance first.

And Nathan would deal with him. That strange guy with dark hair and freaky heterochromatic eyes would regret ever speaking to his woman.

Chapter 10

“ I think my favorite right now is *Is It Wrong to Pick Up Girls in a Dungeon?*”

It was later in the day. The light from the sun had turned reddish orange, setting the sky ablaze. Lilith was still sitting at the table with Christian, speaking to him about her first and guiltiest pleasure. She would occasionally nibble on her food, but most of her time was spent talking.

This was the first time that she had met another person who shared this particular interest—at least, he was first person that she knew who shared her interest. Lilith would readily admit that she was too embarrassed to ask the few people she spoke to if they also read Japanese light novels.

The knowledge that this young man shared her passion made her joyous. Was it fate that she would meet him? Or simple luck? She didn’t know, and she wasn’t sure if she cared. All that mattered was that she’d finally found someone with whom she could discuss the one aspect of herself that she had never shared with anyone, not even Maria.

“You do realize that *Is It Wrong to Pick up Girls in a Dungeon?* has a harem in it, don’t you?”

"No, it doesn't." Lilith fiercely defended her current favorite light novel. Her companion looked skeptical. He even raised an eyebrow at her!

"Really? Because it seems to me that Hestia, Aiz, and Lilliluka all have a thing for Bell."

"Well, they do," Lilian admitted before her eyes burned with the fire of her convictions. "But that doesn't mean it's a harem. Everyone knows that Bell and Hestia are meant for each other, even if Bell is too dense to notice Hestia's feelings. The other two are just there for the sake of comedy."

He held his hands up in surrender as she leaned over the table and got in his face. "Easy. I didn't mean anything by it. I was just surprised to hear that you liked this particular series since it has a har—I mean, since it's more of a male-oriented story. I actually like *DanMachi*," he said, using the abbreviated name for the series.

"Really?" Lilith narrowed her eyes.

"Of course. I've read all of the volumes that have currently been translated." His cheeks suddenly turned bright red. "I've even, um, seen the animated series."

"Well." Lilith sat back down and crossed her arms, feeling only slightly vindicated. "So long as you're a fan, I guess I can forgive your rude comments."

"Right, right. Sorry for making that mistake. Though in my defense, it's an easy thing to do."

"I suppose…"

Her companion paused as he seemed to realize something. "You know, we've been talking here for a while now, but I don't think I ever gave you my name, did I?"

Lilith opened her mouth to respond, and then quickly snapped it shut as she realized that he was right.

Her cheeks heated up almost against her will as she realized her situation. She had been sitting here, talking to this man for a long time now, and she didn't even know his name! How embarrassing was that?

"I'm Christian."

Heterochromatic eyes stared into hers. Even though he was sitting so close to her, there wasn't a single sign that he felt enamored or enchanted by her presence. She had thought it was some kind of fluke at first, but now she knew the truth, and a part of her wondered why. Why was this man not affected by her like every other man? Lilith supposed that she could ask him, but she didn't think that would be a good idea. She didn't want to sound conceited.

"My name's Lilith," she said at last. Then she blinked and glanced around the café. The café was nearly empty. The only other people present were the employees.

Where did everyone go? And more importantly...

"Where's Maria?"

"She left about two hours ago," Auntie Kay supplied with a smile as she approached their table. "Didn't you see her leaving?"

The way Lilith's face lit up like a Christmas tree confirmed that, no, Lilith had not noticed that her friend had left a long time ago.

"Oh, Lilith. I can't believe you actually forgot about your friend, especially since she paid for your meal." Despite her words, it was clear that Auntie Kay was just teasing. The large smile she wore belied her exasperated tone. "Though I suppose I can't blame you. Your friend here is quite handsome. Ah, if only I were a few decades younger."

Christian coughed into his hand while Lilith hid her face with hers. Auntie Kay just chuckled before looking fondly at her.

"I'm happy for you. I'll admit that I had been, well, not exactly afraid, but concerned for you and your future. It's good to see that you're beginning to move past your fear of men." Auntie Kay's gaze flickered to Christian, who sat there, silently watching the interaction. "Or maybe it's just because of *who* you're talking to that you're not afraid."

Auntie Kay's words caused more color than was probably healthy to appear on Lilith's already pink cheeks. Despite the rather prominent blush, she didn't try to hide her discomfort, since covering her face with her hands wasn't working too well for her. She did, however, give the older woman a very powerful pout.

"Please stop teasing me. I'm gonna have more than enough of that when I get home. I don't need it from you, too."

She could just picture Maria standing in the living room, wearing that infuriating smirk. Lilith could even imagine what her friend would say, something along the lines of destiny and how she and Christian had been fated to meet.

"I'm sorry," Auntie Kay smiled amiably. "I didn't mean to embarrass you. I'm just so happy for you. Really, it's nice to see you actually talking to this young man. It does my heart good. I really do worry for you, you know?"

"I wish you two wouldn't talk about me like I'm not here," Christian grumbled, though his voice lacked any real heat.

Despite her red cheeks and obvious feelings of mortification, Lilith gave the elderly woman a dazzling smile. "Thank you."

Auntie Kay returned the smile. She then looked out of the window, taking note of the setting sun.

"You two had best be off now." She turned to look back at the two. "The café has actually been closed for a while. I'm afraid that you two have to leave so my staff can finish cleaning and go home themselves."

"Is it really that late?" Lilith looked out of the window as well, her eyes widening in surprise when she saw how dark it had gotten. "I had no idea... how long have we been talking?"

"About four hours," Auntie Kay supplied. "The shop's been closed for the last fifteen minutes."

"If you guys have been closed for so long, why didn't you tell us?" Christian's frown held nothing but concern. "We would have left if you'd mentioned it."

"And possibly dispel whatever magic helped Lilith overcome her fear of men enough to speak with you?" Auntie Kay scoffed. "I think not. Seeing the girl who's always been so frightened of the opposite sex that she runs away at the mere sight of a man, sitting down and talking to a man, is worth more to me than a few extra minutes at work."

Lilith looked down at her sandal-clad toes, her hair draping her face like a curtain. It did a decent job of hiding her features from view. She imagined her hair as a shield that could block out the rest of the world.

Now if only the rest of the world would play along with me.

Christian looked between Lilith and Auntie Kay. His brow furrowed, and then relaxed after a few seconds. Slowly, he nodded.

"Yes, I suppose I can see why you would feel that way. In that case, thank you for allowing us to continue our conversation." From behind her hair, Lilith saw the slightly crooked smile that gave him a somewhat roguish appearance. "I'll admit, it was... nice, talking to someone who shares my passion for light novels. There isn't anyone back home who has the same taste in reading material that I do—actually." He paused, his face scrunching up. "I don't even know if the people back home even read."

"You're welcome, young man. Now, the both of you really should be off." She made a shooing gesture at them. "This table isn't going to clean itself."

With such a pronounced dismissal, Christian and Lilith could do nothing but stand up from their chairs, and quietly leave the establishment. When they exited the building, the two turned around just in time to see Auntie Kay walk up to the front door and turn the sign adorning the glass from Open to Closed. She tossed them a quick wave before walking back into the café, where she began cleaning.

Now that they were alone and the enlightening conversation that they'd been so engaged in was finished, awkwardness returned with a vengeance. They gazed at each other for but a moment, then just as quickly looked away, unable to even open their mouths, much less speak.

"Well," Christian broke the tense silence, scratching at his cheek with his right index finger, "I guess now that we've been officially kicked out, it's time for us to part ways."

"Yeah…"

He looked at Lilith, and saw that she was looking anywhere but at him. Now that whatever spell had been cast over her was gone, she realized that she had just spent a whole four hours talking to a person that she was supposed to be afraid of.

"Would you like me to walk you home?" he asked suddenly.

"E-excuse me?"

Lilith finally turned to face him. When she did, their eyes locked, and his unwavering gaze pierced her. She hadn't noticed it before now, but his eyes felt almost like they weren't looking at her, but through her. It felt like they cut through all the surface features that most others couldn't look past and saw the real her.

I wonder what he sees when he looks at me?

"I asked if you wanted me to walk you home," Christian repeated. "Seal Beach isn't a very dangerous place, from what I have seen, but I still wouldn't feel right leaving a young woman to walk home by herself."

Lilith looked back down at the ground, her hair hiding her face, which was good, because she didn't want Christian to see how his words made her cheeks feel like they'd been set on fire. It wasn't a bad feeling. It was actually rather pleasant, but it made her uncomfortable. She had never felt this way before, and she didn't know how to respond.

"Thank you," she said after taking several seconds to regain her composure. It took some willpower, but she lifted her head and gave Christian a smile. "But, I think I would rather walk home by myself. It's nothing personal," she added upon seeing his frown. "I'm still not very comfortable with all this—being in the presence of a man, I mean."

Christian took a second to compose his words. When he did speak, it was slowly, as if he was carefully considering each word before pronouncing them. "I suppose I can understand how you feel, sort of. I sometimes feel uncomfortable around women as well."

"Really?" Lilith was surprised. Christian felt uncomfortable around women? With his looks? She certainly hadn't expected this. Maybe they had even more in common than just a love of light novels and manga.

"Well, it's not like I'm afraid of them or anything," he admitted. "It's just that a few of my, um, work colleagues, I guess, get kind of pushy at times, and it makes me uncomfortable."

Did that mean he had women hitting on him at work? She guessed that's what he meant, though she could be wrong.

I guess men aren't the only ones who have problems controlling their desires.

"Well then," he started. "I guess this is goodbye."

Turning around, Christian began to walk away. Lilith watched him go, worrying her lower lip between her teeth. He had only taken a few steps forward when she raised her hand and called out to him.

"W-wait!"

Christian stopped walking and turned around. "Yes?"

"Doyouwannagooutwithmetomorrow?!"

He blinked, then scratched the side of his head, the expression he wore more than adequately conveying his confusion.

"Um, what?"

Realizing that Christian couldn't have possibly understood her fast-paced dialogue, she endeavored to try again. Closing her eyes, Lilith took several deep breaths, pushing her fear and anxiety to the side. A few seconds later, she opened her eyes again, uncertain and timid.

"Do you want to… to go out with me… tomorrow?"

She had no clue why she was asking this, or where it was even coming from. She was supposed to hate men, wasn't she? Why was she asking a man if he wanted to spend time with her tomorrow?

I-it must be because he likes to read Japanese light novels, she told herself. *And he hasn't tried to get fresh with me. Yes, those must be the reasons.*

"I'm… I'm sorry, but, did you just say you wanted to spend time with me tomorrow?" Christian looked gobsmacked. That expression, more than anything else, allowed Lilith to harden her resolve.

"Yes."

"You want to go out with me?"

"Yes."

"Me?"

"Yes. You."

Lilith thought this would have been the perfect time to roll her eyes, but she was far too worried that he would say no.

Christian scratched the nape of his neck. "You do realize that I'm a guy, right?"

Lilith nodded, her eyes flitting away from his for about a second before looking back. "Well, yes, but I... you... you're the first boy... the first man, who hasn't tried to do anything vile to me..."

When Christian just continued staring at her, an uncomfortable Lilith squirmed in place.

"I mean, whenever guys see me, most will just stop whatever they're doing and stare. It's unnerving, but not so bad. But a few of the bolder ones will actually try to hit me up. Sometimes—" she shuddered "—Sometimes, they don't take it very well when I tell them that I'm not interested."

"I see." Christian ran a nervous hand through his hair. Lilith bit her lip. "Well, I guess we could spend some time together tomorrow. I'm not really doing anything. It could be interesting." He smiled. "I've never spent any time with a female outside of work."

"Really?"

"Yeah..."

"... Oh..."

The two stared some more, the tension between them building once again. It was so thick that Lilith was sure she could have cut through it with a falchion—a broad, slightly curved sword with the cutting edge on the convex side.

"So I'll... I'll see you here tomorrow?" Lilith asked, breaking the uncomfortable silence.

"Yeah, see you tomorrow," Christian said.

"Okay then," Lilith breathed out, and then presented him with a shaky and nervous smile. "Bye."

"Bye."

Christian and Lilith parted ways, stopping only once to turn around and look at each other. When they realized that the other person was looking at them, they both blushed and looked away.

As she turned a corner, the slow hammering of Lilith's heart settled into a steady beat. It was only after she had walked several meters that her brain caught up to her body, and the slow realization of what occurred set in. She had just asked Christian on a date. She had asked a man on a date. A man. A date. She was going on a date with a man.

I am so screwed...

***

It was evening when Lilith arrived home. The sun sat low on the horizon and a multitude of colors splashed against the sky. Artistic swirls of red and yellow, combined with light purple streaks, made for a breathtaking scene.

Lilith would have normally enjoyed such a lovely sight. Indeed, under different circumstances, she would have loved watching the setting sun light the sky and ocean on fire. But, at that particular moment, her mind was a million miles away, focused on something other than setting suns and beautiful scenes. She only had one goal in mind, and it wasn't watching the sunset, but rather, getting through the door to her apartment, her bastion of safety.

She was quick to walk up the stairs, and quicker still to take out her key and unlock the door upon reaching her apartment. The door opened and Lilith slipped through. After closing it behind her, she leaned against the doorframe and closed her eyes.

Her body was shaking.

She had just asked a man to go out with her. What had she been thinking? What had possessed her to do something so foolish? She must have been out of her mind when she asked that question!

The sound of footsteps alerted her to someone's approach. Her eyelids fluttering open, Lilith was greeted to the sight of Maria walking up to her.

The sporty woman wore a large smile, a Cheshire cat grin that went from ear to ear as she slinked toward Lilith like a jungle predator. She stopped several feet in front of Lilith, placed her hands on her hips and leaned over slightly, her wide smirk making Lilith more than a little uncomfortable.

"So, did you have fun talking to your new *friend?*"

"Why did you leave me like that?" Lilith ignored the question and glared at her friend, a tint of red flaring to life on her cheeks. She did her best to ignore the burning of her face, however, as she had done enough blushing for one day, thank you very much.

Still wearing her "cat that ate the canary" grin, Maria shrugged. "You had pretty much forgotten all about me the moment you started talking to that guy. You and he were so deep into your discussion, and you looked so content, that I didn't want to interrupt. When the food came, I asked them to set yours next to you and left."

Lilith looked away guiltily. "Sorry," she murmured softly. "I didn't mean to ignore you like that."

"It's all right." The smile on Maria's face showed no hard feelings. "I'm honestly pleased to see you talking to a guy. I was worried you'd never find a man that didn't make you want to run away screaming. And besides, if it had been me talking to that piece of eye candy, you can be sure that our situations would have been reversed. In fact, I would probably still be with him… perhaps after asking him to show me around his house…"

"M-Maria!" Lilith thought her face couldn't burn more fiercely than it already did. She'd apparently been wrong, as her face now felt like it had been shoved into the sun. Maria's giggling did not help matters at all.

"You two looked so cute together, sitting there and talking about your favorite Japanese books."

"They're called light novels," Lilith muttered almost too softly for Maria to hear.

"So defensive," Maria snickered at her friend, while Lilith did her best impression of a turtle and hid her face in her shirt. It didn't work very well. If anything, it only served to make Maria even more amused.

Clapping her hands, Maria switched subjects. "So, I remember you saying something about needing help with your math homework?"

Lilith sighed in relief at the new topic. The bright red flush receded from her face, and she smiled at her friend.

"Yes, I'm having a bit of trouble with the word problems."

"All right, then! Let's see if this goddess of intelligence and beauty can help you solve those problems." Maria led Lilith into the living area. "And after I help you with your homework, you can share all the juicy details about your encounter with that beautiful man, and whether or not you plan on dating him."

Lilith's face felt like it was being steamed.

"I-it isn't like that!"

"Right, right, I believe you."

It was clear to Lilith that her friend did not believe her, not one bit. And for some reason, she had the strangest feeling that Maria was never going to let her live down what had happened. Call it a woman's intuition, but she just knew that this wouldn't be the last time she heard about it.

***

Christian walked to his hotel at a slow, measured pace. He thought about going faster, of arriving at the sanctity of his room sooner, but the cool night air felt nice against his skin and helped to clear his mind. And he had a lot on his mind.

Lilith had asked him out. Lilith had asked him out and he had said yes. What had he been thinking? He wasn't supposed to get close to his target. Going on a date with her definitely qualified as getting close. What would

Samantha think when she found out that he was spending quality time with the person he was supposed to kill?

But then, there was no guarantee that Lilith was a succubus. He'd never heard of a succubus who was afraid of men. The chances of her actually being his target seemed slim to none.

And even if she was the succubus that he needed to kill, would it really matter if he went somewhere with her? Wasn't he supposed to learn as much about her as he could? That's how all those assassins he'd read about in books and light novels worked. They befriended their target, learned everything they could about them: their habits, their personality, what they did, and where they went. Knowing all of that would be important if he did end up having to kill her, as it would make doing the deed that much easier.

This wasn't like killing vampires, werewolves or demons. Succubi weren't fighters, and they preferred remaining in civilized areas that were populated with many people, making it harder to just outright dispose of them. If she did turn out to be a succubus, this confrontation wouldn't end in battle but an assassination.

With those thoughts in mind, Christian cleared his head and looked up at the sky. The sun had gone down. The twilight sky greeted him. It was dark out. The streets were lit only by the lampposts lining the sidewalk, a few of which buzzed and flickered. He marveled at how he could actually see the stars from where he stood. The night was so clear, so unlike the big city he lived in.

What I wouldn't give to live in a place like this...

While he was looking up at the sky, several people stepped out of a small alley that he had just passed and surrounded him. Christian looked back down, and studied them with a casual glance. There were six in total, and all of them were guys.

He took in their expressions, noticing the intense glares they directed his way. Some of them clenched their hands into tight fists, their knuckles turning white. Others held makeshift weapons. None of them looked happy with him, though he couldn't fathom what he might have done to upset these people.

"Can I help you?" he asked mildly.

"You're the guy who was talking to our angel," the one in front said with narrowed eyes. He was a big guy, not quite fat, but definitely pudgy. His slicked back brown hair looked greasy, and his small dark eyes glared ferociously from underneath a thick unibrow.

"Angel?" Christian tilted his head, his brows furrowing. What were they... ah. "Are you talking about Lilith?"

"You think you can just waltz into this town and claim our angel's heart for yourself!" another guy yelled from behind him. Christian turned his head and saw a skinny man wearing baggy clothes, with blond hair and a beanie. "We've been in love with her far longer than you have! We won't let you have her!"

"We're going to teach you a lesson for trying to take away our angel!"

"You're dead meat, pal!"

Christian sighed as he realized what this was. Men like these must be the reason that Lilith feared the opposite sex so much. These people seemed to possess a very unhealthy obsession with her.

A part of him wondered why. Lilith was beautiful. Even Christian, who never really thought about women romantically, couldn't deny that she was the singular most stunning example of a woman he had ever seen. But, really, that shouldn't be reason enough to have such fanatical interest in her.

Unless she really is a succubus. But if she is, then why is she so afraid of men?

"You guys really don't want to do this," Christian warned them. "Please, just walk away."

"No, we really do want to do this," a voice to his left said.

Christian turned his head. Exiting from the same alley as everyone else was another man, making the group now surrounding him seven.

The one who spoke, and who Christian felt might be the ring leader, was a giant of a man. He towered over everyone there, his large, hulking body reminding Christian of steroid-enhanced body builders. His arms and legs were nearly twice the size of his head, which looked absolutely tiny on his disproportionately large body. His thick limbs strained against his t-shirt and jeans. Christian was sure the man's clothing would rip the moment any strenuous movements were made.

The man grinned at him. It wasn't a very nice grin.

"We really, really want to do this. Get him, boys!"

Six men rushed him at the same time, their battle cries ringing in the night. Some carried makeshift weapons, others just had their fists. Either way, their intention to commit violence was clear.

Not that it mattered. These men were far. Too. Slow. Their movements were like molasses running down a tree in the middle of winter. What were a few humans when compared to the monsters that he had faced?

Once they reached him, all six men attacked. Those who weren't carrying a weapon swung their fists, while those who were tried bashing him over the head.

None of the attacks hit.

Christian wove through the hailstorm of fists and makeshift weapons. A closed fist to his face was redirected over his left shoulder by an open palm. A strike to the back of his head was dodged entirely when he ducked, the fist barely ruffling his hair. One of them tried swinging a bat at his midsection, but Christian diverted the attack with his shoe, bringing his left foot up and kicking the weapon away. His left hand then reached out, even as his body moved to the left, and grabbed onto a steel bar that someone tried thrusting into his spine.

With a grunt, Christian yanked on the bar. A surprised cry came from behind. He spun around to face the person who tried landing a crippling blow on him. The man holding onto the steel bar was off balance and stumbling toward him—a perfect opening.

Christian didn't hesitate to attack. While he normally disliked harming the humans he should be protecting, he wouldn't hesitate to defend himself if attacked. These guys had attacked him first. That made them fair game.

His left fist shot out in a straight jab. Rather than aim for the man's face, as most rookies did, Christian hit his adversary in the throat with the knuckles of his middle and index finger. Strangled choking sounds emitted from the man as he stumbled backward, his hands moving up to his neck, as if trying to unclog the now blocked air passage.

Wanting to finish the man before he recovered, Christian stepped into his guard, grabbed him by the head with both hands, and then yanked his face down until it met Christian's knee. A loud *crunch!* preluded the spray of blood that splattered across the front of Christian's left pant leg.

The man's head snapped back as Christian let go of him. His eyes glazed over. He blinked several times. Then he fell backward, his eyes rolling up into his head, as pain and shock overloaded his senses. He hit the ground with a dull thump.

Christian was moving before the man hit the ground. Utilizing some incredibly complex footwork, he shuffled around a blow meant to rattle his brain. It was a sloppy punch, easily dodged. As the man who threw it stumbled past him, off balance from putting all of his strength into that single swing, Christian stepped in behind him. Once in position, he grabbed the man by the arms and spun him around.

He could have taken him out with a chop to the neck, but doing that would have served no purpose other than removing him from the fight, which this particular move accomplished with an added benefit.

When Christian swung the man around, it wasn't just to toss him, but to throw him in the way of someone wielding a bat, effectively using him as a shield. Already in mid-swing, the bat wielder was unable to stop his attack from cracking harshly against his friend's skull. The sound of wood cracking against bone rang through the empty street. This noise was followed by the thud of a body hitting the ground.

Gaping at his friend's motionless body, the bat wielder could do nothing as Christian moved swiftly into his guard and attacked. A jab to the stomach doubled him over, while a cross to the face sent him reeling.

Before the man could stumble too far backward, Christian leapt into the air, his body spinning like a top, his left leg extending. The sound of flesh meeting shoe was loud as he kicked his adversary in the face. The attack had enough power behind it that the man he kicked spun out of control before hitting the ground with bone-jarring force. He didn't get back up.

Three down. Three more to go.

As he landed on the ground, Christian tucked himself into a forward roll, avoiding the man coming in from his left, who'd clearly been intending to attack him while he was unprepared. He then kipped up to his feet right in front of another attacker, whose eyes widened upon seeing him pop up.

Poke.

"Oh, God! My eyes!"

Those same wide eyes were forced closed when Christian jabbed a finger into each one. The man stumbled around like a drunk, his hands covering his eyes, as if doing so would block out the pain.

Christian's left foot slid across the ground. His center of gravity lowered as he crouched down. Bringing his fists in to his torso, Christian took a deep breath, and then expelled it in a loud shout. His fists shot out at the same time, moving so quickly they blurred.

Like a gunshot going off, Christian's attack crashed into the man. One fist hit the solar plexus. The other pounded into the lower abdomen below the belly button. Both attacks connected harshly, slamming into the man like a bullet train speeding down a track.

The force behind each punch was powerful enough to knock the man clean off his feet. He soared through the air, then hit the pavement, bounced, and proceeded to ragdoll across the ground before coming to a stop. He then lay motionless, completely dead to the world.

Breathing out slowly, Christian straightened up. He turned and looked at two of the three people left, the pudgy one and the skinny guy with baggy clothes. Both took a step back, their eyes wide in fear as he eyed them with an expressionless gaze.

"It looks like you two are the only ones left." Christian wasn't normally one for banter with his enemies. There was no point in talking to people who were already dead and just didn't know it yet. But these two were not enemies, not really, just misguided humans. And Christian didn't kill humans. "I would suggest running away and never coming near me again, but know that if you do decide to fight me, then I won't hold back."

He then slid into the southpaw stance, a fighting stance he had learned in his training with the Executioners. The two men nervously looked at him, then at each other. Christian didn't speak. He didn't move, nor did he act. He simply waited and watched as the pair held a silent conversation. After several seconds of nothing but quiet, the two came to a decision.

In less time than it would have taken Christian to say succubus, the pudgy man and the skinny man were running away, speeding down the street, screaming their heads off as if an Ancestor was chasing them. With those two out of the way, Christian turned to the last person who had confronted him.

The musclebound brute stood off to the side, his arms crossed over his chest as he leaned against the wall of a building. He didn't look particularly concerned for his comrades sprawled across the ground, nor did he appear frightened by the fighting prowess that Christian had displayed.

A part of Christian felt disgust for this man, who didn't seem to care for the people under him. This man was not a leader. Leaders were supposed to protect the people who looked up to and followed them. He had done neither.

Christian shunted these thoughts to the side. They wouldn't do him any good right now. Instead he focused on the man before him.

"You didn't attack me."

"Tch, course not. I saw the way you moved before we decided to take you on. I knew you had martial arts training. Really." He shook his head. "What kind of idiot do you take me for?"

"I see." Christian frowned. His gaze swept across those he defeated. All of them were laid out, unconscious on the ground. They would all be waking up with one hell of a headache come the next morning. He then focused back on the man before him, and his frown deepened. "You used these guys to observe my fighting style before battling me yourself."

"That's right," the brute said, grinning as he pushed himself off the side of the building. He walked forward, his gait confident, cocky. "I wanted to see what you have to offer. And now that I've seen it, let me tell you, I'm not very impressed. You've got some skill, no doubt, but it's clear to me that you're not a martial artist of any kind. You just have some basic training."

Christian frowned at the true statement, but didn't answer him. "You're not a very good comrade, forcing these guys to fight me when you knew they had no chance."

"Comrade," the muscle-head scoffed. "Boy, these fools mean nothing to me. They're just a means to an end. Their only purpose was to fight you so that I could find out what kind of fighter you are." He paused before chuckling. "Well, actually, I originally wanted to use them to help me corner Lilith so that I could finally make her my woman." He frowned. "But then you showed up and I had to change my plans. Now I'm gonna have to find a new group of idiots to help me. I should kill you for that."

While the brute continued talking, Christian was gritting his teeth and balling his hands into fists so tight that his knuckles turned white. The way this brute talked about making Lilith his woman… did that mean he planned to rape her? To even think of committing such a sin was abominable, but to talk about it so easily? Even if Lilith was a succubus, no one deserved to have that happen to them. What this man suggested was unforgivable.

It was clear to Christian now. This man did not deserve the title of human. He would be shown no mercy.

No more words were spoken. Christian slid into his fighting stance. Leading with his right hand and right foot, he raised both hands, one in front of his face, and the other near his left collarbone. His knees bent as he lightly bobbed up and down, keeping on the balls of his feet. While the southpaw and orthodox stances often had boxers keep their feet flat and planted firmly on the ground to generate more force, Christian relied more on speed than strength, and thus preferred keeping his footing light.

"Hmph," his muscle-bound enemy snorted when he saw the stance. "Just as I thought. You have some training, but you're no fighter."

He uncrossed his arms and slid into his own stance. His left foot slid forward and further to the right until his feet were shoulder width apart. He bent the forward leg at a forty-five-degree angle while the rear leg remained straight. Both his hips and shoulders remained squarely facing forward, oriented toward Christian.

Christian recognized the stance. Often called the front stance, it was also referred to as forward-leaning stance and sometimes just the forward stance. It was a facet of combat used primarily in Japanese and Korean martial arts, such as karate and its many variants. Some of the Executioners who specialized in hand-to-hand combat used it when they fought. It allowed them to generate more power moving forward, but very little in any other direction.

"Now come on, you little pansy!" the hulking brute roared in challenge. "Let's see what you're made of!"

Despite the challenge being issued, Christian didn't move forward. He instead opted to narrow his eyes at his opponent, recalling everything he knew about the front stance.

That stance, while dangerous in the hands of a skilled practitioner, limited how much a person could move. A fighter could only go forward, any other direction required them to shift their body in such a way that all the power they generated was lost, and any attack made became ineffective. Either this man was incredibly arrogant in thinking that he could beat Christian with a stance like that, or this monstrosity of muscle actually knew what he was doing.

Given his earlier words about Christian not being a fist-fighter, he was inclined to believe the latter. And so he remained where he was, waiting for his enemy to make the first move.

"Tch, fine. If you won't attack me, then I'll attack you!"

The large fighter blasted off the ground, utilizing all the forward power granted to him through the front stance. He bulldozed toward Christian at speeds that shouldn't have been possible for someone so large. He was faster even than most Olympic sprinters.

Christian's eyes widened as, within less than a second, his enemy was upon him and preparing to launch a devastating attack. He saw the man's hulking muscles bunch and tense, like a coiled spring just waiting to be unleashed.

When the attack came, his eyes almost missed it—no, they did miss it. It was only thanks to his heightened reflexes and spatial awareness that he managed to dodge, ducking down and rolling along the ground.

He kipped up to his feet and turned around, hoping to use the man's reliance on the front stance to his advantage. If he could just launch a powerful jab at his opponent's spinal column, he could easily paralyze the brute and deal a finishing blow.

His plan to deal with the hulking brute swiftly and efficiently was all for naught. That plan had failed the moment the fight started. He just hadn't realized it.

By the time Christian turned around, the man's stance had shifted from front stance to back stance, a reverse variant of the forward-leaning stance, but designed to generate power by moving backward.

The brute's right foot slid along the ground, his left leg lifting up to his chest at the same time. The left foot was then launched at Christian with speed as the man extended his leg, which appeared as nothing more than a brief flicker of movement. Christian only had enough time to bring his arms up in a cross guard before the kick struck.

Like the rumbling of thunder, the heel of his enemy's boot slammed into his arms with bone-shattering force. Christian bit back a cry of pain as his guard broke. Rather than let himself be felled by another brutal attack, he moved with the blow in order to mitigate the damage as best he could. He rolled backward along the ground, landed back on his feet, and then threw himself to the side, as the clearly dangerous man tried ramming into him.

Dust kicked up as his enemy's hulking form stomped along the pavement. When he came to a stop, he did so by putting his left foot forward, bending his knee to absorb the shock of impact and force kinetic energy to build up in his leg. He then used that energy to launch himself at Christian with blistering speed that was just barely within human parameters.

It was still too fast for Christian to follow. There was no time to respond as the man lashed out with his fist in a lightning-quick jab. The attack smashed against Christian's chest, knocking the wind out of him and sending him flying backward for several meters. Even after he struck the ground, Christian's body continued moving, rolling along the pavement, each impact jarring his bones and sending jolts of agony like electric currents straight to his brain. It was only after crashing into a brick wall on the opposite end of the street that his body's momentum halted, painfully.

As he lay there on the ground, all Christian could do was gasp in asphyxiated agony. His chest felt like it had been compressed, like a large building had fallen on it. He was sure that last attack had broken a few ribs. At the very least, he would have some serious bruises tomorrow morning.

Coughing and gasping as he tried sucking oxygen into his air-depraved lungs, Christian slowly clambered to his feet. He had to get up. There was no telling what his opponent would do if he didn't. When he finally stood up, his body almost gave out, forcing him to lean against the wall for support.

Footsteps alerted him to his enemy's approach. Looking up, Christian glared at the hulking man with narrowed eyes and gritted teeth.

His short blond hair shone briefly as he stood under a lamp. The brute grinned maliciously, as if the pain Christian felt intoxicated him.

It was in complete contrast to Christian, who felt like an entire pantheon of angry gods had been whaling on him.

"Is that all you've got?" the brute asked in a mocking tone. "I didn't expect much, but I at least expected you to be better than that."

"You want more?" Christian grunted as he forced himself to stand without the wall for aid. His legs wobbled precariously, but he forced them to keep still. Taking a deep breath, he held it, and then let it out as he calmed his racing heart. "Fine. I didn't want to use this on you, but it looks like I have no choice."

"So you were holding back, were you?" The brute grunted as he raised his right hand to his shoulder and tilted his head from side to side. Loud cracking issued from his neck. He then set himself in the front stance again, that unholy-looking grin still plastered on his face. "It doesn't matter if you were holding back, there's no way you can beat me."

Christian didn't say anything. There was no longer any need to talk. He slowly walked onto the street. stopping several meters from his opponent. He didn't raise his hands, nor did he set himself in a stance. Instead, he closed his eyes and slowed his breathing.

His heart rate plummeted rapidly as he focused on stilling his body and expanding his spatial awareness. The world became still. Neither opponent moved from their spots. Christian's posture relaxed further as he sank deeper and deeper into his trance. He could feel his heart beating a slow, steady rhythm. He could hear the breeze as blew through the street, and feel the directional shifts in the wind as it brushed against his skin. He could even hear the steady yet agitated breathing of his opponent, and sense the minute atmospheric changes as the brute shifted from one foot to the other.

Stillness such as this could not last. The pause was broken when his enemy grew impatient and charged him. Like a bull seeing red, the man rushed forward, no doubt intent on ending the fight now. He was upon Christian in less than a second, his left fist already extending in a swift, earth-shattering jab.

It never hit. Moving as if he had known the attack was coming long before his opponent launched it, Christian flowed around the fist. He moved to the left, leading with his left foot and sidestepping. At the same time, his right hand shot forward, pounding against the brute's torso. His left hand followed, launching another strike against the man's back. And then the hulking fighter was running past him, stopping only a few feet away.

Christian hissed in pain, bringing his hands up to his face and looking at them. Even in the dim light provided by the streetlamps, he could see how swollen his hands were, red and throbbing, his knuckles battered and bruised. It wasn't a pleasant sight. By the Almighty! Just what was that brute made of? Stone?

The brute turned around and chuckled at him.

"Heh-heh, did you honestly think such a weak attack would hurt me? My body is far tougher than most. A pathetic pinprick of an attack like that won't do a thing to me."

Christian clenched his teeth and narrowed his eyes. If an attack like that didn't do anything, then he needed to take more extreme measures to beat this man. Christian's hope had been to inflict enough damage on the brute that he passed out, but it didn't look like that would be possible.

He needed to do something else. Something extreme. It wasn't something that he was going to enjoy, but it seemed like he might actually have to kill this man.

God, please forgive me for what I'm about to do.

Calming himself again, he watched as the brute charged him, stepping into his guard within seconds. He left his right flank deliberately open, and the brute took the bait just as he had expected.

Like water flowing around the rock impeding its path, Christian swerved around the speeding fist. He sidestepped to the right, his hair ruffling from the breeze that the fist generated. He then grabbed the extended limb, and used the strength of his arms and torso to lift himself over the fist.

He flew into the air, twisting and flipping until he stood on his enemy's outstretched arm. When his feet touched the extended limb, his right hand flew into his shoe and pulled out the butterfly knife. Quicker than greased lightning, the blade extended, and Christian plunged it into his enemy's throat.

The brute's eyes widened as the knife pierced his larynx. Blood gushed from the wound, spilling down his neck and staining his shirt.

Christian hiked himself off his enemy's limb and, like a professional acrobat, flipped over the brute. He landed on the ground some distance away. When he stood back to his full height, he turned his head to watch his enemy.

The brute brought his hands up to his throat, as if trying to plug the wound spilling carnelian liquid down the front of his shirt. It wouldn't do him any good. Christian had pierced his left subclavian artery. There was no way to stop a wound like that. He would bleed out within a few seconds.

True to Christian's prediction, the man soon fell to his knees. For a moment, he struggled to get back up, but after several seconds passed, his arms dropped limply to his sides and he fell flat on his face. His body lay still after that.

Christian sighed. Closing his eyes and turning away from the sight, he said a quick prayer to God, begging forgiveness for the sin of killing another human. It was all he could do now.

When he finished praying, he slowly walked away from his makeshift battleground. He would call Headquarters when he arrived at the hotel, and have them send someone to pick up the body before anyone noticed.

"He… he… he…"

He stopped.

"He-he-he…"

His eyes widened. Impossible!

"Ha-ha-ha!"

The corpse was laughing!

"Hahahaha!"

Christian turned his head in shock and horror as something that shouldn't have been possible happened right before his eyes. The corpse moved. The muscles in its back twitched, its left hand raised and planted itself firmly on the ground, the right hand following suit. Slowly, the body pushed itself onto its knees, and then its feet. It soon stood to its full height, its back facing Christian.

And then it turned around.

"Ha… you're good." The brute's grin reminded him of a deranged serial killer. "I didn't expect you to bring a weapon to a fistfight. It looks like I underestimated you." His eyes narrowed. "Don't think that'll happen again. From this point on, I'm going to be taking you seriously."

Taking him seriously? Did that mean he hadn't been taking Christian seriously before? Well, obviously, if the man was still alive after having his artery stabbed, then he must have some tricks up his sleeve.

While he was thinking this, Christian noticed that the wound he had inflicted, the one that should have killed the brute, was gone. Vanished. As if the wound had never been inflicted in the first place.

Christian narrowed his eyes. "You're not human."

"Got it in one," the brute applauded mockingly. "I'm surprised you came to that conclusion so quickly. But then, I guess there are some humans who know about our existence. It would make sense. I hope you don't think this knowledge will give you a leg up on me or anything. Like I said, I'm getting serious now."

The man soon proved how true his statement was when his body suddenly changed. Doubling over like his body was experiencing incredible agony, the man's muscles rippled and expanded as blood started pumping through them at an increased rate. His clothing ripped—first his shirt, then the bottom legs of his pants. The front of his boots also tore open, revealing clawed, hairy feet.

More changes took place. His face grew longer, the nose and mouth expanding outwards to form a muzzle. His eyes sank into his head, and his brow ridge thickened, becoming more prominent. His teeth, once human-looking and ordinary, suddenly became razor sharp and looked like they could easily rend flesh, muscle and bone.

The last change that took place was his body sprouting massive quantities of fur. Starting from his head and working its way down, thick brown, almost black, fur grew out of his pores, covering almost every part of his body, the exceptions being his chest, stomach, triceps, and the palms and soles of his hands and feet.

"A werewolf," Christian whispered, already cursing his luck. Intelligence had really dropped the ball on this. Not only had they possibly mistaken Lilith for a succubus, they either didn't know of, or had neglected to mention, a werewolf. Whoever was in charge of gathering information in this city was obviously an idiot.

At least now he knew how that man had brought those other six guys together. Werewolves always traveled in packs, and lone werewolves had the ability to make pacts with humans through their innate charisma.

"Hahahahaha-ha! That's right, boy!" The werewolf cackled and growled, his voice far deeper than before. It sounded more animal than human. **"I'm a werewolf! And now I'm gonna tear you apart!"**

Chapter 11

There were many different creatures inhabiting the world that presented a grave threat to humanity: Vampires, werewolves, demons, succubi, incubi, mermaids, and sirens were only some of the more prevalent monsters lurking in the shadows cast by humans.

Of those many species, a few stood near the top of the food chain. Vampires were one of them. Werewolves were another.

There were many legends concerning the origins of werewolves, but no theories had ever been confirmed. What the Executioners did know was that werewolves had several powerful abilities that allowed even the weakest of them to stand a cut above most monsters.

Foremost among those abilities was their insane speed. If vampires were the pinnacle of physical strength, with boulder-shattering capabilities, then werewolves were the embodiment of speed. They could travel faster than the top speed of most sports cars, and rumor had it that the fastest werewolf in recorded history could outpace a drag racer.

And it was a werewolf that Christian found himself running from. Fighting a werewolf wouldn't normally be a problem for him. Despite their capacity for traveling at an incredible velocity, a werewolf's movement was notoriously predictable. They could only move linearly, meaning the laws of physics and motion worked heavily against them. Only werewolves that had mastered their speed became truly dangerous.

Christian didn't believe this werewolf was particularly dangerous. Wily perhaps, but not dangerous. That hardly mattered given his current situation. Injured and unarmed as he was, he might as well be just another human. He had no special attributes, and he didn't take enhancement drugs to increase his physical abilities.

What made Christian so deadly on the battlefield wasn't any special power or enhancement, but his unique fighting style. However, without his swords and his guns, that fighting style meant nothing. He might as well attack his enemy with a stick for all the good it would do him.

He'd managed to escape from the werewolf with a well-placed flashbang to the face. Werewolves had incredible senses, not just an extreme sense of smell but also perception. The flashbang would keep it blinded for a good while. Hopefully, that action would buy Christian enough time to grab his weapons and lead the beast to a battlefield of his choosing, one where he would hold all the advantages.

Thankfully, his hotel wasn't far from where he'd been attacked. Despite how his muscles ached and his chest felt like it was being stabbed with a hot, rusty knife every time he took a breath, Christian still made it there in record time.

Rushing into the hotel, ignoring the person behind the front desk who tried to greet him, Christian disregarded the elevator and ran up the stairs. He arrived at his room and almost ran into the door in his haste. He slid his card through the slot. When the door gave a soft click and the light turned green, he opened it and ran inside.

His weapons were exactly where he left them; hidden in a case attached to the underside of the bed. He swiftly pulled out the case, which was almost half the length of the bed, and set it on the floor. It had a combination lock that his hands fumbled with in his haste. Opening it took far too long for his liking. When he finally did manage to open the stubborn lock, he undid the latch and lifted the top.

His carrying case wasn't the standard issue that most Executioners were given. Expensive velvet lined the inside. Imprints shaped like a pair of swords and guns showed where his weapons were to be placed. They sat there, gleaming in the minuscule moonlight entering through the window, reflecting silver and black. Strapped across the inside of the top were his sheaths and holsters, which he grabbed first.

Acting with haste, he placed his swords in their sheaths, and then put the sheaths over his head and around his shoulders before tightening the straps. They were uncomfortable and aggravated his injuries, but there wasn't much he could do about that. After strapping his swords to his back, he grabbed his holsters and strapped them to his thighs. He then grabbed Gabriel and Phanuel, shoving them into their holsters.

As his final preparation, he slid the last of his flashbangs into a small pouch on his waist. He only had one left, so he would need to be careful when using it. It wouldn't be good if he used it hastily, and ended up wasting it when a better opportunity to use it presented itself.

The sound of footsteps coming down the hall made him tense. Closing his eyes, he blocked out all of his senses except for hearing. It was a unique talent those who underwent Executioner training gained, and one of the talents that he had cultivated to perfection from many years of practice.

His ears twitched as noises that he wouldn't normally hear filled his senses. His own breathing was almost invisible to all of his sensory perceptions as he stilled it. Outside he could hear the rustling of leaves from the tree next to his window, the chirping of crickets, and the barking of a dog from across the street. Inside the building his ears picked up the sound of breathing from the room on his immediate left, and also the light, almost nonexistent sound of footsteps in the hallway.

Frowning, he placed his hands on the ground, canceled his focus on his ears and focused instead on his sense of touch. By focusing hard enough, he could feel the vibrations produced by the footsteps. Judging from the force of impact and the timing it took for each step, the person getting invariably closer to his room was very large. They were also stooped over, as if their frame didn't fit in the hallway.

That confirmed it, then. The werewolf had found him. He really shouldn't have been surprised. A werewolf's sense of smell was amazing, nearly twenty times better than trained police dogs. It was no great shock that it would eventually sniff him out, but he had been hoping for a bit more time.

Too bad his time was up. All he could do now was act.

Christian didn't have any talent in stealth. He wasn't an Assassin, but he was still light on his feet. He slipped over to the window quickly and without making too much noise.

The footsteps had already stopped. He could tell that the werewolf was right next to his door. As if to prove his point, the handle rattled as the person on the other side tried opening it. They didn't have a card key, so it would take a while, and the beast was clearly trying to keep its existence a secret from the other residents of the city. It wouldn't do something to jeopardize that. That was the only advantage Christian had.

He opened the window and hopped onto the ledge. Not even taking a moment to judge the distance between him and the tree, he leapt.

His hand caught a tree branch, latching onto it with a tight grip as it swayed and bounced. Christian winced as his rib cage rattled painfully; he could feel several ribs that had gotten loose scraping against his lungs. He ignored the pain and swung himself across the branch and over to the trunk. Once he reached the trunk, he wrapped his arms and legs around it and, using cracks in the bark as handholds, climbed down.

A loud crash alerted him to the fact that the werewolf had just lost its patience and busted his door in. That was not good. He needed to hurry.

Seconds later, he dropped to the ground and took off running. He didn't turn back to look at the window. He didn't need to. Not even a second after he hit the streets, a loud thudding sound let him know that the werewolf was on the ground.

And thus the chase was on. Christian ran through the silent and empty streets, avoiding the places that he knew were busier during this time of night, cutting through alleys and side streets to avoid being spotted by civilians. He also turned as many sharp corners as possible so the werewolf couldn't take advantage of its speed.

"You can't run from me forever, boy!"

"Tch!"

Christian could hear the werewolf catching up to him. He needed to force it back, needed to put some distance between them. Should he use his guns? No. That might work, but it would also draw attention. Even if these streets looked silent, he knew there were people sleeping in some of these buildings. The last thing he wanted was to have innocent civilians getting caught up in this and killed because he was being reckless.

While running through an alley, he caught sight of a trashcan sitting against the wall, a lid leaning against it. His body ached as he pushed his legs harder than he should. He reached the trashcan and leaned down, grabbing the lid. He then spun around 180 degrees and tossed the impromptu projectile at the werewolf like a Frisbee. Then he finished his spin and hit the ground running.

It didn't do much. The werewolf simply swiped it with his claws, not only knocking it aside, but also slashing it apart like grated cheese. The loud sound of metal being ripped to shreds caused Christian to wince. He hoped that whoever lived around here would simply think the noise came from a cat smacking into a trashcan or something. Still, the lid had served its purpose and distracted the werewolf from the real attack.

"Gah!"

The alley lit up with the brilliance of a sun. Christian grimaced at being forced to use his last flashbang so soon but didn't lament its loss for too long. He needed to focus on running, not crying over the loss of his last flashbang.

With his foe busy trying to rub what had to be some nasty spots from its eyes, Christian was able to make some excellent headway. He reached a small park several miles out from the more populated parts of the city. There wouldn't be anyone there at this time of night. It was the perfect place to battle a monster of this caliber.

The park wasn't very big, maybe several hundred square feet altogether. A sandlot with a playset sat to his left, and an even larger grassy area with a sparse population of trees lay on his right. He had actually scouted this place out when trying to find a spot that he could take Lilith to and kill her should she turn out to be a succubus.

He reached the grassy area of the park and slowed his run to a jog, then a trot, and then a walk. By the time he stopped moving, he was standing in front of the sandlot.

He gazed at the playground, even as the thumping of feet reached his ears. They stopped a second later. His foe had arrived.

"So you finally decided to stop running?" a deep voice growled behind him. **"About time. And I see you've even chosen the place that will become your grave."**

Christian turned around to face the werewolf. His eyes locked onto the monster's bright, glow-in-the-dark yellow orbs. They were the eyes of a rabid animal, a beast that needed to be put down, and he had every intention of wiping this abomination from the face of existence.

"What's the matter? Got nothing to say?"

Christian didn't respond. Words were no longer needed. This thing was already dead and just hadn't realized that yet. "Phew, fine. If that's how you want it, you can just keep that mouth of yours shut. You'll be screaming in a few seconds anyway."

A pause followed, a lull that extended to one second, then two, and then three. Like an old-fashioned showdown Christian and the werewolf glared at each other.

A soft breeze whistled through the park, carrying several leaves that crossed the space between them. And still the two stared.

And then, on some unspoken signal, the werewolf charged him. Its clawed feet thudded against the ground, spitting chunks of earth and grass in all directions. In response, Christian drew his handguns and laid down a barrage of gunfire with unnerving accuracy. The bullets didn't do much to slow down the creature; the werewolf just raised its arms, protecting its face and, more specifically, its eyes. The tiny balls of steel penetrated its flesh, but even then, the bullets were pushed out seconds later and the wounds healed.

Christian cursed. Without silver bullets, his guns wouldn't do any real damage. He might as well be shooting at the thing with a BB gun.

Gritting his teeth, Christian holstered his guns and unsheathed his swords. They weren't made of silver, but Orichalcum could kill a werewolf just as easily.

The werewolf came in fast and hard. Christian ducked under a claw swipe and counterattacked, trying to take its hand off with Raphael while simultaneously impaling it through the stomach with Michael. Neither sword found its mark. The werewolf retracted its hand too quickly for Raphael to take it off, and then swerved left, avoiding the twenty-four inches of Orichalcum attempting to penetrate its gut.

Christian backpedaled after his attack failed. He sidestepped, barely avoiding the claws that tried impaling his chest. He then spun in a circle, both of his blades singing in his hands as they sliced through the air. The attack forced the werewolf back to avoid being bisected. Even then, one of Christian's swords managed to draw a thin line of blood from its chest. The wound didn't heal.

The werewolf's glare narrowed at Christian, whose body had already grown heavy. His wounds from before were finally catching up to him, so he was grateful for the pause.

He knew what had the werewolf so wary about attacking him after their initial exchange. No doubt it had seen the many holes in his guard, and was now wondering why it couldn't exploit them.

He called it the fake opening style. It was a method of fighting that he had created after years of blood, sweat, and many broken bones. The style relied on deliberately presenting his enemies with openings in order to predict where they would attack next. It was based on the theory that, so long as he knew where the attack was going to land, he could respond to it well in advance, counterattacking with blistering speed and leaving his enemy unable to fight back. It essentially allowed him to control the flow of any battle by deliberately exposing himself to danger.

Christian didn't attack when the werewolf began circling him. His style did not rely on attacking first. And so he stood there, legs bent, swords held loosely at his sides, eyes carefully studying the werewolf's movements.

The werewolf seemed to grow tired of watching him and charged in to attack. It came at Christian with a claw swipe to the opening he presented on his torso. He twisted his body, barely avoiding the attack that would have sliced a deep furrow in his flesh. At the same time, the sword in his left hand swiped out in a flash, nearly taking the clawed hand off had the werewolf not hastily jerked its appendage back.

Continuing with the motion offered by the momentum of his swing, Christian rotated. Michael made a diagonal slice starting from the ground and traveling up, forcing the werewolf back just as it came in to attack the opening on his left flank. Blood spurted out of a new wound, as the sword's incredibly sharp blade sliced through the bridge of its nose.

"**You...**" the werewolf snarled as it wiped at the blood running down its face. The wound was not healing, much like the one on its chest. "**You are a member of the Executioners, aren't you?**"

Christian said nothing. He merely stood there, waiting for the werewolf to attack again. The beast had learned its lesson, however, as it appeared extremely wary of attacking him now that he had injured it twice. That would not do at all.

Deciding to finally go on the offensive, Christian used one of the dirtier tricks in his arsenal: kicking up a clod of dirt into his opponent's eyes. It wasn't the most elegant of attacks, but at this point, all he cared about was killing this creature before it could harm another innocent person.

"**Graaa! My eyes! My eyes! Damn you!**"

With its eyes closed, the aberration began flailing its arms about erratically, hitting nothing but air. Christian carefully avoided the clawed hands and tried to find an opening that he could exploit, ducking and dodging and weaving through the whirlwind of swipes and swings. He moved with a dancer's grace, all the while studying his enemy's movements, searching for an opening that would allow him to end this fight.

Finally, he found it, a small gap in his opponent's defense. Christian took it. He ducked under a swing from his enemy's left hand, twisted his body to avoid being impaled by the right hand, and then moved in. A single step took him into the werewolf's guard, too close for the thing's claws to attack him.

Feeling a surge of victory, Christian made to thrust Michael and Raphael into the werewolf's chest—only to gasp as sharp agony flared in his stomach.

Christian looked down, baffled when he saw the werewolf's tail, which had curved around its body, sticking in his stomach. The tail's hair follicles shredded his shirt, sharp and hard like a thousand needles. They penetrated his skin, their tips stained red with his blood.

He would have cursed if his mouth was working. How could he have forgotten about a werewolf's ability to harden its fur on any part of its body?

The werewolf yanked the tail out of Christian's flesh. The swift movement knocked him off balance and sent him spiraling to the ground. Michael and Raphael flew out of his grip. His left shoulder smacked against the grassy field, the impact jarring him.

He rolled onto his back and coughed as something coppery filled his mouth. *Blood.* That meant he had internal injuries. More blood leaked from the several dozen holes in his stomach. It ran down his sides and stained his shirt.

He tried to get up, but before he could do so much as move, the werewolf lunged at him, its snarling visage trying to tear into his flesh. Only quick thinking and reflexes saved Christian. He lifted his legs, pressing his feet against the werewolf's chest, keeping it from biting his head off. Yet despite the advantage of added leverage from lying on the ground, Christian knew this was a losing battle. His strength was ebbing.

"You're finished, Executioner," the werewolf howled its victory. **"I'm gonna kill you! It's only a matter of time now. And once I'm done with you, I'm gonna make Lilith my woman! I'm gonna break her, Executioner! I'll break her and there's nothing you can do about it!"**

Christian snarled. How dare this filthy, disgusting, flea-bitten mongrel dare to even think of putting its filthy hands on someone like Lilith! Bad enough that she feared men! She didn't need this *thing* coming after her, too!

With strength that he didn't know he possessed, he shoved at the werewolf with his feet. It stumbled backward, allowing him enough room to maneuver his hands. Before the creature had time to recover, he pulled out his guns and unloaded a barrage into the inhuman beast at point-blank range.

Holes appeared in the werewolf's chest. Blood erupted from the wounds like miniature geysers, splashing against Christian's face and body. Yet even as the wounds appeared, they began to heal. The bullets were pushed out, the wounds hissed, and then they were gone, as if they had never been there to begin with.

Click. Click.

Christian grimaced as his guns clicked empty. He had run out of ammo.

"Heh, looks like you're out of bullets." The malevolent grin spreading across the creature's face was filled with a lust for blood. His blood. **"It's been fun, boy, but I've got better things to do then play around with you. Like making Lilith my woman."**

Gritting his teeth hard enough to make his gums bleed, Christian looked around for something, *anything*, that he could use to get him out of this situation. He couldn't let this be the end, and he couldn't let this... this disgusting thing hurt Lilith.

As if God was answering his prayer, Christian saw his sword, Michael, lying just a few feet away. Thinking fast he kicked the werewolf in the face, eliciting a loud snarl of rage. He then scrambled out from underneath the monster and wrapped his fingers around the sword's hilt.

The feel of cool metal against his palm filled him with confidence. He'd faced worse creatures than this. The aberration before him wasn't even the strongest werewolf that had died by his hands. He would not be defeated here!

"Oh no you don't," the werewolf growled at him, its snarling face showing a rictus of sharp teeth. **"You're finished!"**

It lunged at Christian as he lifted Michael from the ground. Turning, he used both hands to thrust the sword forward.

"Urk!"

He watched in satisfaction as the weapon penetrated his enemy's chest, slicing through hardened flesh like it was warm butter. Blood ran down his blade. It gleamed bright crimson in the moonlight, contrasting with Michael's silvery sheen.

Silence blanketed the park, broken only by Christian's heavy breathing and the pained rasps of the monster looming over him. The werewolf's disbelieving yellow eyes stared into his. It then looked down at the sword penetrating its chest right where its heart was. Copious amounts of blood leaked from the wound, running down its torso like a river. Through the handle, Christian felt the monster's still beating heart grow fainter with each passing second.

This beast was finished.

"Heh," it laughed. **"To think I would be done in by an Executioner..."** It coughed, carnelian liquid dribbling down its mouth and chin. **"How... disgraceful..."** With those parting words the monster died...

... And fell on top of Christian.

"Gurk!" He grunted as the monster's now-dead weight bore down on him, aggravating his injuries even more, sending lances of agony tearing across his chest. It felt like his ribcage was being crushed. To make matters worse, the hilt of his sword was jabbing painfully into his stomach, making him increasingly uncomfortable.

He struggled to push the beast's corpse off. It took far more effort than it should have, but he eventually rolled the bleeding corpse onto the grass by his side. He then gulped in deep several breaths of air, even though each breath felt like a hot poker stabbing his lungs.

Lying on his back, Christian felt too tired and sore to move. Everything hurt; his chest felt like it had been compressed in a trash compactor, and his leaden limbs shook with exhaustion. His head was pounding and his ears were ringing. It had been a long time since he'd felt this awful. He'd not felt this much pain since earning his title of *Christian the Quadra.*

He wondered what Lilith would think if she knew that he had the same title as her favorite light novel character. She would probably get a kick out of it.

Knowing that his body had reached its limit, Christian decided to just get some rest right there. An hour or two of rest wouldn't hurt anything. After he rested, he would burn the werewolf's corpse.

There wasn't much he could do about the blood splatters. Those would have to stay. He just hoped the Church would be able to deal with the media. He didn't doubt that they *would* find out that *something* happened here, and Christian had no desire to deal with the aftermath of an unaccountable werewolf attack happening in a city where no werewolf should have been in the first place.

Chapter 12

"Are you certain this is accurate?"Samantha's narrowed eyes gazed at the man standing before her. She waved a sheet of paper in her hand. Her voice was tinged with a sense of urgency and unease.

"Yes, everything is one hundred percent true. I triple-checked this information myself," Tristin told her. "There has been an increase in disappearances across the US for the past two months, and California was hit with two dozen disappearances just two days ago. Most of them are girls in their late teens to early twenties. If you look closely enough, you'll see that all the disappearances are creating a trail of sorts."

"A trail leading directly to Seal Beach," Samantha finished, her lips pursed. "Has Intelligence been able to figure out what's causing these disappearances?"

Tristin shook his head. "No, but we have been able to determine that none of them are from mundane causes, nor are they runaway cases."

"So what you're basically telling me is that something supernatural is killing people, and we don't have the slightest clue as to what." Samantha tried not to let her frustration show, but it was hard. So much about this situation was worrying. What kind of monster was killing these people? And why did it appear to be heading toward Seal Beach?

"Have you informed Christian about this?" Samantha placed her forearms against the desk and leaned forward to fix Tristin with a look. "If there is something dangerous heading his way, then it is imperative that we let him know as soon as possible, regardless of whether we know what it is or not."

"I haven't had a chance to inform him yet," Tristin admitted. "I was going to tell him immediately after informing you of my findings."

"I see." Samantha watched in minor satisfaction as her glare made Tristin shudder. He should have known how important it was to let Christian know of this danger first. If her subordinate was hurt because of him, then she would make sure to let her displeasure fully known. "I suggest you call him as soon as possible then."

"R-right." Tristin breathed sigh of relief as the intensity in Samantha's eyes lessened. "I'll do that once I'm—"

His cell phone chose that moment to ring. He looked down at the phone attached to his belt, which was playing "Thunderstruck" by AC/DC. He then looked at Samantha, who had raised a single, delicate eyebrow, as if asking, "*Why the hell is your cell phone ringing?*"

"*I was caught, in the middle of a railroad track!*" the ring tone proclaimed.

"It's Christian," he told her.

"*I looked around, and I knew there was no turning back!*"

The eyebrow rose some more. "How can you tell?"

"*My mind raced, and I thought, what could I do!*"

"He's the only one who I gave that ringtone to."

"*And I knew, there was no help, no help from you!*"

"Uh-huh," Samantha said before falling silent.

"*Sound of the drums! Beating in my heart! The thunder of guns, tore me apart!*"

After several seconds in which nothing happened and no one moved, the woman frowned and spoke again. "Well? Aren't you going to answer it?"

"*You've been thunderstruck!*"

"I… didn't think I was allowed to answer it while in a debriefing." Tristin scratched the back of his neck and grinned sheepishly when Samantha rolled her eyes.

"I give you permission to answer that call."

"Right." Tristin reached for his phone and pulled it out of its holder. He pressed a button on the touchscreen and then held it to his ear. "This is your friendly neighborhood Intel Agent. If there is any way that I can be of assistance, please do not hesitate to let me know. I shall do all in my power to provide you with the most accurate intel available."

Samantha's right eyebrow twitched. She gave no other indication of her annoyance, and instead simply watched as Tristin's eyes lit up in a way that thoroughly disturbed her.

"What do you mean you were attacked by a werewolf?" asked a startled Tristin. Samantha's eyes widened. Christian had been attacked by a werewolf? At Seal Beach? But there hadn't been any reports of a werewolf living there! What was going on?

She almost leaned forward to see if she could pick up any more of the conversation. Almost. It would have been undignified of her to try and listen in on a conversation like some kind of gossip, but it was a near thing.

"Hey, hey, hey, don't take your anger out on me," Tristin protested. "I had no clue there was a werewolf there. None of the reports I had on hand mentioned anything about a werewolf."

There was a pause while Tristin listened to the other end.

"Okay, just calm down. Now, explain to me what happened, slowly this time." Tristin's grim expression grew more pronounced the longer he listened. Samantha clicked her teeth. "So he was after your target? That's not unusual. Human women are often raped by werewolves, though I've never heard of one wanting a succubus before... well, yes, if the girl actually turns out to be a succubus... no, I haven't had a chance to look into it. Hey now, don't get snappy with me. I've been busy."

As Christian spoke again, Samantha tried piecing together what they were talking about from Tristin's words. She wasn't successful. The only thing she knew was that it had something to do with Christian's target.

Once Tristin is finished speaking, I believe he and I are going to have a long conversation about keeping information hidden from his superior.

"I've been busy dealing with a possible problem that's heading your way is what," Tristin said into the phone. "Listen, there's been a string of disappearances lately. Yes, yes, I know that's not unusual in and of itself and—would you let me finish! —right, so anyway, these disappearances form a trail leading to Seal Beach. Whatever is causing these people to vanish is coming your way."

Tristin stopped talking for a moment, and then shook his head, causing his blond hair to sway.

"Yeah, we can send more munitions and equipment. With everything that's going down right now, you're going to want to be loaded with as much firepower as we can give you... right. I'll see to it that you get some supplies. They should come some time tomorrow morning. Okay. Yeah, you too."

With a sigh, Tristin ended the call and put the phone back in his holder. Samantha raised an eyebrow.

"Well?"

Tristin scratched the back of his neck.

"So, as you probably just heard, Christian was attacked by a werewolf. He killed the thing, no surprises there, but got pretty banged up in the process. He's asking for some extra supplies: ammo, flashbangs, smoke grenades, and the like. Oh! And he wants some knives that he can hide on his person in public.”

“Very well,” Samantha said without giving it much thought. It was a reasonable request, given what had happened. “See to it that he gets everything he asked for, and also make sure to include some of our medical supplies in there; the Science Division just came up with a new healing cream that’s far more advanced than anything else we have. It should work wonders on his injuries. I’ll also send one of our doctors there to help apply it.”

“Got it, anything else you want me to do?”

“Not at the moment.” Samantha shook her head, but then remembered something. “What was that thing you and he were talking about? You mentioned how you were looking into something for him.”

Tristin rubbed his jaw thoughtfully.

“That? Christian doesn’t believe that Lilith girl is a succubus. She’s apparently got a serious case of androphobia. Can’t stand being in the same room as a guy, and runs away in fright whenever she bumps into one.”

Samantha felt pensive. An unsettling feeling wormed into her gut.

“That doesn’t sound right. Succubi are creatures of lust and sex. They live to feed off men through primal acts of passion. Just like a vampire can’t live without blood, a succubus can’t live without sex. For a creature like that to be afraid of men… it’s unheard of.”

“Those were his thoughts, too.”

Samantha closed her eyes, contemplating this new piece of information. There was a lot wrong with this mission, and it seemed there was even more wrong than she initially suspected. The Catholic Church requesting Christian be sent on this mission. Bishop Virtrous’ words. A succubus who might not be a succubus. And a threat possibly heading to Seal Beach. Were these all connected somehow?

“Tristin.”

“Ma’am?”

“It seems there are several large gaps in our intelligence that cannot be allowed to go uncorrected.” Something was going on here. Samantha didn’t know what, but the entire situation was starting to smell rotten.

“Commander?”

“I want you to work more closely with Christian and ensure that nothing happens to him on his mission,” Samantha continued. “See to it that he is constantly given the most up-to-date information regularly. I also want you to pull up everything you can on Lilith Vie. If that girl really is a human, then we need to know.”

Samantha grimaced when Tristin's eyes lit up at the prospect of working more closely with Christian. It disturbed her, those sparkling eyes that gleamed with childish joy.

If only I knew someone who was willing to help Christian with the same zeal as this man, but without the disturbing fascination.

There was something seriously wrong with Tristin—and she didn't just mean his larger than average libido. His unhealthy interest in her favorite subordinate bothered her.

"Your will be done!" Tristin said with so much fervor that Samantha almost rescinded her order. The blond pretty boy placed a hand over his heart and bowed before her. He then straightened up, spun on his heel, and walked out of the door, whistling a jaunty tune. Samantha watched the door close, feeling even more pensive than she had at the start of the debriefing.

"I'm pretty sure that I just made Christian's life a thousand times more difficult," she said before going back to her paperwork.

Chapter 13

The walk home was long and arduous. Christian's hotel was less than fifteen miles from the park, yet it took him nearly two hours to arrive there.

His body ached in ways that it rarely had before. All of his muscles felt like they had been put through a meat grinder. His bones felt brittle, as if even the most minute of movements would cause them to snap. Just walking was a chore.

When he finally arrived at his hotel, he avoided going through the front door. His clothes were torn and covered in blood. Entering through the lobby would be a terrible idea. He could just imagine the front desk clerk freaking out and calling the cops. Christian didn't want to deal with whatever problems would arise from that happening.

A fire escape on the west side of the building provided him with the means of entering his room. If he thought walking hurt, then climbing up the ladder felt like someone trying to tear his arms off with iron prongs that had been dipped in molten lava. Even after making it onto the roof, he still had a hell of a time getting into his room. It took far more effort than it should have to climb down the other side of the building and lower himself through the window.

Grunting, Christian slipped just as he slid through the window. He hit the floor with a loud crash, groaning as his face scraped against the carpet. That was definitely going to leave a rash come tomorrow morning.

"Hey! Keep it down up there! Some of us are trying to sleep!"

Christian ignored the shouting. It wasn't important, though he did take some consolation from the yell. It meant that, if nothing else, the werewolf had been smart enough to avoid the other people staying at this hotel. It had probably snuck in through a window in the hallway to avoid being seen. Most of the other residents likely assumed the loud crashing was one of the guests getting angry and smashing a fist against a door.

A glance at the door confirmed this. It was still intact, if a little dented. He was honestly surprised the door was still closed.

Even monsters like werewolves were smart enough to realize that letting regular humans know of their existence was a bad idea. With humanity being the most prevalent species on the planet, they had an advantage over any supernatural force, be they vampire, werewolf, succubus, or mermaid—in numbers if nothing else.

And that wasn't even going into the new weapons that were constantly being developed. Few, if any, supernatural creatures could survive having a nuclear bomb dropped on them, barring maybe an Ancestor or one of the Seven Demon Lords.

Placing his hands on either side of his body, Christian tried to push himself to his feet. His teeth gritted and his muscles strained. His limbs shook with exhaustion and pained spasms, yet he continued pushing. If he could just stand up, then he could crawl into bed and get some sleep.

A second later, he yelped, his arms giving out and his face slamming into the floor for the second time that night. There was some more yelling from the person below him, but he ignored it. It seemed he had pushed his body too hard. His muscles were no longer responding to his commands.

He chided himself for getting so complacent; if he had just kept some of his weapons on his person at all times, this wouldn't have happened. The next time he went out, he was bringing at least one of his main weapons. That werewolf wouldn't have stood a chance if he'd had even just one of his swords. The battle would have been over the moment it began.

He wouldn't be able to carry a sword, though, as that would be too conspicuous. But, if Tristin came through and procured some silver knives as he had asked, then he would at least have a means of defending himself from supernatural attacks.

He closed his eyes and breathed deeply. There was no use cursing himself over what had happened. He couldn't change the past. All he could do was take the lesson this experience taught him to heart, and not make the same mistake again.

Christian's breathing evened out, and he soon enough fell asleep on the floor of his hotel room.

***

Christian awoke from his dream of flames and burning bodies to the sound of knocking. He was so startled by the abrupt wake-up call that his body jumped from asleep to awake in seconds. In the process of doing this, he sat up far too quickly for his body's taste, and it had no trouble letting him know that.

A hiss of pain escaped his mouth, air whistling through gritted teeth. While his body didn't feel the sharp, overwhelming pain like yesterday, it still hurt. A dull ache had spread throughout his body, permeating his cells, and letting him know just how hard he had pushed himself the previous night.

The knocking persisted, and Christian thought about ignoring it and trying to get some more sleep. According to the view outside his window, it wasn't even morning yet. The sun had yet to rise, and the stars and moon were still out. Yet as the knocking continued, growing more insistent by the second, he knew that sleep would not be returning.

"Hang on," he called out, his throat dry and hoarse, as if he hadn't used it in months. Was this strange dryness of mouth what some of the Executioners referred to as cottonmouth? What an unpleasant sensation. "I'm coming!"

His body groaning in complaint, Christian gingerly rose to his feet and stumbled to the door. He carefully peered through the small peephole to see who was knocking, only to be met with a pair of green eyes.

"Christian, you had better open this door right this minute!"

Fear overriding pain, Christian swung the door open hastily. Standing on the other side was a woman who appeared to be in the prime of her life. She had long, straight blond hair and green eyes. A black knee-length skirt covered her legs, and a long white overcoat was worn over her white t-shirt. On her feet were a pair of tan heels that added an extra inch to her height.

"D-Dr. Adams," Christian stuttered. His heartbeat accelerated as adrenaline began pumping through his body. He should have realized that

Samantha would send a doctor to see how he was doing, but why-oh-why did his commander have to send *her* of all people?

Anastasia Adams was a member of the Executioner's Medical Division. She helped members of the Warrior caste heal after they were injured. She was also Christian's personal physician, having taken it upon herself to heal whatever injuries he suffered after every mission, ever since his battle with Abaddon the Destroyer. At the moment, Dr. Adams was wearing her patented "*I am so amazed by your stupidity that it is only this smile that is holding me back from coming over there and beating the aforementioned stupidity out of you*" smile.

Dr. Adams had some very emotive smiles.

"Hello, Christian," she said. His shuddering increased.

"W-what are you doing here?" He gulped as Dr. Adams took a step forward. He took a step back, followed by another, and then another, as the woman continued striding into his hotel room. He absently noticed the large traveling case trailing behind her. Several more briefcases were being brought in by another person, someone in the uniform of the Science Division.

Dr. Adams took a single glance around the room, and then dismissed her surroundings to penetrate Christian's soul with a glare so intense that he felt like he was back in the orphanage, being scolded by the nuns because he had let Tristin convince him to raid the pantry.

He still hadn't forgiven Tristin for that.

"Why, I am here because I was told you allowed yourself to get mauled by a werewolf," she replied. Christian opened his mouth, but no words came out, just a terrified choking noise. The look Dr. Adams gave him was absolutely petrifying. "I can see that *mauled* was a bit of an understatement; you look like you were eaten by Satan and shit back out."

Not only were Dr. Adam's smiles emotive, but she had a foul mouth to boot.

"Uh… are you… mad at me?"

"Of course not. Why would I be mad at you?" she asked, her smile growing so wide that her eyes were literally forced shut. Was it just him, or had the room's temperature taken a sudden nosedive? "Because you allowed yourself to be injured by a mere werewolf? Or perhaps it's because you decided it would be a good idea to walk around without a weapon while on a mission? Mad? Don't be absurd. I'm not mad. I'm furious."

Christian gulped.

This is not going to end well for me.

***

"Take off your shirt," Dr. Adams commanded as she forced Christian to sit on the bed. They were the only ones in the room. The man from the Science Division had already left, his task of delivering the various ammunition and weapons that Christian had requested done.

Christian followed his physician's orders, reaching for the hem of his shirt. He began to lift it over his head, but dropped it with a hiss of pain the moment he lifted his arms. By the Almighty! Just trying to lift his arms hurt!

"Oh, honestly," the woman growled. "Are you really so weak that you can't even take your own damn shirt off?" Without waiting for his answer, she grabbed his shirt and yanked it over his head and off his frame.

"Yeowch!" Christian yelped as his arms moved far too quickly and in a direction they were not ready to go. Shock coursed through him as the nerves in his arms flared up like someone had shoved them onto a bed of burning coals.

"Don't be such a baby," Dr. Adams chided. "You've been injured worse than this before. Fuck, remember when I had to heal you after your battle with Abaddon? You were way more injured back then. Or did you forget how you almost died?"

"No, I didn't forget. And just because I've had worse doesn't change the fact that I'm still injured." Christian winced as the socket joint in his left shoulder sent a sharp jolt to his brain. "Couldn't you be a bit gentler?"

"Gentle? With you?" Dr. Adams snorted. "The only way you'll ever learn a lesson is if it's beaten into that thick skull of yours, you reckless idiot. Now lie down on your back."

Christian wanted to grumble in complaint, but knew that he would just have more pain inflicted upon his person by the sadistic doctor. So he did what she asked, lying on his back and allowing the woman to check him over. After several moments of giving his body a standard check-up, she walked over to one of the cases on the floor and opened it.

She then came back with what appeared to be a giant brick with a speaker system on one side and a monitor on the other. She held the device over his body, moving it from his head to his toes, then back up to his head.

"You have no broken bones," she announced at last, "though your ribs have been bruised very badly. A number of your muscles have also been torn, and it looks like the ligaments in your wrists have snapped. I suspect the reason for this is due to you swinging those swords of yours around while already suffering several injuries." She gave Christian a look of mixed exasperation and annoyance. "Honestly, must you always be so reckless?"

"It's not like I had much choice." Christian grunted, then yelped when she pinched the flesh under his left pectoral, hard.

"There is always a choice," she scolded. "You could have chosen to be more careful and carried a weapon with you. I know you, Christian, and I know that the only reason you're this injured after fighting a measly werewolf is because you contracted a serious case of stupidity and decided not to carry any weapons."

"There isn't much I can do about that," he told Dr. Adams as she walked back to her case, and pulled out a jar containing some kind of white cream. "You know carrying weapons would draw unwanted suspicion. And besides, I didn't expect to run into a werewolf on this mission. There haven't been any reports of werewolf sightings in Seal Beach."

She walked back over to him, popped the lid open, and scooped a good deal of cream onto her fingers.

"I fail to see how that matters." She sat down on the left side of the bed. "You're always taught to expect the unexpected. You should have known to always keep at least one of your weapons on you at all times. Honestly, Christian, what am I going to do with you?"

Christian didn't have an answer for that, so he didn't say anything.

Silence followed as Dr. Adams proceeded to smear the cream, which he noticed was thick like a paste, onto his skin. He stifled a hiss as it burned when it touched his skin. After a moment, however, the pain faded, and was replaced by a soothing coolness that numbed his body.

"What is this stuff?" asked Christian.

"A new experimental product," she answered, as she continued applying the cream to his body. "This cream contains several million nanites; tiny, microscopic machines that are designed to heal injuries from inside your body. They're the latest in medical innovation. Turn over."

When he did as instructed, she started applying the cream to his back. Christian grunted when Dr. Adams applied an almost painful amount of pressure to his left shoulder blade, just enough to make her displeasure known without aggravating his injuries.

"Sounds like those guys in the Science Division are as busy as ever. Though I don't know how I feel about having tiny machines inside my body." He'd read one too many sci-fi novels where nanomachines ate their host from the inside out to feel comfortable with them inside of him. The images those thoughts evoked did not help any.

"The nanomachines don't have a long lifespan, they'll dissolve in a few days," Dr. Adams informed him primly. Christian grunted, but didn't say anything else. After a few more seconds, she finished rubbing the cream into his calves. She then straightened up, and wiped her hands, ridding them of any residue. "There, all done. Tell me, how do you feel?"

Christian tentatively sat up, using his hands to act as support for his body. He made sure to take it slow, just in case his arms gave out on him again. They didn't, something that he was thankful for as he sat all the way up.

"I feel… a lot better," he admitted. Moving about experimentally, he placed his right hand on his left trapezius and rotated his entire left arm. After a moment, he smiled. "I don't feel any pain." Just then a jolt ran up his shoulder, causing him to wince. "Well, not too much pain."

"Your body is still going to be very sore for a while," Dr. Adams informed him. "The nanomachines need time to work, and you've sustained a lot of damage. I would suggest taking it easy. You should probably stay in bed today."

"I can't." Christian shook his head. He slid off the bed and stood up. He moved slowly, cautiously, taking one step and then two, making sure that his legs were in working order. "I've got a date today."

"A date?" Dr. Adams perked up. It was only after seeing the amused quirk to the woman's lips that Christian realized what he'd just said.

"D-did I say date? I meant I was going to observe my target and learn more about her behavioral patterns."

"So you're going on a date with your target?"

"That isn't what I meant," Christian snapped, then took a deep breath. "This isn't a date. I'm doing this to protect her."

Dr. Adams raised an inquiring eyebrow.

"To protect her? Isn't she a succubus?"

"No." Christian shook his head. "She can't be. That werewolf I ran into was obsessed with her, too. You know as well as I that supernatural creatures are immune to the passive abilities of other supernatural creatures."

"That is true," Dr. Adams admitted. "Though I believe *resistant* is a more accurate term. If this Lilith's *Aura of Allure* is powerful enough, she can override another creatures' resistance."

"Then wouldn't I be affected as well?" Christian questioned. "I haven't felt a single desire to do something with Lilith since meeting her. Not even the desire to kiss her. If I, a human, do not feel the desire to have sex with her, then a monster wouldn't feel that desire either. Humans do not have a monster's resistance."

"Hmm… you do bring up a good point." Dr. Adams decided to drop the subject. "So, about this date…"

"Oh, for the—it's not a date!"

"Calm down." Dr. Adams smiled disarmingly. "I don't think there's anything wrong with having a little fun. Just make sure you don't fall in love with her. I would hate for you to be excommunicated because you ended up committing lascivious acts on a pure, innocent young maiden."

"Don't talk to me about lascivious acts! The only person I want to hear something like that from even less than you is Tristin!" He paused for a moment, but only to catch his breath. "And it isn't a date!"

Chapter 14

Lilith awoke from her slumber with a gasp and jolted upright. The sheets fell away to reveal the pink spaghetti strap shirt that she had worn to bed. She shivered as the chill from the fan overhead hit her skin, creating goosebumps on her flesh. The air was much colder than it should have been, even with the fan blowing. It took her several seconds to realize why. Her body was covered in a light layer of sweat.

And that wasn't the only thing covering her body. Lilith's already flushed cheeks rapidly gained more color as she realized that her legs were coated in another kind of fluid. So were her bed sheets.

Taking her fingers out of her panties, nearly ripping the undergarment in her haste, Lilith brought her hands up to her eyes. Her face burned like the sun as she studied the clear liquid coating her fingers. She knew what it was, but she was still surprised. She had been… and in her sleep… God, this was so embarrassing!

It was a good thing she didn't share a room with Maria. Lilith knew there would be no end to the teasing she would have to endure if her friend knew what she had been doing in her sleep.

And just what had she been doing in her sleep? Lilith, despite her embarrassment still being very prominent, tried to shunt such feelings to the side, and focus on what she could remember before waking up.

A dream. She had been having a dream, that much she knew. The problem was that she couldn't remember what she had been dreaming about. The only image her mind could conjure up were two colors: red and green. Everything else remained elusive, out of her reach, as if it was just beyond the edge of her perception. Every time she tried to focus on recalling more of the dream, it slipped away into a hazy fog.

She soon realized this was getting her nowhere, and decided to forget about the dream for the moment. There were other things that she needed to do. It would behoove her to get a quick start on her day, so she could wash her sheets before Maria or—heaven forbid—Stacy woke up.

Lilith slipped out of bed, then pulled her sheets and comforter off the mattress. The thick fabrics were bundled into a ball that she could just barely wrap her arms around. She then hauled them to the washing machine, where she dumped everything in, along with two cleaning pods, and started it up.

As the washing machine hummed and rumbled with life, Lilith went into the bathroom. She turned the water onto its coldest setting, and stepped in immediately after stripping her clothes off.

The spray hitting her body chilled her to the bones, freezing her skin and making her shiver. She didn't complain or yelp. She *needed* this. Her body felt hot, like she'd been slowly baked inside of an oven. The frigid water running down her body was exactly what she needed to cool herself off. Upon finishing her shower, she wrapped a towel around herself, and headed to her room.

Lilith ran into another dilemma after putting on her underwear. She didn't know what to wear. Whenever she normally went out, she wore the most unflattering clothing that she could think of—unless she was going to work, in which case she would wear a knee-length skirt and button-up shirt, or one of her sundresses.

Her preferred outfit was dark-brown pants, a large overcoat with an even larger collar, and a bucket hat that hid the rest of her head from view. They worked wonders to hide her face and body, though they never seemed to work like she wanted them to.

Some part of her really wanted to wear that ugly outfit for today. Even if it didn't completely stop the stares, she felt almost safe while cocooned in that ridiculously large coat. Another part of her wanted to wear something special to commemorate the first day that she willingly spent time with a man. And still another part just wanted to call the whole thing off and stay in her room. That last desire became stronger the longer she stayed in her closet, staring at her rack of clothing.

"Having some problems?"

"Meep!"

Lilith spun around in shock, then promptly crashed to the floor, bum first, when she tripped over her own feet. Sitting where she had fallen, her left hand rubbing her now sore backside, she looked up to give Maria a glare.

"Now there's a scary look." Maria's cheerful smile greeted her. "You should wear that more often. I'm sure at least half the male population would be too frightened to go near you then."

Lilith huffed and turned her head to the side, determined not to pay attention to her friend. As far as she was concerned, this entire predicament was all Maria's fault anyway.

"Aw, come on. What's with that look?" Maria placed her hands on her hips and grinned down at Lilith. "I decided to do my run a little later just so I could help you pick out something sexy to wear on your first date, and here you are ignoring me."

"D-d-date?" Lilith stuttered, her face threatening to spontaneously combust. "T-t-this isn't a date!"

"It's not?" Maria's devilish grin was in full bloom. "Then what do you call it when a man takes a woman out somewhere?" The grin widened and her eyes gained a delightfully frightening gleam that had Lilith shivering in terror. She looked up at the ceiling, and tapped her chin in a mock-thoughtful manner. "Although, I do seem to recall you being the one to ask him out... still, if you're not willing to consider this a date, then perhaps I could—"

"All right, all right! It's a date!" Lilith practically shouted. "There, you happy now?"

"Very," Maria chirped.

"Would you two keep it down?" Stacy asked as she walked into the room. The goth girl looked like she had just rolled out of bed; her eyes were nearly glued shut, dark rings surrounded them, and her hair was in complete disarray. "Seriously, you two, some of us are trying to sleep, and I've got to work tonight."

"Right, sorry." Maria had the decency to look sheepish. "I guess I got a little excited because Lilith's going on her first date."

"Maria!"

"And I don't think she wanted me to tell you that."

Stacy stared, first at Lilith, and then Maria, then back to Lilith again. Maria grinned wickedly while Lilith felt like her head had been stuck in a deep fryer. It took the youngest girl several seconds of doing nothing but staring to comprehend the words, but eventually, Maria's statement finally penetrated her brain. She looked back at Lilith, who wanted nothing more than to crawl back into bed and hide under the covers, and then at Maria one more time.

"Did you just say *date*?"

"It's not a date." Lilith sounded sullen.

"Yes." Maria smiled a brilliant, beautiful, absolutely terrifying smile. While Lilith started shivering in abject fear, Maria gave Stacy a wink. "A very important date."

***

Christian frowned as he stood in front of The Crema Café, where he and Lilith had agreed to meet. He was leaning against the window, his arms crossed over his chest, and trying not to show any of his discomfort.

His body still felt like it had been put through the wringer. Maybe Dr. Adams had been right and he shouldn't be out of bed. Still, he couldn't just stay in the hotel room, could he? He had agreed to meet up with Lilith.

He still wasn't entirely sure why he had actually agreed to spend the day with her when she asked him out. Actually, he wasn't really sure of *anything* when it came to this mission, so that told him something right there. That aside, he still couldn't figure out why Lilith had asked him out, especially after he took her fear of men into consideration.

At least he now knew that she wasn't a succubus. Supernatural creatures had an innate immunity to a succubus's *Aura of Allure*. That werewolf shouldn't have been affected by her, and in fact, it should have been repulsed just by standing in her presence. Monsters of different breeds never got along.

So why am I still agreeing to go out with her? I should leave before she arrives. It's not like I'll ever see her again.

"H-hey… um, C-Christian."

Well, shoot.

Lifting his head and looking to his left, Christian was treated to the sight of Lilith standing before him. A light shade of pink dusted her cheeks, enhancing her gorgeous face. She had donned a simple black cami top with a V-neckline and thin straps. A red skirt that stopped at mid-thigh wrapped around her hips, and tan gladiator sandals adorned her feet. It was a modest outfit, nothing all that special.

Christian wondered if the breathlessness he felt was natural.

"Lilith… that outfit…"

"D-does it look okay?" Lilith looked increasingly embarrassed as he continued staring at her. "I've never worn something like this before… the skirt isn't it too short, is it?" She grabbed the hem of her skirt and tried pulling it down. Christian watched for several seconds before shaking his head.

"No… you look fine," he said.

"You think so… it… it doesn't look bad or anything?"

"Not at all." Christian shook her head. "You look, uh, nice?"

The two stared at each other for several seconds, then looked away with matching blushes.

***

"Oh, for the love of—come on, you two! Get a move on already!"

Hiding behind a lamppost several feet from the mutually embarrassed duo, stood Maria. Her hands gripped the metal railing in front of her. She stared at them with a hard glare, as if doing so would make them start their date.

"Why are we doing this again?"

Standing several feet behind Maria was Stacy. The youngest of Maria's boarders looked like she wanted to be anywhere but there. Wearing her usual gothic outfit and an expression of the utmost annoyance, the pale-skinned girl stared at her eldest roommate's back in disgust.

"Ugh, what are they doing just standing there! They're wasting daylight!" Maria shouted, mostly to herself.

Stacy's right eye twitched. "Are you ignoring me?"

"Why aren't they moving?"

"You are ignoring me," Stacy deadpanned.

"Huh?" Maria looked behind her to stare at the seventeen-year-old girl. "Did you say something?"

"Not a thing," Stacy grunted, before gesturing at something over Maria's shoulder. "By the way, I thought you might be interested to know that those two are leaving."

"What?!"

***

Christian and Lilith eventually left The Crema Café. It became immediately clear once they started moving that not only did they *not* have a destination in mind, but neither of them had a clue as to what they were supposed to do. Lilith had never gone anywhere with a man, and Christian's entire life consisted of killing monsters or training to kill monsters.

This would be a first for the both of them.

They walked side by side. Christian would occasionally ask a question, and Lilith would answer, but for the most part, neither spoke much.

"So… what do you think we should do?" Christian asked. Lilith looked at him. She then turned her head to look back down at the sidewalk.

"I… I don't really know," she admitted with endearing bashfulness. "This is the first time I've ever done something like this. I mean, I've gone out before, but I was always with Maria. I've never…" Lilith fidgeted with her hands, her voice growing softer as she spoke, until it was little more than a whisper. "… I've never been anywhere with a man before."

Christian coughed into his hand, more to cover his face than for any other reason. He didn't know why his face felt so hot, but it was completely unbecoming of an Executioner. He was a Warrior who specialized in the extermination of aberrations. He didn't blush.

"What do you normally do when you and Maria go out?"

"Um." Lilith pressed her index finger against her lower lip. "We usually go out to get a coffee and then do some window shopping. We did go to the movies a few times, but…"

"I've never been to the movies before," Christian admitted.

"You haven't?"

"No." Christian smiled a bit at the shocked look Lilith was giving him. "My job never leaves me much time for recreation, and if I'm being honest, I'd much rather find a nice, quiet place to sit down and read a good book."

The stare that Lilith gave him made Christian feel a little self-conscious. And when her face broke into a smile that could part storm clouds, his heart skipped a beat.

"Yeah, I can understand that," she said. "While I do like watching movies, I usually only go to the theater because Maria drags me along when she wants to see one."

The young woman tapped her chin in thought for a moment, her nose scrunching up cutely and making her look a bit like a chipmunk. Christian wondered how someone so gorgeous could look so cute.

"So, the movies are out," she said after thinking about it for a moment. "I guess we could walk around and I could show you some of the sights…"

She trailed off and looked around apprehensively. He noticed the expression and wondered what was wrong before he, too, observed their surroundings and realized what the problem was. While they had been discussing what they should do, every male within a twenty-five-meter radius had stopped what they were doing and began following them. Some stared at Lilith with slack-jawed expressions. Those who had more willpower than the average male leered at her, lust gleaming in their eyes. More men arrived by the second, as if they'd been enchanted, and maybe they had.

Christian remembered that werewolf who'd been enamored with Lilith. A succubus's allure didn't affect other supernatural creatures, but Christian knew that certain supernatural creatures could, indeed, control other supernatural creatures. Ancestors, the Seven Demon Lords, and a few others had the power to do that.

He didn't think any of those were present in Seal Beach, but he also remembered Tristin's words about how something was coming this way. Christian also remembered what Samantha had said, about how many creatures were migrating to the west, almost as if something had spooked them. Could all of these incidents be related? Could this creature who was supposedly coming to Seal Beach be the reason that Lilith received so much unwanted male attention? If it was, then it must be powerful. A curse of this magnitude took a lot of power to cast and even more to maintain.

"C-Christian." Lilith pressed herself into his back, and Christian realized how frightened she was. Her body was shaking like a leaf trapped within a tornado.

"Don't worry," Christian reassured her. "I won't let any of these guys lay a finger on you."

Lilith said nothing, merely nodding against his shirt. Christian looked around at all the men, drooling and moaning like zombies lusting after brains. His hands clenched into fists, the knuckles turning white as they shook.

I have to protect Lilith... but how?

***

"Uh-oh," Maria muttered, biting her thumb as she stared at the scene before her. Christian and Lilith were surrounded by a large group of men— no, not a group. A group would imply three or more. This was a *horde*; there had to be at least fifty men surrounding them. "Not good, this is so not good."

Stacy was also staring at the sight of Christian and Lilith being surrounded, though her focus was more on Christian than Lilith. The sound of rustling drew her attention to Maria, who stood up from her crouched position behind the bush that they had been using as urban camouflage.

"What are you doing?"

"I'm going to help them." Maria dug through her purse. "I should have suspected something like this would happen. Those clothes that Lilith is wearing really are too much for most men to handle."

"Then why did you force her to wear them?"

"Because I wanted her date to be special," Maria informed her younger compatriot. "This is the first time she has ever gone out with a man, and she's going out with him willingly. I wanted her to look nice for the occasion."

"I suppose I understand that," Stacy murmured. She then turned to look at Maria when the older woman released an "ah-ha!" and her expression became dryer than a desert, "Is that a Taser?"

"Yep!" Maria answered proudly. Stacy stared some more.

"Where did you get it?"

"Bought it on the Internet." Maria winked at her friend. "A girl's gotta have some way to protect herself."

Without waiting for a response from Stacy, Maria dashed out from behind the bush and started shouting. Stacy sighed and silently followed her roommate. She would have been better off staying in bed today.

***

Things were not looking good. He and Lilith were surrounded by a bunch of guys, and he didn't know what to do. He could fight them, of course, but that meant injuring them. They might have been filled with unimaginable amounts of lust, but they were still human, and he was loath to hurt another human—self-defense purposes notwithstanding.

Christian felt Lilith pressing herself against him for protection. A part of him was surprised, but the greater part recognized that out of all the people surrounding them, he was the only one that didn't look ready to drag her into a dark alley and have his wicked way with her. He was her only means of protection, even if he and the people surrounding them shared the same gender.

His eyes flickered across the sea of heads. He couldn't tell how many people there were, but he estimated over two dozen at least. That was a lot of people, too many for him to fight off without causing potentially grievous injury.

A soft sob captured his attention. Something wet stained his back. Tears, he realized. *Lilith's tears.* These men scared her so much that she was crying.

I have to do something! I have to, but what should I do? What can I do?

"Hey, you! The guy with two different colored eyes!"

He and Lilith turned toward the source of the shout. It was a woman that he had never seen before, though Lilith recognized her immediately.

"Maria?!"

"Here! Catch!"

The woman, Maria, tossed something over the sea of people. It was small, black, and rectangular in shape. It traced a parabolic arc through the air before being caught by Christian.

"A Taser?" he wondered out loud as he looked at the device. He recognized it as a standard Taser that almost anyone could buy off the Internet. They were used mostly by women who needed protection from muggers and rapists while walking the streets at night. What a woman in a city with relatively little crime was doing with a Taser was beyond him.

He supposed he could think about that later. The most important thing was to get himself and Lilith out of this mess. This Taser would help him do just that.

"Lilith." Christian waited until Lilith nodded against his back to continue. "On my signal, I want you to make a break for it. I'll create a path for you and keep these guys off your back."

"But, what about you?" Despite her own fear, Lilith sounded concerned for his safety. Christian felt surprise, but he didn't let the feeling last long.

"I'll be fine," he assured her. "Once I'm positive that you're out of harm's way, I'll make my own getaway, and meet up with you."

Christian turned his head to look behind him. Lilith had closed her eyes and took a deep breath. Then she opened them again and gave Christian a determined look.

"Right. I'm ready."

"Okay then." Christian steadied himself and prepared for the coming confrontation in much the same way that he did for combat. "We'll do this on the count of three."

Lilith nodded and got ready. The group of men no seemed longer content to just stand there looking like a bunch of idiots. Like a group of zombies out of a horror film, the mass of drooling males walked toward them with a slow, stumbling gait.

"One."

Christian heard blood pounding in his ears, and he knew that Lilith must have felt the same. A trickle of sweat made a trail down the left side of her face, and her wide eyes darted back and forth like a frightened rabbit staring down the barrel of a shotgun.

"Two."

Christian gripped the Taser tightly in his left hand. What he wouldn't give to have another Taser so he could dual-wield them. He was always more comfortable with a weapon in each hand.

"Three."

The mob finally reached them. They were practically knocking on the two's doorstep. Their hands were outstretched, as if attempting to reach out and snatch Lilith from Christian's side.

"GO!"

Lilith bolted at the same time Christian slammed the Taser into the nearest man's chest. The man's body twitched and spasmed before he fell to the ground with a thud. At the same time as he tased the man, his fist lashed out and caught another in the temple, knocking that guy unconscious as well.

Christian and Lilith shot through the mass of people swiftly, with Christian leading the way. He became a whirlwind of activity, zapping people left and right. His fist blurred, knocking people down as well, helping clear a path for Lilith to run through. It wasn't long before he had cut a large swath through the crowd.

Lilith burst out of the gathered mob and bolted down the street, her legs carrying her with the swiftness of fear. Christian stayed behind and continued knocking out everyone who dared to follow. One man received a chop to the neck that sent him face-first to the ground. Another got a boot to the face, and still more were given a powerful shock from the Taser. Minutes after Lilith left, the once large group had dwindled to just under a dozen.

Bzzzz! Christian mercilessly stuck the Taser into the next guy who tried passing him. He then pulled back and, before the man could fall to the ground, grabbed him by the arm and swung him around. He let go a second later, sending the unconscious body flying into two others, sending all three of them to the ground.

After taking a quick headcount of the men still conscious, Christian decided that it was time for him to make his own escape. He chucked the

Taser at the nearest guy. The close-range-weapon-turned-projectile hit its target with unerring accuracy, and the man was felled seconds later.

With his task done, Christian bolted. He needed to find Lilith before another group of men found her first.

***

"Wow!" Maria whistled as she stared at the young man running from the scene. Her eyes were wide and her mouth wanted to drop. "That was…"

"Hot." Maria looked over at Stacy. They eyed each other for a moment. The younger of the two shrugged. "What? We both know you were thinking it, too."

Maria giggled. "Am I that obvious?"

When Stacy just deadpanned at her, Maria turned back to look at the large group of unconscious bodies lying haphazardly on the ground.

"But really," she said with a contemplative gaze. "I've never seen anyone move like that before, except for people in those action movies. I wonder if he's an actor, or maybe some kind of stunt double."

"He could be a martial artist," Stacy suggested. "You know, like that Jackie Chan guy."

"Hmm… maybe. In any case, I think we're done here." Maria stood up.

"Please tell me we're going home?"

Maria paused to look at the other girl. After silently contemplating what had just happened for a moment longer, she said. "You can go home if you want. I think I'm going to stick around and make sure those two don't get into any more trouble." There was an extra Taser in her purse, and she could use it to preemptively zap any male who came too close to Lilith. It was the least she could do for the threatening her friend had endured this morning.

"Thank God." The goth girl slumped in relief. "I'll see you later."

"Yeah, later."

Maria watched Stacy walk off, then turned and ran in the direction that Lilith and the young man had gone. As she tried catching up to the duo, a grin spread across her lips. This was the most exciting thing that had ever happened in this dull town!

Chapter 15

Lilith didn't know how long she ran. It could have been minutes. It could have been hours. With adrenaline pumping through her veins, and fear coursing through her body, crashing against her like a tidal wave and spurring her onward, she ran much harder and for far longer than she would have thought possible.

However, fear and adrenaline can only give a person so much strength. It granted a massive boost in stamina and athletic ability, but the effects were notorious for not lasting more than a few minutes.

It was no surprise that Lilith's run slowed down to a jog, and then to a walk. Her body eventually became incapable of going any farther, and she found herself leaning against the wall in a nearby alley. She could only hope that no one found her while she rested.

She gasped for breath, her chest heaving as she used the wall to support her exhausted frame, which was covered by a light sheen of sweat. That full-on sprint had drained whatever stamina she may have possessed. Perhaps her lack of athleticism was what allowed so many men to catch up to her with ease.

Maybe I should start running with Maria in the mornings.

Her legs finally giving out, Lilith slid down the wall, until her bottom hit the hard cement. Her breathing evened out, but she still felt shaken from her ordeal. She wrapped her arms around her legs, her body shivering like those times when she had nightmares about her time before coming to Seal Beach.

She wondered what had happened to Christian. Was he all right? Had the mob caught him and decided to hurt him for helping her escape? Lilith still didn't know what to feel about him, but she couldn't deny that he was pleasant company… for a man. He didn't ogle her like other members of his gender did. He didn't strip her with his eyes, didn't act like an idiot whenever she was around. She could even talk to him and not worry about him trying to take advantage of her. It was a rather novel experience.

Lilith leaned her head against the wall and closed her eyes. Even though her breathing had become more even, she suddenly felt a lot more tired. A thick haze clouded her mind, making her drowsy. She felt the temptation to just close her eyes and drift off.

"Lilith?"

"KYA!!"

She nearly fell over in her haste to scramble back to her feet. With her back pressed against the wall, she stared at the person who'd walked into the alley, her heart hammering in her chest. It was only after several seconds had passed, and her pounding heart had slowed down, that she recognized the person before her.

"Christian?"

As the familiar green and red eyes gazed at her from underneath strands of messy midnight hair, Lilith slowly relaxed.

"I'm sorry." Christian sounded contrite. "I didn't mean to scare you."

"No, no." Lilith shook her head. The shaking increased. "It's okay. I was just… just a little startled, is all."

"Are you okay?"

"Fine." Lilith sniffed. "Why do you ask?"

"Because you're crying."

It was only after the words were spoken that Lilith felt it, the wetness running down her cheeks. She brought a hand up to her face and tried to wipe away her tears to no avail. Like a small stream that never ceased, her tears refused to be stopped.

"Sorry…" she apologized in a soft whisper, still wiping her eyes. "I must look unsightly."

"You don't need to apologize, and I don't think it's possible for you to look unsightly." Christian walked up to Lilith, causing her to tense. When nothing happened, she relaxed again. She looked into his eyes and saw nothing but concern for her. "Are you sure you're all right?"

Lilith started to nod her head, only to quickly change the motion and begin shaking it. Along with shaking her head, the rest of her body shook as well. She wrapped her arms around her waist, as if doing so would cause the shaking to cease. It didn't.

"I… I was so scared," Lilith whispered. "When those men surrounded us… I was so afraid. I didn't know what to do. If you hadn't been there…"

"Has it always been like this?" Christian made a vague gesture toward the exit. "Are most men always that crazy around you?"

"Yes." Lilith sniffled as she sank back to the ground. She brought her knees to her chest and wrapped her arms around them. "It's been like that ever since I turned thirteen. I hadn't noticed it at first, the stares, but eventually people began coming on to me: boys, men, students, teachers. It wasn't so bad at first. I even used to think getting all that attention was nice."

Christian walked over and sat down beside her, his back also against the wall. Lilith didn't look up at him. Her eyes gazed at the ground, but they weren't looking at the ground. They were distant, staring, lost in memories of a past that she wished to erase.

"What changed?" he asked.

For a few moments, his question was met with silence. The only sounds that permeated the small alley were Lilith's sniffles and hiccups as she relived the past that she'd tried so hard to forget.

"It was just after I turned fourteen." she started. "It was after school, and one of my teachers said that he wanted to talk to me about something. When I got there, he asked me to sit down. I didn't think anything was wrong at the time, so I did what he asked of me. It was only after he started talking that I realized something was wrong. He kept… touching my leg, and every time I pushed it off, he would put it back on and begin rubbing me. I got really uncomfortable and told him so, but he just laughed and said that there was nothing to be uncomfortable about… and then he… then he…"

As she trailed off, the tears in her eyes turned into full-fledged waterworks. They poured down her cheeks like a river. She tried stopping the flow, but they refused to end.

"Here."

Lilith blinked through blurry eyes as a shirt-covered arm appeared in her view. After several seconds of staring at the dark-black fabric of the sleeve, she turned her head to look at Christian, who looked at something off to their left. He seemed uncomfortable.

"I don't have a handkerchief or anything for you to dry your eyes with," he explained, as if he could tell that she was staring at him, even though he wasn't looking in her direction. "You can just use my shirt instead."

After several more seconds of staring, Lilith made a noise that was half-hiccup, half-giggle. Christian looked at her, but she just shook her head. She grabbed the fabric in both hands, and hesitantly used it to wipe the tears from her eyes.

"Feel better?" Christian asked, as she let go of his shirt.

"I do." She knew that she probably didn't look good right now, her eyes felt puffy and irritated, and they were probably bloodshot, too. Despite that, she smiled at him. "Thank you."

"Anytime." Christian's half-smile was surprisingly endearing.

She looked back at the alley. Trash littered the ground. Several sheets of crumpled paper fluttered in the air, as a soft breeze blew through the small space between buildings.

"That teacher—" Christian choked on the words. Lilith looked at him curiously. He hesitated, and then coughed into his hand and continued. "He … he didn't … rape you, did he?"

"No." Lilith's long blond locks swayed in front of her face as she shook her head negatively. "He tried. He almost succeeded, but a passing teacher heard me scream and came in. The teacher who tried to rape me was arrested, and I never saw him again."

"I'm sorry," Christian said sincerely. "I can't imagine how hard that must have been to deal with."

Lilith smiled at him but didn't say anything. She looked up to stare at the clear blue sky wistfully. The cloudless sky with the sun shining its radiance unto the world presented a stark contrast to her own tumultuous emotional state.

"Ever since that moment, I've been deathly afraid of men." She paused, then shook her head. "No, that's not quite true. There was one guy that I thought I liked once, but he turned out to be even worse than that teacher." She frowned, but quickly got back on track before Christian could ask her to elaborate. "After that I've always been frightened of men and took great pains to avoid them. The few times that I had no choice but to interact with them, they would try doing… things to me, and I became even more afraid as a result."

"Sounds like a vicious cycle."

"It is," Lilith agreed. "To be honest, I'm afraid of what will happen to me once I graduate college. Right now, my teachers let me do most of my work at home, and then I send all of my assignments to me via e-mail. I don't think an employer would let me do that, though."

Christian nodded. "Probably not. Considering how afraid you are of men, I'm actually surprised you're even talking to me."

Lilith was startled by the observation. Not just because he made it, but because she agreed with it. Why was she talking to him? Why had she asked him out? It didn't make sense.

"I couldn't tell you why, either," she admitted. "I don't know why I can talk to you, or why I'm spending time with you. I guess… I guess it's because I don't feel afraid. It's weird, but when I'm with you, the fear that I normally feel whenever I'm around a man isn't there."

"I see."

Silence engulfed them for a time. A slight breeze kicked up a sheet of paper that blew down the alley. It flew into the street and was whisked away by a passing car.

"I guess this date was a bust." Lilith felt oddly dejected. "And I was actually looking forward to today, too."

"You were?" Christian asked in surprise.

"Well, yeah." Lilith could feel her cheeks becoming warm as Christian glanced at her. "I-I mean, you're the first man I've spoken to in years. And you… you haven't stared at me, or tried doing anything untoward to me, so I… I was kind of… really looking forward to this."

"I-I see." Christian coughed into his hand. Lilith thought the way that his cheeks lit up in a blush was cute. "Anyway, I wouldn't say this day has been completely ruined." She felt her confusion mount, but then he turned and presented her with a small, sincere smile that made her want to melt. "I mean, it's still pretty early, right? We could still do something."

"I-I don't know what we could do," she admitted. "I've never done this before."

Christian gave an eloquent shrug in response to her words. "I haven't either, so why don't we just do something that you want to do?"

"Something that I want to do?"

"Yeah. What do you like doing when you go out?"

Lilith thought about all the activities that she enjoyed doing. There weren't that many—at least, none that involved going out. She didn't like going out. There were too many men in public, especially the more populated places like the mall and the movie theater, and don't even get her started on the clubs. The few times that she had hit the town were all at

Maria's behest, and her only consolation about those times was that her best friend had been present.

Maria had no trouble pounding in the face of any man who came too close. Her friend was really strong. She also had a mean right hook.

That still didn't solve her problem, namely, figuring out what she and Christian should do on their date.

Thinking on it, there was really only one thing that Lilith truly enjoyed doing. And fortunately for her, she already knew that the young man sitting by her side also happened to appreciate this singular activity.

"Well"—an idea formed within her mind— "there is one thing that we can do."

Chapter 16

Jason Stolle sighed. He stood behind the counter in the comic book shop and surveyed the small store. Nothing exciting ever happened here. Man, what he wouldn't give for something interesting to come along, if only to break this monotonous life.

The chime of a bell signaled the arrival of a customer. He turned his head to greet whoever had just entered … and his jaw promptly dropped.

Two people had entered the store. One of them was a young man with unruly black hair and two different colored eyes. He wore blue jeans and a black, long-sleeved shirt. While the man was noteworthy thanks to those freaky eyes of his, he wasn't the person who had attracted Jason's attention. No. That particular feat belonged to the man's companion.

The girl walking at the man's side was the most gorgeous creature that he had ever seen. Better than any of those girls that he saw in those pornos that he illegally downloaded off the Internet. Her long blond hair cascaded past her shoulders, framing a face that was simply too beautiful to be human. As corny as it may have sounded, her face had the alluring innocence of a fairy-tale princess and the unblemished perfection that could only be found on a goddess.

It wasn't her face that he admired the most, however. Why would he look at her facial features, attractive as they were, when there were much better things to look at? Like her rack. He had never seen a girl in real life who had such beautiful boobs. They were big, but not too big. They sat high on her chest, perky and proud, and they also looked real. God, what he wouldn't give to grab those things on her chest, stick his face in them, and…

As if noticing the eyes on her, the young woman looked at him. He noticed how her body began shaking, or rather, he noticed how the shaking of her body caused her breasts to shake. God, he was getting so hard. His dick could probably cut glass!

Just as that thought entered his mind, a strange sensation came over him, like a weight was pushing down on his soul. It snapped him out of whatever trance had been caused by the sight of such a sexy woman, forcing him to look away and seek out the source of this feeling.

And that's when he saw it.

His mind froze as two glowing orbs bored into his soul. One was green and the other possessed the color of fresh blood. Terror washed over him as those eyes glared into his own. It felt like he was being drowned, smothered. Images filled his mind. He saw himself getting slashed apart by a pair of gleaming swords, of being shot several times by two handguns, one a gleaming silver and the other darker than a black hole.

He saw blood…

He saw death…

He saw *his* death…

And then, just like that, the feeling disappeared, the images vanished from his mind like a wavering breeze, a dark fantasy caused by playing one too many hack-n-slash video games. All he saw was a young man with black hair and two different colored eyes glaring at him, and a beautiful young woman practically burying herself into the guy's back. Another moment passed before the young man led the beautiful woman farther into the store, tossing him one final glare.

With the threatening presence of the raven-haired man gone, Jason fell face first onto the counter, his breathing heavy and his chest heaving. Sweat poured from his scalp like a river, running down his face and pooling onto the counter.

That had been the single most terrifying confrontation of his existence.

His bladder seemed to agree.

***

Christian led Lilith past the store clerk, who lay shivering face down on the counter. They wove through several miniature bookshelves with a variety of comics lining them. He recognized some of them, but as American comics weren't really his thing, he only vaguely recognized the more mainstream ones like DC Comics and Marvel. The rest he couldn't make heads or tails of.

"What just happened?" Lilith asked. "What did you do to him?"

"That guy?" Christian looked back at the boy, who appeared to have released his bladder. He turned back around and shrugged. "Nothing really. I just didn't like the way he was looking at you. Maybe my glares are just really frightening."

He didn't tell Lilith that what he'd done was release his killing intent—the physical manifestation of someone's intent to kill or cause harm. All sentient beings could do it, even humans, though it took years of training. Christian didn't release killing intent often, but he could when he felt it was necessary.

"Thank you for doing that, Christian," Lilith said softly. He looked at Lilith, and couldn't help but gently smile at her.

"It's no problem. I know how much you dislike it when men ogle you, and I didn't like how he was looking at you either."

Lilith giggled, causing him to quirk an eyebrow. She squeaked and hid her face against his arm, which he noticed she had been clutching ever since they'd left that alley.

He wondered why she was still holding his arm, but figured it was simply because of the safety his presence offered. He decided not to let it bother him too much, even though he felt uncomfortable with her being so close. He could put up with it. The discomfort that he felt was probably nothing compared to how she must feel, especially when in the presence of people like that teen manning the front.

"So what exactly are we doing in here?" he asked.

"I sometimes come here to buy more light novels when I finish reading the ones I already have," Lilith told him. "I... usually come in disguise, which is probably why that boy didn't recognize me."

Christian filed away the knowledge that she apparently disguised herself whenever she went out. He then put the information off to the side with a reminder to ask her about it later. There was something else she had said that he felt was more important at the moment.

"There are light novels in this store?"

"Uh-huh." Lilith finally began taking the lead. She grabbed his hand in what Christian felt was an unconscious gesture, because he highly doubted she realized she was doing it, and led him to a small corner of the store. "This is the only place that sells them. None of the mainstream bookstores have any."

The light novel section consisted of several shelves in the back corner of the room. There were many titles that Christian recognized. Some he'd already read, and others were on his To Read list. He even saw a few that he'd never heard of.

Lilith seemed to know a good deal about all of the light novels present, though, and she was more than happy to let him know which ones she liked, and which she felt were not worth reading.

"*Is This a Zombie?* is okay, but it's not very original," she told him. "*Sword Art Online* is also decent, but *Accel World* is a much better series and written by the same author. Of course, if you want something truly original, then you should read *The Devil is a Part-Timer*."

They stayed there for nearly an hour, discussing light novels and looking for something that one of them might like to buy. Christian had a lot of fun. He couldn't remember the last time he'd been in a bookstore, and he'd never entered one with another person. He discovered that shopping for something that he actually enjoyed, with a person who shared his passion to be a novel experience. It made the whole activity several times more enjoyable.

They eventually settled on buying the sixth volume of *Spice and Wolf,* and were soon standing in front of the cash register, where the teenager rang up their purchase with shaking hands. The clerk looked torn between staring at Lilith in obvious lust, or Christian in abject terror. Every time the teen's eyes strayed to Lilith, who responded by hiding further behind Christian, he glared at him, dousing the pimply child with a healthy dose of his irritation.

They soon left the store, and the nearly comatose clerk, behind them.

***

Upon leaving the comic store Christian and Lilith went in search of a nice, quiet place to read their new acquisition. After much searching, they found a park several miles from the store. Only a few children were playing there and, more importantly, there were no men in the vicinity.

Christian felt some ironic amusement when he noticed that the park they'd chosen was the same park where he and Lilith had met for the second time. This feeling of déjà vu peaked when Lilith led him to exact tree that he had been sitting under the last time he'd been there.

The grass was slightly damp, but neither of them minded. They sat side by side, shoulder to shoulder, as Christian pulled out the light novel they had bought and flipped it open to the first page. He and Lilith soon lost themselves in the story of a merchant and the wolf deity who accompanied him—or at least, Lilith did.

Why am I doing this?

Christian carefully flipped the page as Lilith gently tugged on the sleeve of his shirt, letting him know that she had finished reading. She smiled at him in thanks, and then became engrossed in the story once again.

I shouldn't be getting so close to this girl.

It felt odd holding a book in his hand instead of his tablet. Even his Bible was located inside of the sleek little device. And yet, at the same time, there was something inherently nice about holding an actual book instead of an electronic storage device. Maybe it had something to do with the feel of paper beneath his fingertips. It had a certain charm to it, this feeling, though he couldn't figure out why.

Members of the Executioners are not allowed to become intimate with others. Or at least, they shouldn't.

He and Lilith rested with their backs against the tree. They sat with their legs straight out in front of them, their respective left and right thigh almost touching. Another centimeter or two and they would have physical contact.

Intimacy breeds conflict with our creeds and laws.

Christian knew that few Executioners followed this creed anymore. It was inevitable, he supposed. With the increase in supernatural activity, the Church had to recruit people other than those raised in their orphanages. Many of these newer Executioners didn't believe in God, followed no religion, and therefore didn't believe that the laws their organization upheld applied to them.

When you fall in love with someone, you're forced into choosing between your duty to God and the person you love. That's why romantic relationships are not allowed within the Executioners.

He'd never really thought about romance himself. Having been raised by the Church since he was six years old, the idea of falling in love, of getting married and starting a family, had never occurred to him before.

It shouldn't be occurring to me now.

"Christian…"

I shouldn't be thinking about this, especially not about a girl who I just met a few days ago.

"Christian."

What is wrong with me?

"Christian!"

"Huh?" Christian's attention snapped over to Lilith, whose frown spoke of concern mixed with mild annoyance at being ignored. "I'm sorry, Lilith, I was distracted by the story. You were saying?"

"I said I was ready for you to flip the page," she informed him, still looking at him with an odd tilt to her head. "But if you're not finished..."

"No, no, I just finished." He flipped to the next page. Lilith stared at him a moment longer before shrugging off his behavior and focusing on the unfolding story. Christian tried to do the same, but his mind remained unable to focus on the words.

Of course, it's not like I'm in love with her or anything. No. Of course not. This isn't like some kind of light novel, where the hero and heroine fall in love on their first meeting, but, still... He looked at Lilith, who was focused intently on the story. Her small tongue poked out from between her lips, and her brows were furrowed in a cute gesture of concentration. Shaking his head, he looked back at the lines of text, seeing and yet not seeing them. *It's only been a day, and I'm already beginning to enjoy her presence more than I feel comfortable with.*

He had never been in this position before. Even if forming romantic attachments weren't against the Executioners' creed and laws, his job as an Executioner didn't leave him enough time to pursue romance. When he wasn't on a mission, he was training for missions. That was all his life consisted of. He wouldn't even know how to go about creating something as important and meaningful as a loving relationship with a member of the opposite sex.

"Okay, now I know something is wrong. You're not even paying attention to the story anymore."

Christian's thoughts were shattered by Lilith's voice. He looked at her again, at the frown on her face, the open concern in her eyes. He tried ignoring the way his heart felt like it was melting. He really didn't want to deal with this unusual sensation right now.

"I'm sorry; I guess my mind's preoccupied with something."

"Preoccupied with what?"

"Oh, this and that."

The pout Lilith gave him in response was adorable. Her cheeks swelled like a blowfish and turned an appealing shade of pink. He felt a strange urge to place his hands on her cheeks and push the air in them out.

"That's not a very good answer."

He smiled. "I was just thinking about my job. I'm always so busy that I almost never have time to just sit back and relax like this."

"That reminds me, you never did tell me what your job is."

"No, I didn't, did I?"

"Are you being purposely vague with me?"

"Heh… maybe."

The two stared at each other for a long moment. Several seconds passed in which their eyes never left the others face.

"He-he-he-he …"

"Hahahaha …"

They broke out in simultaneous bouts of laughter. Several older ladies walking past them looked at the two and smiled. Several comments about how cute they looked together were made, but he and Lilith ignored them in favor of continuing to laugh. Light laughter soon trickled into the occasional snicker, before even that died down.

"You know something? I had a really good time today," Lilith told him.

"Yeah." Christian's smile was, much to his surprise, completely genuine. "I had a pretty good time as well." He paused, and then made a small amendment to his statement. "Except for when we were surrounded by all those guys. That wasn't much fun."

Lilith shuddered. "Agreed."

"Anyway, it's getting pretty late." Christian looked up at the sun. It was nearly halfway down the horizon line. An array of colors splashed against the sky; a streak of orange, a touch of purple, and a hint of red, all of which mixed together and made the sky appear reminiscent of multicolored flames. It looked like God had gone all out on this evening's sunset. "We should probably get you back home."

"Yeah, I guess."

Christian looked over at Lilith as she released a breathy sigh. He didn't know how, but somehow, he knew that she wasn't looking forward to the walk home.

"I'll escort you home this time, if you don't mind. After what happened to us this afternoon, I'm not entirely sure that I feel comfortable letting you make the trip by yourself."

"I'm not helpless, you know." Lilith turned her head to the side. Christian thought he saw some color on her cheeks, but it could have just as easily been the light from the sunset playing off her face. "I've made the walk home hundreds of times before."

"I never said you were," Christian gently told her. "I just don't feel comfortable with you being on your own after what happened. Even if you can take care of yourself, I would still like to walk you home, for my own peace of mind."

Lilith regarded him curiously, silently contemplating his request. Christian watched as several cute expressions crossed her face, and then watched as her cheeks turned a captivating shade of pink.

"Well," she started, her head tilting toward the ground to look at her feet. The heel of her left foot drew circles in the grass. "I guess it would be okay if you walked me home. It's… it's not like I didn't enjoy your company today."

Christian smiled. "Thank you."

"D-don't mention it."

***

Lilith watched Christian out of peripherals as he escorted her back to her apartment. The young man who'd begun to fascinate her was looking straight ahead, though he would occasionally glance in her direction, as if he could feel her eyes on him. Every time this happened, she would look away and pretend that she hadn't been staring at him.

They walked down the sidewalk, which was surprisingly empty at this time of day. Only a few people were present, the vast majority being women. She guessed that most of the men had been at the incident this morning, and were likely staying in their hotel rooms, nursing a major headache and wondering what had happened to them. Or maybe they were still unconscious. Christian had smacked them around pretty hard.

As they continued to walk in silence, she thought about how this day had panned out. It was almost odd how, after spending just a single day with Christian, she already felt comfortable in his presence. She was still deathly afraid of men. She knew this because every time another man came within viewing distance, she froze up and attempted to hide behind Christian. But for some reason, she wasn't afraid of him. She actually felt safer in his presence than she did in Maria's!

And she couldn't help but wonder: What made Christian different? What separated him from other men? Why did she feel so comfortable around him? And how did it happen in such a short amount of time?

She didn't have an answer to any of those questions. She just didn't know. Lilith couldn't pinpoint the precise reason she felt this way.

Regardless of that, she wasn't going to question it. She had finally found a member of the opposite sex who wasn't affected by her, who didn't drool over her like some kind of idiot, who could actually hold an intelligent conversation, and who shared in her guilty pleasure.

That last reason was a definitely plus in her book. A true silver lining. Just what were the chances that the only man she felt safe around also enjoyed reading light novels?

***

The trip to her apartment was short, no more than fifteen minutes. When they arrived, Lilith led him up the stairs and to her front door. She reached into her purse and pulled out a set of keys. Instead of opening the door, however, she turned around and favored Christian with a lovely smile.

"Thank you for today," she said. "I had a really great time."

"Me too." Christian answered back. Lilith fidgeted with her keys. Her face was beginning to feel warm, which he seemed to notice. "Is something wrong?"

"Mm-mm." Lilith shook her head. "I was just wondering if we could… do something like this again?"

Christian shifted uncomfortably. Lilith watched his face flicker through several different emotions. She wondered what he was thinking, but didn't get a chance to ask as his face cleared mere seconds later.

"I think …" He paused, shook his head, nodded, and then smiled. "I think I would like that."

"Really?" Relief swept through her. "Okay. Great. That's great. So, um, I don't have work tomorrow, but I do have some homework that I need to get done. How about we meet up at The Crema Café again to grab lunch. Say, twelve?"

"Twelve sounds fine," Christian said. "I'll be there."

"Okay."

The two stood together in awkward silence. Lilith squirmed as she wondered how this day should end. Should she just say goodbye? But most dates usually ended with a kiss, didn't they? That's how she figured most of them ended at any rate, but she didn't really feel comfortable with the idea of kissing him. While she enjoyed spending time with him today, the idea of Christian kissing her was still more than a little frightening. Maybe a simple goodbye would do for now?

"So, I'll see you tomorrow?" Lilith said unsurely. Christian looked almost as relieved as she felt. His shoulders visibly relaxed.

"Yeah, see you tomorrow."

Lilith watched as Christian walked down the stairs. When he turned the corner and was out of sight, she unlocked the door and stepped inside the apartment. There she was greeted by the sight of a grinning Maria, who had her hands on her hips and a look on her face that promised nothing good.

"So did you have fun on your date?" she asked.

"I-it wasn't a date." Lilith's face lit up like an oil lamp.

"Of course it wasn't," Maria said in a mocking tone. "It was just two people of the opposite sex going out together, having fun, just the two of them and no one else." She then snapped her fingers, a look of faux realization spreading across her face. "Oh, right. That's called a date."

Lilith tried to scowl, but with the way her cheeks felt like they were on fire, it probably wasn't very effective. "You're not going to let this go, are you?"

"Nope!" Maria chirped. "I'm going to keep embarrassing you, until you admit that you and Mr. Tall, Dark, and Dual-Eyes were on a date."

"F-fine." Lilith walked farther into the room, trying to ignore the way the other woman leered at her. "You can do whatever you want. It's not like I care."

Maria's giggle sent a shiver down her spine.

"Oh, Lilith, you are just too cute." While Lilith felt her face turn into a miniature nova, Maria continued throwing fuel onto the metaphorical fire. "By the way, I noticed that you washed your bed sheets again. Didn't you just wash them just a few days ago? Is there something you want to tell me? Perhaps you would care to share the steamy dream you had that stained your sheets with your best friend?"

"Maria!"

Interlude 2

He flew overhead, the moon and stars at his back, while the earth passed by underneath. From his vantage point he could make out all the buildings, streets, and parks that made up Seal Beach. This city appeared much smaller than the one's he'd visited thus far. He didn't sense much life in it—maybe a little over twenty-thousand or so humans at most.

That was good. It would make finding *her* much easier.

He soared through the sky, his large wings flapping and creating powerful gusts that kept him aloft. While passing over a building, his eyes caught sight of something interesting. His wings retracted, and he angled his body down to descend in altitude. This allowed him to get a better look at the sight that attracted his attention.

Several police officers stood in a park that was blocked off by caution tape. They walked around the area, flashlights in hand, as they surveyed what he recognized as battle scars. Gouges from what he guessed was a sword, claw marks from a creature with clawed feet, torn up clods of dirt and grass, not to mention the bloodstains along the ground. The blood was black, dried. Whoever had fought in this place had likely done so some time ago.

How curious.

He swooped down with speeds that rivaled a fighter jet. His silent descent carried him to the nearest police officer, who only had enough time to look in his direction before sharp nails sank into the pliant flesh of the officer's throat.

The officer gurgled as he was lifted off his feet. His body jerked and twitched several times, and then went still. His arms and legs dangled limply as blood dripped from them and splashed against the grass.

One of the other police officers spun about. He moved his flashlight back and forth, but found nothing.

"Kyle?" he called out. When he received no answer, he shouted again, louder this time. "Dammit, Kyle, this isn't funny! Stop hiding!"

His shouting drew the attention of the others. The two officers standing beside a large scorch mark—no doubt where the body of whatever creature had fought here was destroyed—looked up from their investigation.

The other officer continued waving his light around frantically, searching for his missing partner, the dead one that the winged being held in its grip.

"Something wrong, Stan?"

"I don't know," the officer said with narrowed eyes. "Kyle was right behind me and now he's gone. He's probably just being an idiot and hiding to try to freak me out."

One of the other officers looked around, his flashlight making a sweeping motion of the area. *They won't find anything,* the watcher mused to himself, *not unless they look up.* Humans really were a foolish bunch.

"There aren't many places to hide. I wonder where he could have gone?"

A malicious grin split his face, and he dropped the corpse in his grasp. It hit the ground and made the other three officers spin around, their flashlights illuminating the cooling body. Their horrified faces amused him. Humans were only good for two things: food and entertainment.

"Shit! Is that Kyle?!"

The officers began running up to the body, but they stopped when he flapped his wings loudly to draw their attention. Their heads swiveled about like owls, searching but unable to find the source. Idiots. He flapped his wings again, and they finally pointed their flashlights into the sky.

He wondered: what did these humans think when they saw him? Were they awed by his magnificent presence? Terrified by the feeling of death that he exuded? What thoughts flashed through their mind when his form, wreathed in darkness and cloaked in despair, appeared before them?

Perhaps they believe that I am a fallen angel come to wreak vengeance upon them.

He continued staring at them, watching as they shook, observing as they lost control of their bodily functions. Fear it was, then. They feared him so much that they'd actually pissed themselves.

Understandable. They should fear him. Gazing upon him meant death. The only one among the rabble who need not fear death was *her*. His beloved *Eve*. Everyone else was simply food.

Chapter 17

Fire. *My entire body felt like it was on fire. Electricity coursed through my veins, and sensations that I never knew existed sent my body into fits of ecstasy.*

A pair of lips pressed against my own, kissing me with enough passion that I could feel my toes curling. A tongue filled my mouth, wrestling with mine and nearly sending me over the edge. It pushed and pulled and rubbed against my tongue to create a delicious friction, further fueling the fire burning between my thighs. The moan that escaped my mouth was hampered by this tongue and the pair of lips that claimed this territory for themselves.

Hands explored my body, touching me in places that I had never let anyone touch before, not even myself. The gentle, feather-light caresses left goosebumps on my flesh, as calloused hands glided across my skin. Noises escaped my throat as skilled fingers roamed across my breasts, traveled down my torso and slid across my hips.

One of those hands soon found its way between my thighs. My hips bucked as sensations unlike anything I had ever felt before filled me—like a jolt of lightning traveling up my spine and shooting straight into my brain.

My body writhed in rapture. It felt incredible. Unbelievable. A fire burned inside of me, and I knew there was only one way it could be quenched; only one person who could put out the raging inferno that my body had become.

"Please," I whimpered as the lips left my mouth after giving them a thorough ravishing. A string of saliva connected them for but a moment, before it broke when he raised his head further. I looked into his eyes, red and green orbs that gave me a glimpse into his soul. "Please... I need you... I need you inside of me... right now..."

He did not say anything, but I saw his eyes soften. His smile became tender and loving. That look caused another wave of heat to spread through my body. I knew in that moment that this was the only man that I would ever allow to claim me like this.

His head came down, his lips pressing against mine in a voracious kiss. I responded eagerly. My arms wrapped around his neck, and my legs opened as he guided himself between them. Breathing soon became a necessity, and he took his lips reluctantly off mine, only to begin paying homage to my neck, sending a delicious thrill through my body.

"I love you so much..."

Not even a moment later, I felt him inside of me, and I wrapped my legs around him. I nearly cried out in joy as our bodies, our hearts, and our souls became one. It was the single most glorious experience I had ever felt.

"... Christian."

***

Like a drowning person breaking the water's surface, Lilith woke from her slumber with a loud gasp. She shot up in bed, her body kick-starting awake with a jolt like she'd stuck her finger in a socket.

Her eyes gazed wildly around the room, yet hardly saw anything at all. Her body twitched and spasmed, remnants of her erotic dream. Lilith tried coming to terms with what she had seen, but her brain refused to function, like a computer whose motherboard had short-circuited.

It took her far longer than it should have, but she eventually recognized her location. She was in her room. On her bed. Christian was not there. It had been a dream.

Despite knowing that what she had just experienced was nothing more than a dream, her body still shuddered like an electric current was running through her, sending blissful jolts of pleasure that traveled along her nerves, until they had spread through every region of her body.

She could still feel Christian's hands exploring her body, tending to her flesh with delightful caresses and gentle fondling. Just the feeling of his phantom limbs stroking her skin caused her entire body to flush with delight. It was all kinds of embarrassing.

Lilith looked down. Her left hand was stuck inside of her panties, showing that she'd clearly been playing with herself in her sleep... again.

Carefully extracting her hand from the white cotton undergarment, Lilith both blushed and grimaced before she wiped it on her bed sheets. They were already sullied anyway, so it wasn't like getting them dirtier would make much of a difference.

Slipping out of bed, the first thing Lilith did was slide the window to her room open and turn on the fan. This would hopefully drive away the smell that pervaded the room. After that she put her dirty sheets in the wash.

How many times does that make now? Three? Four?

Back in her room, she stripped out of her clothes and stepped under the spray of the shower, although the water felt like sub-zero on her skin. Only then did she allow herself to contemplate her most recent dream.

It wasn't the first time she had dreamt like this. The dreams had been occurring ever since her date with Christian. However, none of them had ever been this vivid before. Even now, she could still clearly feel his hands as they caressed her body, recall the details of his face, his expression as he stared into her eyes while plunging his—

Whoa, girl! Lilith placed her hands on her cheeks. *Slow down. Stop right now. Don't even go there!*

Lilith didn't want to continue thinking about this. She needed to think of something else, something that would help get her mind off her latest dream.

Perhaps it was a side effect of her dream, but when she tried thinking about something else, thoughts of Christian immediately speared through her mind.

Nearly a week had passed since their first date. Since that day, when they had sat in the shade of a tree and read light novels together, they'd been spending all of their free time with each other. Whenever she wasn't at the preschool or working on her schoolwork, she was spending time with him, either going to The Crema Café or finding a nearby park. Sometimes they would read, other times they would talk. Lilith couldn't deny how much she looked forward to seeing him again each time they parted ways.

Maria had begun teasing her even more, claiming that Lilith had finally found the man of her dreams. Her friend's words made her self-conscious at first, but she had learned not to let the teasing bother her... too much. And it wasn't like she hadn't entertained the thought. She would just never admit to having those thoughts … out loud.

She and Christian would actually be going out again today. They were going on what Lilith considered their first official date.

A real date. Her first date. Just the knowledge that she would be going out to dinner with a guy gave her shivers that, for once, were not of fear. Lilith wouldn't deny that she was worried. What if something went wrong? What if they arrived at the restaurant and had a repeat of what happened the first time they went out? She tried not to let this bother her, however, because she knew that Christian wouldn't let anything happen. He'd become very protective of her, and she was sure that they would have a good time.

After stepping out of the shower and donning in a light purple sundress and sandals, Lilith entered the living area.

Maria stood in front of the stove cooking breakfast; eggs and toast, it looked like. Stacy was nowhere to be seen. When Maria noticed her enter, she gave her a knowing smile.

"I see that you're cleaning your sheets again." The comment was so innocuous and innocent that Lilith immediately knew it was anything but. "Pleasant dreams? Perhaps you were thinking of a certain raven-haired young man with intriguing eyes and lady-killer looks?"

Lilith did her best to ignore her friend's words, and strode into the kitchenette to begin grabbing plates and utensils. She wouldn't allow herself to be teased anymore. She had no reason to feel embarrassed… or did she? Surely the phenomenon happening to her was a natural occurrence … or was it? Did other women not have erotic dreams that caused them to stain the sheets? She didn't know, but Lilith was determined not to let Maria get to her.

"Well, good morning to you, too, sunshine." Maria chuckled when Lilith refused to respond in the usual manner. "So how do you want your eggs? Unfertilized, I hope."

Now *that* got a reaction. After Lilith finished choking on the oxygen that she had inhaled, she turned around to glare at her friend.

"How long are you going to keep teasing me like this?" she scowled at her friend.

"Oh, so you can talk," Maria chirped. "That's good. I was beginning to worry that you'd forgotten how."

"Whatever," Lilith replied morosely.

"Aw, come on. Don't be like that. You know I'm just messing with you."

"I know that." Lilith didn't look at Maria as she set the table. "But that doesn't make it any easier to deal with, and it's no less embarrassing either."

Maria walked over to the table as Lilith finished setting it. She put the pan of eggs onto a cooking mat, then walked behind her, arms wrapping around Lilith's neck. Because Maria was taller than her, the brunette's chin rested on the crown of her head.

"I'm sorry. Forgive me?"

In spite of herself, Lilith sank into the comforting embrace of the first female she'd befriended since junior high.

"I guess I can forgive you this once, but only if you stop teasing me." She tried pouting, but since her friend couldn't see it, she realized that there wasn't much point and stopped.

"All right, I'll stop teasing you."

"Thank you."

Unspoken between them was the unstated "for now" that they both knew Maria was thinking.

***

"… And in other news, there are still no leads in the disappearances of Officers Stan Malaci, Kyle Ferdinand, and Kenny Kreimer, and Deputy John Holland, the four police officers who mysteriously vanished while investigating the site of what appears to be a battleground. With us live is news anchor Lisa Solvers who may be able to shed some light on this strange case."

"It looks like they still haven't found those cops." Maria said to Lilith. She chewed her food with a thoughtful expression as she watched the TV. Unlike Lilith, who sat at the table while she ate, Maria had taken her plate to the living room after turning the television to the local news station. "This is so strange."

Though Lilith didn't say anything, she agreed with her friend. Seal Beach had no real criminal activity. There were a few gangs, but they mostly consisted of high school kids who thought vandalizing property was funny. The disappearance of four cops was definitely an unusual occurrence.

She wondered what had happened to them, but most of her thoughts were on the coming date with Christian. The disappearance of four cops, while troubling, didn't really involve her.

Interlude 3

The room was dark. No light could be seen from inside. No light could enter from outside. The cracks in the doorway had been sealed shut, the windows were boarded, and the curtains sewn shut and lined with duct tape. The person who did this for him, a young woman that he had found wandering the streets and enthralled into doing his bidding, lay on a couch several feet away. Her pale and unbreathing body was deathly still.

As he basked within the darkness, his mind turned over matters of the utmost importance. He'd only been in this city for a few days, but several problems had already come to his attention, courtesy of his slave.

The first issue came from those cops that he had killed. An area-wide search had begun. He conceded that feeding on them might have been a hasty decision. He could ill afford to have someone discover the truth.

Another issue came from all the rabble that he'd run into; werewolves, incubi, undines, succubus, and several low level vampires had noticed his presence. He'd been forced to kill many of them, but that had only created more problems. The Executioners had cottoned on to his presence, or rather, the fact that someone powerful was stirring up trouble. He couldn't afford to have them discover him yet, so he needed to remain ever vigilant—vexing.

Of more importance, however, was the matter of his Eve. He had located his Queen easily enough. Her presence glittered like a diamond in a landfill, but even that news, which should have been monumental, did not please him.

It seemed his Queen had found herself a plaything. This was not necessarily wrong; he'd had plenty of those, but she had become far too attached to hers for his liking. He would have to do something about that, and soon. A King such as himself could not allow his Queen to be sullied by the likes of anyone else.

Chapter 18

The afternoon sun blazed overhead. Christian had spent much of his day reading—or trying to. He'd actually been staring at the same page for the last few hours while thinking deep, complex thoughts on his newest moral dilemma. He had tried to read, really, and even finished two chapters of *Stigma of the Wind,* volume two, but that was about it.

Thinking back on this past week made Christian wonder if all this, traveling to Seal Beach and meeting Lilith, was nothing but a dream. It certainly seemed so in some ways. Aside from his battle with the werewolf, and a minor footnote at the beach where he'd been forced to fight against an undine, the rest of his time here had been relatively peaceful.

A part of him wished his life could remain like this. Another part was just waiting for the hammer to fall, and this life of tranquility to end.

Christian looked around his hotel room, just as neat and tidy as it had been when he had first moved in, maybe even more so. His bags were now stashed away in the closet. The clothes they contained had all been neatly folded and put away in the dresser that served as a television stand for the wide, flat-screen TV that he had never bothered using.

Realizing how fruitless his reading attempts were, Christian took a quick shower and got dressed for the day. He had a date with Lilith this evening. They were going out to a small Japanese restaurant called Restaurant Koi for sushi.

Had anyone told him several weeks ago that he would be going on dates with a woman, he would have shot them in the face. The idea, the notion that he would allow himself to become *that* close to someone, to *anyone*, was preposterous. At least it had been.

The twists and turns that life can take is funny sometimes. God must have a sense of humor.

Worse than simply going on dates with his target, Christian was beginning to really like Lilith. He loved spending time with her. She was intelligent, compassionate, and determined to live her life to the fullest despite the hardships that she had—and would—face. That they shared the same passion was just the icing on the proverbial cake.

Whenever they were together, he and Lilith spent hours just reading or talking. Sometimes they discussed light novels, other times they discussed topics that had nothing to do with books, but shed light on the other person.

Through these conversations, Christian had learned that Lilith was an incredibly bright and passionate individual. She was enrolled in Fullerton College for Graphic Design and Illustration. Her dream was to be a freelance web designer. She'd shown him some of her designs and they were all stunning. She had a keen eye for detail and drew impressive illustrations. Her hand drawings were some of the most beautiful that he had ever seen.

He had also discovered that she worked part-time as a preschool teacher. She apparently loved working with children, and enjoyed coming up with new and fun ways to help facilitate their learning. Christian found this to be an endearing quality. He understood the importance of educating the young well—better than most, in fact.

He really was growing fond of Lilith. *Too fond.* Even though he no longer worried about having to kill her, the knowledge that they would eventually part ways tore at him. He didn't know what to do. What would he do when Tristin called and confirmed that Lilith wasn't a succubus, and that he could go home? Leave the idyllic life that he and Lilith shared? Could he do that? Did he even *want* to leave?

Christian didn't know. He thought about it often, what would happen when the call came. His mind always came up with the same answer, and it never failed to leave him shaken.

He looked at himself in the full-length mirror, more to dispel the thoughts clinging to his mind like winter's chill than to check on his appearance. He wasn't wearing anything too fancy, just a white long-sleeved button-up shirt, a black coat, black dress pants, and a pair of comfortable black shoes. The shoes clashed a bit with the rest of his clothes. They were running shoes. But, having already nearly died once because he was unprepared, Christian felt determined not to make the same mistake twice.

After ensuring that he looked nice, Christian walked to his bed and stared at the weapons laid out on it: his handguns, Gabriel and Phanuel, and two longer-than-average knives, both shining a bright silver under the sunlight streaming in through the window.

After nearly getting killed by a single werewolf, Christian had made sure to keep several weapons hidden somewhere on his person. He wouldn't allow himself to be caught unaware like that again.

He picked up one of the knives and twirled it around in his hand. He really wished he could bring Michael and Raphael with him, but they were too conspicuous. They couldn't be hidden on him like these knives. At least the blades were made of silver. They weren't as strong or effective as his Orichalcum swords, but they still worked against most abominations.

Lifting his left foot and setting it on a nearby chair, he pulled his pant leg up to reveal a holster strapped to his calf. He slid the knife into it, and then repeated the process with the other knife on his other leg. After rolling his pants legs back down, he picked up his guns and slid them into his new holsters.

The holsters strapped across his chest as opposed to his thighs, which meant that his guns were hanging from his back instead of his front. They were a pain to unholster. After years of merely reaching down to unholster his guns, having to reach behind him required conscious thought. He actually practiced unholstering them for two hours each night to ingrain the action into muscle memory.

After securing his weapons to his person, he slid on his jacket, and looked himself over in the mirror again. The last thing he needed was for his weapons to be visible.

Vibrating suddenly erupted from his pocket and music started playing, alerting him to an incoming call. Pulling his phone out, he glanced at the caller ID and grimaced. On the screen was an image of Tristin's grinning face as he held up two fingers in the peace sign. Just how that idiot had managed to put this photo on his phone was beyond Christian, never mind the fact that Tristin somehow made his ringtone "Dirty Deeds" by AC/DC.

Clicking his tongue, Christian accepted the call and held the phone to his ear. He opened his mouth, prepared to demand an explanation as to why this idiot was calling him—

"Hey, hey, hey! How is my favorite cold-blooded killer doing?" The loud, obnoxious voice emerged, cutting off the snappish words that had been on the tip of his tongue.

"Tristin," Christian grunted. "What do you want?"

"What kind of greeting is that? Here I am, calling in to see how my best buddy and partner in crime is doing, and all you can say is 'what do you want?' like I'm some kind of annoyance."

"You are an annoyance."

"You're so cruel! How could you be so mean to this humble intelligence agent, who has done nothing but offer you the most accurate and up-to-date information available?"

Christian gritted his teeth, his aggravation reaching a new peak. He quickly tried to calm down by taking a deep breath, holding it, and then releasing it. It worked, at least a little bit.

"Is there a reason you're calling me, or are you just trying to get on my nerves?"

"Um... a little of both?"

"I'm hanging up now."

"Hold on!" Tristin's voice erupted into a panicked shout.

Christian stared at the phone, and then slowly brought it to his ear again.

"I do have some information for you," Tristin said.

"Does that mean you've discovered whether Lilith is a succubus or not?" Christian didn't know if he wanted an answer. Confirmation would mean leaving, and leaving meant he wouldn't be able to see Lilith anymore. The thought of not seeing her again hurt, even if he didn't want to admit it.

"No, I haven't even had a chance to look into that," Tristin admitted, causing Christian to sigh, though whether in relief or vexation was unknown, even to him. *"The information I have is on the disappearance of those cops."*

"Disappearance of the cops? When did this happen?"

... He was met with several seconds of awkward silence.

"Christian." Tristin's voice was incredulous. *"Are you telling me that you didn't know several cops disappeared after investigating the site of your battle with the werewolf?"*

Christian felt his face grow hot.

"You know that I neither watch nor read the news."

"Right, I forgot. The only thing you're interested in reading are those light novels of yours... Geek."

Christian scowled at the phone.

"Anyway," Tristin continued, *"we have reason to believe that their disappearance was not because of mundane reasons."*

Christian sucked in a breath. He didn't need to be a genius to know what Tristin meant.

"You're saying there's another monster in Seal Beach?"

"Pretty much. I haven't been able to find out much. There are no bodies, no autopsy reports. Just about the only information that I've been able to get is that the disappearances I told you about earlier have all stopped."

"So, basically, what you're telling me is that we know the creature that's been killing across the United States is here, but we don't know what kind of creature it is."

"Essentially." Tristin at least had the decency to sound sheepish.

"Without knowing what I'm up against, there isn't much that I can do." Christian paused long enough to sigh. "I guess there's nothing to it. I'll stay alert on my end. You keep me up to date from yours."

"Of course. You know that I would do anything for my best friend."

Christian twitched.

"Whelp! Now that all this heavy stuff is out of the way, I want to wish you luck on your date. Don't do anything I wouldn't do! Actually, don't do anything I would do either! That'll get you into a lot of trouble with the boss lady! Hehehe, see ya!"

Christian's eyes widened as the phone went dead. He stared at the object in his hand like it was a foreign entity that he'd never seen before, one thought plaguing his mind.

How did Tristin know about my date with Lilith?

***

Anticipation is a killer. There was nothing worse than being stuck waiting. Lilith was finding this out the hard way.

During her time at the preschool, Lilith had been unable to concentrate or focus on anything. Several times during class, she'd been forced out of her daydreaming by one of the children or by Janice, when the woman noticed that she wasn't paying attention. It had actually gotten so bad that Janice had taken over for Lilith and delegated the task of grading the children's artwork to her.

The mindlessness of the task did nothing to ease her anticipation, nor her anxiety. She had actually stopped paying attention to what she was grading and taken to tapping her index finger against the desk, hoping it would somehow help while away the time. It eventually became so bad that Janice had gotten annoyed and, after telling her to stop several times with no success, told her to go home early.

Not that arriving home early changed anything. It just meant that she would be waiting at home instead of at work. At least Maria was there to help her get ready for her date. The instant Lilith arrived home, her friend pushed her into a chair in front of the large vanity mirror in Maria's bedroom.

"You've got such beautiful hair." Maria ran a brush through Lilith's hair, the bristles gliding through silken locks without finding a single knot. "I'm so jealous. I wish my hair was this pretty."

"I don't see why you're jealous." Lilith resisted the urge to shake her head. "You turn more than few heads of your own. To be honest, I'm jealous of how athletic you are. You look so fit."

"You could become just as fit as I am, if you wanted to. The only reason you're not is because you don't want to put in the effort." Maria smiled when Lilith shrugged. "And besides, if you became as athletic as I am, that gorgeous figure of yours might disappear."

"Sometimes I think that would be a blessing." Lilith's response put deserts to shame with its dryness.

"I bet you won't be thinking that tonight," Maria teased in a sing-song voice. When Lilith's face became inflamed with red, Maria laughed in delight.

"Ugh, would you two please shut up," Stacy moaned from within the closet. She emerged seconds later, decked out in full gothic regalia. "I really don't want to hear you two going on like a couple of middle-grade schoolgirls. Also, your date's gonna hate you if you keep doing that."

Lilith tried not to glare at the younger girl. "Doing what?"

"That thing you do with your finger. It's fucking annoying."

Looking down, Lilith saw her right index finger tapping against her knee. Weird. She hadn't even noticed.

Tilting her head back up, she frowned at the younger girl's blazing-eyed reflection in the mirror. She didn't know why, but ever since Christian had walked her home that first night, Stacy had become even more unpleasant. When not outright ignoring her, the goth was giving Lilith the death glare. It was, in all honesty, beginning to get on Lilith's nerves, and was something that she didn't need right now.

"Come on now." Maria gave the goth an amiable smile, even as she artfully twisted Lilith's hair into a style of her choice. "You shouldn't be so grumpy all the time; it'll give you wrinkles."

"Whatever." Stacy's scowl grew even more prominent. "I'm out."

"Have fun!" Maria called as Stacy stormed out of the room. The goth didn't reply. Unless slamming the door shut with a loud *bang!* counted as replying.

"Is it just me, or is she even grumpier than usual?" asked Lilith.

"It's just you."

"… Right…"

***

Christian stood at the door to Lilith's apartment. He was beginning to have second thoughts. He knew that he should knock on the door, knew that Lilith was waiting for his arrival. He had already agreed to this date, and all that was left to do was see it through to the end.

I shouldn't be doing this.

And he shouldn't. He and Lilith were getting too close. *He* was getting too attached. Executioners were never meant to fall in love.

I should just leave and pretend this never happened.

But he couldn't turn back now, could he? Doing so would hurt Lilith, and he couldn't stand the thought of hurting her. The notion churned his insides. He liked her, he enjoyed spending time with her, enjoyed reading with her, enjoyed holding long conversations with her. He just enjoyed being around her. It was far too late to turn back.

Christian knocked on the door.

"Just a minute!"

A blink. He recognized that voice. It was not Lilith. Maria, then. Lilith's roommate, a woman who was far too pleased about his and Lilith's relationship. Christian sometimes thought that Maria was happier about their relationship than Lilith herself.

The door opened. Maria stood in the doorway. Her ear-to-ear grin almost split her face in half. She eyed him once, traveling up, then down, then back up again. When her eyes landed on his, Christian saw how they twinkled like the star on top of a Christmas tree.

"Hello there, handsome," she purred. Christian almost twitched, but quickly mastered himself before he said something that he would regret later. This girl's teasing personality reminded him so much of Tristin that it was almost reflex to snap at her.

"Evening," Christian said.

"You don't sound happy to see me." Maria pouted. Christian almost rolled his eyes. Almost.

"It's not that I am not pleased to see you. I'm merely... anxious, I suppose."

"So even someone as cool and collected as you can feel nervous about something," Maria observed with a casual mien. "How intriguing."

This time Christian couldn't quite contain his eye roll. "Is Lilith ready?"

"She will be in just a minute. Why don't you come inside?"

Maria moved out of the way and beckoned him in. Christian stepped past her into the apartment. He had not actually been inside before, despite walking Lilith home every day since their first time out. While he wasn't exactly sure what he expected the inside of Lilith's residence to look like, he decided that this place was probably pretty standard for three girls living on their own.

Maria turned to face him. "Hold on just a second and let me get Lilith for you."

"Thank you."

Maria walked into a small hallway on his immediate right. Christian absently wiped a small trickle of sweat from his brow. He tried not to let his anxiety get the best of him.

While he waited for Lilith, he studied the room. Pale carpet shifted to white tiles. A couch, coffee table, and television sat in the living room, along with several plants. The kitchenette had a table, long, rectangular in shape. Nothing seemed out of place or eccentric. Christian could imagine three women living here quite easily.

The sound of a door opening and closing alerted Christian to someone entering the room. A soft voice spoke up a second later.

"Christian."

Christian turned, his mouth open and prepared to greet Lilith... when he promptly forgot to breathe, as a creature so ethereally magnificent that she simply couldn't be of this world appeared before him. Her long blond hair had been pulled up, each lock delicately twisted and secured in place by several pins, making the entire style look like an intricately woven tapestry. Several strands looked to have been left purposely lose to frame her face, directing all of his attention to her delicate features, to the light pink lips that were arched in a soft smile.

If it had been just her face that captivated him so, Christian might have been able to resist this angel's beauty, despite his inexperience when it came to dealing with matters of the heart. However, the gown she had chosen for that night was almost as incredible as the one wearing it. Or maybe it was simply the young woman wearing it that made the dress look out of this world.

She wore a light blue chiffon dress that matched her eyes. There were no sleeves, just a simple strap that looped through the dress proper and went around her neck. A triangle-shaped cut-out appeared on her bust as the left strap crossed over to the right. It had a hemline that dipped low in the back and rose in the front, showing where the fabric split and crossed over. A simple band the same color as the dress held it together and showed off Lilith's amazing figure. The ensemble was topped off with a pair of silver gladiator sandals that looked like someone had set diamonds into the straps.

"Oh... oh, wow..."

Lilith blushed at the barely whispered words. A hint of pink rose to her cheeks.

Stepping out from behind her was a grinning Maria.

"See?" she proclaimed, pointing at Christian with her right index finger. "I told you this outfit would knock him dead. I think you actually broke him."

Christian shook himself from his stupor long enough to glare at Maria.

"I am not broken," he informed her, almost scowling. "I just..." he trailed off, becoming speechless as his gaze once more landed on Lilith.

"Please stop staring. It's embarrassing," Lilith whispered. Christian shuddered at the delicate sound of her voice, even as he wondered how someone's voice could both soothe and torment him as hers did.

Taking a deep breath, Christian tried to calm himself. He tried telling himself that this was just Lilith, and that it didn't matter how gorgeous she was. He also told himself that this would be no different from the other times they had gone out together. It didn't work out as well as he'd hoped.

Christian sought Lilith's baby-blues, and he gave her an apologetic smile. "I'm sorry. I guess I lost myself for a second there. It's just that you look so... so..."

Maria's grin was like a cat that had been given a bowl of fresh cream. "Beautiful? Stunning? Incredible? Sexy enough to eat?"

Christian gave Maria a blank stare, "First off, I don't think something can be sexy enough to eat. Second"—he looked back at Lilith— "I'm not sure any of those words are an apt description."

"Then what would you use?"

"How about ..." Christian struggled to find the words that could properly describe Lilith. In the end, he could only think of one line from a book that he'd read—his second light novel. "She looks so ethereally beautiful that every angel in heaven must be turning green with envy."

"Wow." Maria looked suitably impressed. "That wasn't too shabby. Did you come up with that all on your own?"

"No," Christian admitted, only feeling mildly sheepish when Maria gave him a flat look. "I read it in a book."

"*A Goddess Falls to Earth.*" Lilith's face wore a soft smile. As Christian offered her a smile of his own, Maria looked back and forth between the two.

A moment later, she sighed. "You two really are a match made in heaven."

Christian and Lilith both blushed bright red. They looked at each other, and then looked away just as quickly.

From the way she was grinning, Christian had a feeling that Maria was never going to let Lilith live this down.

Interlude 4

The sun had long since disappeared behind the horizon. Night had fallen on Seal Beach.

Sitting on a train taking her home, the seventeen-year-old runaway stewed in anger. This night had been horrible.

After leaving her apartment, she had gone to Up Lounge for her shift, only to find that the manager had discovered that she had used a fake ID and falsified documents to work under an assumed name. He hadn't sold her out, but he did tell her that because she was a liability, he couldn't afford to keep her. She'd then been summarily fired.

Without a job and nothing to do but drown herself in a pity party of such epic proportions that emos everywhere would have shed tears, Stacy had gone to the nearest bar and convinced the first man she met to buy her some alcohol. It had been ridiculously easy. Even if she wasn't fit like Maria or a sex bomb like Lilith, she was still quite the catch, and a little skin on her part had gone a long way.

She didn't know how many drinks she had consumed, but it had been enough that she almost blacked out. Actually, she was pretty sure she had blacked out. There was a gap in her memory. Or at least she thought it was a gap. Stacy couldn't be sure of anything at the moment. Her head was still spinning.

At some point in between the time that she started drinking and now, she must have left the man and gotten on the train. She didn't remember leaving. Nor did she remember getting on the train. It was strange, but she didn't let it bother her too much. With the amount of alcohol in her system, complex thought processes were a little beyond her.

"Attention, all passengers. The train has now arrived at Seal Beach station. For those of you getting off, please be careful when stepping out of the train. Thank you, and have a great night."

The announcement from the overhead speakers blared obnoxiously loud in Stacy's ears. She groaned, holding her head as she rose to her feet.

She exited the train, nearly tripping when her left foot hit the lip of the walkway. Cursing and grumbling after she finally managed to find purchase, Stacy stumbled out of the train station and onto the city streets.

The nighttime air hit her like icy stakes. The cold seeped into her skin. She wrapped her arms around herself, a feeble attempt at keeping warm. Maybe putting on just her black lace bodice, a black skirt, and stockings hadn't been such a good idea after all.

She stumbled through the darkened streets, passing only an occasional street lamp. A shadow fell over her. Stacy barely noticed it.

At least, not until a hand wrapped around her throat from behind.

She felt her breath leave her as that hand pulled her into an alley.

She felt her back hit a wall.

She felt panic as her breath was driven from her lungs.

Felt sharp fangs sink into her jugular.

After that, Stacy Moon felt nothing at all.

Chapter 19

Lilith couldn't wipe the silly little grin off her face when she woke up the next morning and got ready for work. She felt like she was gliding on air. There was a vibrancy within her that hadn't been there before, a glow about her that had not existed until now. Other people noticed this glow as well.

"You're in an awfully chipper mood this morning." Lilith stopped humming and looked up from the paper that she was grading.

"Oh, hi, Janice," she said, a curious look replacing her smile. "What do you mean chipper? I'm always like this."

"Oh, I don't think so." The older woman's eyes twinkled, and her smile was that of a sly fox about to play a prank. "I'm guessing that date of yours went well?"

Like a single ray of light penetrating the clouds of a massive thunderstorm, Lilith's face broke out into a smile. Last night, she and Christian went on their first date, and it had been everything that she could have ever hoped a date would be. Christian had been a little awkward—she got the feeling that he wasn't used to these kinds of situations—but he was also a perfect gentleman. He treated her with respect and dignity, never tried pushing her into doing something that she didn't want to do, and made no attempt to take advantage of her. This was in spite of the fact that he obviously found her attractive, judging from the way he had been staring at her the whole time.

A stray thought occurred to her. Whenever men stared at her, Lilith always felt a deep sense of fear and loathing. She felt dirty, unclean, and tainted, as if a layer of filth and grease covered her body. Yet when Christian had stared at her last night, she had felt attractive and warm and wanted and, well, sexy. In spite of her looks, Lilith had never felt like that before. Ever.

But why? she wondered. Why did she feel like this when Christian looked at her, but not when other men looked at her? Did it have something to do with Christian? Because he wasn't affected by her? Or did it have something to do with her? Because something about him affected her?

These questions and more passed through her head. Stray thoughts with no answers. There was no way for her to know the answers to these questions. It wasn't like a manual on romance existed, and as much as she loved reading light novels, she knew they did not have the answers she sought either.

Fiction never was good for solving life's problems.

"Hello… Earth to Lilith. Come in, Lilith."

"Oh!" Lilith shook herself from her stupor and tossed Janice an apologetic smile. "I'm sorry. You were saying something?"

Janice shook her head, the smile on her face growing wider. "Ah, to be young and in love again."

Lilith felt the blush appear, tiny spots of warmth on her cheeks. She didn't deny Janice's assumption, however, which she supposed was an improvement from the last few times that *someone*—Maria—had mentioned that she was in love.

"Ms. Lilith!" one of the children called out. "Can you help me find the wight color for my dwawing?"

"I'll be right there, Alex." Lilith looked at Janice, who made a shooing motion. Nodding, she stood up, and made her way over to where Alex sat, making a mess of the table with several markers.

The class assignment that day was creating artwork they could take home. All the children sat at the round tables spread around the room. Most were busy concentrating on their work, either scribbling over a sheet of paper, or using a pair of safety scissors to cut out shapes. As Lilith knelt down next to Alex and helped him choose a color for his drawing, she wondered how many of these boys would be giving her proposals of love and marriage that day.

I'm afraid all these boys are bound for heartbreak. The thought filtered through her mind, making her smile. *And for some reason, that doesn't bother me.*

***

As it turned out, by the end of class Lilith received no less than five proposals of love and ten of marriage. She hadn't broken her highest record of ten and ten, but she honestly felt like that was a good thing. These crushes may have just been the passing phase of young children, but she didn't want them to get their hopes up, and then have those same hopes crushed.

Once all the children left, Lilith tidied up the room. Because the children were, well, *children*, they left a big mess whenever they did arts and crafts. Cut up paper lay scattered about the floor, and several marker spots marred the tables. While she cleaned, Lilith's thoughts turned toward Christian.

It hadn't been that long since their first disastrous meeting, and yet, within just a little over a week, he had become one of the most important people in her life. She could no longer imagine a day where they did not sit down in The Crema Café and talk, or sit under the shade tree and read together. The idea of him possibly leaving her was something that she could no longer fathom.

Considering that Christian was a man, and she *still* feared men, that really said something about how special the enigmatic male was. Only someone truly special could invoke this kind of feeling within her, despite how she feared every other member of the same sex.

As she cleaned off a particularly stubborn mark on the table, Lilith thought about everything she knew about Christian who had, dare she say it, claimed her heart. Truth be told, it wasn't much. She knew very little about Christian's past. She didn't know what his job was or even where he came from.

Lilith had the distinct feeling that Christian was hiding things from her. Whenever she asked about what he did for a living, or anything relating to his past, he would become uncomfortable and clam up. She didn't want to lose him because she was nosy, so she often changed the subject when this happened, but she still desired to know more about him.

She did know a few things, though. He wasn't completely closed off to her. Christian had told her about how he had been orphaned at the age of six, when a large fire ravaged the small town that he lived in. He'd shared how he had been saved by members of the Catholic Church and raised in a Catholic orphanage.

That explained why Christian was such a devout follower of the Catholic faith. If there was one thing that she had learned about him, it was that despite not always acting like it, Christian was a faithful Catholic. He believed wholly in the existence of God, even if his beliefs in the Bible were a little flexible.

Lilith didn't know how to feel about that part of him. She wasn't religious, but she supposed it was his right to believe in whatever he wanted, and it wasn't like she couldn't understand why he believed in God. If the Church had saved her like they had Christian, then she might well have been religious, too.

The door to her classroom clicked open. The sound startled Lilith from her contemplation.

Janice stood in the doorway. "Your young man is here," she said.

"All right," she said. "Please tell him that I'll be out soon. I just need to finish cleaning this room."

"How about I clean the room, while you go out and tend to your man? You know that men get awfully needy if you're not constantly there to look after them." Lilith opened her mouth to protest, but Janice cut her off. "I'll be fine finishing up here. You should go and enjoy your time with your beau. You're only young once, you know."

"Thank you." Lilith smiled warmly at Janice, then went to her desk and grabbed her bag. A short walk down the hall took her to the preschool's entrance, where she found Christian waiting for her.

He looked the same as always. A pair of blue jeans rode comfortably on his hips. The dark-blue long-sleeved shirt that he wore was hidden by the black leather jacket that he had taken to wearing. She wondered why he wore something like that with such warm weather, but figured it was just some kind of fashion statement. Surprising, since she knew that Christian didn't know a thing about fashion.

"Christian." As she called his name, Christian turned around. He smiled at her, but she immediately noticed how strained it appeared, as if he was simply smiling for her sake. She slowed to a stop as she reached him, and gazed at him in concern. "Are you okay?"

"Yes, I'm fine. Just thinking about... things."

Christian's answer didn't convince her, but she knew him well enough by now to know that he would clam up faster than she could say his name if she pressed too hard.

"So are you all ready to go?" he asked, no doubt his attempt at changing the subject.

"Yes."

Her arms wove around his right arm and clutched it close to her chest. It was strange how, not even a month ago, Lilith would have laughed if someone told her that she would enjoy being this close, this *physical* with a man. Now she could barely imagine life without this closeness that she and Christian shared.

Christian shifted again, but didn't make any attempts at forcing her to desist in her actions. He relaxed in her grip, and his smile became more genuine. Good. Lilith didn't like his fake smiles.

"All right then," he said. "Let's go."

***

As had become their custom, they took a leisurely walk to The Crema Café. The place was bustling with activity. A cacophony of voices rose over the din as dozens of different conversations took place. More than half the tables were full, as both tourists and locals sat down with friends and family and spoke of the usual topics.

Christian and Lilith stood in line, waiting for their turn to place their orders. Lilith's arms were still wrapped around Christian's right arm, but now her head also rested on his shoulder. She appeared so content, so happy, that Christian didn't have the heart to tell her how uncomfortable her close proximity made him.

He peered down at Lilith, her face alight with a content smile. She appeared oblivious to everything around her. She didn't even notice how every man in the room stared at her. She didn't even notice when one passing man tried to cop a feel, though Christian did, and that man nearly suffered a broken hand when he grabbed it and squeezed.

"What was that noise?" Lilith asked.

"What noise?" Christian played innocent. Lilith's face scrunched up in confusion.

"I'm not sure. It sounded kind of like someone was screaming."

"Well, it is pretty noisy in here."

"I... I guess it is," Lilith murmured as her eyes peered around the room. Christian felt guilty when he saw the uncomfortable look on her face, the way her body almost unconsciously moved closer to him, as if doing so would protect her from the leering eyes of men.

"Don't worry." Christian pulled his arm from her grip and wrapped it around her shoulder, drawing her close. He ignored his own feelings, the ones screaming about how wrong this was, and instead focused on comforting Lilith. "I won't let anything happen to you."

"I know."

Lilith snuggled into their new position, and Christian knew that she had forgotten about the stares. Mission accomplished.

Their turn soon arrived, and they stepped up to the register. Auntie Kay smiled at them, her eyes almost glowing when she saw Lilith.

"What'll you two have?"

"I'll have the Crema burger and a small iced tea, please, and Lilith will have the Bananas Foster crepes," Christian ordered without thinking. Auntie Kay's lips twitched.

"Look at you, young man. You've only known Lilith for a week and already know what her favorite food is."

Christian looked away. "W-well, it's not hard. She orders the same thing every time."

"I do not," Lilith muttered, then squirmed in Christian's grasp when both he and Auntie Kay stared at her. "... Okay, so maybe I do. In my defense, the Bananas Foster crepes are the best."

"Right."

"They are!"

"And I believe you."

"Are you making fun of me?"

"Of course not." Christian's gentle smile made Lilith bury her face in his shoulder.

"You'd better not be," her muffled voice said.

Aunty Kay chuckled as she rang them up. After ringing sliding Christian's credit card through the card reader, she said. "Your order will probably take a little while. Just find yourself a seat, and I'll have someone bring your food to you."

"Thank you," they said in unison.

They walked out of the line and made room for the next customer. After looking for a place to sit, they eventually decided on an empty table near the entrance. Christian directed Lilith toward a chair, pulling it out for her. The smile she bestowed on him made him feel like a million hummingbirds had taken up residence inside of him. He didn't much care for the feeling, so he ignored it.

Conversation was sparse as they waited for their food, which didn't take long to arrive. Upon receiving their meal to-go, they stood up and quickly left the café.

As they were leaving, Christian stopped and turned to look back at the bustling bakery. He frowned when he saw something on the roof. The shadows seemed to waver, almost like … but no, it must be the clouds blocking the sun overhead.

"Is something wrong?" Lilith asked.

"No," Christian said at last. "Nothing's wrong."

While strolling to their destination, they made conversation. Despite having spoken with each other every day since Maria's fateful decision to push Lilith in Christian's direction, they had yet to run out of topics to discuss. Today, they spoke of the differences between tropes used in Japanese stories and those used in American stories.

As the day wore on, the budding couple found themselves sitting under what Lilith had jokingly referred to as *their tree*. It was the same one where Christian had reimbursed her for breakfast, the same one they sat under during their first day out together. No novel was situated between them this time. Lilith leaned against Christian, her head on his shoulder, her eyes closed, and a content smile playing on her lips. Even though Christian knew it was wrong, he didn't stop her. Maybe he couldn't stop her. Or perhaps he just didn't want to stop her.

"Christian?" she murmured.

"Yes?"

"Could you tell me a little about yourself? I know so very little about you. I'd really like to know more."

Christian remained silent for several moments. When he did speak, his voice was much softer than usual.

"I think I already told you about how I was orphaned when a fire destroyed my hometown, and that I had been taken to live in an orphanage owned by the Catholic Church." Lilith nodded against his shoulder, and Christian gathered his thoughts before continuing. "Life at the orphanage was hard. There wasn't a lot of room, and so ten or more of us would often have to sleep in a room that was meant for five. Our mornings were spent praying, and the rest of the day was usually spent doing chores. I guess they wanted to teach us responsibility."

Lilith scooted closer to Christian until her arms wrapped around his torso. He stiffened as his mind and body were bombarded with so many sensations and emotions that he didn't know what to do with them. After a moment, however, he relaxed into her embrace, as a strange warmth engulfed him, starting from his chest and spreading to the rest of his body.

"It must have been tough," Lilith murmured.

Almost without thinking about it, Christian closed his eyes and rested his cheek against the crown of Lilith's head. The scent of vanilla ticked his nose, overwhelming his senses. He'd always loved this particular scent. It reminded him of home, of safety and security, of when his mother used to bake vanilla brownies and then scold him when he tried eating one before dinner. Some small part of him longed for those simpler times.

"It was, but I think I turned out better for it. It taught me the meaning of hard work, and I learned how to take care of myself."

Christian paused again, this time in confusion. What was he doing? Why was he telling her so much about himself? Why was he sharing his past with her? He didn't understand how this young woman, who he should have never gotten so close to, could pry this much information out of him. Not even Samantha could make him talk about his past, but all Lilith needed to do was ask and he felt like spilling some of his darkest secrets. It was maddening.

"That's not to say we didn't have problems," he added after a moment. "Not every child who lived there subscribed to the teachings of the Church, and not all of those children were benevolent."

That was an understatement if he ever heard one. Children as a whole were greedy and selfish. It was part of being a kid. They never thought about how much their next meal cost, or how expensive that blanket was. They wanted what they wanted and didn't think about what others went through to get them that favorite toy or buy that expensive new play set.

This wasn't a slight against children, just a natural part of their maturation. He'd been no different. Christian didn't learn about how difficult their caretakers truly had it until he'd grown older and more mature.

"Were you bullied?" Lilith asked.

"I wasn't, but my… my friend was." Christian grimaced. Much as he didn't want to admit that he and Tristin were friends, he really had to. The slightly older man had stuck with him through thick and thin, in spite of Christian's many attempts at pushing him away. "He wasn't very well-liked because he was different."

"Different how?"

"I'm not sure, to be honest," Christian admitted. "Tristin has always been a bit of an oddball. It isn't just in the way he acts. When you're with him, you just feel like there's something off about him. I always feel like he's hiding some great secret that he's not sharing with anyone. Anyway, because he wasn't liked very much by the other kids for being different, they would often pick on him."

"And you were the one who stood up for him." It wasn't a question.

"Yes, I stuck up for him." Christian's eyes had closed by this point. His body was beginning to feel heavy for some reason. "Even if he hadn't been my friend, I would have still stuck up for him, I think. It's hard to say, but I never liked it when people picked on others just because they were different."

"So what happened? To those boys, I mean, and you. Did you get in trouble?"

"I did get reprimanded, at least at first."

"At first?"

"Mmm. Because the fight was in the defense of someone else I got off with a warning. The other boys didn't. I remember they were given kitchen duty, and one of them, the oldest boy who lived in the orphanage, was kicked out when the nuns tried to make him work and he cursed them out… at least, that's what I had heard," Christian added, almost as an afterthought. "I wasn't there when it happened."

"Oh."

Silence reigned as the conversation came to a halt. It was a comfortable silence, nothing at all like the awkward and stifling stillness that had been prevalent during their first day out together.

Lilith was sitting perpendicular to him, her legs resting over his lap. Her arms around his waist had gone slack. Deep breaths escaped her parted lips, and her shoulders and chest rose and fell in time with her breathing.

She was asleep.

Christian's eyes opened and he looked down at her radiant blond hair. He knew that he should extricate himself from this position. She was too close, getting too physical. This was the kind of intimacy that the Church had forbidden Executioners from having.

But he couldn't bring himself to make her get off him. Or maybe he just didn't want to. His mind felt fuzzy, as if a fog had filtered into his head, addling his mind and dulling his senses. All he wanted to do right then was pull Lilith into his arms, hold her tight, and fall asleep.

Green and red eyes slowly slid shut. Christian's breathing evened out, and his body relaxed. Out of instinct, or perhaps need, his left hand sought out Lilith's, and he laced their fingers together.

As Lilith's hand unconsciously tightened around his, Christian fell asleep, his mind growing dead to the world around him.

***

Darkness had descended upon Seal Beach as Christian and Lilith walked up the stairs and stopped in front of the door to her apartment. Her blond hair shifted over her shoulder as she turned to face him. Blue eyes sought his with an unwavering gaze.

She smiled at him, and Christian felt his heart stop. He then felt it speed up far beyond what could be considered normal while at rest. A hummingbird had replaced his heart, and it was beating against his ribcage at a hundred miles per minute.

"Christian." Lilith's voice, soft and angelic as always, made his attention focus completely on her.

"Yes?"

"I want you to know that I've been having a really great time with you these past few days." A pair of small, delicate hands reached for his, clasping them in a surprisingly firm grip. He had never noticed it before, but her hands were tiny compared to his own. And as they slid into his, he couldn't help but marvel at how they felt, as if his calloused digits were being caressed by the softest silk.

He searched her face. Lilith's smooth, unblemished skin truly was flawless. Her eyes, large and innocent, were enchanting, vibrant irises of the purest blue. Even her nose, that cute little button nose, was breathtakingly attractive in ways that a nose simply shouldn't be.

"I know this seems strange, but despite how we haven't known each other for very long, I feel like I've known you my whole life. Like a part of me has always known you, and was simply waiting for you to arrive in my life."

His eyes strayed to her lips. They were moist and pink. As he took in the sight of those perfectly shaped lips, his mind conjured images that he would have never thought of before meeting this woman.

My arms wrap tightly around her body, pulling her against me. Despite both of us being clothed, I can feel her against me. The contours of her hips, the feel of her flat stomach, the swell of her bosom as it presses against my chest. All of this I can feel, and it nearly brings me to delirium.

Her eyes, which had been staring into mine, slowly flutter shut as she tilts her head upward. Her lips part. She's waiting, waiting for me to make the next move.

Slowly, I lean my head down...

"Christian?" a voice called to him. "Christian?"

"Huh? W-what?"

Blinking several times caused the images to vanish. Lilith still stood in front of him, looking expectant.

"Are you okay? You were staring off into space?"

When he didn't speak, she worried her lip.

He shook his head, opened his mouth, closed it, and then opened it again.

"I… I have to go. I'll see you tomorrow, okay?" Without even waiting for Lilith to respond, Christian walked down the stairs and onto the street.

"C-Christian? Wait!" He heard her call out to him, but Christian didn't wait. His walk became a run. Even as his mind yelled at him for being a coward, he ran. Even as his heart felt like it was being stretched the farther he got from Lilith, he ran.

What's wrong with me?

There had to be something wrong with him. That was the only explanation that he could come up with. These thoughts, these feelings, these desires. They couldn't possibly be his.

For a moment, he wondered if perhaps these strange urges and feelings were being caused by Lilith. Maybe she really was a succubus in disguise.

He dismissed the thought a second later. There was no way Lilith could be a succubus. She had no aura, and she still feared men. Any man that was not him, at least. He should know, as she had used him as a shield more than enough times when they were together.

So then, all these thoughts, all these feelings, did that mean they were his? But how could he feel this way about someone, about *anyone*? He had never wanted someone like this before. Never felt this kind of desire for someone else before. His body craved Lilith's touch, it wanted to feel her body pressing against it, to feel her lips on his own. It was frightening, how much he desired her. It also disgusted him.

Lilith already had enough men lusting after her. Everywhere she went they ogled her, stripped her bare with their eyes. Some even tried to take advantage of her, not content to stare at a distance. More than a few men had been on the receiving end of his fists this past week.

He was supposed to be different. She trusted him. She felt safe around him. She had told him so during their second day out together.

It was sickening. He was such a hypocrite. Even though he was supposed to be different from those other guys, he was just like them.

Winded from running so far and for so long, Christian leaned his back against the nearest building, and slumped to the ground. His teeth were clenched as his chest heaved, and tears of frustration threatened to leak from his eyes.

Guilt set in. What was he supposed to do now? How could he face Lilith again when he felt all these desires and urges welling up inside of him?

He couldn't. The thought of facing her like this, of seeing her with these disgusting and amoral thoughts running through him was abhorrent. He couldn't face her again now that his mind and body were beginning to betray him.

These thoughts of guilt and remorse were interrupted by footsteps. Moving at a slow, measured pace, the sound of booted feet thudding against concrete made Christian's ears twitch. Each step became louder than the next. They were coming closer.

Christian looked up as a shadow covered him. Silhouetted against the light from a nearby lamp post stood a figure clad in a dark-red cloak. The face was hidden by a cowl that created a layer of darkness that couldn't be penetrated by the eyesight of a simple human.

That cloak…

Christian only had enough time for his eyes to widen in recognition before the figure's left hand shot out, and five thin strands of wire glinting in the light of the moon were launched toward him at incredible speed.

Chapter 20

Upon seeing the thin metallic strands flying toward him at near-blinding speed, Christian reacted with reflexes honed by years of training and life-and-death combat. His body moved long before his mind could catch up to the events happening around him. Using both his hands and feet, he pushed off the ground and wall, and tucked his body into a roll.

The wires came into contact with the surrounding surfaces he had been resting against seconds later. Belying their thin size, each wire left a deep, long furrow in the wall, showing that these weapons were not just unique, but also impossibly sharp.

"Who are you?!" Christian demanded, his glare set firmly on the person before him. All thoughts of Lilith and his own self-loathing were pushed aside. He couldn't afford distractions.

The figure—man, woman, he didn't know but decided to simply say his attacker was male for convenience' sake—attacked him again. The right hand made a gesture that caused the wires to shoot straight at him like bullets fired from a gun. Christian leapt backward to avoid being eviscerated by the thin wires. He slid along the ground, coming to a stop several meters away.

"I recognize that cloak. You're a member of the Assassins. Why are you doing this?" Christian's demand went unanswered as his attacker came at him again. As thin wires were launched at him once more. Christian skillfully dodged each attack. His hands twitched toward his guns, hidden within his coat, but he didn't take them out. Not yet. He still didn't know what was going on.

Christian was so busy focusing on dodging the obvious attacks, that he never saw the one coming in from his blind side until it was too late.

Pain erupted from his back as something hard and sharp struck him. His body rolled forward, traveling with the strike to help mitigate the damage. It allowed him to avoid being bifurcated, but the attack still tore into his back, which stung as the cool night air hit it. He felt warm blood leaking down his skin, and knew that he'd only survived because his Orichalcum guns blocked most of the attack.

He jumped back to his feet and ran to the left, circling the person before him. His guns finally came out as he realized that talking to his attacker wasn't going to work. Now was not the time for hesitation.

Gunshots rang out, sounding obnoxiously loud in the stillness of the night. Christian winced as the noise pierced his eardrums. There was no way people hadn't heard that, but it was too late to stop now. All he could do was keep firing and hope that he killed this new enemy before someone came to investigate.

Reacting in an amazing display of swiftness, precision, and dexterity, the cloaked figure raised his hands and manipulated his fingers. The moment the gunfire sounded out, nine wires appeared in front of him, moving so fast they appeared as flashes of light. The wires moved faster and faster until the flashes converged into a seemingly solid form that took on the shape of an oval. Less than a tenth of a second later, the bullets slammed into the shield of fast moving wires and were sliced to pieces.

Christian's eyes widened. Now that he had a small moment to catch his breath, he could clearly see the weapons his enemy was using. They were a pair of gloves, one black with silver veins running along its surface, and the other silver with black veins. Attached to each finger were a set of strings, and on the back of each hand was the crucifix of the Catholic Church, with the number *XIII* embedded in the center.

He recognized those weapons. Among the Executioners, there were thirteen members who, due to the distinction of their service, had received personalized weapons designed to suit the wielder's personality and style. Handguns and swords were his. These gloves belonged to another—Anthony Trekovski.

They were called Uriel and Barachiel. Like his own weapons, those gloves were made of Orichalcum. The wires were not only indestructible, but also sharp enough to cut through any substance known to man, including diamond. Only another object made of Orichalcum could withstand their bite.

Christian's bullets were made of silver and steel.

God would surely forgive the expletives that he released, given his circumstances.

"Is that you, Anthony?" When the man didn't respond to his question, Christian lost his patience. "Answer me, dammit!"

His answer came in the form of nine wires flying at him. Christian moved, his feet taking him backward. He zigzagged back and forth across the alley, dodging razor-sharp wires as the red-clad figure manipulated them to attack. Those wires he couldn't dodge were knocked aside by his guns.

A wire came in for his head, threatening to slice the top half of his cranium clean off. At the same time, four more wires came in from either side in a pincer maneuver. Another two shot straight at his chest in an attempt to pierce his heart. While he couldn't see them, Christian was almost positive that there would be at least another two coming in behind him. That was nine. This meant there was one more wire hidden in the wings. Would it come from below or above?

Acting with the kind of speed born from adrenaline and desperation, Christian reacted to the threats coming in from all sides. He leaned back to avoid the first wire that whizzed by a little less than a centimeter from his nose, close enough that he could feel the tip grazing against his skin and slicing through the outermost epidermal layer. Almost immediately after he dodged the blow, he twisted his body, turning it in a full rotation. His arms extended as he spun, knocking away the four wires coming in from his sides. The two that threatened to stab him in the chest were dodged when his body rotated enough that he presented a profile view to his enemy. The gun in his left hand, Gabriel, came up and swatted the wires away for good measure. Meanwhile, Phanuel lashed out and smacked the wires that tried piercing him from behind.

It was in that moment, just as he finished dealing with the last wire, that the one his enemy had hidden came into play. The ground in front of Christian split, a thin crack appearing as a wire emerged from the ground. Christian had no idea how this person garbed as an Assassin managed to hide his weapon underground like that, but he didn't bother asking questions, or trying to come up with answers. He merely reacted.

Gabriel slid back into its holster and a second later his knife was sliding out of its sheath. The knife was made of silver, not Orichalcum. It could not stand up to the wire. That was okay. It didn't need to. While Phanuel struck the wire and knocked it aside, Christian threw the knife at the red-cloaked figure with unerring accuracy.

Christian observed how the Assassin manipulated his fingers to bring forth the wire shield that had protected them from his gunfire. Even as the dagger was sliced apart as if they were made of soggy paper, he couldn't help but admire the complexity of the maneuver. He could only imagine how dexterous someone's fingers needed to be to use such a move.

He tried to escape, but a yank on his arm that made him stumble forced Christian to look down at his gun. Wrapped around the barrel was the wire that he thought he had knocked away. It appeared his enemy had been prepared for him to try using a distraction in order to escape, and responded accordingly. While he had thrown the knife, the figure had manipulated this last wire into wrapping around his gun while he'd been distracted by the shield. Ingenious.

Not ready to give up just because he had been outmaneuvered, Christian pulled on the arm holding Phanuel, hoping to yank the other figure off balance. If this person was who Christian thought he was, then his strength should be the greater of the two. Assassins were not the most physically able, which was why they were sent to kill creatures that relied on illusions and deception instead of martial combat. He should be able to easily overpower this person in terms of strength.

He was not.

Mouth dropping as the figure before him didn't budge an inch, Christian let out a loud yelp of astonishment when the cloaked figure yanked back. The force and strength of the pull was such that Christian couldn't maintain a firm stance. He was yanked forward and thrown off balance. Eight of the nine wires not attached to Phanuel were then launched at him in a straight-forward, frontal assault. This person obviously thought they had finished him, but Christian wasn't ready to concede defeat.

Rather than allowing himself to be pulled along, Christian rushed toward his adversary, regaining his balance by shoulder rolling along the ground and kipping up to his feet. He quickly moved past the wires, which were manipulated to curve around and pierce him from behind. He could tell from the way the Assassin's fingers moved.

Christian had already noticed several weaknesses in his adversary's fighting style. One of them was that they could only control the strings via the tips of the wires. They couldn't move the rest. Or they could, but doing so ran the risk of causing their own weapons to get tangled up in each other. They probably *could* make the wires move more freely, but that would likely require them to use only two or three.

This person was using nine.

Christian's body moved faster than it ever had before, as he forced the muscles in his legs to work overtime. Faster. Faster. He picked up more speed. His muscles strained and still he moved faster. His legs felt like they were going to tear and he moved faster still. His breathing came out in sharp, pained gasps.

And still he continued increasing his speed.

Then he was there, right in front of his enemy. He still couldn't see the upper portion of their face, just the lower. Their jaw was strangely delicate for a male's, and their mouth was set in a grim, emotionless line.

Time to change that.

Reaching behind him, Christian pulled out a flashbang. He pressed the small button on the top, and shoved it directly into the figure's cowled face.

And then Christian was moving past him. His body sliding along to the right, gliding across the ground. His now free hand dug into his coat. He pulled out Gabriel and pulled the trigger, firing half a dozen bullets. The bullets didn't penetrate flesh. The wires arrived and made that shield again.

That was fine, so long as they didn't destroy the flashbang.

A second later Christian ran out of the alley. A second after that, the flashbang went off, lighting the entire alley with the brilliance of a sun. A loud cry like the yowling of a vengeful spirit then emerged from that same alley. Christian felt a grim smile tug at his lips.

He ran down the street. All around him, he could see lights turning on and hear shouting from nearby buildings. He didn't know what they were saying, but he could imagine the topic.

His ears picked up another sound, too. *Sirens.* Someone must have called the police, who were now coming to investigate.

This isn't good.

He couldn't afford to get caught, and he couldn't let his enemy get caught. Not by the police. There was no telling what kinds of chaos that would unleash.

He ducked into another alley, his feet splashing through a puddle. Christian ran swiftly to his apartment. If he could just reach his apartment, then he could grab his swords, and deal with this new threat.

Several times, he was forced to double back as cop cars sped down the street, sirens blaring. It looked like they had brought out the entire police force. Judging from the way they were circling the area, Christian determined that they had not caught the figure who'd attacked him.

That was fortunate. The police were used to dealing with mundane problems, not ones of a supernatural nature. What's more, the police force of Seal Beach was one of the least experienced in California because of the lack of real crime in their city.

Seconds later, an explosion rent the air. Christian's head snapped to his left, where a large plume of fire and smoke rose above a building, the sight and sound bringing up distant memories that he wished to forget. The direction of the sirens changed as all the cop cars converged on that location.

He felt like swearing. One of the police cruisers must have run afoul of the red-cloaked figure and been destroyed. That explosion was probably from their car getting sliced apart and the fuel ignited by sparks that were emitted when the wires struck the engine.

This was not good. It would be a slaughter. The police stood no chance against that Assassin, regardless of whether he was or wasn't who Christian assumed him to be.

But he couldn't do anything about that. His guns were ineffective against Uriel and Barachiel unless he had Orichalcum bullets, which were in his hotel room. His only hope to beat this person was to reach his apartment and grab his swords and ammo.

The only silver lining that came from the police running into his enemy was that they had delayed the figure long enough for Christian to arrive at his hotel.

He didn't bother using the ladder this time. He ran straight up the tree near his window, as if he was defying gravity. He jumped off the trunk and latched onto the nearest branch, which he then used to swing himself like an acrobat to the next one. He grabbed that branch, flipping around until he landed on top of it, then proceeded to jump off that branch and ascended to the next one and then the next one, until he reached his room.

Upon leaping through the window, he hurried over to his bed, pulled out his swords and sheaths, and then strapped them on. Afterward, he exited the room the same way that he had entered, hitting the ground and rolling forward before bursting to his feet in an all-out sprint.

More explosions sounded out like the rumbling thunder in the distance. The sky lit up multiple times as police cars blew apart one after the other. Christian could see the smoke and flames rising in the distance.

He said a prayer for those officers who had been killed. He hoped that they and God would forgive him for not being able to save them, for once more committing the sin of living while others around him died.

It wouldn't be long before his adversary caught on to his trail. He needed to find a place for the upcoming battle. The park where he'd fought the werewolf was out of the question. There were too many trees, and the playset would put him at a disadvantage. The Assassin wielding Uriel and Barachiel was good. He had no doubt his adversary would be able to use those weapons to their fullest in a place littered with obstacles that could be sliced and thrown at him.

He needed a more open space. He did know of a place, a soccer field near Lilith's apartment complex. It was about the size of a football field and had no trees or obstacles that could be used against him. The terrain was also mostly flat, which would give him the advantage by allowing him a wider range of motion.

He didn't want to use the soccer field, though, because it was so close to Lilith's apartment. Christian didn't know how long this guy had been stalking him, but it must have at least been since he and Lilith had left The Crema Café. That meant this unknown enemy knew about her. The last thing that he wanted was for her to get hurt because someone seeking his life used her as a shield.

But Christian also knew he didn't have a choice. If he wanted to defeat this mystery Assassin, that soccer field was the only viable option, the only battlefield in which he held the advantage.

And so he ran to the soccer field, arriving in record time despite the ache in his back. The wound didn't sting as it had when he first received it. Those nanomachines from the cream Dr. Adams had smeared on him must have still been working, though they should have disintegrated by now. Odd though it was, he was grateful to know that he wouldn't be passing out from blood loss mid-battle.

Several minutes after his arrival, his enemy showed up. With that red cloak fluttering about him, the man using Uriel and Barachiel raced down the soccer field from the opposite direction. In response, Christian slowed his breathing and relaxed his body. This fight wouldn't be like the one he had with the werewolf. While a decent fighter, that creature had been easily dealt with after Christian retrieved his weapons. The only reason it had been such a hard-fought battle was because of the injuries that he had sustained during their fistfight.

Whoever was wielding those gloves had more talent than Nathan Storm—the werewolf that he'd fought—ever would. They were clearly a master at using them. If Christian wanted to come out of this battle intact, then it was imperative that he be at his best.

As the cloaked man sent three wires toward him, Christian's hands reached over his shoulders, and his fingers wrapped around the hilts of his blades. Michael and Raphael left their sheaths with a soft hiss.

The wires converged, striking at him in three directions. Michael met the wire on the left, while Raphael struck the wire on the right. Both wires tried to wrap around the blades, but Christian was prepared this time and threw the wires off his swords with a flick of his wrists.

Coming in behind him was the last attack. Christian avoided serious injury by twisting his body to the right and using some fancy footwork to move out of the wire's path. It still nicked him in the side when the wire changed direction at the last second, but it was just a scratch and not something to worry about.

Seven more wires came in as the other three retreated. They were moving faster than before. Christian could only see them because of the moonlight flashing off their surfaces.

His enemy manipulated the wires to move in random patterns designed to throw him off. It was an effective strategy for fooling most opponents, but Christian could already see the weakness of this maneuver. Constantly changing the direction of the wires at random meant that the wielder had to focus all of their attention on manipulating their fingers to get the desired results. Even the most minute of mistakes could cause the wires to collide with each other and become tangled.

That must be why his attacker was using only seven wires instead of the typical nine. His enemy probably couldn't use any more while still keeping track of all the paths that the wires were following.

Reaching his position at speed, the seven wires split and twisted around each other in complicated patterns that most people could never hope to predict. Christian was not most people. Thanks to his fighting style, he knew where all the wires were going to attack and responded accordingly.

One wire veered off course when Raphael struck it with great force. The wire tangled with another one when Christian twisted his blade and redirected its path into the path that he knew the second wire would take seconds before it happened.

He dodged the third wire when he took one step to the left and spun his body ninety degrees. He brought Michael up into a guard position and allowed that wire to wrap around it. Then, with a great heave, he slashed his sword into the fourth wire coming in from his left. Christian wove a quick circle with his sword, entangling another wire with his blade, and then slipped the sword out through a small gap. The two wires became twisted together and fell to the ground.

Realizing that four of the seven wires he'd sent were no longer usable, the cloaked man retracted the other three. At the same time, he yanked his left hand into the air, where he soon revealed that the other three wires had been hidden right underneath Christian's feet. Christian threw himself into a shoulder roll to avoid having himself cut into quarters. When he came back up, six wires came in hot, all set to spear his body through different locations.

Christian became a blur of activity. His body moved like never before, as he focused entirely on keeping himself alive. Wires came in and were sent back as they met one of his swords. Loud clangs rang through the air, as the two battled each other in a ferocious life-and-death struggle. Each time one of Christian's blades met a wire, sparks erupted between them.

As if in a choreographed dance, they moved across the soccer field—Christian spinning and weaving and ducking and dodging, his swords lashing out at blinding speeds. Meanwhile, his opponent's fingers danced to an unseen rhythm, like a puppet master playing with a marionette.

As the battle wore on, Christian realized something important. He and his opponent were evenly matched. His speed and reflexes combined with the ability to predict his opponent's attacks made it impossible for the Assassin to hit him. But, his enemy was a ranged fighter, and he was doing a damn fine job of keeping him from closing the distance. Every time Christian tried getting close, the Assassin would backpedal just as fast. Those wires moved in even more erratic and unpredictable patterns the closer Christian got.

A fight of this level would not be decided by who had the greater skill, but by who slipped up first. It was going to come down to luck.

There was no telling how long the fight wore on. As far as Christian knew, it could have been hours, or it could have been minutes. The elapsed time could have even been mere seconds and Christian wouldn't know how long he had fought.

His muscles aching with the strain of keeping up with his opponent, Christian continued to fight. Each breath he took came out as a loud gasp that rang harshly in his ears. Every move he made caused droplets of sweat to fly from his hair. Perspiration ran down his face and got in his eyes, burning them.

He didn't dare close them, though, as doing so would mean death. And he could not afford to lose. Not until…

A change in his opponent's pattern forced Christian to backpedal. His opponent's wires flailed about in a chaotic dance. He zigged to the left. This motion halted abruptly as he placed all of his weight on his left leg, then swerved to the right, avoiding a wire that crashed into the ground that he had been standing on, slicing through it and uplifting several dirt clods that exploded into the air.

Christian was just about to make another attempt at closing the distance between them, when his opponent stopped, the wires going slack.

His enemy tilted their head curiously, as if listening to something that only they could hear. Christian eyed the figure warily. His opponent might be trying to lure him in, so he needed to remain on guard.

But there was no trap. A second later the Assassin struck the ground with his wires, kicking up a large cloud of dust and dirt that forced Christian to shield his eyes. When the makeshift smokescreen cleared, his enemy was gone.

With narrowed eyes and a fierce expression, Christian moved cautiously forward. He kept a firm grip on his swords, ready to attack or defend as needed. Soon enough, he reached the spot where his enemy had been standing. After taking a moment to look around, he found nothing. Nothing at all that would indicate where his opponent had gone.

Confusion set in. Why had that man retreated? He hadn't been winning, but he hadn't losing either. That battle could have gone either way. Why give up an opportunity to kill his enemy? Unless…

Unless I was never the real target to begin with!

Like a lead weight, an unsettling feeling caused his stomach to drop, as he realized that only one person could be the real target.

***

Christian raced up the stairs to Lilith's apartment, only stopping to stare at the door that had been flung wide open. His heart nearly stopped beating as he rushed into the apartment.

"Lilith?!"

He surveyed the living room but found nothing out of place. He saw no signs of a struggle—no broken furniture, no overturned tables, nothing at all to indicate that anything was wrong. The sight only made Christian worry that much more.

"Lilith?!"

He rushed farther into the apartment, going straight for Lilith's room. There, he found the first signs of trouble. The bed was a complete mess.

The sheets lay tangled, half on the bed half off, twisted in a macramé of knots. He could see indents in the mattress where several springs had been broken. Two springs poked straight through the fabric of the mattress. The headboard was cracked, as if someone had been slammed against it repeatedly, and there were several chunks of different colored hair. He could make out at least three different colors.

Not wanting to jump to conclusions, Christian searched the rest of the house: Maria's and Stacy's bedroom, the bathrooms, the closets, everywhere that he could think of. He found nothing to disprove his theory.

Returning to Lilith's bedroom, Christian sat on the bed and buried his head in his hands. As the icy fist of realization clenched his heart in its ironclad grip, he came to a terrifying conclusion: Lilith had been kidnapped.

Chapter 21

Christian didn't know how long he'd stayed in Lilith's apartment. Time seemed inconsequential to him now. Only one inconsolable fact penetrated the haze that he'd been in since its realization set in.

Lilith was gone.

As he sat there on Lilith's bed, cursing himself for his stupidity, he surveyed the decorations that made up the bedroom, taking note of the room's feminine touches. Everything about this room had Lilith's unique signature to it. When he looked around, he could imagine Lilith sleeping in the bed that he was sitting on, or sitting behind her desk as she did homework or read a light novel.

His hands clenched the fabric of his pants and his teeth gritted into a snarl of frustration. Something wet ran down his cheeks, dripping off his chin to splash against his hand. Blinking, he swiped his hand underneath his eyes.

Tears?

He was crying. How strange. Christian had not cried in years, not since the destruction of his home and the death of his parents. Yet he was crying now, and over a girl that he'd known for barely over a week. There was something inherently wrong about that, crying over the girl that he'd been sent to kill, but he couldn't find it in himself to care.

Standing up, Christian made to stand in front of Lilith's desk, where several picture frames covered its surface. After picking one up at random, he gazed at the image contained within the frame.

It was a picture of Lilith as a child. Her cherubic face was framed by short blond hair, and her blue eyes contained the same mystifying innocence, though they lacked the current Lilith's melancholy. Standing beside her, with one arm wrapped around her shoulder, was a woman–Valerie, Lilith's foster mom.

They looked so happy in the photo. Lilith wore a mile-wide smile and the woman that she called mother was also smiling gently into the camera. It was a beautiful photo meant to showcase what he could only consider to be the perfect family, one that had been destroyed by hardships beyond their ability to control.

***

The walk back to his hotel was slow. Christian had a lot on his mind; worry for Lilith, questions about what he should do now, and what Headquarters' response would be when he reported in. So much had gone wrong on this assignment. What should have been a simple assassination had snowballed into a mess that he could scarcely comprehend.

The streets were eerily quiet. He didn't miss the dichotomy between now and several hours ago, when sirens blared and explosions went off like fireworks at a festival. He could see smoke rising from between the buildings. The police cars must still be on fire.

All of the police were likely dead now. That Assassin had been good. Christian didn't doubt that he was also thorough and had ensured that no one could report back about him.

After reaching his hotel and climbing in through the window, Christian sat on the bed, the mattress creaking. Weariness overcame him. The weight of his failures mercilessly crushed him, causing his shoulders to slump as his hands covered his face.

Lilith was gone. He had failed to protect her. He'd allowed himself to get drawn into a fight, not even stopping to contemplate that he might not be the real target. Hindsight was always twenty-twenty, but Christian felt like he should have realized that he wasn't the person being targeted after the first few minutes of their battle. Now Lilith was paying the price for his failure.

The sound of his phone ringing snapped him out of his pity party. He reached into his pocket, accepted the call, and held the phone to his ear.

"Tristin." His voice was devoid of emotion.

"Christian, is something wrong? You sound like someone just took one of those light novels you're so fond of and threw it in a furnace."

A snappish reply was on the tip of Christian's tongue, but he held himself back. With a sigh, he closed his eyes and thought through Tristin's words before coming to a conclusion.

"No," he said. "I am not all right."

There was a long pause.

"Tell me what happened?"

And Christian did tell him what happened. Despite his misgivings, he told Tristin everything that had occurred in the past several hours. He mentioned his run-in with the figure whose entire body had been obscured by the red cloak of an Assassin. He didn't hesitate to mention how that same person had used both Uriel and Barachiel, two weapons that should have been in the hands of Anthony Trekovski. He even informed his fellow orphan about his greatest failure that night; Lilith's kidnapping.

"It sounds like you've had a rough night," Tristin said after a moment. *"I guess it makes sense. Nothing about this mission has been going right: finding out that your target is afraid of men, running into a werewolf, and now this strange figure wielding one of the Executioners' most powerful weapons. Not to mention whoever kidnapped your target."*

"Speaking of which, have you found out whether or not Lilith is, in fact, a succubus?"

"No, I've finally managed to pull up all the relevant information I can find. I even went ahead and hacked into the government's database and pulled up the files they have on her; blood work, incident reports, hospital records, the works, but I haven't actually gotten the chance to search through them."

"I see." Christian didn't think going through the files mattered anymore. It was clear to him that Lilith wasn't a succubus. She was just a girl who had issues with men. A succubus not only wouldn't have any problems with members of the opposite sex but would revel in their attention. They also had their *Aura of Allure*, which caused men to lust after them.

Lilith didn't have that aura. He hadn't felt any desires upon meeting her. Christian wasn't exactly sure what the *Aura of Allure* was supposed to feel like, but that hardly mattered. The fact was that he should have felt *something* from Lilith. The Aura was always active. Succubi couldn't just turn it on and off like a switch, or even control who it affected. Every male within a certain radius of a succubus was affected by her, regardless of who he was or how strong a will he possessed.

The Science Division had actually experimented on succubi to discover this information. According to reports written by people who'd been under its effects, the Aura induced *"an intense need to copulate with the woman producing the Aura."* People trapped by a succubus's Aura became inundated by lust, their minds caught within a haze of ecstasy that banished all other thought beyond procreation impossible.

Christian's thought processes were just fine. Throughout the entire time that he had spent with Lilith, he'd never once felt anything like what those reports described. The closest instance was when he and Lilith had fallen asleep under the tree, but that hadn't been lust or the desire to have sex. That moment with Lilith had been comforting, reminding him of better times, soothing the agony that his soul bore, healing the scars brought about by his sin. It felt nothing like lust.

Even that time when he had imagined kissing Lilith, it hadn't felt like that. It had been lust, certainly, but there'd been other emotions as well. Compassion. Understanding. The desire to protect. It was nothing like what those men who'd undergone the experiment had described—one of which had been Leonne, another member of the XIII and someone that Christian respected.

"Ignoring that for the moment, I do have some information for you." Tristin's voice snapped Christian's mind back into the real world. *"The Church was unable to cover up what happened in Seal Beach in time to stop the media from finding out. They're currently having a field day. Reporters all across the US are talking about how the entire Seal Beach police department has been destroyed in a single night."*

"So the entire police department was destroyed," Christian muttered. "The media found out pretty fast. It's only been a few hours since the incident happened."

"The news first came from the Seal Beach Channel Four news station." Christian could hear the shrug in Tristin's voice. *"I imagine one of their reporters heard the explosions and reported the event. Thankfully, the Church was able to get in contact with the Los Angeles police department and they've cordoned off the city. All trains and subways within Orange County have been stopped. No one will be coming in or out, which means national media stations have been forced to watch from a distance."*

"I suppose that's better than nothing." Christian rubbed his eyes. He was so tired, which wasn't surprising after the night he'd just had. "At the very least that will keep the media from getting too close and possibly discovering the truth behind these attacks."

"Those are my thoughts as well, but that doesn't mean we're out of the woods quite yet."

"Problems?"

"Of a sort," Tristin replied vaguely. *"While we were able to get the cooperation of the police department, they have demanded that we let them take part in this mission."*

"I can't see Samantha letting that happen."

"Right. We would normally never allow them to take part in our missions because of the inherent danger involved when dealing with the supernatural. However, the boss lady's hands are currently tied. If she denies them the ability to take part, they'll wash their hands of this case, and then the media will have free rein to go and do whatever they please."

"I see." Christian grimaced. "So I'm going to be stuck working with the police?"

"Yes. The good news is that the people you're to be working with won't be going in unprepared. You won't be dealing with the standard police, but a branch of the LAPD known as the Supernatural Investigations Unit."

Christian frowned. "I've never heard of them."

"That's because they're a relatively new unit," Tristin explained. *"It was created some time last year when a rookie Executioner screwed up on a mission, and a security camera in a subway station caught her killing an undine. The Church was forced into negotiations with the LAPD and informed them of everything they know about the supernatural world. After that, the LAPD created the SIU to deal with supernatural threats."*

"But that's the Executioners' jurisdiction."

"As far as the rest of the world is concerned, the Executioners don't exist. No one is supposed to know about us. Even if they did, we wouldn't hold any real authority, though that would probably be the least of our problems."

Christian blew out a low breath as he realized that Tristin was right. Most governments around the world, and the United States in particular, kept religion as far from positions of power within their government as possible. It was a galling aspect of their society, but there was little that Christian or anyone else could do about it.

"As things stand, we're lucky the LAPD has agreed to work simply with us and not reveal our existence to the world at large. I doubt the Church would be able to survive the backlash they'd receive if that

happened, especially because we're keeping our existence a secret, even from our own followers."

"Yeah, I guess you have a point," Christian said. He had never thought about the potential political ramifications involved with keeping a religious sect that had been created to slay monsters a secret. But then, that's probably why he was a Warrior and not a politician.

"Of course I have a point." Christian heard the scoff in Tristin's voice. *"Now let's get down to business. Several members of the SIU should be arriving in Seal Beach sometime today. They've been given your number and will send you a text message stating the time and place you are to meet with them. From there, you will work with them to deal with whatever creature has shown up in Seal Beach."*

"Right. Is there anything else that I should know?"

"Not at the moment, but if something comes up, I'll be sure to contact you. Now you should get some rest. You sound like you're about to pass out."

"Gee, thanks."

"Anytime." He could practically hear the grin in Tristin's voice.

***

After speaking with Tristin, Christian took a quick shower to rinse off the grime and blood from the day's events. There were dozens of cuts running along his body, and if he didn't want them to get infected, he would need to clean them as best he could.

Once he finished, Christian then proceeded to do exactly as Tristin suggested and get some sleep. By the time his head hit the pillow, it was already early morning, and he'd been up since the sun had first risen yesterday. It was no wonder that he passed out almost immediately.

He slept all through the early morning. By the time he finally awoke, the sun rode high overhead.

Christian groaned as the last vestiges of his nightmare vanished. Even so, the visions of his parents and Lilith blaming him for not protecting them continued their haunting chant, making it impossible to ascertain his present location. It wasn't until the fog clouding his mind dispersed that he noticed where he was. His hotel room.

Lilith. Christian's eyes clamped shut and his teeth clenched, as yesterday's events bombarded him with the weight of his failure. Lilith had been kidnapped because of his inattentiveness and stupidity. She was no longer with him, and he didn't have the slightest clue where her kidnapper could have taken her.

It was a bitter pill to swallow, knowing that she had been taken and he'd done nothing to stop it from happening. Worse was the fact that he couldn't do anything for her. Until he ascertained her current location, the only thing that he could do was wait, and hope nothing happened to her.

There was also the small issue of the SIU. Christian had been told that he was to remain on standby while the Supernatural Investigations Unit of the LAPD arrived on scene and sent him a message, informing him of the time and place they were to meet. While the thought of sitting around waiting galled him to no end, it wasn't as if he had much choice in the matter.

And speaking of the SIU...

Christian reached over to the nightstand and picked up his phone. Upon pressing the *on* button, the screen lit up and revealed the image of his screensaver: a black background with a silver crucifix. Gazing at the top of the small screen, Christian saw that he had a text message, which he quickly opened.

The text message was small, no more than a few lines. It said: *"Meet me at the Starbucks on Bolsa Ave at 12:30 pm."*

After closing the text message, Christian looked at the time. He had less than an hour to get there. That wasn't a lot of time, especially since the walk would take at least twenty minutes unless he decided to run.

Climbing out of bed, Christian groaned as his body told him that it was still sore from last night. He would have to forego a shower and focus on stretching if he wanted to be working at one-hundred percent efficiency during this meeting. It was never a good idea to go into a meeting where you neither knew nor trusted the person that you were going to meet with.

Chapter 22

The streets were quiet. Despite it being a beautiful day with a clear blue sky and mild weather, there wasn't a single person walking down the streets. All the stores that Christian passed on his way to the meeting point were also closed. He didn't know if this had been a conscious decision by the people of the city, or if the SIU had something to do with it. Christian assumed it was a combination of both.

This worked out well for him. Clad in his full Executioner uniform of dark pants and shirt with a black cloak that trailed down to his ankles, he would have undoubtedly drawn a lot of attention if there were people around. The handles of Michael and Raphael poked out of his cloak, making him even more of a spectacle.

He arrived at the Starbucks without incident. Upon making a quick scan of the surrounding area, he counted half a dozen police officers. Four stood guard along the streets, and two hid on the roofs of two buildings several meters away. He could see them looking down the scopes of their sniper rifles.

Their uniforms were different from those of standard police officers. They were not blue, but a dark gray that consisted of military fatigues, a long-sleeved turtle-neck shirt, and what appeared to be a modified SWAT bulletproof vest. Although the officers wore the LAPD badge on the right side of their chests, a patch with the infinity symbol containing the acronym *SIU* was located on their shoulders.

One of the officers noticed his arrival and approached. He was a giant of a man with a hulking frame, yellow eyes, and shaggy brown hair that reminded Christian of a dog. The uniform he wore stretched taut across his bulging muscles. Christian assumed they didn't have a larger size that fit him.

"Are you Christian?"

"Yes."

"You look a little too young to be one of those Executioners." The man's deep voice rumbled like a bass. "How old are ya, kid?"

Christian bristled at being called *kid* as if he was nothing but a boy playing cops and robbers.

"I'm not a kid. I may only be twenty years old, but I have a lot of experience when it comes to dealing with the supernatural, and certainly more than someone who's been with a unit that was only formed a year ago."

"You don't say." The man's chuckle made Christian bristle. "Well, I'm not gonna argue with you. I'm sure you know how to fight, otherwise the Executioners wouldn't have sent ya. Follow me. My commander is waiting for you."

Christian followed the giant to where a youthful woman was sitting at a table with a tablet in her hands. Her long brown hair was pulled back into a bun, but several tendrils had escaped to frame her face. She had brown eyes and sharp features, which were complemented by the dark-purple business suit that she wore. She looked like the no-nonsense type. He could only hope that meant she would act in a more professional manner than her subordinate.

As he approached the table, the woman looked up, and her eyes locked onto him. Much like the police officer had done, she checked him out from head to toe. Christian was thankful when she didn't make any cracks about his age but instead directed him to take a seat with a gesture of her hand.

"My name is Catherine Siegal," the woman said without preamble. "I'm the current head of the SIU, and the one who'll be working with you on this mission."

"A pleasure to make your acquaintance," Christian replied cordially. "I'm Christian, member of the Executioners."

"Charmed," Catherine said. She then proved herself to be a consummate professional by getting right down to business. "My department is currently canvassing each block of the city and making door-to-door inquiries to see if anyone has seen any suspicious activity. So far we haven't found anything, but we're hoping to get a lead soon."

"Are you sure going door to door is a good idea?" asked Christian. "Asking people if they've seen anything unusual is a good way to make them curious. They might end up digging more deeply into things and uncovering something that's better off remaining hidden from the public."

"Do you have any better ideas?" Christian said nothing, causing her to nod. "I thought not. You have to understand that we're not only working under a tight budget because of how new our department is, but we also haven't been able to gather any information through the few channels that we *have* cultivated in the past year. Most of our information network is located within Los Angeles, and Seal Beach is far removed from the larger cities in Orange County like Anaheim."

"I see your point," Christian admitted. "I'm not much for investigative work, so I'll defer to your experience here."

"I'm glad you understand," Catherine said. "Since you're going to be working closely with us, I'd like to discuss how our temporary partnership is going to work."

***

A soft groan escaped Lilith's parted lips as her eyelids fluttered open. Her mind was lost between the waking world and the world of dreams. Her surroundings were nothing but blurry shapes and fuzzy images. Everything appeared to be covered in fog.

She was tired, so tired. All she wanted to do was go back to sleep… But she couldn't. Something was wrong. The bed that she was lying on was comfortable, and the silken gown that she was dressed in gently caressed her skin, sending pleasurable shivers across her body, but her mind felt nothing but unease.

Lilith blinked several times, trying to make her eyes focus. The blurry images sharpened and the once fuzzy outlines became crisper. She soon realized that she was staring at a ceiling. The paint had long since faded into a dull gray. Cracks like spider webs ran along the ceiling to form intricate patterns that followed no known geometry. This was not her ceiling.

Even though her mind still felt sluggish, she processed this fact relatively quickly. If this wasn't her ceiling, then it meant that she wasn't in her bedroom. And if she wasn't in her bedroom, then this was not her apartment. The thought awoke her further like an electric jolt.

Lilith sat up. She tried to move quickly, but her body, like her mind, was slow to act. It felt like she was wading through wet cement.

Something was wrong. Something was very, *very* wrong. What had happened? What was she doing here? Where was *here*? And why couldn't she remember?

Lilith struggled to recall the last thing that had happened before waking up. She remembered spending the day with Christian, remembered how they had fallen asleep in the shade of a tree. That had been nice.

What hadn't been nice was when she had more or less confessed her love for him and he ran away. It seemed their situations were reversed. Wasn't it the woman who was supposed to do the running?

A shake of her head brought her focus back on trying to remember the rest of that night. Bits and pieces of what happened returned, slowly forming an image that allowed her to understand more about her current predicament.

She had entered her apartment to find both Maria and Stacy waiting for her. They had been acting odd; Maria hadn't teased her about her date, and Stacy just being there when she should have been at work or out partying was strange in and of itself.

When she questioned them on their unusual behavior, both had assured her that they were fine. She had accepted their answer at face value, figuring that they must have just been tired or something, and she had honestly been in a rush to get away from them before they could question her. She hadn't wanted them to see how distraught she was.

That had been a mistake.

After quickly dismissing herself, Lilith had retreated into her room. There, she had shed the tears that she'd been holding back, as she tried to understand why Christian ran out on her like that. Had she done something wrong? Did he not like her and just didn't have the heart to say so? No reasons popped into her head despite the amount of thinking she had done, and Lilith had been forced to concede defeat. She had then gone to bed, emotionally exhausted from crying, and mentally drained from trying to understand the actions of the man she had fallen for.

She'd been abruptly awakened some time after falling asleep by the feel of someone grabbing her. She had kicked and struggled and tried to fight back, but then someone else had joined in, and the fight turned against her. She didn't remember much after that; just a pair of brown eyes turning a sickly shade of red before everything went black. And now she was here —wherever *here* was.

She glanced around the room. The walls were bleached white and faded with age. More cracks appeared along their surface, and some mildew grew near the bottom. A stain on the wall to her left stood out starkly against the white backdrop, dirty red, like dried blood. The blinds at the single window were taped shut and boards were placed over it. A small flickering candle stood on a nightstand next to her bed of red velvet covers and satin pillows, the light from its flame her only source of illumination. Her exquisitely furnished bed presented an anomaly to the rest of the room, a dichotomous oasis of beauty in a sea of drab colors.

This bed, with its obvious elegance and the equally obvious intentions behind its placement in the room, did little to steady her nerves. Lilith tried to force back the fear threatening to overwhelm her, but the task proved difficult. She could feel shock rage through her like a maelstrom. Her body started shaking as the full extent of her situation became clear. She was a captive, helpless and weak from whatever method her captor had used to knock her unconscious.

The door to her room creaked open, and Lilith's eyes widened. Did her captor know that she was awake? What would they do if they found her conscious? Would they… would she be… Lilith couldn't even think it. The thought of what they might do to her, the fear of what they could do, was too much to bear.

While Lilith sat paralyzed by a combination of indecision and fear, the door opened fully. No light spilled into the room. The area beyond her bed was even darker than the bedchamber. Two shapes eventually formed out of the darkness, solidifying into a pair of silhouettes, as the sound of footsteps echoed through the room. The figures soon became visible as they stepped into the light cast by the small candle, and Lilith could only stare in surprise when she saw who the figures were.

"Maria?! Stacy?!"

Relief flooded her at seeing them alive, and at knowing that she was not alone, but she also felt worry. If these two were here, then that meant…

"Whoever kidnapped me must have taken you two as well," Lilith reasoned, her mind boiling over with a surprising amount of anger, which almost completely negated the fear. Someone had taken her friends. It was one thing to kidnap her, but to kidnap her friends was something else entirely. If she found out who did this she would… would…

Well, she didn't actually know what she would do, but it would not be nice.

Shaking her head and ridding herself of those negative emotions, Lilith made to climb out of bed and stand up. It wasn't long after making this attempt that she realized how impossible the task was. She could hardly sit straight, never mind stand up.

Unable to so much as move from her position, she looked imploringly at the two girls standing on the left side of her bed.

"Help me up, you two. We need to hurry if we want to get out of here before whoever kidnapped us realizes that I'm awake."

The two girls did not move. They stared at Lilith with blank, dead eyes.

"Maria? Stacy?" When they still didn't answer her, Lilith knew that something was wrong. It should have been obvious from the beginning. Had they been themselves, Maria would have already said something about pounding the person who kidnapped them into the ground, and Stacy would have been complaining. "What's wrong, you two? Why won't you help me?"

"The reason 'tis because they cannot help you."

Lilith's entire body froze. An icy cold chill rushed through her veins, freezing her blood. Terror filled her, causing her body to tremble in trepidation.

That voice. She knew that voice. It was one that had haunted her nightmares for years; a voice that she had hoped to never hear again.

Lilith looked up, dread welling inside of her. Above her, standing on the ceiling as if it were the floor, was a frighteningly familiar figure—a creature who appeared as a young man with ghost-white skin and long black hair. His black suit conformed to his slender frame and ended in a pair of coattails. Large black wings, like those of a bat, were folded against his back. Long elven ears parted his hair.

His dark-red irises were surrounded, not by the usual white, but black. His entire sclera was the color of darkness, blacker even than his hair. As Lilith stared into those carnelian orbs reminiscent of blood, the urge to flee nearly overwhelmed her.

Those eyes were inhuman. Unnatural. Monstrous.

He stared at her, his eyes filled with hunger.

"My dearest Eve." His voice sounded like velvet, smooth and rich. Lilith shuddered as her heart threatened to explode from the absolute, indefinable terror that threatened to overwhelm her. "You look exquisite. Truly, thou hath grown into a beauty beyond compare."

"Don't... don't call me that..."

The man tilted his head. "Don't... ah, right. I hath forgotten. You no longer go by that name, do you?" He chuckled. "You call yourself Lilith now. Very well, then. I shall indulge thee, *Lilith*." He smiled, and Lilith nearly hyperventilated at the sight. "Anything for my Queen."

"I'm not..." Lilith gritted her teeth as tears gathered in her eyes and began running down her cheeks. "... I'm not your Queen."

"I see that you are still being stubborn." The man appeared remorseful. "It seems that I will need to reeducate you."

Lilith's eyes widened as the man who inspired more terror in her than anyone else vanished, his form dematerializing in front of her eyes. Not even a second passed before he stood in front of her, staring down at her with a look that made Lilith want to vomit and scream at the same time.

"Allow me to remind you, my dear *Eve,* that you belong to me."

His hand reached out toward her. Sharp, claw-like nails inched closer to her skin until they made contact with her face.

Lilith's screams echoed throughout the mansion.

Chapter 23

Christian woke up with a gasp. Sitting up in his bed, he looked around wildly, his eyes scanning the vicinity for the source of his unease. When he saw nothing, he relaxed and closed his eyes. Then he pressed a hand to his sweaty face and tried to calm his racing heart.

What was that? A dream? Where had that scream come from? It had sounded like Lilith.

The cold morning air from the open window hit his sweat-covered body and caused goosebumps to break out on his flesh. Christian walked into the restroom and took a quick rinse. Then he dressed in his Executioners uniform sans his weapons, which he began checking and double-checking to ensure they worked properly. It was a mindless task. It was also the only thing he could do to occupy himself and keep from going mad.

Two days had passed since Lilith had been kidnapped. The SIU had been working to uncover her location, but so far nothing had come of it. It seemed that whoever had taken her was not within city limits, or was just doing a phenomenal job of remaining hidden. The police had expanded their search, but Catherine had informed him that he shouldn't expect anything to come of it for at least another few days.

Christian was not an investigator. He was good at tracking his prey through the streets, but gathering clues to deduce someone's location wasn't his forte. Because of his lack of talent in this specific field, he'd been sidelined until they had need of his strength.

It was so frustrating! They had forced him to remain on standby, unable to do anything for Lilith. He felt helpless! Seldom had he felt so weak, so powerless—not since his hometown had been burnt to the ground. He hated this feeling. He never wanted to feel this helpless again.

On the nightstand, his phone began vibrating. He rushed over as it jittered across the nightstand and grabbed it, noting the caller ID.

"Catherine. Have you found anything?"

"We think we've got a lead on the kidnapper's location."

Christian's spirits rose. "That's good."

"You would think so, wouldn't you? But we've also found some information that might be cause for concern."

"What kind of information are we talking about?"

"There have been a few sightings of the creature that we believe kidnapped your friend, and it looks like we're not dealing with some standard monster. Judging from the description we've been given, I can only conclude that we're up against a No-Life King."

***

No Life King—the title coined for vampires who had lived for over five centuries and gained incredible power. Known for their overwhelming physical strength, which could pulverize entire buildings with a single punch, No Life Kings were nearly at the pinnacle of vampire strength. Only the Ancestors, the oldest vampires in existence, were more powerful. Tristin had put it best when he said, *"No Life Kings are like vampires on steroids."*

***

Christian walked beside Catherine as they made their way toward the suspected hideout of the creature that had kidnapped Lilith.

As they moved up a steep roadway carved into the side a small mountain, Christian wondered why the No Life King hadn't left yet. He already had Lilith, and if she was his objective, then leaving before they could find him was the most prudent course of action.

Perhaps he's too preoccupied with something… or someone.

At the thought of what that thing might be doing to Lilith, a chill ran up Christian's spine and rage boiled in his heart. Images of Lilith, helpless, naked, and chained to a bed as the No Life King raped her over and over again filled his mind. Just by existing, that monster had signed its death warrant, but if it hurt Lilith in any way, harmed even one hair on her head, then he would make sure it suffered greatly before meeting its demise.

"We're here."

Catherine's voice snapped Christian out of his vengeful thoughts. They had arrived at a large set of gates, iron-wrought and imposing. Beyond the gate lay a road.

"It took us a while to find this place," Catherine said. All around them, police officers were securing the perimeter, checking to make sure no one could catch them unawares. "No one's come near this mansion in years because of what happened to the last occupants."

"And what happened to the last people who resided here?"

"They died, of course," Catherine said. "According to the reports, the eldest son was taking hallucinogens. His visions slowly drove him insane and made him think his family were a bunch of monsters. One day, his paranoia became so great that he came home with a gun and killed his parents and younger sister. He's currently imprisoned in a psych ward for the criminally insane."

"I see."

"Ever since then, this place has been abandoned. No one dares to go near it."

"Which would make it the perfect place for a vampire." Christian nodded his head toward the gates. "Especially for a No Life King. They despise humans. They would want to stay as far from humans as possible, until it's time for them to feed."

"Those were my thoughts exactly."

Just then, a police officer came up to them and saluted Catherine. "Ma'am, we have just finished securing the perimeter."

"Excellent." Catherine clapped her hands together and began barking out orders. "All right, people! This operation will be starting at exactly oh-nine-hundred hours. We've got one hour to get ready. Check your equipment, and check your weapons. I don't want any of you getting yourselves killed because your gun wouldn't fire!"

"Ma'am!"

As the officers saluted before returning to what they'd been doing, Catherine turned to him.

"Christian, I'm going to want you on standby for now. My men will secure most of the house and search for this No Life King, and then call you in to deal with it."

"Catherine, I really don't think—"

"I am not leaving you out of this mission." Catherine forestalled Christian's protests by raising her hand. "Your job will be the most important one here. My men are good, but they don't have the training necessary to take on a creature like this. After they find him, it'll be your job to engage him and take him out."

Christian frowned at her. "I'm sorry, but I can't do that."

Catherine returned his frown with one of her own. She opened her mouth to say something, but he cut her off.

"Lilith and her friends are somewhere inside. Before I even think about engaging the No Life King, I need to make sure they are safe and out of harm's way."

The look on Catherine's face said that she disagreed. "I can assure you that my men will find them and—"

"Your men will not go near Lilith." Christian's eyes narrowed dangerously at the woman.

When Catherine took several shaky steps back, he realized that his emotions were getting the best of him, and he took several calming breaths. "I am not questioning your men's ability to locate the girls who were kidnapped. You need to know that Lilith has androphobia. Men terrify her. I'm actually the only man whose presence she doesn't seem to fear. If your men go in and find her, her panic will escalate."

Christian stared into Catherine's eyes, willing her to understand why he needed to be the one who rescued Lilith.

After several seconds passed between them, Catherine looked away and sighed. "If that is how it is, then I suppose there is no choice but to let you locate and rescue the girls."

Christian sighed in relief. "Thank you."

She tuned back to look at him with a small smile. "I can see that this girl means a lot to you."

The words made Christian pause. Lilith did mean a lot to him, that much he wouldn't deny. But her words also made him wonder: How much did Lilith mean to him really? What were his true feelings for her? He honestly didn't know how much she meant to him, but he knew one thing for sure.

"She is more important to me than anyone else."

There was no point in denying it anymore, not after everything that had happened. Christian didn't know what this meant for him, or for Lilith, but there would be a time to figure that out later. The only thing on his mind in that moment was rescuing her.

"I see." Catherine paused long enough to show him a bitter smile that must have a story behind it. "To be honest, I think I'm a little jealous of this girl. I doubt there are many people who are willing to face such a powerful creature for another person's sake."

"I-it's not like I'm doing this just for her." Christian's excuse sounded flimsy even to him. "I'm also an Executioner. Slaying monsters is my sworn duty. And besides, there is more than just a No Life King in there. I can't say for sure, but I believe it has an accomplice."

"An accomplice?"

"Yes. This person might not be as powerful as the No Life King, but he's definitely much stronger than any normal human. I'll have to deal with him as well as the No Life King. Chances are this person will be guarding Lilith, so it would be best if I take point."

"If you say so." Catherine shrugged in resignation. "In any case, you had better get ready. Our assault begins in fifteen minutes."

Christian nodded and began mentally preparing himself for the upcoming mission. He would need to be at his best.

***

Getting past the front gate was a simple matter. The SIU had apparently brought plastic explosives with them. A little C4 glued to the lock granted them easy access.

A large fountain sat in the center of the driveway, once elegant, but having since fallen into a state of disrepair. Chips and cracks ran along the surface of the beautiful woman, the fountain's centerpiece. The basket she held, from which water used to pour, had crumbled, along with half of her left arm and right hand. Water no longer ran in the fountain. The interior, cracked and pitted, showed where the water had leaked onto the driveway.

Much like the fountain, the mansion looked like it had been a grand and stunning example of European architecture reminiscent of Victorian homes owned by nobility. Dull gray tiles sloped down from the roof, weathered by age and ravaged by time. Two large towers jutted from the earth like giant monoliths, spires that speared through either side of the manor. The light tan bricks composing the walls were chipped and pitted, old and worn. Columns lined the front porch, lifeless marble that had long since lost its luster.

Chances were good the No Life King was already aware of them, and Christian told Catherine as much. "No Life Kings have the ability to sense life, which helps them track down humans when they need to feed. The stronger a No Life King is, the greater their range at sensing humans."

As if emphasizing his point, the doors leading into the mansion burst open and almost a dozen people dressed in blue police uniforms rushed out. Even though all of them had guns strapped to their holsters, none of them grabbed their weapon. They simply charged at the SIU members.

"W-what the hell?! Those are the uniforms of the Seal Beach police department!"

"They've probably been turned into ghouls." Christian's eyes narrowed in disgust as his hands reached for his guns. "When a person has all of their blood sucked out, a No Life King can inject them with their own to reanimate the corpse. When this happens, the person becomes a ghoul, an undead monster that's under the thrall of the one who created it."

"I wish you would have told us that sooner," Catherine snapped as she whipped her own gun out of her holster.

Christian shrugged. "You are aware of what a No Life King is, so I thought you already knew."

"Tch!" Catherine peered at the charging group of ghouls. Christian studied her, and then observed the other officers. None of them had their guns out, no doubt hesitant to open fire on fellow officers. "Christian, are you telling me it's okay to open fire on these things?"

"Yes," Christian said. "they aren't human anymore, just empty shells."

"Right. Open fire, men! These aren't your comrades anymore! Just a bunch of soulless slaves!"

Turning words into action, Catherine fired several rounds into the group of ghouls. Several fell as they were shot in the leg, or spun around as they received a bullet to the shoulder, but none of them stayed down for long.

"I would suggest aiming for the head."

"Tell me these things sooner!"

Seeing their commander fire at the incoming horde caused the other SIU members to overcome their own reluctance. Watching one of their own getting ripped apart may have also played a hand in snuffing out their inability to open fire.

"Can you handle things from here?" Christian asked over the sound of gunfire. Catherine grunted as her gun, a magnum, blasted a hole through one of the ghoul's heads.

"Yeah. Sure. Just leave these things to us. Don't worry. We've got it all covered."

"Your sarcasm is unneeded," Christian said, "and you should be thanking me. The creatures I'm going to be facing inside that mansion would tear you and your men apart without even slowing down."

"Just get in there already!"

Christian didn't answer the woman's annoyed shout with words. He rushed out from behind the fountain and toward the ruined doorway, avoiding the ghouls by circling around them, letting the SIU officers grab their attention. He reached the door in record time and charged into the building without looking back.

Inside, dust coated the black marble floor of the foyer. The once-grand staircase in front of him had rotted away and was missing several steps. A number of doors to the left and right led to other areas of the house.

Christian tried to determine where he should search first. No Life Kings preferred living in darkness. Their hatred of light was one of their few weaknesses. If a No Life King was going to hold a captive, it would want her somewhere with little to no light.

Lilith is probably in the basement.

Making a quick decision, Christian traveled through the first door on his left. It led to a large dining room with a long table. He ignored the fancy decor as he ran across the room and burst through the door on the other side of the room.

The next area was a hallway with dark-red carpet and white walls. Several paintings that must have been expensive at some point lined the walls, their canvases torn and the paint cracked. Christian ran down the hall until he came to the first door and opened it. Seeing that it was nothing more than a parlor, he shut the door and continued running.

It took more time than he wished, but he eventually found a flight of stairs leading down to the basement. Christian knew very little about the layout of old Victorian mansions like this, but he knew they sometimes held more than one basement level. He hoped this route would lead to Lilith.

Christian fumbled as darkness engulfed him. His hands ran along the wall before he found a light switch. He was pleased to see that the bulbs still worked. The area lit up, revealing a hallway made entirely of dull gray stone. He was tempted to say the room looked like a dungeon, except it was too nice to be a dungeon. A wine cellar, maybe?

Christian moved cautiously. The sound of his feet thudding against the floor and his slow breathing was accompanied by soft creaking that echoed down the corridor.

The hallway eventually opened up into a large room, a cylindrical chamber with several doors. His gaze swept across the interior while his stride took him further in, until he stopped within the center.

Instincts screamed at him, warning him of impending danger. Yet he could see nothing that might be dangerous. Just an empty room with—

A feeling surged through him, the tingle along his spine telling him of impending attack. Christian rolled forward, the attack missed, along with several other attacks that manifested in the form of thin wires lashing at the ground, creating thin slash marks in the stone.

As he rolled onto his feet, Christian whirled around, whipping out Phanuel at the same time. He fired a barrage of bullets that were sliced to pieces by thin, razor sharp wires that moved around a red-cloaked figure like a shield.

Deciding that even more firepower was needed, Christian pulled Gabriel out of its holster. The silver gun added to the amount of gunfire being unleashed. The wires whipping around the red-cloaked figure moved faster in response. While the wires were busy slicing apart his bullets, Christian rushed forward.

The Assassin tried to move backward, but doing so caused several of his wires to slip and become tangled. If Christian had been a more conceited person, he would have smirked at the sight. It had taken him a while to work out a way to beat those gloves, but he had eventually figured it out.

Uriel and Barachiel offered their wielder the ability to attack from many directions at once in the form of ten Orichalcum wires. However, while the gloves allowed their wielder to attack from ten places at the same time, it was very difficult for the user to keep track of everything: the wires, the paths they moved in, the position of the opponent, their surroundings, and their wielder's own movement. There too many variables for even the most talented of combatants to keep track of at all times.

As Phanuel ran out of ammo, Christian clicked a switch on the side, causing the now empty cartridge to fall out and clatter to the ground. He continued firing Gabriel, his finger pulling the trigger fast enough that it seemed like he was shooting an automatic pistol.

The hand holding Phanuel dipped into his cloak, where he kept several cartridges of ammo strapped to his thighs. With practiced ease, he pressed a button that caused the cartridge to slip out of its holder, then swiftly moved his gun so the cartridge slid into it. He hit his thigh with the butt, locking the ammo into place, then brought it out of his cloak and began firing again.

Putting more pressure on his opponent, Christian forced the cloaked figure to back up against the circular wall. The Assassin was obviously not paying attention to his surroundings, busy as he was trying to deflect Christian's constant barrage of gunfire. The wires smacked against hard stone, gouging out several lines and, more importantly, halting the wires' continuous motion. This was the chance Christian had been looking for.

Rushing forward, Christian slid his guns back into their holsters before drawing Michael and Raphael. A second after that he reached his opponent.

He thrust his blades forward, penetrating flesh, muscle, and bone, along with the wall behind the cloaked Assassin. Blood spurted from the wounds, a clear sign that he had sliced into arteries or veins. The crimson liquid ran across his blades, dripping off and splashing against the floor.

A second passed. Then two. Finally, a breathy sigh escaped the cloaked figure. It was light, airy, and slightly high pitched, as if the person was just going to sleep instead of dying.

As the figure slumped over his swords, he pulled them out and took a step back, letting the body crumple to the floor. He waited for a second to see if it would get up, but when nothing happened, he knelt down next to the figure and took a long, hard look.

The corpse was lying on its front, so Christian turned it over. When he did, the hood fell away to reveal the person he had killed.

"That is not Anthony," he stated to himself as long crimson hair spilled out of the hood to halo the body. Aside from Anthony having brown hair, he was also a male. This person was clearly female, an Assassin he didn't recognize.

He dismissed the idea of her being a ghoul, as she'd been far too capable a fighter. While ghouls were physically stronger than humans, they were also stupid. Nothing more than soulless husks, they possessed a limited intelligence. They could follow simple orders but were incapable of complex thoughts beyond *kill this* or *guard that.* Ghouls were cannon fodder at best.

This woman had fought him with a strength, ferocity, and cunning that no ghoul could match. Another vampire? Unlikely. An enthralled human? Maybe. No Life Kings were more than capable of cursing or enthralling humans. Christian supposed he would never find out now.

Since there was no point in staying there, Christian left the room and continued his search. This battle might have been finished, but there was another fight awaiting him. The battle that he had just fought would be nothing compared to the one he was knowingly walking into.

But, before he engaged in mortal combat with a No Life King, he had to find Lilith.

Chapter 24

Lilith wasn't in the basement, which he had discovered was indeed a wine cellar. He didn't know how long he'd searched through that basement, but according to the reports coming in through his headset, it had been long enough that Catherine and her team had dealt with all the ghouls.

From the small bits of dialogue he allowed himself to listen to, the SIU members had only lost two members, which was good, considering they were all a bunch of wet-behind-the-ears rookies when it came to dealing with supernatural monsters.

After leaving the basement, Christian began a more thorough search of the first floor. Several SIU members were inside, including Catherine. Upon spotting him walking down one of the mansion's many hallways, she ran to catch up.

"Christian!"

Turning around, Christian waited for Catherine to reach him. Then, together, they started moving once more, with the SIU police officer trying to keep pace with his long strides.

"I see you've taken care of the ghouls," Christian observed.

"We have. And I take it you haven't found the girl Lilith, or her friends?"

"I think the answer to that should be obvious." Christian was not often one for sarcasm, but his frustration at failing to find Lilith shortened his fuse considerably.

"Yes, I suppose it is." Catherine seemed unaffected by his snappish reply, or perhaps she simply chose not to openly show her annoyance. "What about the No Life King and his partner?"

"I've already killed his partner." Christian turned down another corridor. Catherine stuck to his side as they walked. "It was a woman that I've never seen before. She wasn't a ghoul. Her body is in the wine cellar. I know it's an unusual favor to ask, but could you see to it that the body is sent to the Executioners Headquarters?"

"I take it there is something special about this person?" Catherine inquired.

"Not the person so much as what she's carrying, a weapon of the Church. It belonged to another Executioner, so the fact that she has it is cause for alarm. The church will want to retrieve her body and the weapon."

Catherine thought about his request before slowly nodding. "I don't see why I can't do this for you. I'll have my men retrieve the body and deliver it to the Catholic Church once this operation is finished."

"Thank you."

"*Ma'am.*" A male voice came over the communication devices inside of their ears. Catherine didn't break stride as she followed Christian down the twisting maze of corridors.

"What is it?"

"*We've found a really large door near the back of the mansion that looks like it might contain something important. The locks on this thing are pretty impressive. We plan on breaking through to see what's inside, but it's going to take a while. We're out of plastic explosives.*"

"That's probably the No Life King's sleeping chamber," Christian informed Catherine. "It and its human accomplice probably enthralled several people to install that door before killing them. I would tell your men to leave it alone. If it's locked, then it means the No Life King is inside. Breaking into the beast's chamber wouldn't be a wise move."

"Right. You hear that? Don't try getting past that door. Wait until Christian and myself arrive before—"

Catherine was interrupted by the squeal of tearing metal from the other end, which was so loud Christian and Catherine almost ripped their headsets out of their ears. Christian could only imagine how the officers in close proximity to the sound were dealing with it.

However, the noise gave way to a much bigger problem. He and Catherine were forced to listen to the sound of gunfire and screams.

"Oh, God! What the hell is that thing?!"

"Wings! It has wings!"

"Fire! Fire!"

"Delta squad? Delta squad, come in!" Catherine stopped walking as she shouted into her headset. Christian followed suit, turning around to watch the woman's frantic calling. "Delta squad!"

"Come on." Christian grabbed her by the arm and started dragging her behind him as he ran through the hallway. "I know it's difficult, but we've got to keep moving or this entire mission is a bust."

"Delta squad! Come in, Delta squad!" Catherine continued yelling into her headset.

"Delta squad is gone," Christian told her. "They just had a meeting with a No Life King. There's no way they could have survived that encounter."

"Dammit!" she swore before speaking into her headset again. "Alpha squad! Omega squad! The enemy is on the loose. I repeat, the enemy is on the loose. Keep your eyes peeled, your guns at the ready, and make sure you've got your squad-mates' backs."

The comlink crackled with static. *"Ma'am!"*

"We were completely unprepared for this." Catherine clenched her teeth, air whistling through them as she and Christian rushed swiftly down hallway after hallway. They blurred passed several doors, their frames barely lit by the almost-burnt-out bulbs glowing overhead.

"That's to be expected." Christian made a sharp turn as they rounded a corner. "You're not only new to all this, but your group is working with standard equipment meant for dealing with humans, not supernatural monsters."

Catherine scowled, but didn't say anything to dispute the claim.

They rounded another corner. This one opened into a larger-than-average hallway with a single door at the end. As they ran to it, Christian's danger sense warned him of an impending attack.

"Look out!"

He shoved Catherine away, and then rolled across the floor just in time to avoid getting impaled by a small throwing knife, which embedded itself into the carpet. Coming back to his feet while Catherine scrambled to her own, Christian pulled Phanuel back out of its holster and aimed it at the person who had attacked them.

He hesitated when he saw who it was.

"Maria? Stacy?"

The two women dropped from a small hole in the ceiling, where they had obviously been lying in wait. It looked as if they'd set this area up as an ambush point, which meant Lilith was likely on the other side of that door.

"You know these two?" Catherine's gun was trained on the two girls, one of whom held a knife in her hands, revealing her to be the culprit who'd thrown the other knife at them.

"They're Lilith's roommates."

"And why are they attacking us? Are they ghouls as well?"

Christian shook his head.

"No, look at their skin. It's still healthy, and they're still breathing. Their movement is also too natural to be a ghoul's. I'm pretty sure they've been enthralled. It's one of the two abilities unique to a No Life King, the other being their ability to curse people."

"Curse?" Catherine eyed the two stationary women. Christian wondered why they weren't attacking. "You mean like spells and stuff?"

"It's not a spell. By injecting a person with its blood, it has the ability to do one of two things: control them through the phenomena known as enthralling, or curse them to create a passive phenomenon such as giving someone really bad luck. We call it cursing, but really, all they're doing is forcibly changing a person's genetic structure through the power of their blood."

"Sounds nasty." Catherine walked sideways, keeping the two women in her sights. Christian also watched them. Maria looked ready to throw her other knife, while Stacy took a combat stance. "Any suggestions on how to deal with these two?"

Christian readied his swords. "The only thing we can do is knock them unconscious. It won't break them of their enthrallment, but so long as they remain unconscious, the blood in their system will be rendered ineffective."

"And how do we break the enthrallment?"

"The only way to break their enthrallment is by killing the No Life King who enthralled them."

"… Great—"

The two girls attacked. Maria flung her throwing knife at Christian while Stacy charged Catherine. Knowing that she couldn't use her weapon on them, Catherine holstered her gun, and brought her hands up in a guard position just as Stacy reached her.

Christian rushed at Maria, dodging to the left and letting the knife sail past him. Then he was in front of her, unloading a powerful yet swift jab to her temple. The woman dodged by tilting her head, but all that meant was that, instead of getting punched in the face, she received a knee to the stomach.

Christian gave Maria no reprieve as she stumbled backward. His fists shot out in blurring corkscrews and powerful straights. Despite being enhanced by the No Life King's blood, he was clearly the superior fighter.

He slipped a punch through her guard, knocking her upside the temple and rendering her unconscious. He caught her before she could hit the ground, gently laying her against the wall. With his opponent taken care of, he turned to see how Catherine was holding up, and saw that she had already knocked Stacy out cold.

"Call your men and have them come pick these two up," Christian said. "Have them sent to the hospital, and tell the doctors to keep them sedated. So long as they're unconscious, the No Life King can't send them commands."

"Right." Catherine frowned at him. "I don't like taking orders from you, but it's clear to me that you have more experience with this than I do. We'll do things your way for now."

"Thank you." Christian gave her a nod. "I'm going to go on ahead. Please wait here. We need to keep an eye on these girls. It would be a pain if they woke up and attacked us from behind."

"I got it." Catherine waved him off. "You go rescue your girl. I'll stay with these two."

That was all the answer Christian needed. He raced down the hall and, before even reaching the door, pulled out Gabriel and took careful aim at the handle. Two precise shots struck the brass knob, destroying the locking mechanism and allowing him to kick the door in and rush inside.

The room, much like the rest of the mansion, was dark. The vampire had obviously gone to great pains to keep this place sealed from natural sunlight and radiation. A small candle on a nightstand next to a bed served as the room's only illumination.

Christian's eyes were drawn away from the candle when something on the bed moved. A shivering lump—that's what it looked like, until his eyes adjusted to the room's low lighting and he discovered the lump to be a person.

Her knees were drawn to her chest, and she wasn't facing him, but he'd recognize her anywhere.

"Lilith!"

Christian was beside the bed in a matter of seconds. Lilith didn't seem to have heard him, but her body had become still, as if she were petrified. He leaned over and placed a hand on her shoulder.

"Lilith? Lilith, it's me—"

A loud wail of terror erupted from Lilith the moment he touched her. He jerked backward as the girl kicked and struggled like she was locked in combat against aggressors' unknown. His surprise only lasted for a moment before he moved back, wrapping his arms around her middle and trying to calm her with his presence, only to be forced off when an elbow slammed into his gut.

"No! Get away from me! Don't touch me!"

"Lilith, you need to calm down! You're safe now!"

He tried to reassure her, but Lilith wasn't listening. If anything, his words only seemed to fuel her desperation, increase her struggling. She lashed out with a fist that caught Christian straight in the nose, drawing blood. The heel of a bare foot smacked his right eye, and he knew that he'd be sporting a shiner tomorrow. Another hand crashed against his chin, his teeth clacking together harshly from the force of the blow.

"Lilith! Stop it!"

Lilith didn't stop, and Christian did the only thing that he could think of. When she tried attacking him again, he grabbed the offending limb, yanked the girl off the bed, and pulled her into his chest, where his arms wrapped tightly around her. Her struggling grew even more desperate, but he continued calling out to her.

"Lilith! It's me! It's Christian!"

Lilith's struggles lessened as the name struck a chord within her. He looked down at her as she stared at his chest, her eyes fluttering rapidly. She then looked up at him, staring into his face, her own a rictus of confusion.

"Christian?"

"Hey." Christian's heart went out to her. She seemed so small against his chest. "You finally back with me?"

"Christian…"

Lilith's face scrunched up in a grimace. She sniffled once, then twice. Tears gathered in her eyes, and then spilled over, small droplets of crystalline liquid running down her perfect skin.

Christian's eyes widened.

"Lilith, I…"

"Christian!"

Without warning, Lilith shoved against him. He fell backward as she pushed him off the bed, landing on his backside with a loud *crack!* Two arms wrapped tightly around his waist, and she buried her face against his chest.

With the realization that she was in his presence, the floodgates seemed to open. Lilith lay on top of him, straddling his thighs as her fingers clutched his shirt, the front of which grew wet with tears. Her body shook, the combination of her wracking sobs, the overwhelming fear she must have felt upon realizing she'd been kidnapped and, hopefully, her relief at being rescued by him.

Christian's own relief was an almost palpable thing. Lilith was alive. He didn't know what had happened to her, but in that moment, nothing mattered to him except the girl in his arms.

He hugged her back, one arm going around her waist. With his other hand, he gently combed through her hair as he whispered reassurances in her ear, telling her that everything would be all right, that he was with her now, that she was safe. At some point, the tears stopped coming, though she still occasionally sniffled. The entire front of his shirt was soaked.

"Are you all right now, Lilith?"

"Idiot…"

Whatever he had been expecting her to say, calling him idiot was not it.

"P-pardon?"

"You… idiot! Idiot, idiot, idiot!" The insulting words were followed by the gorgeous blond repeatedly slamming her fist into his chest. While Christian sat there, blinking like some kind of fool as he tried to discern the reason for her continuously calling him an idiot, Lilith pushed herself off his chest so she could glare at him through red-rimmed eyes. "You left me! You left me standing there in front of my apartment, you jerk!"

Christian opened his mouth to speak, only to snap it shut before he could get a word out, when he found himself receiving the full brunt of Lilith's glare. The fact that she had tear tracks staining her cheeks did nothing to lessen the expression, which kept him from saying something he might regret later on.

Christian pulled Lilith back into a hug, resting his chin on the crown of her head. She didn't resist, which he was thankful for. He was also thankful that she had stopped insulting him.

"I'm sorry. I don't have any excuse other than my own discomfort with the situation. I know I shouldn't have run out on you, especially after you… after what you told me."

"You had better be sorry," Lilith snapped, and then sniffled. She hugged him again, her grip surprisingly strong. She turned her head, placing her ear against his chest. "I was so scared. I was attacked by my own roommates. They knocked me unconscious somehow and brought me here. And then I found out that Damien is the one who kidnapped me and—"

"Wait," Christian interrupted. "Who?"

"Damien." Lilith shuddered, as if just saying that name brought its own special brand of fear. "Do you remember the guy I told you about? The one that I used to think I liked?"

"Vaguely." Christian took a moment to recall that conversation. "You mentioned a guy that you thought was different from everyone else, kinda like me, I guess, except you found out that he was using you."

"He wasn't just using me," Lilith said. "He was obsessed with me. He was always watching me. It wasn't noticeable at first, but it became more obvious after I turned fifteen. Sometimes, when I was doing homework in my room, he would be standing outside of my window staring at me. Other times I'd wake up, and he would be in my room watching me. I eventually began to feel uncomfortable with it and told him so, but he would just laugh it off like it wasn't a big deal. Then he said that I was his, that I belonged to him. When I told him that I didn't want to be with him, he… he…"

"Lilith?" Christian tried pretending the tremor in his voice wasn't there. He needed to be strong for Lilith's sake. "What happened? What did he do?"

"He killed my mom!" More sobs tore their way up Lilith's throat. "He tore her throat open and made me watch! I ran away after that, but he told me that no matter where I ran, he would always find me! And so I kept running and running and I even changed my name in the hopes that it would throw him off my track! But it didn't work! He found me again! And he's controlling my friends somehow! And he's got wings! Wings, Christian! Like some kind of monster! And I… and I…"

"It's okay," Christian whispered as his fingers ran through her hair. "You don't need to worry about your friends. I've already rescued them."

Lilith relaxed as his calloused fingers caressed her hair.

"You did?"

"I did. They're currently being taken somewhere safe. All that's left is for me to get you out of here, and take care of the guy who kidnapped you."

"Take care of him?" It looked like Lilith needed several seconds to wrap her mind around that statement. When she finally seemed to realize what he meant, she removed herself from his comforting embrace to stare at him in horror. "But you can't! Listen, Christian, I don't think Damien is human!"

"I already know that he's not human," Christian admitted.

Lilith looked startled. "You do?"

Christian nodded.

"Then you should know that you can't beat him!" Lilith cried. "I know that you're a skilled fighter. I remember when you fought those men who surrounded us, but you're still only human! Damien was standing on the ceiling, Christian! He stood on the ceiling like he was defying gravity! And he has these big wings and sharp claws and strange powers. You can't... fighting against him... it's hopeless! Please don't do it!"

"Lilith—"

"I love you!" Lilith blurted out. "I know that we haven't known each other long, but I love you so much! So you can't fight him! You can't fight him because if you do, you'll die! And then I'll be all alone! And if you leave me alone, then I won't get to see you anymore! I just can't... I can't bear the thought of losing you like I lost Mom!"

Hearing Lilith's passionate declaration of love caused Christian's heart to throb painfully. This painful feeling, this fist that clenched his heart... it mixed with the warmth of her words, easing the doubts that he'd been facing, the dilemma that made him run out on her before. He knew what his feelings for her were now. He couldn't deny them any longer.

"Lilith." Christian prepared to confess his own feelings. "I—"

"I slumber for a few short hours and look at what happens." A voice spoke above them, and they both stiffened. "Several disgusting humans hath attempted to break into my room, my new maids were stolen from me, the bodyguard that I hath procured for my Queen was killed, and I find my Queen straddling the body of another man. I must admit, I am feeling most displeased by this recent turn of events."

"No... oh, please no," Lilith whispered, her body shaking like a leaf. Her eyes, wide and frightened, looked more terrified than Christian had ever seen them. "Please don't let it be him. Don't let it be him."

As terrified tears fell from Lilith's eyes, Christian glared up at the creature that had caused such a reaction. The person standing on the ceiling as if defying gravity was as simple as breathing looked almost human, like a young man barely into his twenties. Crimson eyes like blood glared down at him. Translucent white skin lent the creature an ethereal air, which contrasted with its dark suit. Long pointed ears sat on its head, and pinions jutted from its back.

This was the first time that Caspian had ever seen a No Life King. He didn't know what he should have expected, but vileness radiating from those eyes, the blackness of its wings, and the overpowering and tainted aura that it released caused a cold sweat to break out on his brow.

"You're Damien, I'm guessing?" Christian asked.

Damien's malicious grin revealed sharp fangs. "I am he. And I am assuming that thou art the one responsible for all this ruckus. You need not say anything. There is no point in denying your complicity in this. For the crimes of killing my bodyguard, stealing my maids, and attempting to take my Queen, I shall sentence thee to an eternity of suffering and damnation."

Chapter 25

This was one of those times where Christian wished that his glares could cause physical harm. He stared up at the monster disguised as a handsome young man, who defied gravity by standing on the ceiling. The being met his stare with a look of bland annoyance. Lilith still lay on top of Christian, her body shaking and her face pressed into his chest. Feeling how frightened she was caused rage to well up inside of him.

"So you're Damien." Christian narrowed his eyes. "The creature who treated Lilith like some kind of object and killed her mother."

"An object?" Damien tilted his head to the left, his hair swishing. "Of course not. Eve is to be my Queen."

"Don't…" Lilith's shaking intensified. "Don't… call me that…"

"Thou hath no need to be so obstinate, my Queen." Damien said the words as if he truly meant them. "Everything that I do is for you. Now then, my dear sweet Eve, come here so that I might deal with this intruder."

"Stop calling me Eve!" Lilith screamed, emphatically shaking her head. "That's not my name anymore! And stop calling me your Queen! I don't want to be your Queen! I don't want to be your anything!"

Damien stared at her for several seconds, his expression bland. Then he sighed and closed his eyes.

"You still refuse to see reason." He sounded almost apologetic. "After I deal with these intruders—that man in particular—I will need to resume your reeducation. Your responses are most unbefitting of a Queen."

Lilith's grip on Christian tightened, something that he did not fail to notice.

"Lilith," Christian whispered into her ear. "I want you to reach into my cloak. Find the strap that has several objects attached to it. Grab the spherical one, and hit the button on it twice."

Damien scowled as he watched Christian whispering into his Queen's ear.

"You would do well to stop acting so close to my Queen. You're already slated for an eternity of suffering. Believe me when I say that you do not want to exacerbate your already tenuous predicament."

"Can you do that?" Christian continued, carefully watching as the monster's glare intensified. Lilith nodded against his chest. "Good, then do it quickly."

"I'm warning you, human. Do not make your situation any worse than it already is."

He felt Lilith's hand slip from around his waist and dive into his cloak. Feminine digits roamed over his chest, searching for the object he had mentioned. It didn't take long before they closed around the spherical item in question.

"That's the one." Christian's arms loosened around Lilith as he prepared to act. "Now, the button on top, hit it twice."

"If you don't stop talking so familiarly to my Queen, human, I am going to make you regret it," Damien continued. Christian ignored him. So long as Lilith was on top of him, that creature wouldn't do anything.

"I've done it," Lilith whispered softly.

"Good, now give it to me." His left hand slid around Lilith's frame so she could place the item into it. He then tilted his head to penetrate Damien with a glare. "I don't know who you think you are, but I will never let something like you take Lilith!"

The scowl on Damien's face deepened. "You're saying that as if thou hath some kind of choice in the matter. Tell me, human, what do you think you can possibly do to me?"

"How about this!"

With lightning-quick speed, Christian threw the tiny sphere at Damien, whose eyes were drawn to the device in curiosity.

"Lilith! Close your eyes!"

Doing as she was told, Lilith shut her eyes tightly, and Christian followed suit. Moments later, the room lit up with the brilliance of a thousand suns, visible even behind his eyelids.

"GAHHH!"

Christian couldn't see anything, but he didn't need eyes to hear the screams of anguish as Damien's corneas were burned.

"Time to run," he shouted as he scooped Lilith into his arms and shot to his feet. Even without his eyesight, Christian's spatial awareness showed him the door's location, and he burst through it without a backward glance. Several seconds later, the brilliant white light abruptly vanished, and darkness returned.

Christian opened his eyes. He raced down the darkened hallway. The lights had blown out. He could scarcely see where he was going, but he didn't rely on his eyesight to move. He rushed through dark corridors, taking turns seemingly at random, yet knowing exactly where he was going, having memorized the route out.

"What was that?" Lilith asked as she clung to Christian's neck.

"Sun grenade," Christian answered. Even from this distance, he could hear the pained wails of the No Life King. "It's a new invention that captures and releases sunlight. It works quite well on vampires and, as you can see, it works just as well on No Life Kings. I doubt it hurt him, but it's definitely going to leave him blinded for a while."

"Oh." Lilith's voice told Christian that she clearly didn't understand what he was talking about. "Wait. Did you say vampires?"

"DAMN HUMAN!!" The roar that echoed through the hall kept Christian from answering.

"Tch! I guess this guy really is a No Life King. No regular vampire could have survived getting hit with what amounts to a supernova-worth of UV rays." Christian grunted as he put on a burst of speed. "Hang on, Lilith!"

Lilith did hang on. She tightened her arms around his neck as Christian burst through into the foyer, dashed across the open space, and then peeled out of the entrance like Cerberus was nipping at his heels.

The midday sun stung Christian's eyes after spending nearly three hours in the darkened corridors of the mansion. Catherine stood near the fountain along with squads Alpha and Omega. Several large transport vehicles, including an emergency ambulance, gleamed brightly as the sun reflected off their metal hulls.

"I take it this is the girl," Catherine stated more than asked, as Christian ran up to them. Lilith's grip on his neck tightened when they entered the large circle of men surrounding the SIU captain.

"She is." Christian glared at all the men when he saw how they were affecting Lilith. "And I would like to suggest that you order your men to stop looking at her."

Catherine turned to glance at her men. All of them stared at Lilith with the hungry leers of a teenager visiting his first porn shop. They appeared to have completely forgotten their purpose.

"Don't you all have something that you need to be doing?!" Before Christian could even blink, the men ogling Lilith were suddenly doing something else. Wearing a rather prominent smirk, Catherine turned back to look at him. "Better?"

"Much." Christian nodded as Lilith relaxed in his arms. "Thank you."

"So, you're Lilith." Catherine leaned down to get a closer look at Lilith, who buried her face against Christian's chest, causing the SIU captain to laugh. "She's awfully shy."

"Yes, well, getting kidnapped by a madman would make anyone a little skittish, I think," Christian replied.

"Yes, I can see how that would make a person wary of others." Catherine straightened up and dusted off her suit. "Did you take care of that No Life King?"

"No." Christian shook his head. "I can't fight a No Life King *and* protect Lilith at the same time. I decided that getting her to safety took precedence over fighting off a creature that I may not even be able to defeat on my own."

Catherine raised an eyebrow. "Are you sure that was a wise idea?"

"Yes," Christian said. "I'm sure. Now that Lilith is safe, we can begin making plans to dispose of the No Life King, and I can fight without holding back."

"And what if he decides to flee?"

"He won't." For the first time since she and Christian joined Catherine, Lilith spoke up. "Damien's egotistical and arrogant, and Christian humiliated him by escaping with me. There's no way he'll just cut his losses and run. He's going to come looking for revenge."

Christian didn't know Damien, but he knew that No Life Kings were generally an arrogant bunch. It came with the territory. Living as long as they did and becoming as powerful as they were would make anyone arrogant.

"And besides," Lilith spoke again, her voice soft. "Damien is obsessed with me. Now that he's found me again, he won't rest until he has me in his grasp. He's not leaving."

"If what you say is true, then we can definitely come up with a plan to deal with him." Catherine appeared thoughtful. Christian just frowned at the thought of Damien remaining to continue chasing after Lilith. "We'll need to come up with a detailed plan, but I think we can make this work. Come on, you two. You both look exhausted, and I want you, Christian, to be at your best once we've got a plan to deal with this Damien."

***

Christian frowned as he stared at his bed and, more specifically, the many items that lay strewn across it. It was all the ordnance he had left. Next to the bed, his black weapons case seemed depressingly empty without any of its contents inside.

He'd taken to separating all of his munitions by type. Some of these items wouldn't serve any purpose other than slowing him down. Very few weapons worked on No Life Kings. Silver didn't affect them as it did werewolves, poison didn't work on them since blood no longer pumped through their veins, and regular lead bullets were about as effective as pellets from an airsoft gun. The only ammo he had that would work were liquid nitrogen bullets, which were designed to deal damage to heavily armored opponents, and Liquid Sunlight bullets, the Science Division's newest invention.

Just what possessed the Science Division to come up with such a stupid name was beyond him. There was nothing liquid about these bullets. They were specialized bullets made with Orichalcum shells that contained upwards of two-million kW/m^2. A single shot to the heart from one of those should be enough to put even a No Life King down—at least that's what he was banking on.

Michael and Raphael lay next to Gabriel and Phanuel. His four specialized weapons gleamed silver and black. Lying next to his weapons of choice was the sniper rifle, which he *still* didn't know what to do with. He honestly wasn't even sure why he'd brought it anymore. The thing was useless.

One by one, Christian loaded the ammo clips that he would be using, placing them in the straps that would go around his thighs. He'd only be taking the nitrogen and sun bullets with him. He put everything else away. it was too bad he didn't have any more sun grenades. He placed his guns on the nightstand and leaned his swords against the wall. As he finished his preparations for the coming conflict, his cell phone started blasting *Dirty Deeds*.

"You need something, Tristin?" he asked.

"Wha... how'd you know it was me?"

Christian deadpanned, even though the other man couldn't see it. "You're the only one in my phone with an AC/DC ringtone."

"Oh, so you kept my ringtone? Yay! I'm so happy!"

"Is it just me? Or have you gotten even more childish since the last time we spoke?"

"It's definitely you," Tristin said before getting somewhat serious. *"So, this is it, huh? You'll be taking on that No Life King soon?"*

"Yes," Christian answered. "I would rather deal with it during the day, but I doubt that monster is stupid enough to fight against us when it's at its weakest. I suppose we could go back to its mansion, but it would hold all the advantages there. Maneuvering in the enclosed space is difficult, and I need all the space I can to utilize my style to its fullest."

"Right. I would wish you luck with the upcoming battle, but considering you're you, I doubt you'll need it. Anyway, listen, I just got through checking over Lilith's information and wanted to tell you—"

"Could you tell me a little later?" Christian interrupted before the man could speak. "I think Lilith just got out of the shower."

"The shower? Is she there with you?"

"We'll talk about this after my battle, okay?"

"Wait, Christian—"

But Christian ended the call, and set his phone on the nightstand. Behind him, the bathroom door opened. He turned his head just as Lilith stepped out.

She walked into the room, drying her hair with a towel. Pearlescent drops of water trailed down her skin, glistening in the light. She still wore the nightgown from when he had rescued her. The damp red silk clung to her body, showing off her well-proportioned figure, while maintaining a semblance of modesty.

Catherine hadn't let her return home to get a change of clothing, claiming that it was too dangerous, and that it would be better if she just stayed at Christian's hotel. He thought the woman was being a tad paranoid, but couldn't really blame her. They were going up against one of the strongest abominations in the world. Paranoia could only be a good thing in this instance.

And it's not like I mind her staying with me.

"Who was that on the phone?" Lilith asked as she walked further into the room, curious eyes glancing around at the sparsely decorated interior.

"Just a friend," Christian answered automatically.

"I see…"

"You know, I never got the chance to ask this before, because of all the excitement, but are you okay?" Lilith looked at him, her head tilted quizzically. "I mean that you were with Damien for two whole days before we found you. It must have been a frightening experience."

Lilith smiled and walked up to him. She stopped in front of him and grasped his hands in hers. Bringing them up to her face, she pressed her lips against them. It was a surprisingly bold move on her part, but Christian couldn't find it in himself to complain.

"I'm fine." Lilith's voice was only slightly muffled by their hands. "It was terrifying. Just being in Damien's presence scares me. But, no matter how scared I was, I never gave up hope, because I knew that you would come for me."

Christian had once heard the saying *"The eyes are the window to the soul."* He'd never believed it until now. Lilith's eyes were twin pools of azure, filled with her love. As he stared into those gorgeous and innocent eyes, he felt like he could see Lilith's heart laid bare. It made him feel warm, and the smile that he gave her was a reflection of that feeling.

"Lilith… thank you."

"You're welcome."

Lilith's return smile was dazzling. Christian could honestly say that he had never seen anyone who possessed such an enchanting smile in his entire life. It caused his heart to hammer loudly in his chest. His mind nearly blanked as a strange urge overcame him, one that he dared not disobey.

Slowly, following a set of instincts that were more mimetic than anything else, Christian tilted his head. Lilith saw what he was doing, and tilted her head up in response, her eyes slowly fluttering closed.

The first contact was soft, fluttery, more of an ephemeral caressing of lips than an actual kiss. Contact only lasted for one second, maybe two. Despite the kiss's brevity, Christian marveled at the feel of Lilith's lips, like someone had slipped velvet on his mouth. When they pulled back, he stared at Lilith in astonishment.

"That was my first kiss."

Lilith, the lightest of blushes complimenting the fair skin of her cheeks, smiled ever so slightly. "That was my first kiss, too."

Christian could believe that. With her fear of men, it stood to reason that she had never kissed someone before, either.

"Lilith, I…"

"You can kiss me again, if you want to." Lilith's cheeks began coloring, yet she did not look away. She stared at him with those bright, vibrant eyes that were so full of life. "I don't mind."

Christian's mouth felt strangely dry. He raised his left hand, and rested his calloused palm against her cheek. She closed her eyes and leaned into his touch, humming pleasantly. When she opened her eyes again, they contained a look that he acted on without hesitation.

He leaned down again and pressed his lips to hers. He caught her lower lip between his, while his left hand slid from her face down her neck, across her shoulder and arm, before eventually coming to rest on her hip. His right hand also found purchase on the shapely curvature of her waist.

With a possessiveness that he didn't know he had, he pulled her close. Lilith moaned into his mouth, stoking the flames of passion that appeared with startling suddenness and frightening intensity. Her hands found their way to his head, her delicate fingers threading through his hair. They grasped his wild locks and pulled him down to capture more of the sensations that his mouth was giving her.

Being new to kissing, Christian couldn't say he knew what to do. He didn't know what he liked, didn't know what she liked, and just had no experience with the act in general. That hardly seemed to matter right then. Guided as he was by humanity's instinctual need for physical intimacy, he basked in the electric feeling this singular act generated within him.

He wanted more of this feeling. And so did Lilith, apparently.

Lilith walked forward, as if doing so would grant her more access to his mouth. Christian's response was for his hands to tighten around her waist as he moved back. His legs eventually hit the bed, causing him to tumble backward as he lost his balance. Neither of them stopped. Even as he and Lilith fell onto the bed, their lips remained firmly locked together. They didn't even stop when their teeth clacked together as they landed.

Lilith's hands traveled from his hair to his face. Then they slid down his neck, moved over his chest to his navel, before slipping underneath his shirt. Her two hands wandered, mapping out the hard contours of his body, feeling the small bumps of his six-pack, and traveling over the defined bricks that were his pectorals. Her fingers left goosebumps in their wake.

In response to this angel's delightful ministrations, Christian gained his own case of wandering hands. His calloused palms moved from Lilith's hips to her backside. She really did have an amazing butt, he marveled. Her cheeks were shapely and small, fitting perfectly in his hands, almost as if they were made to fit within his grasp. He grabbed the plentiful flesh and began kneading it as a baker kneads dough. Lilith's loud gasp was muffled by his mouth, and the deep moan that followed sent reverberations through his body, stoking the fire that blazed within him and turning it into a raging inferno.

Christian's enthusiasm got the better of him. The hands that grasped her delicious bum pulled her down. A jolt surged through him as her center rubbed against his erection. He felt it even through his pants and her dress. It caressed him, made him want more, made him want to pull her back down and feel her lips stroking him in ways that he'd never felt.

It also made him keenly aware of what they were doing.

"We… we should stop this," Christian muttered in between the small, intermittent pecks that he continued giving Lilith.

"We really should," Lilith moaned out before the last of those annoyingly unsatisfying pecks were caught in a voracious kiss. Her tongue plunged eagerly into his open mouth, stimulating him as it rubbed against his tongue and stirred up saliva between them. When they broke the kiss, a small liquid connection remained, until he licked his lips and broke it.

"This… this is wrong…"

"I agree…"

While the words spoken were against what they were doing, neither of them stopped. Christian's tongue pushed Lilith's back into her mouth and then chased after it, and she seemed all too happy to receive him. Her mouth closed around his tongue and she sucked on it, the action tipping him over the edge.

He ground his erection against her nether lips, which he could feel clearly through the thin fabric of her nightgown and his shorts. She was wet, and her wetness was beginning to stain his pants. That only served to make him want more.

Sometime after their mutual agreement to disengage from their activities, he and Lilith lost their clothing. Lying against each other, he and Lilith shared another round of passionate kisses.

Even within the haze of passion, Christian was amazed by how warm Lilith felt. Her body felt hot. Or maybe he was the one who felt hot. His tongue played with hers, exchanging saliva, hooking and pulling and pushing. Her hips ground into him, and he could feel her nether lips rubbing against his erection, hot and slippery, coating him in her juices and creating a euphoric feeling that he wished would never end.

"Christian…" Lilith moaned his name into his ear when they broke away for breath. Not satisfied with how they had stopped, she began nibbling on his earlobe. He had no clue where the idea to do such a thing came from, but he couldn't deny that feeling his ears being nibbled on and coated in her saliva drove him crazy.

Christian didn't know when their activities took that last, irrevocable step, but sometime during their satiric engagement, he and Lilith decided that they wanted more.

Straddling his waist, Lilith lined herself up with Christian and, without even a hint of hesitation, impaled herself on him, breaking through her hymen in one swift go. She must have forgotten about that protective membrane, because the second it broke, a loud cry escaped her lips and tears sprang to her eyes.

Hearing her pained cry and seeing the liquid silver leaving a trail down her cheeks had the same effect as dumping a bucket of ice water on him. The passion was replaced with worry. The need for continued sexual stimulation was doused by the knowledge that Lilith was hurting.

"L-Lilith, are you okay?"

"No." Despite her whimpers, and the tears running down her cheeks, Lilith smiled at him. Her right hand reached up to caress his face. "But I will be."

Now that the haze of lust induced by their passion had left him, Christian was perfectly aware of what they were doing. He could feel himself inside of her, feel their connection. Guilt settled in his stomach like a demon that refused to die.

"I-I don't know if we should continue," Christian gasped, resisting the urge to lose himself inside of Lilith's warmth. The tightness of her inner walls clamping down on him made it hard to think. "This... this isn't right..."

"Please don't say that." Lilith looked ready to cry again. "This is right. It is. I love you, and I want to be with you, not just spend time with you, but be with you like this, joined together as one. Please don't say this is wrong. Please don't reject me."

Christian looked away from Lilith's disturbing stare. Who knew that Lilith could be so adamant about something like this? Certainly not him. He had to wonder why she was comfortable enough to be connected with him like this. Even though he knew that she wasn't afraid of him, never in a million years would he have expected her to be comfortable enough with him to engage in this particular act.

"I would never reject you," Christian whispered. A pair of hands cupped his cheek, smooth palms turning his head and making him face Lilith.

"Then don't reject me now. Let be with you. Let me make love to you."

In the face of such an honest and heartfelt request, he found himself incapable of resisting. His defenses, worn down by days of being in this girl's presence, of seeing her every day, talking to her, walking her home, getting to know the woman behind the enchanting fairy tale princess facade, couldn't resist. His defenses crumbled as if they had never existed, and all that remained was his desire to please this young woman who had stolen his heart.

That night he and Lilith made love for the first time. It was awkward, stymied by the fact that neither of them had ever engaged in anything like this before, not just having sex, but also in regards to their relationship. They had taken a backward approach to things, he knew, sleeping together before becoming what most people would consider an official couple.

It also bothered him that they weren't married. What must God think of their actions? However, he couldn't deny his feelings and his desire to join with Lilith.

Besides, he reasoned with himself, *marriage is a shallow term these days. It means less than the paper it was written on. Marriage of the heart the important thing, of becoming one in both body and spirit. Who cares if the government officially recognizes our union? They're not God.*

In spite of their odd relationship, he found peace within her arms, within her touch, within her. He didn't know what lay in store for them. He didn't know how Samantha and the other Executioners would take this. He didn't even know where they would go from here. But in that moment, he found himself not caring. The disasters possibly awaiting them could wait. All he cared about was the woman in his arms. Nothing else mattered. No one but her.

Lilith.

Chapter 26

Knock. Knock. Knock.

He woke up with a start. Blinking several times, he tried fighting through the hazy fog that clouded his mind. It took him nearly five seconds longer than it should have to recognize the ceiling of his hotel room.

Knock. Knock. Knock.

As he became more alert, several facets of his current situation became obvious. The first was the large weight on his chest. The second was his lack of clothes.

Knock. Knock. Knock.

Looking down, he blinked some more when all he could see was blond. Lots and lots of blond. It took him several more seconds to realize what—no, not what, but *who* all of that blond hair belonged to. Lilith lay on top of him, her hair splayed across his chest and fanning out across the bed. The only thing he could see of her, aside from those beautiful locks of long blond hair, was a bit of her bare back and her butt. That's when he realized they had fallen asleep without covering themselves after their nightly activities. Or was it their afternoonly activities?

Knock! Knock! Knock! Knock!

The knocking reminded him of the reason that he had awakened in the first place. "Hang on," he shouted to whoever stood outside his room.

Knowing that he had to get up, Christian was about to try waking up Lilith, only to notice that she was already stirring. She lifted her head from his chest, her unfocused eyes blinking several times before coming to focus on his face. A second passed as she did nothing but stare, as if she wasn't quite sure what to make of him.

And then she smiled.

"Good morning, Christian," she said, inching upwards to plant a chaste kiss on his lips.

"Good morning." Christian smiled at her. She came in for another kiss, which lasted far longer than the first. "You're being awfully affectionate."

"You think so?" Lilith sighed, laying her head back down on his chest. "Is it so odd that I would be like this after what we shared last night?"

Christian needed a moment to think about that before shaking his head.

"No, I guess not."

"This might sound strange, but now that I'm here with you like this, all I want is to just stay here and kiss the living daylights out of you." Christian stiffened in more ways than one, causing Lilith's delightful giggle to caress his ears. "I wouldn't mind doing that with you again, either, but I'm still a bit sore from last night, so you'll have to give me some time to recover."

"You're also being a lot bolder," Christian muttered, shaking his head. "I've never heard you make a joke like that before. Are you sure you're really Lilith, and not some imposter who's just pretending to be her?"

Lilith giggled some more. She then turned her head and kissed his chest, sending shivers down his spine.

"I don't know why, but I just feel so amazing. I can't really explain it, but I feel almost like I've been reborn, or like I've become a new person."

"Really?" Christian frowned. Reborn? What did she mean by that? Did she feel this way because of what they did last night? Because of what they shared together? That couldn't be it. While he thought last night was amazing, he didn't feel any different.

"I really do." With a contented sigh, Lilith nuzzled her cheek against his chest. "I don't know why, but everything feels so much better now. I feel like I've become complete, like some part of me that I never realized was missing has suddenly been returned."

Christian didn't understand what she meant, but he supposed it didn't matter. If she felt this way, then it could only be a good thing.

"I'm glad." Christian kissed her forehead. "I hope that you'll always feel this way from now on."

Lilith rested her chin on his chest. Her eyes stared into his, and he felt like he could drown within her gaze. She really did have the most beautiful, expressive eyes that he had ever seen.

"I love you, Christian."

He smiled. "And I love you."

Lilith slowly pulled herself up. She leaned over him, her blond hair catching and reflecting sunlight as it draped over him like a curtain. Her eyes fluttered closed as she leaned down to kiss him, and he did the same, leaning up to claim her lips as he had a few short hours ago.

KNOCK! KNOCK! KNOCK!

"Christian! Lilith! Open this door right now!"

Their eyes widened as a shout penetrated the other side of the door. They looked at each other. He could see his wide eyes reflected in hers as their situation became more apparent. They were in a bed, naked, and someone was on the other side of the door, knocking and shouting, sounding about ready to break the door down if he didn't answer.

"Dammit, Christian! I don't know what you two are doing in there, but if you don't answer this door right now, I'm going to break it down!"

And it seemed her patience had worn off. He and Lilith scrambled off the bed, nearly becoming a tangled mess of limbs in the process, and hurried to get dressed. Before the woman on the other side of the door could make good on her threat, Christian, dressed only in his pants, answered the door by opening it just a crack and peering out.

Catherine stood on the other side of the door, hands on her hips, scowling and looking most displeased.

"Uh." Christian tried to think of something to say. "Good morning?"

"Christian," she said, and Christian could practically see the vein throbbing on her forehead. "Do you remember what I told you after we parted ways?"

Christian needed a moment to recall her words. His brain felt oddly fuzzy.

"Um, I think you told me to meet you at five, so that we could create a plan to deal with Damien."

"That's right, I said to meet me at five." Catherine nodded, seemingly pleased that he remembered this. He felt a chill run down his spine. "And do you know what time it is now?"

"Um, no?"

"I thought not. Just so you know, it is now five-thirty in the evening."

"Oh." Christian winced. "I'm sorry."

"You don't sound sorry," Catherine said, trying to peer through the crack in the door. Christian blocked her attempt, which made her frown. "Anyway, can I come in? I need to inform you and Lilith of the plan that we have come up with since *someone* decided not to show up."

"Would you mind waiting for just a second?" he asked. When Catherine's glare intensified, he knew that was the wrong thing to say and quickly elaborated. "I need to, um, get dressed…"

Catherine stared at him. She stared at him so hard that he wondered if she was trying to see whether it was possible to make him spontaneously combust with nothing but a glare. He met her glare head-on, not looking away. It wasn't as if he hadn't seen worse from some of the monsters he had killed. Abaddon's glares had been a truly frightening thing to behold. Compared to that, Catherine looked like a small child throwing a temper tantrum.

"Very well." Catherine sighed and closed her eyes, looking mildly exasperated. "But make it quick. And take this." She shoved a travel bag into his hands through the doorway. He looked from the bag to her. "I took the liberty of having someone head over to Lilith's apartment to grab her some clothes."

"Oh, thank you."

After closing the door, he turned around to see Lilith standing in front of him, wearing nothing but a pair of panties.

"That was the woman from before, wasn't it? The one who was with you when you rescued me?"

"Yes." He allowed himself a moment to admire the vision of perfection in front of him. He then held up the bag for Lilith to take. "Here, there are clothes for you in there."

"Thank you." Lilith took the bag from him with a smile. She then moved over to the bed, where she set the bag down, unzipped it, and pulled out the clothes contained therein.

Christian finished getting dressed as well, pulling a skin-tight sleeveless shirt over his head, and then strapped his guns and ammo clips to his thighs. His ensemble was finished after he slung his swords over his back and tightened the straps. He left the cloak hanging on his door. It would only hamper his movements this night.

"Christian?"

He paused. "Yes?" he asked, turning to Lilith who was biting her lower lip.

"When this is all over," she started, paused, then continued. "Will you tell me more about yourself?"

He didn't need to be a genius to know what she was talking about. Her gaze strayed from his face to the miniature armory on his person, making what she wanted to know about more than obvious.

Christian smiled at her.

"Yeah, when this is all over, I'll tell you everything."

His words brought a smile to her face.

When they finished getting dressed, he opened the door and allowed Catherine to enter. The female officer, her purple suit looking crisp as ever, paused at the doorway, her inquisitive gaze staring at the mess they had made of the bedroom and, more specifically, the bed. After a moment, she shook her head, and then walked to the window, where she turned around and leaned against the windowsill.

"We've come up with a plan to deal with that No Life King." Catherine paused, raising an eyebrow when she saw him and Lilith cuddling on the bed. He was grateful when she decided not to question them and continued. "The plan itself is very basic. We would have been able to come up with a more fool-proof plan if *someone* had decided to show up and grant us the boon of his expertise in supernatural matters."

It was pretty obvious that the jab was directed at him. The fact that Catherine was glaring right at him only helped confirm this fact.

"I wouldn't be able to give you much information." Christian shrugged. "No Life Kings all vary in strength. Some are so powerful that fighting them with anything less than an entire platoon of the best Warriors in the world is suicide. Others can be defeated by small teams of five. The only true weakness a No Life King has is the same weakness that all vampires have: sunlight."

"I see." Catherine looked put out by that piece of knowledge. "I doubt we could lure him out during the day."

"What's this plan you have to deal with Damien?" Lilith asked, speaking up for the first time since Catherine had arrived.

"Like I said, the plan is simple. We're going to have you act as bait to lure him out, and then—"

"No."

Catherine and Lilith looked at Christian, seemingly startled by his single word sentence.

"Excuse me?"

"I said no," he repeated, narrowing his eyes. "I'm not going to let you use Lilith as bait for that monster."

"Be reasonable, Christian," Catherine started. "We need her to—"

"No."

"Christian—"

"Not happening." He shook his head. "I didn't rescue Lilith just so you could put her in danger all over again."

"You are being completely unreasonable." Catherine looked about ready to punch his face in. "Lilith is the only sure-fire way of getting Damien to come out and—"

"And it's very likely she'll be kidnapped again, or worse, killed in the crossfire of the battle that will take place between our forces and Damien." He looked at the woman through narrowed eyes. "I'm not going to let you put Lilith in that kind of danger."

Catherine's right eye began twitching. "Christian—"

"No."

"You didn't even—"

"Nu-uh."

"Listen to—"

"Not. Gonna. Happen."

"Dammit, Christian! Would you stop being so stubborn and listen to me!"

"I'll do it."

Before he could tell Catherine that he had no intention of listening to her, Lilith's gentle voice spoke up. He and Catherine turned to look at her.

"Lilith?" he questioned.

"I'll do it. I'll act as bait."

He opened his mouth to protest, but her smile cut off any words that he might have used to deny her.

"I know that you just want to protect me, and it makes me really happy to know that you care about me. But you have to understand; Damien isn't going away. He's not going to leave me alone. As long as he is alive, he'll continue chasing after me. He'll chase me to the ends of the earth. It doesn't matter how far I run, he'll just find me again. He's already proven that he can track me from one side of the country to the other. I doubt even changing continents would keep him away for long."

"I still don't like it. I don't like the idea of you putting yourself in danger." He didn't like the idea of *anyone* not trained in combat risking their lives. His job was to protect people, like Lilith, who were innocent and couldn't protect themselves. How could he protect her if she put herself in jeopardy?

"I know you don't like it." Lilith's eyes softened as she raised a hand to caress his cheek. "But this is something that I want to do." She paused, then shook her head and began again. "No, this is something that I *have* to do. I'm tired of living in fear. I'm tired of having Damien constantly haunt my every step. I'm tired of always being afraid of the men around me, and letting what he did to me dictate my life. I want to do this, to move past my fear of him and men in general. Please, please let me do this."

He stared at her, his mind a hurricane of conflict. Her eyes contained a silent plea, asking him, begging him to let her do this. He didn't want her to. The idea of putting her in danger repulsed him.

Lilith was innocent, pure, someone whose outlook had yet to be tainted by conflict, despite her own tumultuous past. She wasn't like him, forged in the fires of sin, trained in the art of killing. What kind of person would he be if he willingly let her face such danger?

And yet, as he looked into her eyes, he questioned himself. Lilith was seeking closure, an end to her own suffering by confronting the thing she feared most. What right did he have to deny her this?

"All right." He closed his eyes and took a deep breath. Then he opened them again, and looked at the angelic woman sitting by his side. "I don't like this. I really don't. But, I suppose that, from an objective standpoint, it can be argued that you'll be safer with us than if we left you here, especially since you're Damien's priority. So, if you're really set on doing this, I'll… I'll support you to the best of my abilities."

"Thank you." Lilith smiled. The hand on his cheek slid through his hair. She grasped the back his head, and pulled his mouth onto to hers, pouring her gratitude and love into the kiss that he melted into.

"Ahem."

Jerking apart, he and Lilith snapped their heads over to Catherine, who gave them a look so dry that deserts everywhere were crying in jealousy.

"If you two are quite finished, then perhaps I can explain the rest of our plan to you."

He and Lilith had the decency to look abashed.

"Sorry," he said for the both of them. He made a hand gesture at Catherine. "Please, continue."

"Thank you. Now, the plan requires Lilith to act as bait…"

Chapter 27

From a copse of trees, Christian stared out at the open field where Lilith stood by herself, waiting for the arrival of Damien. He didn't like being forced to wait so far away from her. Catherine had told him that it was necessary for the plan, stating that Damien might realize it was an ambush and break off upon seeing him. He didn't believe that would happen, but Lilith had backed up Catherine, and seeing how she was the leading fount of knowledge on their current enemy, there was nothing that he could have said to change their minds.

Arrayed around the area were the two remaining squads that had arrived in Seal Beach with Catherine. Alpha Squad was on the far east side of the clearing, hidden underneath a large sheet designed to resemble the ground. Omega squad waited among the trees with him.

The plan to deal with Damien was simple. They would lure the No Life King out by using Lilith as bait. When he arrived, squads Alpha and Omega would unleash a barrage of motion-targeting missiles and take him out. While they unloaded their payload on Damien, Christian would run onto the field, grab Lilith, and retreat.

At least that was the plan. He didn't have the confidence in it that Catherine and Lilith seemed to. There was just too much that could go wrong. What if Damien didn't do what they expected? What if the missiles couldn't track him? Would missiles even work on such a monster?

"You worried?"

He craned his neck to see Catherine walk up to him. She wasn't looking at him, but at Lilith. Seeing this, he looked back at the source of his troubles.

"Yes."

There was no point in denying it. He *was* worried. What if he wasn't fast enough to reach Lilith before something happened? What if Damien grabbed Lilith before Omega and Alpha squads could unleash their payload? What if she got caught in the blast? There were so many things that could go wrong, and he didn't like it.

"How could I not be worried? This plan of yours is stupid."

His words didn't seem to be met with a very warm reception by Catherine's men—one of them at least. The titan of a man with the mane of wild hair frowned at him in what could only be described as stern disapproval. Christian ignored the look.

"So you say." Catherine had no trouble letting him know how little she cared. "But this was the only plan we came up with that has the greatest chance of succeeding. Lilith agrees."

He grunted, but didn't say anything else. It didn't matter what he thought anyway; the plan was already under way. All he could do was pray that this whole thing didn't backfire on them in some spectacular manner.

He looked up. The night was dark, but not pitch black. A full moon hung in the sky, acting as a silent witness to the events about to take place, and illuminating the ground with enough light that hampered visibility would not be an issue.

He was very glad they weren't facing a werewolf, whose powers reached their peak on nights with a full moon. He was also glad that Nathan hadn't attacked him on a full moon, as he probably wouldn't have survived.

"Ma'am!" The call came from someone above. He and Catherine looked up to see the spotter, a man whose dirty brown hair was flecked with gray. He was looking through a pair of high-tech binoculars trained on the airspace above Lilith. "He's coming!"

"All right, get down here. We don't want him seeing you," Catherine breathed out. "Okay, people. It's time. On my mark, I want you to open fire."

"Three..."

He looked into the open field, his eyes automatically zeroing in on Lilith. Even if he hadn't come to know her so well, he would have been able to tell that she was frightened. Her body shook from the crown of her head to the soles of her feet. Despite putting up a brave front with him, he had known from the moment she decided to help that the idea of confronting Damien terrified her.

"Two…"

It didn't help that whatever magic made her act so boldly with him that evening had vanished the moment they had left the room. Maybe the reason for her boldness was because she had been in the sanctity of their room, where the only people present had been her, him, and Catherine. He couldn't say for sure. He just knew that after they left, and upon finding herself in the presence of another man, Lilith had reverted to her shy, androphobic self.

"One…"

Looking away from Lilith and into the sky, his eyes narrowed. He could see Damien now. The No Life King was just a small black spot blocking out several stars, a silhouette in the general shape of a human with large wings that grew larger as he came closer.

"Fire!"

If he hadn't been prepared for it, the sound of a dozen rocket launchers going off at once would have been deafening. The entire park lit up as several FIM-92 Stinger Man-Portable Air-Defense Systems illuminated the area in a brief burst of orange and yellow. The rockets traveled at an unbelievable velocity, a tail of smoke trailing behind them.

Christian didn't wait to see if they would hit. The moment Catherine ordered her squads to fire, he dashed out from behind the trees and rushed toward Lilith. In his peripheral vision, he could see the two dozen missiles trying to track their target, who was proving to be extremely elusive, weaving between the missiles and making it look easy.

He knew this wouldn't be as simple as everyone else thought it would be. Damien had probably sensed the life signatures of multiple humans surrounding Lilith. It wouldn't have surprised him if the monster was prepared for an ambush even before everyone had gathered together for this assault.

He was at Lilith's side in seconds. The girl looked mesmerized by the aerial maneuvering of the No Life King. The missiles tried tracking Damien, but were unable to get a lock. The ancient vampiric monster confused their tracking systems with a series of twists and turns, causing them to crash into each other or slam into the ground, igniting in brilliant plumes of fire.

"Lilith," he shouted over the din of explosions, grabbing her arm and trying to get her attention. She turned to look at him, her eyes wide.

"Christian…"

"We need to go. Run toward the trees! I'll cover you!"

His commanding words prompted Lilith to snap out of her trance. With a quick nod, she ran off the way he had come, sprinting toward the copse.

"NO!" A shout came from above.

Eyes narrowing and a snarl ripping its way from his throat, Christian spun around, Phanuel and Gabriel flying out of their holsters. His fingers pulled the triggers, creating a stream of fire that was almost inhuman. Within the first second, he unloaded all the ammo in both magazines, forcing him to hit the release that caused the cartridges to slide out.

His plan for this action had been to force Damien to dodge, moving away from him and Lilith to avoid the hail of bullets. That was not what happened. Unfortunately, he was unaware of Damien's resolve and the lengths that the No Life King would go to in order to recapture Lilith. Rather than avoid the barrage of liquid nitrogen bullets, the powerful vampire took the storm head on, arms crossed in front of his face to keep the most important organ protected.

Holes appeared in Damien's arms and shoulders. Blood flew out of the numerous bullet wounds as the gunfire did its damage. Then each hole froze over as the nitrogen within the bullets activated. Damien wavered in his flight but didn't slow down. The barrage soon ended and he uncrossed his arms, dive-bombing toward Christian.

"YOU WON'T TAKE HER FROM ME!"

Gritting his teeth, Christian was forced to make a choice. Move out of the way and let Damien get a clear shot at Lilith, or stand his ground and prepare to take this monster head on.

What a simple choice.

Holstering his guns and unsheathing his blades, he prepared for a head-to-head confrontation the likes of which he hadn't seen since facing off against Abaddon. Within seconds, Damien was upon him, claws out and set to rend the flesh from his bones. He responded to this by thrusting Michael at his foe, forcing the over-powered vampire to dodge and avoid being impaled through the head. In the next instant, Raphael was there, slicing toward Damien's shoulder.

The stroke missed. At the very last instant, Damien dodged it by twisting into a corkscrew, coming out after flying past him. Upon realizing that he had missed, he sheathed his swords and brought out Gabriel and Phanuel, loading them in less than a second, then unleashing a hailstorm of gunfire.

Most of the bullets went wide of his target when Damien swerved to the right, pulling up into the air, but a few still hit the vampire's back. The No Life King's pained grunts were drowned out by the clapping thunder of gunfire. In spite of the injury, Damien wasn't slowed down in the slightest.

After leveling off, the vampire dove right back down toward him. Like some kind of Kamikaze pilot from World War II, Damien descended on him at speeds that created a sonic boom. The air was displaced and large drafts of wind kicked up, causing dust and dirt to erupt from the ground in a massive spray. Several grains struck his left eye, causing him to close it out of reflex.

That was a mistake. With his left eye covered, his aim was off. His next barrage went wide, and not because Damien had dodged. The vampire flew straight and true, aiming to take him out of the fight by impaling him upon sharp claws.

Christian did his best to avoid the attack, twisting out of Damien's way, but he wasn't fast enough. As Damien passed him, four lines of blood were drawn across his left arm. His body spun like a top from the momentum caused by Damien's immense physical strength. He tumbled to the ground, rolling across the grassy field, and then slammed his uninjured arm against the earth, using the resulting buildup of kinetic energy to land back on his feet.

His right hand went to his injury. The four bloody gashes were deep. Damien's claws had torn straight through his muscles, all the way to his bone. It hurt. He felt pain. But he ignored it. Shunted it to the side. If he let this pain overcome him, then it was all over.

"Christian!"

Eyes going wide, Christian's head snapped toward Lilith, who stood several meters behind him.

"What are you still doing here?!" he shouted. "You were supposed to run!"

"Christian, behind you!" she screamed.

Reacting to her words on instinct, Christian turned around to see Damien not even two feet from him and closing. It was like watching a movie in slow motion. The vampire's sick grin grew larger as he closed the distance between them. His hand was already being thrust forward to impale him through the chest—

"NO!"

—Only for Damien to inexplicably miss.

Christian blinked several times as Damien flew past him, just barely grazing his left cheek and drawing a thin line of blood. Out of instinct, Michael came out in a vertical swing that sheared off the creature's left wing in a spray of gore, which splattered along the ground like a bucket of crimson paint thrown across a canvas by mad painter.

An agonized roar ripped from Damien's throat. Without both wings, the No Life King couldn't remain aloft, and crashed face first into the ground. He then tumbled along the dirt like a rag doll tossed aside by an angry god.

"Lilith," Christian snapped to get her attention. "I need you to get out of here!"

"But I—"

"Catherine!" he shouted to the female officer, who had run up to them sometime during the fight. "Take Lilith and run! Get her to safety while I deal with Damien!"

"Right!" Catherine nodded once before grabbing Lilith by the arm. "Come on, let's hurry up and get away from here."

"What?" Lilith looked at her in surprise before trying to struggle out of Catherine's grip. ""I can't leave! I have to stay here with Christian!"

"Right now, all you're going to do is get in the way," Catherine snapped at Lilith, making her flinch. "Come on! Christian needs to concentrate on this battle, which he can't do if he's constantly worrying about you!"

Lilith bit her lip, looking between him and Catherine. A little way off, Damien struggled to get to his feet. Christian's eyes narrowed as he looked at Lilith, a silent plea that caused her to relent. She nodded at him, and then allowed Catherine to pull her toward the copse, where she would be protected by Omega squad.

"Do you really think I'm going to let you take her from me?!"

Damien surged to his feet and attempted to chase after them, but was intercepted by Christian, who came in with swords swinging. Damien leapt backward to avoid having his throat slit by Michael as the blade soared in from his left.

Rather than give his opponent time to recover, Christian continued with his swing, moving in a complete rotation. Raphael soon appeared near the ground, the blade moving in a vertical swing that was set to bisect

Damien from left hip to right shoulder. That attack was blocked by the vampire's left hand intercepting the blade, sparks flying as Orichalcum met razor sharp nails.

I see, so Damien is so strong that he can even block a sword made of Orichalcum.

Narrowing his eyes, Christian went into a flurry of sword swings. Michael and Raphael became mere flashes of light as moonlight reflected off their polished surfaces. A downward stroke from Michael cut the air with an almost shrill whistle. The lightning quick slash was dodged when Damien sidestepped to the left, feet gliding across the ground like they were hovering.

The powerful vampire would have returned his attack with a counter, but then Raphael was suddenly there, blurring toward the vampire with unerring accuracy. Damien took a single step back, black hair following a second later. The attack, while not quick enough to injure Christian's adversary, did manage to slice off several strands of hair, which fluttered away in the breeze.

As soon as Raphael's sharp edge was no longer in front of him, Damien charged forward. Raising his right hand, he blocked Michael, which attempted to slice off his head, then stepped into Christian's guard. He moved so suddenly that Christian barely had time to react.

A clawed hand moving at ungodly speed tore into Christian's shirt and slashed through his chest. The wounds were not deep, but they most certainly stung as the cold night air hit them. Hissing in pain, he ignored the superficial wounds and spun to the left. A claw slash meant to gouge his eyes out was avoided when he leaned back. His return swing came in the form of Michael rising up from the right side of his body, moving diagonally across the air.

When Damien took several steps back, Christian put Raphael in its sheath and whipped out Gabriel, unloading a barrage of bullets. Damien hissed in anger. His hands blurred, moving so fast that Christian couldn't see them. When Gabriel clicked empty, Damien held up a hand to reveal the bullets between clawed fingers.

He caught them with his bare hands?!

"I hath truly grown tired of your continued interference!" Damien snarled. The bullets in his hands were sliced in half, the liquid nitrogen dripping off the nails and onto the ground, where they froze the grass. "I'm going to kill you for taking my Eve from me!"

It was Christian's personal motto to never share banter with an enemy, believing that doing so was degrading. There was no need to speak with someone who was already dead. However, in this instance, Damien's words angered him to the point where he completely forgot himself and retorted without thinking.

"Don't talk about her like she's some kind of object! She isn't yours!"

"She's mine and only mine!" Damien roared as he charged at Christian. "If not me then who else could she belong to?! Only someone like myself could ever deserve someone like her!"

"You're delusional!"

"You understand nothing! Just a foolish human! Fodder whose only purpose is to be food for those like myself! Eve is the only one who can resist the call of my blood! She is the only one worthy of being my Queen! And I will be damned if I let a brat like you steal her from me!"

Their battle began again with renewed fury. Damien assaulted him from all sides, attacking with lightning-fast strikes that could easily tear his body apart if they hit.

Falling back on his suicidal fake-opening style, Christian left a number of holes in his guard, which the vampire was more than happy to exploit. Or try to exploit. No matter how many times the No Life King attempted to land a decisive blow on him, none of the attacks struck. With apparent ease, Christian avoided or parried each hand-thrust and claw-swipe so that he received only minimal, if any, damage. To Damien, it must have appeared as if Christian was predicting where each attack would come from long before it actually happened.

Christian dodged a hand-thrust set to spear his throat by spinning left. That same hand was also almost lopped off as Michael, already in motion before Damien had attacked, came screaming in, forcing the long-haired vampire to retract the hand quickly.

Another slash from claw-like nails screamed at him, this time aimed at an opening in his torso. The move was so swift and powerful that it rent the air itself, producing a loud whistling screech. It, too, was avoided when he took a single step back and to the right, allowing it to pass by underneath his armpit. His return swing nearly sliced through Damien's throat.

Over and over again Damien attacked. Over and over again Christian moved as if he had the power of precognition. No matter what was thrown his way, he always dodged it. It didn't even matter that each strike came in at speeds that no human should be able to see let alone match. None of them struck true.

"Enough of this!!"

Sick and tired of being incapable of destroying someone who was far beneath his station, Damien raised his left foot into the air, and slammed it into the ground with incredible force. The earth around them cratered. Large cracks spread from where his foot struck, and Christian lost his balance.

The fake-opening style that Christian had created was capable of not only predicting his opponent's next move, but controlling the very flow of battle. Its amazing abilities came at a price, however—anyone who attempted it put their own life on the line… which was why no one but Christian used it.

However, while the style had very few weaknesses when looked at from the standpoint of a martial artist or a weapons user, it did have two major weaknesses: indirect attacks and area attacks. When Damien smashed his foot against the ground and caused it to heave with the force of a miniature earthquake, Christian was knocked off-balance and became vulnerable.

Damien had no issues against destroying an enemy while they were vulnerable.

Eight sharp, blade-like nails penetrated Christian's flesh, four in each shoulder. Christian sucked in a sharp breath as pain overloaded his senses, causing his vision to blur. When his eyesight came back into focus, it was to see Damien glaring at him with a look of complete loathing. A moment after that he realized that Damien was holding him several feet off the ground by the claws embedded in his shoulders.

"I am going to kill you slowly," Damien hissed. "Slowly and painfully. I am going to make you suffer."

Christian would have said something snarky, but his mind couldn't focus past the pain. It wasn't as intense or overwhelming as some of the other wounds that he had received throughout his years of service, but it was enough. The jolts of agony lancing from his shoulders to the rest of his body distracted him, leaving him unable to think up any snappy remarks, or think about much of anything, period.

That pain turned into unbearable agony as Damien clenched his hands, causing the nails to curve their way into Christian's muscles.

"How does that feel?! Do you feel this pain?! This is the pain that I felt when you took my Queen away from me! I'm going to make sure that the pain I felt is returned to you a thousand-fold!!"

With a quick yank, Damien pulled his claw out of Christian's shoulder, making him grunt. That grunt soon turned into loud sucking sounds, as all the air was driven from his lungs after receiving a brutal hit to the ribs that cracked out like a gunshot. That single punch had done more damage to him than any other attack he'd received in the entire fight thus far. He could practically feel his ribs snapping under the localized assault.

The strike also sent him flying backward. He flew through the air, his body moving in a straight line parallel to the ground. It was only after flying backward for several meters that he began losing altitude, his body eventually striking the ground. His vision blurred as he tumbled along the earth, his bones jarring each time they impacted against hard ground.

Seventeen meters later, he finally came to a stop, lying on his back, gasping for breath. The act of taking in oxygen was almost impossible, however. He couldn't breathe for some reason. Each time he tried, his broken ribs scraped against his internal organs, forcing him to grit his teeth, lest he end up screaming in agony.

He ended up doing that anyway when Damien came up to him and stomped on his already broken chest. The power behind the attack was such that the ground underneath him turned into a large crater. Cracks spread out in an intricate pattern like a spider web. The loud thunderclap caused by his body being crushed into the earth drowned out his agonized screams.

And then Damien began digging a heel into his chest. There was no stopping the scream that tore its way out of his throat this time. He could feel the broken shards of his ribcage grinding against his internal organs. The No Life King seemed to know exactly how to maximize the pain he felt without making it fatal.

"You will never go near my Queen again," Damien snarled, continuing to grind his heel against Christian's chest.

Christian tried to grab Damien's foot and push it off, but as a vampire, as a No Life King, the monster before him had strength that he couldn't match on the best of days. And he wasn't at his peak. The pain lancing through his chest overrode everything. He couldn't act. He couldn't think. He could do nothing except wail as Damien's heel ground his bones, muscles, and organs into powder.

Again Damien lifted his foot and stomped it on him with force. Again Christian cried out. He screamed and screamed and screamed, until his throat grew sore and hoarse. Even after he lost his voice, his mouth continued to remain open in a silent scream, as his entire world became immersed in blinding pain.

Damien lifted a foot from Christian's chest once more. Christian tried keeping the No Life King in focus, but his eyesight had become blurry. The figure above him faded in and out. Darkness crept on the edge of his vision.

"Let this pain serve as a lesson to you in the afterlife," Damien said as he raised his foot again. Christian knew in that instant that he was going to die.

Chapter 28

"Let this pain serve as a lesson to you in the afterlife," Damien said, raising his foot once again. This time, he planned on crushing Christian's skull in a single blow. It was more merciful than he would have liked, but there were more important things to do than mess around with this trash.

His Queen was waiting for him.

Before he could drop his foot on Christian's skull, a sharp pain in his back scrambled his concentration and caused him to miss. The attack hit the ground right next to Christian's head, the earth cracking around his foot.

He blinked once, the time it took to process the pain he was feeling. He then looked down at the tip of a blade protruding from his chest in disbelief. Dark-crimson blood dripped off the blade, falling down to land on Christian's face. Craning his neck to look behind him, Damien saw Lilith standing there, the handle of the sword that was stabbing him held in both of her hands.

She gripped the handle tightly, her knuckles turning white, while her entire body shook at being in such close proximity to him. Despite the naked fear she displayed, her eyes were glaring at him, her eyebrows drawn together in a fierce look of determination.

It would have been a beautiful sight in most circumstances. His Queen had never looked more regal than she did right then. However, the blade protruding from his chest, which she had thrust into him, prevented him from being able to admire the sight.

"My Queen…" he whispered, right before backhanding the young woman away. Lilith cried out at the stinging pain in her cheek, as she was sent sprawling to the ground. He looked down at the girl, then at the sword in his chest. Reaching behind him, he grabbed the handle and yanked it out of his body without ceremony.

Damien took notice of the blade's elegance as he examined it closely. It really was a beautiful sword. Were it not for that disgusting crucifix on the guard, it would have been a weapon fit for a No Life King such as himself. Most unfortunately, it had that guard, and as such was not even fit to be used against him.

He tossed it away.

With the weapon no longer an issue, Damien turned his attention back to Lilith. She had recovered from his attack, though he saw how her cheek swelled where he struck. She crawled away from him in fear, her terror-filled eyes filling him with a sense of vindication.

He took a step forward.

"So this is what you've chosen?" he asked, his voice sounding almost upset, *almost* anguished. "Thou hath decided to choose that lowly human over me? You would let your beauty be squandered by those who can't appreciate you? Allow someone as insignificant as that human to taint you?"

Damien took another step forward. Lilith crawled back some more.

"I see how it is." He stopped walking for a moment, and the almost sad grimace on his features twisted into an outraged scowl. "Very well then. If that is your choice, then I shall send both of you to hell together."

Damien moved toward Lilith. He barely made two steps before the thunderclap of a gun rang out, echoing ominously across the clearing. His body stumbled forward, while his left hand went to his right shoulder. Blinking in confusion, Damien wondered why he couldn't feel his arm anymore.

He looked down.

"Oh…"

His right arm from the shoulder down was missing. Gone. *What happened to it? Where did it go?*

Before he could question himself further, three more shots rang out. Each shot caused Damien to stumble. The shock of losing his arm soon wore off, and then he felt it: pain.

He had experienced pain before. Clawing his way up from the muck, fighting against monsters that were much stronger than him in order to claim their power for his own, he couldn't have done those things without experiencing pain.

That pain paled in comparison to this. It felt like his body was being disintegrated from the inside out. Like something was slowly eating at him from the inside. Molten lava dripped in his veins, setting what should have been dead nerve endings ablaze with torment the likes of which his mind could scarcely comprehend.

Where is this pain coming from?

More bullets penetrated his flesh. He spun around, even as he stumbled forward, allowing him to face the source of his pain.

It was Christian. He sat on the ground. One hand had been placed behind him, acting as support for his torso. The other held one of his guns, the silver one, which was pointed right at Damien.

"You...!"

Damien surged forward, intent on killing this annoyance who just would not stay down. He was halted from doing so as Christian unloaded the entire cartridge of ammo into his flesh. His body jerked about as around half a dozen bullets hit him in rapid succession. Each time one of the shells pierced his skin, they went off inside of him like a flare lighting up the night sky. His body began disintegrating. Holes appeared all over him. These large gaps in his flesh expanded, and he could see beams of light coming out from them.

Do those weapons contain the power of the sun?

It was in that moment, as his body disintegrated, as the holes appearing on him grew larger, that he realized he was going to die. Even No Life Kings are weak against sunlight.

Damien's last thoughts were of Eve, his Queen. If he had one regret, it was being unable to make her his.

***

For a long moment, no one spoke, no one moved, they didn't even breathe. Christian and Lilith stared at the space between them, at the area where Damien had been standing. He wasn't there anymore. His entire body had been vaporized by the liquid sunlight bullets. Even a creature as powerful as a No Life King was unable to stand up to condensed light particles containing the power of a miniature star.

"Christian!"

Lilith was the one who finally moved.

Christian would have moved, but he was too injured. The young woman clambered to her feet. She began walking over to him, her feet starting off slowly but picking up pace quickly enough. A walk turned into a jog, which then turned into a full-on sprint.

"Christian!"

With nary a thought Lilith tackled Christian, landing on top of him, where she proceeded to hug the life out of him.

"Oof!"

A pained grunt escaped him, as he found himself at the tender mercies of the young woman. Despite the pain that flared up in his ribs, he returned the hug as best he could, wrapping a single arm around her waist.

"I'm so glad…" she whispered. It was only after he felt something wet dripping on his bare skin, where Damien had ripped his clothes, that he realized that she was crying. "… I'm so glad you're all right."

"Yes." Christian sighed in relief. He didn't know why, but the tears that Lilith shed onto his skin soothed the wounds he'd received on his chest. "I'm all right. Thanks to you. You saved me."

Lilith looked up from where she had been nuzzling his chest.

"I… I didn't do much." Two small beacons of red appeared on her cheeks. Despite what appeared to be embarrassment, it was clear from her smile that she was pleased by his words.

"I would have been dead if you hadn't had the courage to come up behind Damien and stab him," Christian told her. He smiled. "You really saved me back there."

"Well, I… I couldn't let him hurt you," Lilith murmured, her cheeks darkening in hue. "I love you."

"I know," Christian said. "I love you, too."

Lilith looked at him in surprise. Then tears of joy sprang to her eyes and overflowed down her cheeks. A smile that could outshine the sun appeared on her face as she leaned in to kiss him.

Unfortunately, she never would get to kiss him that day. With the battle over, all the adrenaline that had been pumping through Christian's body wore off. Without the chemicals produced by the hormones associated with the fight-or-flight instinct running through his system, the pain of having several shattered ribs became intolerable. It overwhelmed all of his senses, causing his mind to shut down in order to avoid splintering into a thousand irreparable pieces.

The last thing Christian saw was long blond hair and bright blue eyes. The last thing he heard was Lilith's terrified voice screaming out his name.

Chapter 29

I was playing around with one of my action figures, something that I had always enjoyed doing. I was reenacting a scene from my favorite movie. Luke and Leia had just been cornered by Stormtroopers in the Death Star. The bridge that led to the other side had been retracted, and the door behind them was slowly sliding open. In a move of incredible daring, Luke decided to use the grappling hook on his utility belt to swing across the giant chasm. He wrapped an arm around Leia's waist and was about to jump when she kissed him on the cheek "for luck."

It was in that moment, just as Luke and Leia were about to leap across the chasm, that several loud explosions rocked the house. The earth shook like it had been caught in an earthquake, and the loud rumbling of what sounded like bombs going off nearly deafened me.

My parents ran down the stairs, both of them looking frightened out of their minds.

"Mom! Dad!" I stood up, stumbling a little as another explosion, this one even closer,

shook the house to its foundations. My mom caught me before I could fall, and I looked into her frightened green eyes, feeling more scared than she looked. "What's going on? Why are we shaking?"

Mom didn't answer. She just looked over at Dad.

"They've found us," Dad said. I was confused. They? Who were they? "It was bound to happen sooner or later. Quick, take Christian and get out of here. I'll go to where the fighting is, and help hold them off long enough for you two to escape."

"What?" Mom looked startled for a moment, but then shook her head. "You can't expect me to just leave you! I'm going with you!"

"You aren't," Dad snapped. "Someone needs to stay with Christian. I'm sure the others are mounting a defense already, but they'll be outnumbered! And besides"—Dad grinned a sharp-toothed grin— "it's a man's job to protect his wife and child."

"Don't you dare put that sexist attitude on display with me." Despite her narrowed eyes, Mom almost looked amused. "I might not be able to fight like you can, but I'm a damn good shot."

"I know that, but you still can't come. If you go with me, who'll be there to protect Christian?"

Mom bit her lip, but was forced to concede the point.

"Fine. Just know that if you get yourself killed, I am going to drag your ass out of hell and beat the crap out of you."

"Now there's some serious motivation if I've ever heard it," Dad snarked back before kissing Mom on the lips. I never liked it when they kissed. Kissing was yucky. But I didn't mind it this time. I was too scared by the sound of explosions to pay attention to my parents getting all lovey-dovey with each other.

They soon broke apart. Mom rushed upstairs to "grab something important," and Dad knelt down next to me, placing his hands on my shoulders and giving me a warm smile.

"Christian, I want you to listen to me and listen well. When you are older, you will likely find yourself in a position where someone you love is in danger. There are only two choices you can make during times like this: the easy choice and the right choice." His grip on my shoulders became firm. "Promise me that you will always make the right choice."

I didn't know what Dad was talking about. Right choice? What did he mean? Still, even if I didn't know what he meant, I nodded my head dutifully. I felt tears running down my cheeks as I did so, even though I couldn't understand why.

"Good. Now be a good boy and protect your mom for me, okay? She's a stubborn woman and will need your help in the years to come."

I wanted to ask why he was telling me all of this. To ask why he couldn't just protect Mom himself. I had seen him train. Dad was strong. He could break boulders with his bare hands. I wasn't that strong. I couldn't protect Mom like he could.

But I couldn't ask. I couldn't ask why because I was afraid. All I could do was nod my head.

"There's a good boy." My dad gave me that cocky grin of his. His grin always reminded me of Han Solo. "And remember, even if I'm not by your side, a part of me will always be with you."

With those parting words, Dad rushed out of the house.

That was the last time I ever saw him. It was the last time I ever saw Mom as well. Not even a second after Dad left, my entire house became consumed with flames, and I ended up blacking out as a powerful explosion blasted me straight through a wall.

***

Inhaling a sharp breath, Christian woke with a start. His eyes flickered about wildly for a second, trying to see the flames that were devouring his house. Only there were no flames. He was not in his house. All he saw were the white walls and ceiling of his hotel room.

As the tension in his body slackened, his mind put together the pieces of what must have happened after he blacked out. It was clear that someone—likely Lilith, or maybe Catherine—had brought him back after the battle. He wondered how long he'd been unconscious.

A groan escaped his barely parted lips as he thought about what had transpired to land him in this situation... again. It was happening far too often for his tastes. First that werewolf had caught him completely unprepared. Then, after facing down an assassin, he'd wound up in a battle for his life against a creature that he really had no chance of defeating. The only reason he was even alive was due to Damien's arrogance and Lilith's courage.

Speaking of Lilith...

Christian's ears twitched as the sound of running water alerted him to someone in the shower. He assumed it was Lilith, as she was the only person who would take a shower in his hotel...

Well, Tristin might also take a shower at his place just to screw with him, but since Tristin was all the way in Los Angeles, he was betting on it being Lilith.

Wanting to know the state of his physical condition, he ran a mental checklist of the injuries he could feel. There were surprisingly few. In fact, aside from a bit of stiffness in his chest, shoulders and back, he couldn't feel any of the damage that he had received during his fight with the No Life King.

While he checked the extent of his injuries, the sounds coming from the shower cut off. Christian pushed himself into a sitting position, groaning as his muscles stretched uncomfortably after however long they'd gone unused. The door to the bathroom opened and out walked Lilith, a towel wrapped around her curvaceous figure.

Maybe it was because his brain felt more than a little muddled because of having just woken up, but Christian couldn't help but admire Lilith's figure. With nothing more than a towel wrapped around her, he could see the generous proportions that made up her body; her slender shoulders, her incredible bust, her thin waist and flat tummy, her sensual hips that traveled down into even more incredible legs, which ended with a pair of small, dainty feet.

It had never occurred to him before now, not even the other day when they slept together, but Lilith was truly the most bewitching woman that he had ever met.

The young woman in question continued walking, toweling the water off her hair for several more seconds. She strode nearly halfway into the room before finally noticing that he was no longer lying unconscious on the bed. She stared at him, blinking for several seconds, as if she was not quite sure what to make of him.

"Good morning, Lilith," Christian said into the silence.

"Christian…" she whispered. A second later the towel was fluttering to the ground as she bounded toward him. "Christian!"

Christian's eyes widened.

"Wait! Lilith, I'm still—OOF!"

Just like what had happened after his battle with Damien, Lilith bodily tackled him. Fortunately, he was on a bed and not the ground. He also wasn't injured, which was a very good thing, because he didn't want to undergo the feeling of his ribs being crushed by the overzealous woman wrapping her arms around him.

And just like that, Lilith began crying… again. He seemed to have a knack for making her cry.

"You're finally awake!" He could just barely make out the words between her sobs. "I was so worried! You passed out and wouldn't wake up! We took you to the hospital, and these people kept trying to stick you with things, and I didn't like it. And then they tried to revive you, but you wouldn't wake up! I thought you were dead! And then they said that you were healing and that you would make a full recovery, and I was so relieved that I... that I..."

Guilt settled in his gut and refused to leave. Christian felt like a jerk. How many times had he made this woman cry? Two times? Three? Maybe more? He could only hope this didn't become a common occurrence. On their own, women were trouble. Crying women were trouble to the tenth power.

With nothing else to do except comfort the young woman in his arms, Christian did the only thing he could think of. He hugged her back. His arms went around her waist and pulled her in. Her body conformed to his, allowing him to feel all of her pressing up against him. Her head found purchase in the crook of his neck, where she proceeded to continue bawling her eyes out.

He didn't know how long they stayed like that, with him holding Lilith as she cried out her worries. Time didn't seem to have as much meaning in these instances, or maybe the passage of time had slowed down because God was playing a prank on him. He'd never heard of God being a prankster, but with everything that had happened on this mission, someone up there had to be finding entertainment with the utterly ridiculous set of circumstances that he'd been finding himself in.

Christian could only be thankful that the waterworks eventually stopped and, save for a few sniffles and hiccups, Lilith calmed down.

"I'm sorry for worrying you like that," Christian murmured softly, pressing his lips to her forehead.

"You'd better be sorry." Lilith hiccupped. "Stupid man. You could have died. Do you know what would have happened if you died? What that would have done to me?"

"Uh, well, I guess it would have made you sad?"

When Lilith lifted her head and glared at him, complete with dangerously narrowed eyes and thinned lips, Christian knew that he had said the wrong thing.

"I wouldn't be able to live with myself if you died, Christian. I don't think you realize how important you are to me. How much I love you! If something had happened... if I hadn't been able to save you in time... I wouldn't have been able to go on living..."

Lilith fell back on top of Christian, her body going slack, as if she'd expended all of her energy in one go. It reminded him of those short bursts of adrenaline that he felt during combat, the ones that gave him an exceedingly powerful burst of energy, but left him utterly spent afterward.

"I'm sure it's not that bad."

Lilith shook her head at Christian's words. "No, it is that bad. You mean everything to me Christian. I… I know that sounds strange, and I can't even explain why, but you are so important to me. I feel… no, I *know* that if you were to die, then there's no way that I could continue living."

"I see." He really didn't, but if that's how she felt, then maybe it would be better to simply agree. "I'm sorry, I had no idea I meant that much to you."

"Well, you do," she sniffled. "Which is why I don't want you ever doing something that stupid again, okay?"

"Okay."

Silence settled the room for several seconds. Christian held Lilith to his chest, enjoying the feel of her warm body conforming to his. There was something sublimely beautiful about this moment, being able to hold this woman in his arms. Soon, he would have to let go, but for this now, he allowed himself to experience the absolute peace that came from holding the woman he loved.

"How do you feel?" Lilith asked.

"A lot better than I expected to," Christian admitted. "Those doctors did a good job."

"They didn't do anything. All they did was try sticking stuff in you. They also said that you wouldn't wake up for another two days."

"Really?"

Lilith nodded.

"Huh, that's odd," he said. "I guess those nanomachines are still working. I thought they would have dissolved by now."

The room became still once more. Unlike some of the other times they abstained from speech, this silence wasn't awkward or strained. It was tranquil. Lilith's soft breathing calmed Christian's heart and mind, even as the hot breath hitting his neck made his skin prickle pleasantly.

Christian knew that he should have felt like there was something wrong with this situation. He was an Executioner. Romance, love—these words were not supposed to be in his vocabulary. Yet all he could feel as he lay on that bed, with Lilith in his arms, was a sense of peace and contentment.

And he had already made his choice anyway. This was going to be his last mission. He was proud of being an Executioner, proud to have played a part, however insignificant, in the constant defense of humanity. But now he had something else, something more. He'd found a partner in Lilith, a young woman with a troubled past, who still lived her life to the best of her abilities. A woman who shared his passion for reading light novels and manga and, more importantly, the woman that he felt could very well be his other half.

He was positive of this now: he loved Lilith. She was the Eve to his Adam (a fact that he found amusing considering her original name), and just like those two had gone on to create a life together—however screwed up that life may have been—Christian found himself wanting to create a life with her.

Once Lilith and he decided to move from their comfortable position, Christian would call up Samantha and ask for a discharge. She would be displeased by his decision, but he was sure she would grant it to him in light of his service. The Executioners would still assign him a minder, but that was a small price to pay to be with Lilith.

"Lilith." The young woman in question raised her head and looked at him. "I love you."

The smile that she gave him was like rays of light breaking through storm clouds.

"I love you, too."

Epilogue

"And that concludes the report given to us by Catherine Siegal," Tristin finished giving an after action report (AAR) to his boss. As per the usual, Samantha sat behind her ornate desk, elbows resting on walnut top, her hands clasped together in front of her face as she listened to him. She took in everything that he had told her with furrowed brows and a small frown. It was clear to Tristin that the woman was contemplating all of the information that he'd just given her.

At long last, Samantha spoke, but it was clear from her tone that she was displeased with something that he'd said, "So, the creature that's been killing humans and monsters across the country was a No Life King, one that we had no prior knowledge of until now. This monster also almost killed one of our best operatives, and probably would have succeeded were it not for the actions of that… that girl. Is that what you are telling me?"

Tristin managed to withhold a wince. Just barely.

"Yes."

"And how is it that we didn't know about this creature before now?" asked Samantha. "What is the Intelligence Division doing? This thing has been killing humans for who knows how long, and we're just now finding out about it?!" As she continued speaking, Samantha's voice grew louder and louder, as her anger at the situation increased. By the end of it, she was practically shouting.

"I don't know what to tell you," Tristin shook his head, trying not to let his nervousness show. Being around Samantha was nerve-wracking on its own—he didn't know how Christian dealt with it—dealing with an angry Samantha was downright terrifying. "The killings first started happening in New Shoreham, Rhode Island. That region is inside the jurisdiction of the New York Executioners division, not ours, and I don't have permission to access their files."

"Damn them!" Samantha slammed her fist onto the desk, cracking it and causing Tristin to jump. He'd never seen the woman this angry before. Actually, he didn't think he'd seen her angry before period. This issue must be really eating at her.

Visibly shivering in rage, Samantha took several deep breaths to calm down.

"And what about the assassin that Christian killed? Did we uncover her identity?"

Just like Catherine had promised Christian, the assassins body had been transported to Executioners HQ. The Science Division had immediately taken it and performed several autopsies. Tristin had already reviewed the information they had sent him.

"We did, and it looks like the assassin was Michelle Oria. My guess is that the No Life King found her attractive and, rather than turn her into a ghoul, decided to make her his slave."

"I see," Samantha closed her eyes for all of one second, before fixing Tristin with another look, "What of Christian? How is he doing?"

"His wounds have fully healed," Tristin informed her, looking down at the report, "There isn't even a scar. That nanotech the Science Division has is pretty amazing. I'm surprised they were able to make something so useful, given their propensity for creating things that explode in their face."

"It isn't hard to force them into creating something useful. You just have to give them the right motivation."

Tristin took that to mean that Samantha had threatened them into creating it.

"And what of that… girl?" Samantha asked.

"She hasn't left Christian's side except to take showers. From what I've gathered in Catherine's report, not only has she been refusing to leave his side, but she actually attacked several people who tried to make her leave. She even attacked a doctor when he tried attaching an IV drip to Christian's arm."

Samantha scowled for a moment, but then dismissed the knowledge.

"She will be dealt with accordingly soon enough, once Christian wakes up." The attractive woman with dark hair narrowed her eyes at Tristin. "You will tell him when he wakes up, right?"

Tristin shifted uncomfortably.

"Do we really have to do this? I mean, she did save his life, you know? And it's obvious that she really cares for him. Couldn't we let this slide just once?"

"You know the rules, Tristin," Samantha's voice was stern and unyielding, "You will tell him the moment he wakes up. That's an order."

Clenching his hands into a tight pair of fists was the only thing that kept him from gritting his teeth. After taking several slow breaths, he unclenched his hands, placed his right hand up by his heart, and bowed to the woman.

"It shall be as you command."

Have you been turned on to Brandon's books?

Wait. That sounded kind of wrc

If you liked Succubus,
then be sure to check out these great titles!

Book 1 of the
American Kitsune series.

Volume 1
Arcadia's Ignoble Knight
Coming Soon…

www.ingramcontent.com/pod-product-compliance
Lightning Source LLC
Chambersburg PA
CBHW031220120726
47905CB00002B/411